BY LIES BETRAYED

Also by Gwen Madoc

DAUGHTER OF SHAME

BY LIES
BETRAYED

Gwen Madoc

Hodder & Stoughton

A CIP catalogue record for this book
is available from the British Library.

ISBN 0 340 79279 5

Typeset in Bembo by Hewer Text Ltd, Edinburgh
Printed and bound in Great Britain by
Mackays of Chatham plc, Chatham, Kent

Hodder & Stoughton
A division of Hodder Headline
338 Euston Road
London NW1 3BH

To my dearest husband Harry,
my life long friend and companion.

Thanks and acknowledgements to the award-winning Grand Theatre, Swansea, and in particular, Paul Hopkins, marketing manager, who kindly supplied the photograph of the theatre which inspired the artwork for the wonderful jacket.

Chapter One

Sandfields, Swansea, Autumn 1926

Stella Evans locked the shop door, slid the bolt into place, and twisted the closed sign to face the street. As she slipped into her coat and hat, she called out, 'I'm going now, Mrs Ridd. I've locked up.'

Mrs Ridd came out of the living quarters. Her thin features, sharp as a hatchet blade, were more pinched than usual this evening, and Stella, though suspecting trouble, held out her hand for her pay. 'See you tomorrow, Mrs Ridd.'

Deliberately, Mrs Ridd put the pay-packet she was holding into her apron pocket, and stared hard at Stella, her gaze hostile. 'No! I won't see you tomorrow, Stella. I'm finishing you tonight.'

'*What?*'

Appalled, Stella stared at the truculent light in her employer's eyes. 'You're sacking me, Mrs Ridd? But why? What've I done?'

Mrs Ridd brushed a hand over the thin puffs of frizzy hair on either side of her head, and patted the meagre bun at the nape of her neck. Instinctively, Stella knew the woman was about to tell a lie.

'It's like this, you see,' Mrs Ridd began, her tone defiant, 'my Ceinwen wants to come back to work in the shop. Well, the baby's six months now. I can't afford to pay you both. After that awful strike last May, times are lean, and family comes first.'

The muscles in Stella's jaw tightened. 'Well, there's a funny thing, Mrs Ridd,' she replied, her tone caustic. 'I was talking to your Ceinwen only yesterday, and she told me she wouldn't come back to work here in the shop with you for love nor money.'

'Oh!' Mrs Ridd's mouth was round with surprise, and for a moment she looked flummoxed.

Stella felt anger rising, but quelled it. She couldn't afford to lose her job or her temper. Times *were* lean, and getting leaner. Mrs Ridd wasn't wrong there.

'Now, what's this all about, Mrs Ridd?' Stella went on, trying to appear reasonable. 'If you've got a complaint against me, please speak up. I'm sure it's all a misunderstanding. Is it because I split a packet of baccy for old Mr Lewis?' She pointed to Mrs Ridd's apron pocket. 'Take it out of my pay, if you like.'

The older woman's nostrils flared. 'Warned you before about that, haven't I?' Mrs Ridd rapped out, her thin lips narrowing even more. 'I'm not running a charity by here, mind. It's just as well you're going. You'd have me bankrupt.'

'One measly packet of baccy?' Stella was scornful. 'That's like a pimple on St Paul's.'

'Yes, well . . . I'd be entitled to sack you for that alone,' Mrs Ridd said. 'But there's more, much more . . . far worse, in fact.' She glared at Stella, her eyes bright with spite.

'Well, go on, then!' Stella exclaimed heatedly, not under-standing what was behind that look. 'Spit it out, will you? What've you got against me?'

'So you want to know the truth, do you? Well, I'll tell you. First off, there's that no-good brother of yours.'

Ignoring the slur for the moment, Stella frowned, mystified. 'Griff? What's *he* got to do with you sacking me?'

Mrs Ridd's mouth twisted in a sneer, and her tone was scathing, as she said, 'As if you don't know!'

Stella tensed, but still held on to her temper. 'Wouldn't be

2

asking if I knew, would I? You'd better start explaining, Mrs Ridd, if you please.'

'Huh! Playing innocent – bit late for that.' Mrs Ridd sniffed. 'Umpteen times, I've seen him coming in the shop, snatching packets of ciggies and baccy off the shelf, and you turning your back, pretending you haven't noticed. I'm not *twp*, mind.' She gave a satisfied nod. 'And that's why I'm keeping back your pay for this week. You owe me that for stolen goods, and more.'

'You can't do that!' Stella spluttered. 'Against the law, that is. It's my entitlement.'

'Thieves don't get entitlements,' Mrs Ridd retorted sharply. 'Clink is what they get. You keep away from my shop in future, and that brother of yours, too. I don't want to end up burgled, with me and my Fred found murdered in our beds with our throats slit.'

'*What?*' Stella wondered if Mrs Ridd had gone mad. 'You're talking rubbish, woman!'

'Oh, am I?' Mrs Ridd tossed her head. 'And don't you "woman" me. I'm decent, I am, while your brother is a downright bad lot. Everyone knows he hangs about with crooks.'

'I'm not standing for this!' Stella snapped.

'Oh, no?' Mrs Ridd's scornful smile was triumphant. 'Well, I'll tell you something for nothing, then. Your brother's down the Archer's pub every night with that Tommy Parsons from Ysbyty Street, as thick as thieves they are. And that's exactly what they are.' Mrs Ridd's lip curled. 'Scummy, murdering thieves!'

Mrs Ridd had gone too far this time. Hot rage bubbled up in Stella's throat, and she made no effort to stem it.

'How dare you call my brother a thief, you miserable old – old mischief-maker!' she cried. 'We'll have the law on you for defamation of character, so you'd better mind what you say.'

'Law? Don't make me laugh!' Mrs Ridd gave a mocking cackle. 'Griff Stroud keeps well clear of the law. Just a step away from clink, he is, the riffraff he keeps company with. You know the big-time crook Tommy Parsons works for, don't you?'

'No, I don't, Mrs Ridd,' Stella retorted. 'I'm not so well acquainted with the criminal underworld as *you* seem to be.'

'Charlie Pendle!' Mrs Ridd almost hooted. 'Now you must've heard of *him*.'

Stella swallowed. Of course she'd heard of Charlie Pendle. Who in Swansea hadn't, after that fiasco of a murder trial in Cardiff a couple of years ago? The story had been sensational enough to reach the national newspapers when two vital witnesses against Pendle disappeared and he was acquitted for lack of evidence. Rumour had it at the time that, although he was in prison, he'd had the witnesses murdered, their bodies dismembered and dumped far out at sea. She'd never believe that Griff, her own half-brother, would have truck with a man like that.

'It's a lie!' Stella shouted. 'A black-hearted lie! You ought to go to clink yourself for spreading such malicious rumours about Griff – a hero, who lost an arm fighting for his country and the likes of you.' Griff had lost so much: his health, his ability to work, his wife and home. Stella felt riled anew that people like Mrs Ridd could vilify him. 'How can you talk like that about an innocent man after the sacrifices he's made?' she asked.

'Innocent man!' Mrs Ridd's jarring cackle came again. 'Oh, that's a good one! If you don't know what your own brother gets up to,' she said nastily, 'you're either an almighty fool or the biggest liar I've ever met. And we both know you're no fool, don't we, Stella?'

Stella completely forgot herself, and the need to try to keep her job. 'You foul-minded, stingy old skinflint!' she cried, shaking from head to toe with fury. '*You* can talk about thieving. You squeeze every last halfpenny out of your customers. Even your own daughter won't work for you. She knows you too well. She told me how you tried to break up her marriage.'

Mrs Ridd gasped. 'Oh! You lying bitch!'

Stella felt a measure of satisfaction at the consternation on the woman's face. It was time she had a taste of her own medicine. She pressed on relentlessly: 'You've got barefaced cheek, calling *me* names, you old battle-axe, you! I've worked six days a week for three years in this shop, without a day off for illness, and never once has the till been short. Admit it! Never once!' She lifted her nose proudly in the air. 'You owe me an apology, Mrs Ridd.'

'Apology, be damned! I don't give apologies to the likes of you, Stella Evans, a woman no better than she should be.'

'Take that back!'

'Don't make me laugh, you gyppo!' Mrs Ridd waved a hand dismissively. 'I've always thought there was a bit of the gypsy about you, my girl, with that black hair of yours. Black as the devil's tongue. I want no gypsies around here. Get out – go on! Get away from here this minute. I want nothing more to do with you or your tainted family. I'll see to it you're finished around here.'

Stella held her ground. 'Tainted?' she asked, through clenched teeth.

She couldn't believe that this woman, for whom she'd worked so hard, was speaking to her in this way, as if she were dirt. What did she mean, anyway? How could she defend herself, when she didn't know of what she was accused?

'You heard right!' Mrs Ridd's reddening face twisted in disdain. 'Tainted! You know what I'm getting at, all right, so don't come the old soldier by here. When a woman goes bad it shows in her face, and I can see it in yours.'

Bad! Stella could only stare, her mouth open. Mrs Ridd had always been difficult, but Stella was shocked by the malice in her eye.

'We've always been respectable, Fred and me,' Mrs Ridd sniffed contemptuously. 'And we don't want the likes of you or that brother of yours anywhere near our business. Mud sticks.'

Stella felt as if she was in some kind of nightmare. Nothing made sense. What was Mrs Ridd hinting at? She put out a hand pleadingly. 'Mrs Ridd,' she began, 'there must be some mistake.

I've done nothing wrong, and I'm sure you're mistaken about Griff.'

But the older woman flinched away as if Stella were a leper. 'Don't you lay the finger of poison on me, you hussy,' she spat. 'You can't pull the wool over my eyes any longer. Do you think I haven't heard about *your* carryings-on, you dirty little slut? Strange men back and forth at your house at all hours of the night, and you with no husband to call your own.'

'Strange men? It's not true!' Stella was horrified. 'I'm a respectable woman with a young son. Who's been saying such things about me?'

Mrs Ridd's piglet eyes were as shiny as black ice, and just as treacherous. 'Everyone. You're the talk of every chip shop and saloon bar hereabouts. Filth, that's what you are, you and that brother of yours. Filth!'

Shaken by the venom in the older woman's voice and the hatred in her eyes, Stella fled.

'You'll clear out of the Sandfields if you know what's good for you, gyppo!' Mrs Ridd screeched after her. 'Your kind are not wanted around us respectable people.' With those parting words, she slammed the door hard.

Stella tottered to the corner of Lower Oxford Street, her legs stiff and awkward with shock. A slut! A gyppo! What did it all mean?

She swayed on the edge of the pavement, so upset she couldn't remember which way to turn for home. Mrs Ridd's taunting voice rang in her head. No husband to call her own! Stella gave a moan of despair. If only Eddie would come back to her, she'd forgive him everything. But she would never forgive Rose, Griff's wife, for stealing him away. Rose had ruined their lives.

A tram rattling past brought her senses back. She must get home to Danny. It was late. Resolutely she pushed Mrs Ridd's words from her mind. She had more important things to think of, such as where to find another job.

She had only sixpence left in her purse from her last pay-packet. She'd been relying on this week's money, meagre as it was, to see her through. Now she had nothing – no money, no job. And, if Mrs Ridd was to be believed, she didn't have her good name, either.

Shoulders sagging, she turned towards the Sandfields, and her two-up, two-down terrace home in Victor Street. Her footsteps seemed to echo extra loudly tonight: a hollow sound like the bells of doom.

Sacked! Out of work! How would she and little Danny live, and what would become of them if she'd really lost her good name, too?

Chapter Two

Stella hurried down Victor Street. At least she still had a home to go to, but for how much longer? Thank heavens she'd managed to keep the tenancy after Eddie walked out on her, taking Rose with him. But without work, how would she pay the rent?

If only Griff could find a job, earn enough to contribute a bob or two each week for his keep. One arm or not, he ate like any other man, but Stella had never had the heart to ask him for help. If he *could* earn, he'd have kept his own place going after Rose left him, instead of having to live with her and Danny.

When she finally arrived, Griff wasn't home, of course. He spent most of his evenings out, and more often than not, he came home tipsy, sometimes falling-down drunk. She couldn't blame him: he had so little in his life now, his heroism forgotten, his future a desert, his uselessness rankling in his heart and mind. It was a terrible reward for his sacrifices.

She'd assumed that he squandered his dole, if he had any, on drink, or perhaps his pals saw him right, those who had jobs. Now she found herself wondering, despite her faith in him. Surely what Mrs Ridd had said couldn't be true. She wished he was home so that they could talk about it, until she realised, with a sigh, that he'd be in no fit state to talk rationally tonight. It would be tomorrow morning before she could broach the subject.

She wouldn't tell him that Mrs Ridd had called her a slut, or about the shameful accusation she had made against her. She wouldn't tell anyone, not even her best friend, Babs, next door. It was too humiliating, and she was ashamed that such things were being said. If only she could put it out of her mind.

Stella kicked off her shoes and slipped into her old daps, then went next door to Babs's to fetch her son.

'You're late, Stella, love,' Babs said amicably, as soon as Stella stepped into the living room. 'Danny's on with his night's rest, look.'

He was curled up on the sofa under a Welsh wool shawl, his soft brown curls, just like Eddie's, spread on a cushion.

The sight of her sleeping son made her want to burst out crying, but she stopped herself, not wanting to make a fuss.

'He's been no trouble, has he?'

'Don't be daft, Stell, will you?' Babs responded. 'I love having him in by here. He's a little angel compared to my two.'

'Where *are* the twins?'

Babs pulled a comic face. 'In bed, thank God! They're noisy little devils for girls, mun. Two little tomboys.'

Freda Harris, Babs's mother, came out of the scullery, her small-boned, thin figure bustling in that fussy way of hers – it drove Babs crazy. As usual, she wore a flowered wrap-around pinny, and today sported a blue felt hat, decorated with a scraggy feather.

She dumped a large brown earthenware teapot unceremoniously on the table, her dark eyes glittering as she regarded Stella.

'In *my* day we never left our children for neighbours to bring up,' she exclaimed, her mouth prune-shaped in her narrow face. 'It's irrepressible, that's what it is. You ought to be ashamed, Stella Evans!'

'Mam!' Babs's cheeks were pink with embarrassment. 'I'm sorry, Stella, love. I think Mam means irresponsible, but she's talking through her hat, as usual.'

Babs tittered nervously, and Stella almost managed to smile back at her.

Freda had a hat for every day of the week. She was never seen without one, indoors or out, from breakfast until bedtime. Stella often wondered whether she wore one in bed. It was a long-standing joke between the friends, stimulating periodic fits of giggles. But it didn't seem funny today.

'Oh, am I?' Freda's eyes flashed. 'Well, I'm not the one she's taking advantage of, or making a fool of, either. With you looking after her boy, she's free and easy to carry on.'

'Mam!' Babs was aghast, her colour deepening. 'She didn't mean that the way it sounded, Stell, honest.' She turned to her mother. 'You didn't mean it the wrong way, did you, Mam?'

Stella stared at the older woman. As difficult as Babs's mother was, she and Stella got on reasonably well as a rule. But on meeting Freda's flinty gaze, Stella realised she *had* meant every word, and more. Hostility burned in her eyes; even the little greying hairs on her chin bristled with indignation.

Stella's blood ran cold. Had Freda heard the same lies as Mrs Ridd? 'Have I done something to upset you, Freda?' she ventured.

Freda's jaw worked, but her lips were clamped together, as though she was holding back an avalanche of spleen.

Her gaze flickered warily towards her daughter, and in a moment of insight, Stella understood that Freda's grievance had nothing to do with her leaving Danny in Babs's care. Something else had incensed the older woman, and Stella could guess what it was. In trepidation, she waited for her to answer.

'Mam?' Babs said at last, an edge to her voice now. 'Stella's talking to you.'

'Huh!' Freda turned on her heel and marched back into the scullery.

Babs glanced uncertainly at Stella, and ran her hands down the front of her apron, over her round, comfortable, womanly figure – so different from Freda's. They didn't seem like mother and daughter. 'Don't know what's got into her today, Stell, but don't take any notice, mun,' she said. 'She's being nasty because we've had words over Ted again.'

Stella's skin crawled, and she tried to prevent any expression of revulsion appearing on her face.

Babs's husband, Ted, was a pest – more than that, he was a menace, and detestable with it. Stella could think of no other word for him. Well, perhaps she could, but it was too rude to think, let alone mention.

Freda had the measure of her son-in-law, though, but poor Babs was the only one who couldn't see the truth. Stella had decided long ago that Babs was blinded by his handsome looks and superior attitude. Just because he had a good, steady job as park-keeper with the Corporation, money in his pocket, and an athletic build, Ted Thomas thought he was God's gift to women. The slimy rat! If only Babs knew.

'It's no wonder he goes out so much,' Babs went on, 'with her nagging all the time. I wish she wouldn't keep coming over here every day and staying till all hours. Me and Ted's got no privacy.'

'She's probably lonely across the road,' Stella suggested. She was wholly ready to sympathise with Babs over Freda's niggling ways, but this evening Freda's hostility paled into insignificance. 'Babs, listen!' Stella caught at her friend's hand. 'Something awful's happened. I've been sacked!'

'*Never!*' Babs was astounded.

Stella nodded miserably. 'Not even a week's notice. Not even a week's wages in lieu. In fact . . .' Stella gulped '. . . she held back my pay for this week.'

She couldn't bring herself to admit she had only sixpence in her purse. Good-hearted as she was, Babs would try to press money on her that she could ill-afford: she was on a strict budget with the housekeeping her husband allowed her. Ted Thomas was a steady earner, but Babs never had the benefit of it.

'Well, the old cow!' Babs exploded. 'But why, Stell?'

Stella stopped herself blurting out Mrs Ridd's accusations. Neither would she mention the harsh words against Griff. That felt like disloyalty and, besides, she didn't know if it were true. It *couldn't* be true!

'She caught me splitting a packet of baccy for old Mr Lewis,' Stella fibbed.

'Well!' Babs said again. 'The miserable old hag! After all the years you've put in. She won't get another good one like you, Stell. More fool her!'

A sob escaped Stella. Babs put an arm around her shoulders. 'Have a cup of tea, kid,' she said, 'and we'll talk a bit. Perhaps we can think of something.'

Regretfully, Stella shook her head. 'Danny needs to go to bed.'

'Oh! He's all right, mun, on the sofa by there. Kids can sleep anywhere.'

'Your mother—'

'Pot on her!'

'Don't you mean . . . hat?'

They clung together, giggling, and Stella felt the tension ease. She'd get through this somehow. Perhaps Freda's anger had been about something else. Stella tried to persuade herself of this, but in her heart she knew it wasn't true. Not after the terrible things Mrs Ridd had said.

Someone had started a campaign of vicious rumours against her. Somehow she'd made an enemy, who was intent on destroying her. But who?

Stella couldn't wait until morning to tackle Griff, and tired though she was, she resisted sleep, awaiting his return. It hardly mattered about a late night now. She had no job to go to in the morning.

It was well after midnight when she finally heard the key in the front door lock, and Griff fell into the passage, letting rip with a stream of oaths.

Stella shuddered as she got out of bed, and slipped into her old dressing-gown.

All evening she'd been dreading the coming confrontation. These days Griff was like a stranger, and with each passing year he became more and more distant from her. She hardly re-cognised in him the dashing young soldier who'd gone off to war twelve years ago, and his disintegration had speeded up alarmingly since Rose had left.

If she saw this, other people must. No wonder rumours were spreading. And she had to admit to herself that he was a liability now – hadn't she lost her precious livelihood because of him?

She heard him stumble again in the passage and more curses. When he had first come to live with them, Stella had left the gaslight on for him, but too often it was still burning in the morning, and she couldn't afford that.

She put a match to the bedside candle, went out on to the landing and down the stairs.

'What the bloody hell!' he ejaculated.

She must have startled him, appearing suddenly like that. He stood with his back pressed against the passage wall, a tall, lopsided shadow that flickered in the candlelight.

'Stella! What the hell are you doing up at this time of night?'

As she reached the bottom stair, she smelt the drink on him, already turning sour. He looked dishevelled, as though he'd fallen down in the street a few times. Suddenly Stella was irritated by the sight of him; the pity she had once felt was wearing thin. 'Waiting for you, I am,' she answered shortly. 'We need to talk, Griff. Something's happened.'

'It can wait.' He pushed himself away from the wall with difficulty. 'I'm buggered. I'm going to bed. But I got to have a pee first.' He slouched towards the living-room door, making for the scullery and the lavatory out in the backyard. His movements were awkward and unsteady. 'Why can't you leave the bloody gaslight on, mun, so a man can see if he's peeing straight?'

Stella winced at his crudity. Sometimes she could see their father in him, but not often. Percy Stroud had been a small man, given to rotundity in his later years. He'd been upright, though, she remembered; a man of dignity, perhaps a little pompous, but she'd quarrel with anyone who dared say that.

He'd had his weaknesses, of course, like any man. She'd been proud that her father was a porter at the railway station in High Street, although he always liked to give the impression he was the station-master.

He'd be ashamed of Griff now, Stella reflected. She thought about the promise she'd made to her father on his deathbed. His last thoughts had been for poor, wrecked Griff. Even he had seen that Griff's marriage was doomed. She'd gladly given her promise to take care of her half-brother for always. Didn't they all owe him an immeasurable debt?

While Griff was out in the lavatory Stella lit the gaslight in the living-room, blew out the candle, then sat on the sofa waiting, not relishing what she had to say. She was tempted to put the kettle on and make a pot of tea, but she waited to see if Griff wanted something.

He came in at last and stood swaying in the scullery doorway. He looked awful and she wondered if he'd eaten that day. There was a bit of boiled mutton left. She was about to offer to make him a sandwich, when he asked, 'Somebody been in here with you tonight, have they?'

His eyes, though bleary with drink, were strangely alert, too.

'No, why?'

'Ted next door, for instance.'

Stella jumped up, the sandwich forgotten. 'Ted Thomas? Why would *I* have Ted in my home?'

He gave a short, derisive laugh. 'Well, according to him, you two are . . . well, shall we say as close as two coals in a fire, and just as hot?'

'*What?*'

'He was down the Archer's earlier tonight, giving me all the details. He left early, hinted he was on his way to spend time with you.' He swayed alarmingly, almost losing his balance again. 'You sure he hasn't been here, upstairs, like?'

'No!' Stella shouted. 'He has not! How dare you? She clutched her dressing-gown tightly around herself, staring into her brother's bloodshot eyes.

So it was Ted Thomas who was spreading dirty lies about her, and even her own brother believed them. She should've known. It was spite. Revenge. Just because she'd sent him packing with a crack on the head when he'd tried to molest her, and in her own living room, too.

Griff shrugged. 'He said it, not me. But why would he lie, Stella, tell me that?'

Stella hesitated. Should she tell Griff now that Ted had tried to rape her? He would've too, if she hadn't clouted him with a candlestick. But if she did tell, Babs might get to know, and how would she face her best friend then?

'It's not true, Griff,' she said lamely. 'How could you think such a thing?'

Griff took unsteady steps towards the sofa, and collapsed on to it in an untidy heap. 'Because all you bloody married women are the same,' he said, bitterly, 'after one thing only, and if you can't get it from one man, you'll get it from another.'

'That's a disgusting thing to say to me, your own sister!' Stella burst out, then thought of Danny asleep upstairs. She didn't want him awake and frightened. 'And don't lump me with your wife,' she went on. 'Rose did a terrible thing to both of us, remember? She stole my Eddie.'

Griff's features turned even more pasty at her words. 'Don't mention that bloody man's name under this roof,' he thundered. 'Or hers, either. I should've gone after them and killed them both.'

'Don't talk that way, for God's sake,' Stella exclaimed. 'And it's *my* roof, Griff, not yours. Remember that. I pay the rent. I pay for everything.'

Stella paused. She hadn't meant to remind him of that. But she knew what was eating him up from the inside: her sister-in-law had confided that Griff was impotent, and Stella guessed it had been the final straw for Rose, who wanted children.

Stella felt the pain around her heart that always came when she let herself remember the way her life had been with Eddie. They'd been so happy together. At least, she'd always thought they were . . . but had he ever really loved her?

Griff's shoulders were tense with anger. 'What am I supposed to do about money, eh?' he asked, his tone heavy with sarcasm. 'Sit with the cocklewomen outside Swansea Market, begging like a tramp with my tin plate outstretched for pennies?'

'I didn't mean it like that, Griff. It's just that something's happened, and I'm worried sick.'

'Oh, bugger it!' he said, ignoring her. 'I've had enough of this. I'm going up to my bed.' He tried to struggle up from the sofa, but it wasn't easy with one arm, and with legs that wouldn't obey his will. He stretched out an arm to her. 'Give us a hand up, Stell.'

Stella folded her arms across her chest, and stared hard at him.

'I'm not finished, Griff. I lost my job today. I'm out of work, and all because of you.'

He looked bewildered. 'What're you on about?'

'I'm sacked!' Stella heard the shrillness in her voice. 'What are we going to do for money – rent, food? I know things are hard for you, Griff, but I need a hand, too.'

He sank back against the cushions. 'So, this *is* about money. Well, since you haven't got a job any more, you'll have to do like I do. Find other ways of getting it.' He leaned forward, a crafty light in his eyes. 'You're giving it to Ted Thomas for nothing, and others, so I've heard,' he jeered. 'Why not make a bit of money lying on your back instead of giving it away? You're sitting on a fortune.'

Stella couldn't believe her own brother had said that. She was speechless.

He laughed harshly. 'Oh, come on now, Stella, you're not exactly an innocent young girl, are you? You married women know what's what. There's nothing to it, mun. Just do what comes naturally, and make a bob or ten.' He rubbed forefinger and thumb together, grinning. 'Because, there's money in it, Stell, big money.'

Stella still couldn't speak, but her mind was racing.

Perhaps Mrs Ridd had been right about him. If so, she could no longer keep that promise to her father. She had Danny to think of. These were his impressionable years, and Griff was a bad influence now. He'd sunk so low, and she hadn't noticed. The time had come to tell him he must leave. And she must do it now.

Stella wondered how to start, but there was something dangerous and unpredictable about Griff tonight that she hadn't seen before. Instinctively, she knew she must be careful.

'I don't blame you, Stell,' he said, clearly mistaking her hesitation for shame. 'A woman's no different from a man. What with Eddie buggering off, and all, you miss what you've been used to. Mind you, doing it with your best friend's husband, that takes real nerve.'

'Don't say any more, Griff,' she warned. 'Otherwise I won't be responsible for my actions.'

'All right,' he slurred. 'You don't have to get bolshie about it. I'm trying to help you, aren't I?'

He managed to get to his feet, and stood swaying like a tree in a gale. 'Look,' he began again, 'a pal of mine can arrange things. He does it all the time. There are blokes, decent blokes, mind you, who'd willingly pay good money for a bit of companionship and, er, entertainment with a good-looker like you, Stell.'

Stella felt anger race through her veins like a tidal wave. She'd never before felt such rage. She wanted to hit him with something, but held herself in check. 'This pal of yours wouldn't be Charlie Pendle, by any chance?' she asked.

Griff started. 'Where'd you get *that* name from?'

Stella shook her head in sorrow at what had become of him. 'I wouldn't believe Mrs Ridd when she said you were mixing with scum like him,' she went on. 'Charlie Pendle's a dangerous criminal and he's infected you with his filth.'

'Charlie gave me work when your so-called *decent* people wouldn't give me the time of day because I'm useless to them with only one arm.'

'Don't be a fool, Griff!' Stella shrieked. 'Can't you see he's using you? When he's finished you could end up like those witnesses who disappeared, or you'll be found floating in the Tawe with your throat cut. He'd slit a man's throat as soon as say good morning to him. That's what they say about Charlie Pendle. He's evil.'

'You don't know what you're talking about, Stella,' Griff's voice had a dangerous edge, 'so you'd better keep your mouth shut about Charlie – if you know what's good for you, that is.'

'I won't!' Stella was incensed. 'I lost my job because of you messing with him. I'll probably have to whistle for another, because nobody'll give me work, knowing I've a child dependent on me and a criminal for a brother – not to mention the lies Ted's spreading about me.'

'You're just a bit of loose skirt,' Griff taunted. 'I've told you what to do to get money – just lie back and spread your legs. Don't be a fool, Stella. Do us both a favour.'

Stella swallowed her revulsion. Griff was ready to sell her body to anyone with a shilling in his pocket. That things should come to this between brother and sister! 'If Dad could hear you talking now, Griff, he'd be so ashamed,' she said. 'And I'm ashamed, too. I want you to go. Find another place to live. Get your pal Charlie Pendle to put you up.'

He stared at her, disbelieving. 'You promised Dad, Stella, promised on his deathbed.'

'Dad would disown you himself if he were alive. You've got until next weekend to find a place, or your stuff goes out on the street.'

Suddenly his expression was thunderous, and Stella was afraid. 'You whoring bitch!' he bellowed, and took a step towards her. 'I know what you're up to. You think you can keep all the money for yourself.'

'Mam! I can't sleep.'

Stella whirled round to see Danny, barefoot, clutching his teddy-bear, standing in the living-room doorway. She thanked God that he wouldn't have understood the words Griff flung at her, yet he must feel the anger that vibrated between them. She could tell by his eyes that he was frightened.

'Go back upstairs, Danny, *cariad*,' she said, as calmly as she could.

His face puckered. 'There's a bogeyman under the bed, Mam,' he wailed.

She rushed to him and ushered him out into the passage. 'Go upstairs, chick. Mammy'll be up in a minute, now.' She gave him a little push, and he went up the stairs reluctantly.

'Don't walk away from me, you cheap trollop,' Griff roared down the passage. 'I haven't finished with you yet, not by a long chalk.'

'Oh, yes, you have, Griff!' Stella cried, as she rushed back into the room to face him. 'You're not fit to be under the same roof as my Danny. You're rotten through and through, and you're poisoning everything around you. I should've seen it before. I want nothing more to do with you, so get out of my sight now, and don't come back.'

'You're double-crossing me like that bloody husband of yours did, but you'll pay for this, Stella.' Clumsily, he lifted his one arm to strike at her. 'Knock you black and blue, I will, you dirty slut,' he yelled.

He lunged forward, but Stella leaped away, and ran up the stairs into the front bedroom. Shaking with fear, she rammed a wooden chair under the door-handle, then leaned against the wall near the door, breathless, dreading to hear him climb the stairs. But there was no sound. Had he gone out or fallen down in a drunken stupor? For the first time she didn't care what had happened to him, just as long as he stayed away from her and Danny.

She glanced at the bed. Danny was sitting up, staring at her, and she thought she could see silvery traces of tears on his cheeks.

'It's all right, Danny, love,' she said, soothingly. 'Mammy's with you. Get under the covers, now, and go to sleep.'

Obediently, he snuggled down.

Danny must be protected from Griff at all costs, she knew. And, from deep down, a shocking thought came. At that moment she wished Griff had not survived the war.

After a minute or two of self-recrimination, she crept to the bed and eased herself in, holding Danny's small form close. He snuggled into her warmth, his breathing even.

Stella was sleepless, although she was dog-tired. She thought about Ted Thomas and the lies he was spreading. Plainly, if her own brother believed them then so would others, all too ready, like Mrs Ridd and Freda, to see smut. Stella's whole body burned with shame, and she prayed Babs wouldn't hear them. If Stella lost her only real friend she didn't know what she'd do.

Mrs Ridd had been right about one thing: Griff had tainted their family, and now they'd all suffer. He *wanted* to believe Ted's lies so that he could sell his sister as a prostitute for his own profit. How low could anyone sink?

Stella knew she must separate herself from him. Her brother had turned into a stranger, and there was no one to turn to for help.

She dreaded what tomorrow would bring.

Chapter Three

The air in the living room smelt sour. Stella drew back the curtains and opened the sash window a few inches to let in some fresh air.

She wasn't surprised to see Griff lying on the sofa, asleep. She paused at the sight of him, rumpled and crumpled, unshaven and unwashed. He looked so vulnerable with that empty shirt-sleeve. Why had she been so frightened of him last night? He'd been drunk, hadn't known what he was saying.

Guilt assailed her, mingled with pity and remorse. She shouldn't have given way to temper and ordered him out. Losing her job had upset her, and everything had seemed hopeless last night. Today she felt more optimistic, and was determined to go out and find another job.

In the scullery she opened the back door to let in the cat, which twined itself silkily around her legs until she gave it a saucer of milk. 'Morning, Mogs.'

She put a match to the gas ring, which stood on the draining-board at the side of the stone sink, then dumped the heavy cast-iron kettle on to it.

Griff was probably parched for a cup of tea, and she needed something herself. It was going to be a long, tiring day.

Tea ready, she put a hand on Griff's shoulder to wake him. He opened his eyes and stared up at her. Something in his gaze looked like panic, but it passed so quickly that Stella couldn't be sure she'd seen it.

'What you want?' His voice was hoarse.

'Cup of tea, Griff.'

He struggled into a sitting position, and Stella put the cup and saucer on a small table close by.

'What time is it?'

'Half seven.'

He uttered an oath. 'What you want to wake me so bloody early for? Can't wait to get me out of the house, is it?'

Stella sat down opposite, her own cup of tea balanced on her knees. 'I'm sorry, Griff. I must get out early today to find work. Morning's the best time to look. I'll probably have to tramp all over town, as it is.'

She wanted to apologise for the hasty words she'd spoken the night before, and was determined to put things right between them. Apart from Danny, Griff was her only relative. It wasn't right that they should be at loggerheads.

'Look, Griff, what I said last night about finding other lodgings . . .'

'You didn't have to wake me to remind me of that,' he snarled. 'You're in a bloody hurry to get rid of me, aren't you? But I know why you want me out of the house, mind – so you can carry on with Ted Thomas on the sly. You tart!'

'Griff!'

He kicked the small table out of his way, and stood up, upsetting his tea, which splashed on to the linoleum and the rug at his feet.

Stung by his words, Stella sprang up. 'How dare you call me bad names? I'm your sister, for heaven's sake! And don't repeat Ted's lies under my roof. I won't have it.'

'Lies, my backside!' he bellowed. 'I had to sit in the Archer's last night and listen to all the details. Yes, my own sister!'

He struggled to pull his braces up over his shoulders, but Stella made no attempt to help him as she usually would. Looking at his face, contorted with rage, she felt she hardly knew him, and echoes of the fear she'd felt last night came back to haunt her.

'I'm a fool to feel sorry for you, Griff,' she said tightly. 'You're your own worst enemy. No employer will tolerate your bad temper. No wonder Rose walked out on you. You're pathetic!'

A vein throbbed in his temple, his colour rose, and Stella quailed.

'Rose didn't want to go,' Griff rasped out. 'That swine, Eddie, persuaded her. And it was *your* fault, Stella. You weren't woman enough to keep your own man happy.'

'Don't blame me or Eddie, either,' Stella said tightly. 'It was Rose. You knew what she was like. Never satisfied, was she? Always clamouring for things she couldn't have – things you couldn't give her—'

'What do you mean by that?'

Stella realised that dangerous ground lay ahead.

'I – I'm just saying that Eddie isn't the only one to blame.' She wrung her hands in despair. 'And I don't know why you're bringing this up after four years, Griff.'

'You started it! Calling my Rose up in holes. But you must've known what Eddie was up to. You should've warned me.'

'*I* should've known? She was *your* wife, Griff.'

Stella wanted to laugh at the irony of it, but a sob reconstricted her throat. 'When Rose took Eddie from me, I wanted to die, and I hated her with all my heart,' she said. 'But I've learned to live with it. Perhaps Eddie will never come back to me. I have to face up to that. You must do the same.'

'You two-faced bitch!' Griff bellowed. 'You couldn't hold on to your own husband, and now you're scheming to take someone else's.'

'It's not true, Griff.' Stella was shocked. 'Don't say such things. I'm your *sister*.'

'Oh, aye!' Griff exclaimed. 'My sister, who's kicking me out on the street. And Babs Thomas is supposed to be your best friend, but you're betraying her like you've betrayed me, and she ought to know the truth about you and Ted.'

At that moment Stella heard footsteps crossing the scullery flagstones.

'Cooee! It's only me!'

Freda stood in the living-room doorway, a brown hand-knitted cardigan around her bony shoulders, small eyes gleaming inquisitively under the narrow brim of a rust-coloured hat. She held up a teacup.

'Begging a cup of sugar, I am, for the kids' breakfast.' The gleam sharpened. 'Oh! Am I interrupting?'

Stella tensed. How long had Freda been standing in the backyard before making her presence known? How much had she heard?

'No, no, you're not interrupting, Freda,' she answered, her heart in her mouth. 'We're just going to have our breakfast. I'll get you the sugar. Babs and the kids all right, are they?'

Freda snorted. 'They'd be better if that sly bugger, Ted, left home.'

Griff's nose wrinkled. 'They'd be better off still if busybody relatives learned to keep their long noses out,' he remarked. 'Ted's told me a few things about you. Bloody mothers-in-law!'

Stella gasped, but Freda gave a dry laugh. 'Oh! You're a one, Griff!' Her tone was waspish. 'Always ready with a little joke, isn't it? On the bone of your arse, you are, but you don't let it get you down, do you, boyo?'

Griff growled deep in his throat, and shuffled towards the passage. 'I'm going to bed,' he muttered darkly. 'Don't bloody wake me again.'

'Have a swill first, for God's sake, mun?' Freda called sarcastically. 'You stink like a fourpenny herring, ten days old.'

'Nosy old cow!' Griff snarled. 'Somebody ought to knock her on the head. Put her out of her misery.'

Freda spluttered with indignation. Not knowing where to look, Stella handed Freda the cup filled with sugar. 'Mustn't take any notice of what Griff says,' she said awkwardly. 'What he

went through during the war plays on his nerves, you know. He
. . . he imagines all kinds of things.' She pushed a strand of hair
behind her ear. 'I don't believe half of what he says.'

Freda's mouth puckered in a sneer. 'Ah, but you know what
they say, don't you? A drunken man always speaks the truth – as
he sees it, anyway. He just threatened to do me in! Call the
bobbies to him, I should.'

'Griff's not drunk. He's in a temper because I asked him to
find other lodgings.'

'Not drunk! Don't make me laugh,' Freda scoffed. 'Smell the
booze from the back door, I could. And he looks like something
the cat's dragged in, as well.'

'Well, it's none of your business,' snapped Stella. 'Griff's a
war hero, but people like you have short memories.'

Suddenly Freda looked haggard and older. 'I lost a son in the
war, don't forget, so don't you throw the war in *my* face.'

'I'm sorry, Freda. I don't know what I was thinking of.'

Stella was filled with remorse. How could she have forgotten
that Freda's eldest son was killed in Flanders?

Through narrowed eyes, Freda stared at Stella accusingly. 'A
guilty conscience, is it?' she asked. 'Always thought you were a
bit of a deep one, my girl.'

'No, it's *not* a guilty conscience, thank you.' Stella bridled. 'I
don't know what rumours are going around, Freda, but I've
done nothing to be ashamed of. And next time you run out of
sugar, don't come to me.'

With a scornful sniff, Freda turned on her heel and marched
out, slamming the back door behind her.

After that, Stella had to pluck up courage later to ask Babs if
she'd look after Danny while she searched the town for work.

Normally she just pushed open Babs's back door and walked
straight in, though lately she had been wary of running into Ted.
She comforted herself with the thought that even he wasn't fool
enough to try something in his own home.

This morning she gave a perfunctory knock, and called a good morning. Babs answered immediately and sounded cheerful enough. She was in the scullery attempting to bath her twin girls, who were splashing the water about recklessly.

'Liz! Pat! Stop it, you little devils!' Babs scolded. 'Don't waste the water. I've got to use it to have a wash myself in a minute.' She threw a towel around Liz and hauled her out. 'Give us a hand by here with Pat, Stell,' Babs begged. 'Mam's never around when I really need her.'

Relieved that all seemed well between them, Stella lifted one little girl and towelled her down energetically, ignoring her squeals of protest and attempts to break free.

Babs's two were wild ones for sure. Perhaps they took after their father. Stella suppressed a shudder.

'Could you mind Danny for me?' she asked her friend. 'I'm going to look for a job this morning and I might be out longer than usual.'

Babs grinned good-naturedly. 'Don't you worry, Stell. Anything for my best friend.'

Stella felt a stab of guilt about Ted, though she hadn't done anything wrong. What she knew about him weighed on her mind. 'You sound fed-up, Babs. Is anything wrong?

Babs shrugged dejectedly. 'No more than usual. Mam's in a right old mood this morning, and Ted's not much better. Went off this morning without a word.' She looked directly at Stella, a worried expression on her pleasantly plump face. 'I always defend him when Mam calls him up in holes, but lately, well, I don't know, he seems so distant. We haven't . . .' Her cheeks turned pink. 'Well . . . you know, we haven't been together, like, for weeks, well, months even. Do you think he's tired of me, Stell? Break my heart, it would, if he left me for somebody else.'

Stella made a big fuss of hanging the damp towel over the back of a chair. 'Any man who got tired of you would want his head read,' she said firmly. 'Ted knows which side his bread is buttered, don't you worry.' But her heart ached for her friend.

28

She was hiding the truth from her, but one day Babs was sure to find out about Ted's womanising ways. Stella prayed Babs wouldn't blame her. Their friendship meant so much to her, especially now she was virtually alone.

And Babs would need support, too, when she finally learned the truth. It would be tragic indeed if a worthless swine like Ted Thomas should come between them.

Chapter Four

It was well after teatime and getting dark when Stella gave up her search for work and trudged along Victor Street towards home. She'd made innumerable enquiries in the Sandfields itself, and along Bryn-y-mor Road and St Helen's Road, only to learn that Mrs Ridd had indeed blackened her name in every corner shop for streets around.

It was galling to watch people's faces close up and their backs turn on her when she gave her name. She was ready to burst into tears, but wouldn't let herself give way. Mrs Ridd might have won the first round, but she hadn't won the war yet.

Pressing on bravely, Stella walked the town, but there was nothing, not even in Swansea Market. Mrs Ridd had no influence there, but times were so lean that there was no work to be had. Of course, she'd go out again on Monday. She must keep trying.

As she put the key in the lock she wondered if Griff was in and her courage almost failed her, but the house was empty.

She peeped into his bedroom, hoping that he'd already moved out, but his clothing was still strewn about. Griff had apparently never heard of hanging clothes in a wardrobe.

The untidiness looked so permanent. Perhaps he had no intention of leaving. She'd never be able to cope with his growing animosity if he stayed.

If he hadn't moved out by mid-week, she would confront him yet again, no matter how frightened of him she was. She couldn't allow Danny to be affected. He'd already lost his father, and shouldn't be exposed to rowing, drunkenness and perhaps violence. Her son, so precious to her, was all she had in the world.

With a sigh of resignation she made Griff's rumpled bed, then went downstairs to fetch Danny from next door.

Much later in the evening, when her son was in bed, someone knocked on the front door. She glanced at the clock on the mantelpiece. Gone nine.

Since she had learned about Griff's dubious acquaintances, she was nervous about late callers. It might even be Ted Thomas – she wouldn't put it past him to try bursting in on her to catch her unawares.

In trepidation, she leaned against the door and called out, 'Who is it? What do you want this time of night?'

'It's only me, Stella.'

Stella stood rigid, unable to move a muscle. That voice! She hadn't heard it in four years. It couldn't be! She must be dreaming. But her heart leaped in her breast.

'Eddie?'

'Open the door, Stella. Let me in.'

With fingers made clumsy with disbelief, Stella fumbled with the big old key and finally turned it. She pulled open the door and stared out into the darkness.

A man stood there on the doorstep, clutching a bundle in his arms. Stella stared at him, eyes wide. He moved forward into the gas-light, and Stella retreated a step, still in a daze.

'Let me come in, Stella, and close the door,' Eddie Evans said, in a voice heavy with weariness.

Stella stood aside to let him pass, unable to take her eyes off him. 'Eddie! I can't believe it. You've come back to me.'

She stood in awe as he walked past and down the passage to the living room. She'd pictured his return so many times, longed for it, but had never believed it would happen.

Yet here he was! Her Eddie was back. He must still love her!

She hurried after him into the living room and watched from the doorway as he looked around him, then placed the bundle on the sofa. He took off his grey trilby and threw it casually on a chair.

'Place looks the same,' he remarked, turning to her.

'Oh, Eddie!'

She searched his face eagerly for signs of love or happiness that they were together again. She loved him still; he must know that. 'Eddie, love, I can't believe you're here at last.'

Suddenly, her vision was blurred with tears of joy. A sob caught in her throat, and for a moment she couldn't speak. She kept her gaze fixed on his face, afraid that if she looked away for a split second he would disappear again.

Finding her tongue, she said, 'I tried to keep our home as you left it, Eddie, though it's not been easy . . . on my own.'

That sounded like a criticism, but she hadn't meant it that way. She could forgive everything now that he was back. She stepped towards him eagerly, wanting to throw herself into his arms, feel his kiss once more. 'Oh, Eddie, love! It's wonderful to see you. You don't know what this means to me.'

Her heart was singing. Eddie's back, and everything will be all right now. Her problems dissolved into thin air. He still loves you, her heart told her. And he has come back just to make you happy again.

'Take your coat off, Eddie, mun. I'll make a cup of tea.' She couldn't help laughing. 'Oh! This is wonderful!'

Eddie put his hand over the breast of his overcoat as though protecting the buttons from her. The gesture brought her up sharply, and her smile faltered, doubt setting in. She looked into his eyes and saw emptiness. The ground fell away from under her feet.

'No, I won't take my coat off, Stella,' he said, quietly. 'I'm not stopping.'

'What?' The sense of devastation was like a physical pain. She

33

couldn't lose him again. It was too cruel. She fought to speak cheerfully.

'You *must* stay for a cup of tea, Eddie. I can't . . . let you go without that. Come on, mun, sit down for a minute, if only for a chat.' Her voice faltered. 'I think you owe me that, Eddie.'

'Don't push me, Stella.'

'I'm sorry, Eddie, love. I didn't mean—'

Stella pulled herself together. Common sense told her to think straight. They had to work things out; get used to each other again. She shouldn't be so eager. They needed time.

She relaxed and smiled, showing him she understood. 'Of course, Eddie. I'm being *twp*. It's the excitement of seeing you again, right here in our home . . .'

She trailed off as a strange look flitted across his face. She was pushing too hard again.

'Here, let me look at you, Eddie,' she went on, and stepped closer to him.

He looked older, she realised with a shock, much older. Lines marked his face where no lines used to be. Could four years do so much? She touched her own face self-consciously, wondering if he saw changes in her, too.

Then she looked eagerly for the sparkle that had always been in his eyes, that had made her fall in love with him. It was gone, and something else was in its place – pain. He needs looking after, she thought; he needed her at last.

'Eddie, love,' she began, 'I'll make things easier by saying straight out that I still love you. I never stopped, in spite of what happened.' She reached forward to touch his arm. 'Let's forget the past. We can start over again.'

'Stella, listen . . .'

She rushed on – she had to say what was in her heart, had to make him understand before it was too late.

'Danny will be overjoyed to see you.' Her words surged out uncontrollably. 'He's just started school, you know. Getting on well, too. He's got your brains, Eddie, love, and your good looks. Oh! Our son's a real charmer! And he hasn't forgotten

you, because I talk about you all the time.' She was breathless.
'I'll wake him, shall I, and bring him down? You must see him
before you go tonight. He really is a handsome boy, Eddie.
You'll be proud of him.'

'No, Stella!'

A spasm crossed his face. Stella couldn't tell whether it was
anger or anguish, and she stared at him bewildered.

'I don't want to see Danny, now or ever,' he said raggedly.
'There's no point.'

Stella was crushed. 'No point?' she repeated. 'No point in
seeing your son? Eddie, I – I don't understand.'

'It would be cruel for him to see me again,' Eddie answered
gruffly, 'because, like I said, I'm not stopping. I haven't come
back to you, Stella.'

'Eddie! You're not making sense. Of course you've come
back home. Why else would you be here?'

Emotions fought on his face – pain, anger and helplessness
too. Her heart went out to him again, despite the cruelty of his
words.

'I need your help, Stella,' he said, desperation in his voice.
'What?'

'I know I've got no right to ask anything of you, but—'

'I'll do anything for you, Eddie, you know that,' Stella
interrupted. She was too eager again but she couldn't help it.
'Just say you'll stay.' She clutched at his arm. 'Please come back
to me, Eddie. Danny and I need you.'

He withdrew his arm and took a step back. 'It's over, Stella,
between you and me. It's been over a long time.'

'No!' She shook her head emphatically. 'Eddie, please, don't
say that.'

'It's true, Stella. I'm astonished you don't hate me. Most
women would.'

'I've never stopped loving you, Eddie. It's Rose I hate, not
you. Danny and me both love you. Don't you see?'

'And I love Rose. I still do, always will.' Eddie's tone was flat
and lifeless. 'Nothing will change that, Stella. Not now, not ever.'

35

Stella stared at him. He really meant it! Anger seized her, and all the pain and loneliness of the last four years swept over her again.

'If you love her so much why isn't she here with you?' she demanded harshly. 'She's left you, hasn't she? Gone off with another man, I'll bet. Huh! That doesn't surprise me.'

Hatred for her rival swelled, and the misery gushed out. 'Rose was always that kind, wasn't she,' Stella cried. 'Anything in trousers! But neither you nor Griff would admit it.' She took a deep breath. 'Did you know she was meeting the landlord of the Copperman's Arms just months before you ran off together? I know because she told me. But I never told Griff. I didn't want to hurt him. Rose is no good, Eddie! Are you too blind to see it?'

'Stop it, Stella!' Eddie lunged forward, gripped her arms and shook her. 'Stop it, for pity's sake! Rose is *dead*.'

Stella stared up at him, unable to speak.

'She died a year ago,' he went on. 'Tuberculosis. All I have left of her is our child.'

Stella's mouth dried. 'Child?'

Eddie strode to the bundle he'd brought with him, and began to unwrap the folds of a woollen blanket. As the last corner was lifted back, the curled-up form of a sleeping child was revealed. Pale blonde hair spilled out. When the light fell on the child's face, Stella couldn't stifle a gasp of recognition. The girl-child was the image of Rose, the hair, the heart-shaped face, skin like alabaster.

'This is Rosie,' Eddie said softly, a catch in his voice. 'She's all I have left.'

'How old is she?'

'Just over three.'

'Then Rose must've been . . .'

'Yes. When Rose told me she was expecting, I knew it was my child. Griff hadn't been . . . capable for years. She was terrified of what he'd do if he found out, so we went away.'

'You deserted me and Danny, just like that?' Stella cried

passionately. 'Your own wife and child! How could you, Eddie? This child might not even be yours. Rose had other men. I told you—'

'She's mine all right. I'll kill anyone who says otherwise.'

At long last she'd had an explanation from him after wondering and speculating for four years. He'd never felt that strongly about her or Danny, that was clear now. She'd wasted all that time pining uselessly for him, and was incensed at the knowledge. He had deceived her while they were still living together as man and wife. He'd been carrying on with Rose all the time.

'You betrayed us,' Stella hissed at him. 'You broke your marriage vows and turned your back on your family. You're despicable.'

'I fell in love with her,' he declared, as though that excused every treachery. 'I couldn't help myself. She was all I cared about.'

'Were Danny and me that easy to forget, Eddie? Was our few years together all for nothing?'

He didn't answer, and averted his face.

Glancing at the child on the sofa Stella wondered if worse was to come. She'd been prepared to forget and forgive, but now that she was facing the truth, her anger could not be suppressed. 'All right,' she went on coldly, when he didn't answer, 'you didn't love me any more, but what about your son? How could you abandon him for this other child?'

'I regret that, Stella,' he said quietly. 'Honestly, I do. I love Danny. And I'm sorry. I know I've treated you both very badly.'

'Yes, you have!' Stella cried. 'You've behaved abominably, and now you're asking for my help. You've got one hell of a nerve, Eddie Evans.'

Eddie sat down suddenly, perching on the edge of the sofa next to his child. His hand strayed to the golden hair spread out on the blanket. Stella's heart ached for the expression on his face. Even when she had thought he loved her, she'd never seen such tenderness in him. She felt a stab of jealousy.

'Why should I help you?' she asked. 'After all you've put me through. You don't know what the last four years have been like.'

He looked up at her. 'You just said you still loved me.'

'Oh, that was cruel, Eddie!'

His face was set. 'It's a cruel world, Stella. Ask Griff.' He stood up again, facing her. 'Look,' he said, pleadingly, 'you're the only person I trust with my child.'

'*What?*'

'I've given up my job in Bristol,' he said. 'I can't work and look after the child on my own.' There was a catch in his voice. 'Not without Rose. My family and friends are here in Swansea.'

'Are Danny and me included in those?'

'I need to find lodgings and work,' he went on evenly, ignoring her question. 'I can't lug Rosie about while I'm doing that. I've got somewhere to spend the night, with an old pal, but it isn't the sort of place to take a child. Will you keep her overnight, Stella? I'll come for her tomorrow when I've settled something.'

'Why should I?' she asked sharply. 'You tell me to my face you never loved me, then expect me to do you a favour.'

'I never said that,' Eddie said quickly. 'When we married I thought I was in love with you. No more than kids ourselves then, were we? With Rose it was different – real. Oh, God, I can't explain it. You have to experience it to know what I mean.'

'I have.'

'No, you haven't, Stella.'

'Don't try to tell *me* what I'm feeling, Eddie.' Suddenly she was furious with him again. 'You didn't give a damn what I'd feel when you up and left, did you?'

He shook his head. 'You thought it was love, Stella. I'm not the one for you, but there's still time to find the real thing. You're young, pretty. Forget me. Look for someone else—'

'You're talking rubbish, Eddie. And you haven't answered my question. Give me one good reason why I should help you.'

'Because little Rosie hasn't got a mother to watch out for her. And because you're a good woman, Stella. One of the best.'

She couldn't help laughing at the irony. 'You wouldn't think so if you heard the lies about me that are buzzing about like blow-flies.'

'What lies? What are you talking about?'

'Never mind.' She walked to the sofa and looked down at the child, this younger edition of Rose. Rose was dead, but she still held Eddie in thrall, and Stella knew that her hatred of the woman who'd taken her husband couldn't be brushed aside, even by death. She had lived with it for too long. How could she bear to have this child, this painful reminder, with her, even for one night? It was asking too much.

She faced him, ready to refuse. He'd put her through hell already.

'Look, Eddie, I can't—'

'She's an innocent child, Stella,' he interrupted. 'Imagine if it were Danny in need.'

As she looked into his eyes, she felt her resolve weaken. 'Well, all right. But I don't know what Griff will do when he finds out she's here and that Rose is dead. He's been acting strange lately. I'm getting afraid of him.'

Eddie lunged forward and gripped her arms so tightly he hurt her. 'Stella, promise you'll protect Rosie,' he rasped. 'Don't let Griff hurt her. She's only a child.'

'Eddie! You're hurting me!'

He shook her. 'Promise me, damn it! Promise! On Danny's life!'

Shocked at the wild look in his eyes, Stella tried to free herself from his grasp. 'Of course I promise. What's got into you, Eddie? Let me go.'

He released her, panting, his face pale. Stella rubbed her upper arms where his fingers had bruised her flesh. *Her* Eddie would never have done that. She didn't know him any more. He was like a stranger. Why was all this happening? First Griff, now Eddie.

39

'She can stay *one* night, Eddie, that's all,' she said. 'Come for her early in the morning, please. Griff doesn't get up until dinner time – he's usually had a skinful the night before. I'll hide her in my bedroom until you come.'

Eddie reached for his hat. 'I have to go.'

He strode to the sofa and looked down at the sleeping child. 'She's so beautiful, isn't she, Stella? Just like her mother.' He spoke as though to himself. 'She may never know how much I love her.'

'Why do you say that?'

He turned away from the sofa. 'Often it's hard to express what you feel for someone.'

'For some people, perhaps,' Stella conceded. 'Danny knows exactly how much I love him.'

He smiled, sadly, Stella thought. He was probably thinking of Rose again. 'Like I said before, you're a good woman, Stella. And I hope you find love again.'

He put on his trilby, smoothing down the brim in the way she remembered, then went to the front door. 'Thanks, Stella. I knew you'd come through for me.'

Suddenly he bent his head and put a quick kiss on her cheek. In that brief moment, Stella took in his familiar scent and her heart skipped a beat.

He'd thought he loved her once. He might love her again. He'd be back tomorrow. There was still time for a miracle to happen.

'Lock the door when I'm gone,' he said. 'Take care of my daughter, Stella. Protect her. Remember that she's not to blame for anything.'

Stella stood on the doorstep as he walked away. 'Don't leave it too late in the morning, Eddie,' she called after him.

In the light from the nearby street-lamp, she saw him lift an arm in acknowledgement. Then she lost sight of him in the crowding darkness.

Chapter Five

She woke with a start, apprehension pressing on her chest. Someone was crying. Eddie's child.

She was standing up in Danny's old cot, gripping the bars and grizzling, her little face blotchy. 'Daddy!' Rosie mewled. 'Where's my daddy?'

Stella was out of bed in a flash and lifted the child into her arms. 'There, there, Rosie, love.' She held the child close to her heart. 'Don't be frightened. Daddy will be here soon.'

On the double bed, the counterpane erupted and Danny's tousled head appeared. 'What's the matter with her, Mam?'

'She's hungry and frightened, chick. She doesn't know where she is.'

'But she's by here, with us,' Danny said, scrambling off the bed. 'Nothing to be frightened about.'

'Yes, well, you're a big boy, Danny. She's only little, and she doesn't have a mammy to take care of her.'

Stella sat on the bed, cuddling Rosie, willing her to stop crying. Griff was in the next room and she didn't want him coming to investigate the noise.

Danny stood close, tentatively touching Rosie's plump leg. 'Who is she, Mam? Why doesn't she have a mammy? What's she doing in my cot? Where did she come from?'

Stella almost blurted out that Rosie was his sister, but stopped herself. That would be too complicated for Danny and, knowing him, he'd expect a complete explanation. Who, what and why were his favourite words, and often Stella didn't have answers. Besides, Rosie would be gone from their lives soon, and it might be better if Danny knew as little about her as possible.

'She's just Rosie,' Stella said. 'Now, you must mind her while I dress and get the breakfast. Her daddy will be here soon.'

'Why?'

'Danny! Please! No questions now.'

Rosie had quietened down and Stella put her into the bed. 'You get back in as well,' she instructed her son. 'Make sure she doesn't fall out. Talk to her if she cries. Sing to her, you know, that song you're learning in school.'

Danny's face brightened. 'I'll teach her the words, Mam. Listen, Rosie,' and he began, ' "the sun has got his hat on . . ." '

Stella caught sight of herself in the dressing-table mirror and almost burst out laughing. In a moment of vanity last night she'd put rags in her hair to curl it in front, something she hadn't done in a long time. Usually she simply combed it back and fashioned it into a bun at the nape of her neck. She touched her hair – dark, like a gypsy's, she supposed, ruefully. Black as the devil's tongue, was how Mrs Ridd had described it, and Stella grimaced.

She hadn't slept much for thinking about Eddie, planning and scheming, wanting to look her best when he came back for his daughter. It was probably all for nothing, though. He'd told her he still loved Rose . . . but Rose was dead. Eddie was alive and so was Stella. There was still time to get him back, and she had to try.

Stella undid the rags, releasing her hair, which fell around her face in thick, glossy ringlets. She stared at herself again. Now she looked like a sad doll. Pulling a wry face, she combed back her hair as she usually did, and secured it with hairpins.

No job, no prospects, no man in her life and no chance of happiness. Her shoulders sagged. She felt lonely and neglected. But if she and Eddie did get together again, what about Griff?

He would hound them, no doubt about that. He hated Eddie, and when he found out about the child, he'd hate him even more.

Thinking about Griff, it dawned on her that she'd not heard him come in last night as she usually did. She tiptoed out on to the landing, and listened at his door. She heard nothing, so eased it open and peered in. The bed had not been slept in and everything was as she'd left it earlier.

Fleetingly, she felt a twinge of guilt. Was he lying in a gutter somewhere, drunk and ill?

A new worry seized her: she'd counted on Griff being asleep when Eddie came to collect his daughter. But suppose Griff came barging in when he was here? There'd be hell to pay. Someone might get hurt – one of the children, even.

Stella returned to her bedroom and dressed. There was no time for a wash now – she'd do that later. She had to get the fire going, get breakfast for the children, be ready when Eddie came so that she could leave the house with him. Perhaps they could go to the park and have a talk.

Stella almost slipped on the staircase in her hurry to get downstairs. In the passage she noticed a white envelope on the doormat. A letter? She never got letters. And it was Sunday.

Maybe it was for Griff, from one of his shady new acquaintances. Stella felt nervous at the thought that such evil people could have come anywhere near her home, and her hand trembled as she bent to pick it up.

There was no stamp, of course, but she was startled to see her name scrawled across the front. In growing trepidation, she hurried through to the living room and sat down at the table before she tore it open.

As she pulled out the letter, two folded white five-pound notes tumbled on to the table. She stared at them in astonishment then turned to the letter.

It was from Eddie. Her eyes skimmed the words.

He couldn't do this to her! Not again! But there it was. He'd gone! Left the country! Working his passage to Australia, and she must take care of Rosie until he was settled, then he'd send for her. Not a word of affection for herself; not a word of concern for his son, Danny.

Stella's hand flew to her mouth. He'd abandoned her again, but this time with the added responsibility of his illegitimate daughter.

Eyes blurred by tears, Stella read the letter once again, trying to find a message hidden between the lines, some word of hope for her, but there was nothing, and she let it fall from her fingers.

She put her elbows on the table and rested her face in her hands, unable to control the sobs that shook her. When she'd seen him standing there on the doorstep last night, she'd thought her troubles were over, but they were just starting. Oh, God! What was she to do?

She must see Babs: she needed to share this new calamity.

It was still quite early and Babs usually had a lie-in on Sunday morning, unless she decided to take the twins to chapel.

Stella picked up the letter and pushed it with the five-pound notes into the pocket of her pinny. First the children must be fed. That would give her time to think. Then she would go next door to see Babs.

After breakfast, Stella was ready to see Babs. 'Now, Danny, I want you to stay in the bedroom with Rosie while I go next door.'

'But why, Mam? I wants to go down Ysgol Street to see Timmy Jones. His cat's had kittens. He says I can have one.'

Stella sighed. 'We don't need another cat, Danny. We've got Mogs. One cat's enough to feed.'

'When will Mogs have kittens, Mam?'

'Mogs is a tomcat. He won't have kittens.'

'Why?'

'Danny! For heaven's sake!' she shrieked. The worry was getting to her – she must get a grip of herself. Stella forced herself to speak calmly: 'Be a good boy, Danny – please. Mammy has to see Auntie Babs. It's very important. Now, stay in the bedroom, especially if Uncle Griff comes home. Don't . . . don't let him see Rosie.'

Stella gave a swift rap at Babs's back door then lifted the latch and stepped inside. 'Babs! It's only me.'

It was too quiet. No sound from the twins, and where was Freda?

Stella hesitated. Just as she was about to leave, her depression deepening, there was a sound behind her. She spin round to see Ted Thomas's leering face. 'Well, well! The mountain comes to Mohammed.'

Stella's innards stirred with revulsion. 'I'm just leaving,' she said. 'Wanting to see Babs, I was.'

'Gone to chapel. But there's no need to rush away, Stella, darling.'

Stella felt sick. Preoccupied with her worries she'd let herself be trapped.

'Danny's alone,' she gasped. 'I must get back.' She moved towards the back door, but Ted intercepted her with surprising speed, cutting off her way of escape.

His eyes were bright, watching her with something like amusement. A cat playing with a mouse. 'You've been avoiding me, Stella,' he said.

'I certainly have,' she snapped, 'after what you tried to do to me last time we met.'

'Don't know what you mean,' he sneered, as he stepped closer. Dread rose in Stella's breast. Babs complained so often that Freda was always barging in when she wasn't wanted. If only she'd barge in now!

'Are you denying you tried to force yourself on me?' she asked, trying to side-step.

He put a hand against the wall, his arm barring her way. 'Come off it, Stell!' he said, and laughed unpleasantly. 'Your tongue was hanging out for it.'

'You're a dirty beast, Ted Thomas! Babs is too good for you. If only she knew the truth—'

'The truth is, Stella,' he broke in, 'you're a hypocrite. Your man has left you, and you're missing it. Makes women bad-tempered, that does, being without. I know what I'm talking about. I know women all right, what makes them tick. Saying no when they mean yes, just to get a man worked up.'

'You've been spreading lies about me,' Stella accused him. 'Even my own brother believes them. I want nothing to do with a pig like you, Ted. Can't make myself plainer than that, can I? Now, get out of my way.'

'There you go again,' he said, with a snigger, 'egging me on. Come here, you little tease.'

Before she knew it he'd grabbed her wrist and twisted it. Excruciating pain shot up her arm into her shoulder, making her cry out; but Ted laughed and gave another vicious twist.

Stella felt the chill of the scullery wall against her back, and suddenly knew what it was to be a cornered animal. Ted moved in closer, forcing himself against her, his knee thrusting between her legs.

'Let's have a look at what you've got, then, Stella,' he panted, his face against hers. 'It's nothing you haven't done before.'

'Stop it!' Unable to suppress whimpers of terror, Stella struggled to break his grip on her arm, until he forced it against the wall above her head, while his free hand fumbled with the buttons of her blouse.

'Stop struggling, mun,' he muttered, 'otherwise I'll have the tear it off you. Give me a kiss, come on.'

He forced her arm round until her head was pinioned, then clamped his mouth on hers. Stella kept her lips tightly closed, but her stubbornness was answered by a deep growl in his throat, and he drove his knee into her groin.

Stella felt nausea rise in her throat, then heard the rending of material as the buttons on her blouse gave way and his fingers clawed her breast. At the pain, Stella's lips opened involuntarily and Ted thrust his tongue into her mouth.

Stella was helpless to resist, overcome with terror and disgust at what he was doing.

She couldn't let it happen! Suddenly she saw Ted's mistake and bit down hard on his tongue. Ted roared in pain and jumped back from her, both his hands over his mouth, eyes watering.

'There, you swine!' Stella screeched. She edged towards the door, but he barred her way again.

'You could've injured me seriously,' he said thickly. 'What'd you want to do that for? It was only a bit of fun.'

'Get out of my way, Ted, or by God, I'll do more than bite you if you lay one finger on me again.'

A cast-iron saucepan stood on the draining-board. Stella snatched it and, heavy though it was, raised it above her shoulder. 'Get back, Ted, or I'll bash you with this. I don't care if I kill you. I wish I'd finished you off with that candlestick.'

'You're hysterical.' He eyed the saucepan uncertainly. 'You're making a bloody fuss for nothing.'

He put a finger gingerly into his mouth. 'I don't know how I'll explain this to Babs.' He glanced into the shaving-mirror over the sink, and stuck out his tongue. It was swollen and red. 'Strewth! Look what you've done!' He glared at her. 'It was just a bit of fun, I tell you. Slap and tickle, that's all.'

'It was nearly rape!' Stella shouted. 'Perhaps that'll teach you to keep your hands to yourself in future, Ted Thomas.'

His eyes narrowed. 'You're bloody unnatural, you are. Maybe you're one of those pieces that fancy their own kind. He pointed a finger at her. 'You stay away from my Babs. She's a proper woman, she is. You lesbian! Is that why Eddie ditched you?'

She was shocked at his words, but decided it would be better to pretend she didn't understand. 'I don't know what you're talking about,' she said loftily. 'And now you can get out of my way, before I start screaming my head off. That'll bring the neighbours in and you'll have some explaining to do.'

His face was dark with anger. 'You're a right stuck-up bitch,' he snarled. 'You need a good seeing-to, you do. That'll knock the lesbian filth out of you and maybe you'd be in a better frame of mind too.'

Stella edged past him warily. 'Babs is my friend and I don't want to hurt her,' she said. 'But if you touch me again, Ted, I'll call a bobby and have you taken in charge for molesting me. I'm a decent, respectable woman, even if you and Griff would prefer me not to be.'

With that, she flung aside the saucepan and fled.

Back in her living room, Stella felt sick at the things Ted had said to her, and at the remembered touch of his invading tongue and groping hands. She needed a good bath to wash away all memory of the incident. She must be careful to keep out of his way in future. She had the gnawing suspicion he'd do her some harm if he could get away with it.

She felt miserable as she set about doing a bit of dusting and tidying. Ted's treatment of her had set her nerves on edge, and Eddie's new desertion stung her to the heart.

How could he dump Rosie on her, knowing how she felt about the child's mother? Obviously, he didn't give a damn about her feelings. Stella beat at the sideboard with the duster, almost knocking over her favourite vase.

And how would she cope, working and trying to take care of two children? Babs had been good about Danny, but how would she feel about taking Rosie on too?

And then there was Griff. She couldn't hide Rosie from him for ever. There'd be a terrible bust-up when he saw her, looking so much like her mother. Stella trembled anew at the prospect of Griff's reappearance.

Mid-morning, just when she'd decided to calm herself with a cup of tea, Babs breezed in through the back door. She was still wearing her chapel garb, a dark red wool two-piece suit, which she'd bought the spring before last. It was now a size too small, and clung to her plump curves. Her cheeks were rosy from hurrying.

'Listen, Stella, love,' she parted, 'I've got some good news. Ted had a pay rise last Friday.' Babs nodded emphatically, as though Stella wouldn't believe her. 'And he didn't tell me until just now when we came back from chapel. He's the limit, mind!'

Stella could almost suspect Ted of feeling guilty, but she knew him better: he'd broken this news now to make sure of his wife's loyalty, in case Stella was tempted to show him up.

'Oh, that's wonderful, Babs,' Stella said, feeling a fraud. 'I'm so glad. Like a cuppa?'

'Yes, please.' Babs pulled out a chair and sat, her skirt straining against her thighs. 'Hymn singing makes me thirsty.'

Stella busied herself with cups and saucers, waiting for a pause in her friend's chatter so that she could tell her of Eddie's new betrayal.

'Do you know what I'm going to do with the extra money?' Babs said excitedly. 'Buy a piano!'

'A piano?' Stella stared. 'What for? You can't play.'

Quick steps skittered across the backyard and Freda appeared, wearing the hat with the tall, bedraggled feather. It makes her look like Robin Hood, Stella thought.

'Not for want of trying,' Freda said. She'd heard every word they'd spoken, and Stella felt uneasy. 'Wouldn't stick with the lessons, though, would she? More interested in playing hopscotch. Then, later, chasing the boys.' Freda gave a loud sniff. 'And look what she caught!'

'Mam!' Babs remonstrated. 'Don't start again, will you?'

Freda gave her daughter a dismissive glance. 'Cuppa going, is there?' She plonked herself down on the stool by the range.

Somebody's had a change of heart, Stella thought. Yesterday she wanted my guts for garters.

Stella poured the tea. She'd wanted to talk to Babs confidentially, but Freda looked as though she was staying put for a while. And anyway Babs could never keep a secret, so her mother was sure to find out about it. Yes, it would soon get around about Eddie and his child. At least if she told the story

49

now Freda would ensure that the gossips got the facts right. Stella opened her mouth to start, but didn't get the chance.

'Going to see about a piano tomorrow,' Babs said firmly.

'Get a good one while you're at it,' Freda said, with the air of one who knows all about pianos. 'Then it'll last a lifetime and longer. Although I expect the twins'll fight over it when you're dead and gone,' she finished gloomily.

Stella and Babs glanced at each other and, although Stella was feeling very down, she couldn't help responding to Babs's peal of laughter.

'Seriously, mind,' Babs said at last, 'I want the twins to learn the piano. It's an accomplishment, isn't it? Finishes you off, like. You've always got friends when you can play the piano.'

Freda nodded sagely. 'That's true. My youngest sister's girl's boy plays the piano,' she told them. 'Passing one exam after another, he is. They're awash with cerstificats, apparently.'

'Mam,' Babs said wearily, 'Phoebe's boy is only five. Auntie Ethel's having you on.'

'It's true, I tell you. The kid's one of them ingeniouses. Plays like an angel.'

The corners of Babs's mouth drooped in annoyance; 'Well, I'm starting the twins on lessons straight away,' she said. 'There's a lady down the end of Goronwy Street. She's quite cheap, so they say. Perhaps I can get two for the price of one.' She glanced at Stella. 'Why don't you let Danny go with the girls? He can always practise on our piano.'

Stella smiled weakly.

'How can I pay for lessons? I haven't got a job, Babs, remember?'

'Tsk! No, I forgot. There's a nuisance, isn't it? You'll have to go looking tomorrow, kid. Try Swansea Market again.'

Stella knew the time had come to tell Babs her own news. 'It's not going to be that easy, now.' She couldn't keep a sob out of her voice. 'Not since what happened here last night.' Out of the corner of her eye, Stella saw Freda stiffen. 'An awful shock, I had, last night, Babs,' Stella began. 'Eddie came back.'

'*What?*' mother and daughter said in unison.

Babs's eyes were like saucers. 'Where is he? Upstairs?'

Stella shook her head. 'Babs, you don't know the half of it yet.'

'Don't tell me that brazen hussy, Rose, is with him?' Freda asked, scandalised.

Stella took a deep breath. 'Rose is dead. Tuberculosis. But Eddie wasn't alone.'

'Not *another* woman in tow?' Freda shrieked.

'Who was with him, Stella?' Babs asked quietly.

'His little daughter.'

'Eh?'

'He and Rose had a child between them,' Stella explained. 'She's three. Yes, that's right, Freda. Rose was in the family way when she and Eddie ran off.'

There was a deep silence for a moment as mother and daughter digested this information.

'Where *are* they stopping, then?' Babs asked, her eyes still wide and round.

'The child's upstairs in my bedroom with Danny,' Stella said. 'Rosie, her name is.'

'Where's Eddie?'

Stella tried to speak but tears flooded her eyes, and the answer came out as a howl. 'Gone to Australia!'

Babs jumped up and put her arm around her friend's shoulders. 'Oh, Stella, love!'

'I'm a deserted woman,' she wailed, 'not once, but twice! How could he do it to me, Babs? I never stopped loving him. I wanted us to get back together again.'

'He's dumped the child on you?' Freda was aghast.

'I can hardly believe it of him,' Babs said thoughtfully. 'I always thought he was a better man than that.'

'A better man?' Freda expostulated. 'He runs off and leaves his wife flat, then comes back to dump his bast—'

'Mam!' Babs tightened her grip on Stella's shoulder.

Stella pulled herself together. Freda was going too far.

Despite her misery at losing Eddie, she felt a resolve rise up in her to protect his innocent child as she'd promised she would. 'We've got to keep it quiet,' Stella said firmly. 'Right, Freda?'

The old woman sniffed. 'Well, I don't know how you'll do that,' she said. 'People will want to know all about her. Stands to reason.'

Stella pulled Eddie's letter out of her apron pocket, spread it on the table and flattened out the creases.

'He left me ten pounds to be going on with,' she said. 'He says in the letter he'll send more when he's settled.'

'Huh!' Freda's tone was scornful. 'Some hope!' She rose from the stool. 'Do you know what I'd do?' she went on. 'I'd pack her off to the orphanage in Cockett. The Children's Homes is the best place for her. Or the workhouse. She'd be among her own kind there.'

'I'll do no such thing!' Stella said. 'I promised Eddie I'd take care of her, and I'm going to. He might change his mind and come back if he doesn't like Australia.'

'Don't kid yourself,' Freda retorted. 'He's well rid. *Duw! Duw!* You're a sentimental young fool, you are, Stella Evans.'

'I made a promise!'

'Oh, yes! Promised yourself right into the workhouse, I shouldn't wonder.' Freda jabbed a forefinger at her. 'Well, go on, then! Get the child down here. Let's have a look at her.'

Stella pushed the letter back into her pocket. 'The thing is, Griff hasn't come home yet. He might come barging in. I'm dreading him seeing her.'

'Well, it's got to happen some time, hasn't it?' Freda stated. 'She can't stay in the bloody bedroom for ever.'

Stella went upstairs and brought the child down, remembering that she had forgotten to give Rosie a proper wash, and that all she had to wear were the clothes she stood up in. Danny followed behind, chattering away as usual. She put Rosie down, beside the table. Her head was no higher than the top, and she was sucking her thumb. She stared warily at Babs and Freda.

'Good God!' Freda exclaimed. 'She's the spitting image of that . . . Rose.' She glanced at Stella. 'No wonder you don't relish Griff seeing her. He'll have a fit four ways from Sunday.'

Chapter Six

The children were seated at one end of the table in the living room, eating bread and jam. At the other end Stella had spread out an old flannelette sheet to do a bit of ironing.

Without Griff their home was peaceful. Danny was revelling in the novelty of a playmate. He talked incessantly and Rosie giggled at everything he said. Stella was amazed at how quickly she was settling in.

Babs had given Stella some things the twins had grown out of: a coat, some woollies, a couple of cotton dresses, a nightie or two and some underwear, but Stella knew she would have to spare some of the money Eddie had left to rig Rosie out properly.

At least the rent was secure for a few weeks. Griff still hadn't returned and she hoped he never would, though his few possessions were still upstairs.

Stella had washed Rosie's own little dress and was just about to iron it when she heard the front door open and heavy footsteps treading down the passage. Griff had come back.

He lumbered into the living room, empty sleeve flapping like a broken wing. She stared at him, shocked at his appearance. He was unshaven, and his clothes were crumpled. He looked as though he'd slept under a hedge. She thought at first that his face was dirty until she realised that the dark shadows were bruises, and he had a nasty gash over one eye.

He flopped into the armchair and closed his eyes. 'What's to eat, Stella?'

Wordlessly, she hurried to the larder and fetched the mutton, cut a couple of slices, then some bread and butter, and made a sandwich. She dumped the iron kettle on the gas ring, then took the food in to him. He snatched it from her and began to wolf it down.

She wouldn't ask him where he'd been or what had happened to him. She didn't want to know and she didn't care. She glanced at the children. Danny was staring, wide-eyed and silent, at his uncle. Rosie, too, lips smeared with jam, gazed at him with round eyes.

Stella felt a like a rat caught in a trap. Any minute now Griff would become aware of the child at the table.

'How about some tea, then?' he said, with his mouth full.

'I've got the kettle on. Won't be a minute,' she replied, and went into the scullery to wait for the kettle to boil. Her mind was racing, rehearsing how she would tell him that his wife was dead but her child was alive, and had taken up residence with them.

Danny started the ball rolling. She heard him get down from his chair at the table, his stage-whispered words of warning to Rosie as he helped her off the chair, their scuffling feet on the linoleum. He was still trying to follow her instruction: don't let Uncle Griff see Rosie.

As she reached the door and looked into the living room she saw that Griff was lying back exhausted, eyes shut, a half-eaten sandwich on the plate in his lap. The children were tiptoeing noisily towards the door.

He roused, looked at them, and they froze. Stella hurried in, intent on shooing them out into the passage, but she was too late.

'What the bloody hell?' Griff sat up and the plate shot off his lap on to the mat in front of the fire. 'Who the hell's she?'

'This is Rosie,' Danny piped up, before Stella could utter a word. 'She's got no mammy.'

Griff struggled to his feet, staring at the child. His mouth worked, then he swallowed hard. 'My God!' He glanced wildly at Stella. 'What's going on here?'

'Sit down, Griff, and I'll tell you.' She turned to the two children. 'Go upstairs, both of you.'

'No!' Griff thundered. 'That kid! Want to have a good look at her, I do. Come here, you!'

But Rosie hung back, frightened, and drew nearer to Danny, who put an arm around her protectively.

'Please, Griff,' Stella begged, 'don't frighten them.'

'Who is she?'

'You know who she is, Griff. You can see it in her,' Stella answered, trying to steady her voice. 'She's Rose's child.'

'Rose?' He looked around wildly as though Rose might be hiding under the table or behind the armchair.

'Rose died of tuberculosis – last year, I think Eddie said.'

Griff was suddenly still, his face ashen. He swayed, and for a moment Stella thought he would fall. He reached out his hand and gripped the armchair for support. 'Eddie.' His voice quivered. 'You saw Eddie.'

It wasn't a question. Rather, it sounded like an answer, and Stella was puzzled. Griff looked shaken.

'Sit down, Griff. Eddie came to see me last evening. He asked me to look after Rosie overnight.' She paused. 'Turns out, though,' she went on dully, 'that he's gone to Australia.'

'Australia,' Griff repeated automatically, then let out a wild laugh. 'Bloody Australia!' Griff roared. 'That's a good one, that is. Australia!'

'Griff, you're terrifying the children, and me.' Stella wondered if the news of Rose's death had turned his mind.

Abruptly Griff stopped laughing and seemed to pull himself together. 'She can't stay here,' he said harshly.

Stella felt annoyed by his high-handed attitude. He was acting like he was head of the household when he was there merely on her sufferance. 'She's Eddie's daughter, too,' she snapped, 'and I'm going to take care of her, as her father would want. Eddie'll come back for her.'

'Forget it!' Griff rasped. 'There's no place for Eddie Evans's bastard in this house. I'm sick of the sight of her already.'

'Don't use that word in front of her,' Stella said angrily. 'It's got nothing to do with you who stays here. This is *my* home, Griff, Danny's and mine. It's you who doesn't belong. I've had enough of your ravings, your drinking and – and your dirty suggestions. Get your things and get out. Don't come back. You're not my brother. I don't know you any more.'

With a swiftness that astonished her, Griff swept the knick-knacks and ornaments off the mantelpiece, sending them smashing on the hearth. The children screamed and ran from the room.

'Your home!' Griff roared. 'Your bloody home.'

He lunged at the sideboard, and more ornaments flew. Some crashed against the wall, including Stella's favourite vase.

'Stop it, Griff,' she screamed. 'Stop, or I'll run for a bobby!'

'Shut your gob, you treacherous slut,' Griff yelled. 'I'll fix your home for you. I'll make it a pigsty fit for you and that little bastard to live in.' He grabbed the pot of jam off the table and flung it against the mirror on the wall over the fireplace. Broken glass flew everywhere and Stella threw up an arm to shield her eyes. When she lowered it globules of jam were running down the wallpaper. It was the last straw.

She ran out into the passage. The children were standing at the foot of the stairs. Rosie was crying, but though Danny's bottom lip quivered, Stella could see he was fighting to be brave.

'Come on,' she urged. 'We'll go to Auntie Babs,' and hurried them out of the front door. She didn't knock but thrust them inside calling frantically as she went, 'Babs! Babs! For God's sake, help me.'

Her friend rushed into the passage, her eyes round with astonishment. 'What's happening, kid?'

'It's Griff – he's gone mad. He's smashing up my house. Look after the kids while I fetch a policeman to him.' And with that Stella raced down to the street corner, then on to the main road.

Autumn dusk was already deepening into night, and she was cold for she had no coat or hat. She felt almost naked without her hat but there'd been no time to think of such things, not with Griff smashing up her home.

There were quite a few people about, workmen and shop-girls making their way home – and the familiar, comforting outline of a dark-clad helmeted figure strolling with measured tread along St Helen's Road towards the police box outside the hospital. Braving the horses and carts, and a jangling tram, Stella tore across the road towards him.

'Officer! Please, help me.'

As Stella approached her open front door, the policeman at her heels, she heard glass breaking inside the house. The gas-light flickered faintly along the passage. The officer pushed her aside. 'Stay back, missus.'

He put one black-booted foot on the front step, hesitated, and withdrew the truncheon from his belt. Then he rushed down the passage, weapon raised, shouting, 'Now then! What's this?'

Stella stood at the open door, too afraid to venture inside. Sounds of a furious struggle came from the living room, and she winced at the crash of furniture being overturned.

The policeman was shouting warnings at Griff, who howled like a madman and yelled obscenities at the top of his voice.

Out of the corner of her eye Stella was aware of people in the darkness about her, neighbours edging on to the pavement, agog, and shame mingled with her terror of what was happening indoors. This spectacle would've been shaming on a week night, but on a Sunday, with chapel-goers on their way to the evening service, it was mortifying.

Babs was at her elbow, then, and behind her Freda, who craned her skinny neck this way and that in an effort to see what was happening.

Babs took hold of Stella's arm. 'Come away, kid. Come into our house till it's over. Everybody's gawking at you.'

'No, Babs. He's my brother.'

'He's a bloody lunatic,' opined Freda. 'He wants locking up. We won't be safe in our houses with him about.'

As two figures appeared out of the living room Stella stepped back. One was the policeman, red-faced now and gasping for breath. He had Griff's arm twisted behind his back, and his free hand gripped the nape of the miscreant's neck, forcing his head towards his chest.

The pair staggered out on to the pavement. The officer glanced at Stella as they passed her. His nose was bleeding, and he had a cut above one eye. 'You never said he had only one arm,' he said reproachfully, 'but even so he put up a fight.'

He looked around him, agitated. 'Here! One of you men, blow my whistle for me. I daren't let go of the bugger. I need help with him.'

The whistle was blown, several times, with gusto.

It seemed like eternity, although it was only a few minutes before heavy running feet were heard along the street and another policeman appeared.

A jingle of handcuffs, and Griff was tethered to the new-comer's wrist, but the first policeman didn't let go of his neck. Griff looked wretched and had fresh bruises on his face where the truncheon had caught him.

'All right, you lot,' one of the policemen shouted, 'push off home. There's nothing more to see. About your business, or you'll all be had up for loitering.'

It was too dark now to see exactly how many were enjoying the spectacle. Stella envisaged a crowd like at a football match, and her shame deepened.

'You'd best go indoors now, missus. He's coming with us,' the other policeman said to her. 'Looks like you've got a hell of a mess to clean up.'

'You're not going to walk him through the streets like that?' Stella asked.

Griff didn't deserve such treatment: the war, society's neglect and Rose had done for him.

'We're only going as far as the telephone box on the corner,' a policeman assured her, 'to send for the Black Maria.'

Now they had him secure, they were handling him less severely and Griff raised his head. His eyes fell on Stella. In the light from the street-lamp she could see that they were brimming with hatred.

'You've done this to me,' he said hoarsely. 'You've brought your own brother to this disgrace. You've chosen that bastard over me.'

'No, Griff! You don't understand . . .' She could find no words to defend herself. 'I'm sorry, Griff.'

'You will be, my girl,' he promised. 'Keep looking over your shoulder from now on, because one day I'll be there! Then God help you!'

'Here!' a policeman said. 'That's enough of that kind of talk, boyo.' He jerked his head at Stella. 'Get indoors, missus. You've got plenty on your plate already. He's made a right pigsty out of it.'

Babs stepped in through her back door and yawned. She'd spent the last hour helping Stella clear up the debris from Griff's rampage, and now she was tired and ready for bed.

She was sorry for her friend. Things were hard for Stella, with no job, and no man to support her. And now this extra responsibility of Eddie's child.

Babs looked around at her neat little scullery. She had a lot to be thankful for: a steady husband with a good job, two lovely kids. And Ted's pay rise meant little extras for them all. She yawned again, and wished she was curled up in bed against Ted's warm back.

She went into the living room. Ted was sitting in front of the range, reading the Sunday newspaper, stockinged-feet resting on the brass fender, trying to ignore Freda, who was feeding the fire with small coal, building it up to last the night.

'You'll be going now, then, Mam, will you?' Babs looked pointedly at the clock on the mantelpiece.

Freda gazed at her reproachfully, the coal scuttle in her hands. 'Thought I'd stay a bit longer,' she said. 'It's not half ten yet, and my grate'll have cold ashes in it.'

'Should stay home and look after it, then, shouldn't you?' muttered Ted nastily. 'You must be worth a mint, the money you save on coal.'

Freda dropped the scuttle into the hearth, and coal dust sprinkled the tiles and fender.

'Are you saying I'm not welcome in my own daughter's home, Ted Thomas?'

'Course he isn't, Mam,' said Babs, trying to head off yet another row between them.

'I should think not,' she said icily. 'After all I've done for you both. I've worked my fingers to the bone in this house, I have.'

Ted rattled the paper. 'What've you ever done for us, eh? Interfere, that's what,' he exclaimed bitterly. 'It's wicked, as my old mam used to say, when somebody interferes between husband and wife.'

'I never did!' Freda was indignant. 'Tell him, Barbara. Stand up for your mother.'

'Mam! Ted! Please!' Babs put her hands to her temples. 'It's too late in the evening to be bickering.'

'I've been a good mother to you, Barbara,' Freda insisted. 'Of all my children, you're my favourite.' She sent a baleful glance at Ted. 'Aye! And the one most in need of me, too. You wait and see, my girl.'

'Not many men would put up with a meddlesome mother-in-law,' Ted remarked darkly. 'They'd have left home years ago, if they hadn't bumped her off first.'

Freda opened her mouth to retort, but Babs forestalled her. 'Mam, make us a cup of tea, will you, please?' she begged. 'I'm worn out. Me and Stella worked like navvies to get her house straight.'

With a scalding glance at Ted, Freda darted into the scullery.

Babs guessed that she was glad to make the tea: any excuse not to have to return to her silent house across the road just yet. She understood that reluctance, but Freda's carping and her animosity towards Ted were spoiling their marriage.

Dejected, Babs sat down on the wooden chair opposite Ted, and wished he would put away the paper and talk to her. She felt as if a chasm was opening up between them, widening each day. Bridges she built were soon torn down, either by Freda or Ted. But she had to keep trying.

'The wallpaper's ruined next door,' Babs began. 'And the mats in the living-room. We had to nail a bit of plywood over the scullery window. Not a pane of glass left intact. Do you think he'll go to prison, Ted?'

'Who?'

'Griff Stroud, of course. He threatened her, you know. I heard him. He frightened me, I can tell you.'

'Probably will go to prison,' Ted agreed, turning the page with a rustle. 'The Strouds are a bad lot, Babs. I don't know why you bother with that Stella. I've heard things about her no decent woman like you should know about. Smutty things, if you get my meaning.'

Babs was aghast. 'I don't believe it! And I'm astonished at you, Ted. How can you say that when you know that Stella's a decent woman?'

'Don't know her all that well, do I?' Ted said casually.

'Well, she's been my best friend since we were girls,' Babs assured him. 'Stella'd give you the coat off her back if you asked her. She's decent and respectable. It's Griff that's the bad lot.'

'Well, I've heard she's not above making vicious accusations against innocent blokes,' Ted replied obliquely. 'You don't want to believe everything she tells you. The less you have to do with her the better.'

'What *are* you talking about?'

'Well, ask yourself, Babs. Why did Eddie leave her? She's a deep one, she is, and sly with it. I don't trust her, and neither should you, Babs.'

Before Babs could respond, Freda came in with a tray of tea and biscuits, and she thought it wise to let the matter drop.

Babs poured a cup for Freda, who sat at the table. When she handed Ted his tea he indicated, with a sharp lift of his chin, that she should stand it in the hearth.

Babs sat down and sipped hers, thankful that a row between Ted and her mother had been averted. She wanted to plan how they would spend the extra money coming in.

'I've been thinking, Ted. Could you get off an hour early tomorrow?'

'What for?'

'I want us to go into town and look for a piano. I thought we'd go up High Street, see what Snell's in the arcade have got to offer.'

'*What?*' He lowered the newspaper into his lap.

Babs smiled eagerly, pleased to have his full attention. 'We agreed at dinner time, remember? Now you've had this pay rise we'll get a piano for the girls, and lessons, as well.'

'Where *do* you get these fancy ideas from?' Ted asked. 'Piano, be buggered! Do you think I'm made of money?'

'Penny-pinching so-and-so!' Freda interposed.

Babs waved her mother into silence. 'But, Ted, it's for the twins,' she cried, disappointed. 'You promised!'

'No, Babs. We can't afford it.'

'Oh, yes?' Freda's voice crackled like dry leaves underfoot. 'What about that pair of plus-fours you bought yourself, last week? You'll be buying golf clubs next.'

'Mam, please!'

Freda wouldn't be silenced. 'Plus-fours! Bloody waste of money. Trying to impress somebody, are you?'

'Shut your interfering chops, you old harpy,' Ted snarled. 'I've had just about enough of you.'

'Ted! Don't speak to my mother like that!'

He crumpled the newspaper into a ball and threw it on to the floor. 'Don't want to speak to her at all, damn it!' he shouted. He jerked his head towards the door. 'Tell her to bugger off!'

Babs's face reflected the agony of trying to divide herself in two. 'Don't start, Ted, will you?' she pleaded.

'Don't tell me, tell her!' he snapped. 'You're pathetic, you are, Babs. *She*'s made you like that. Huh! No wonder your father died young, poor bastard. He was glad to get the hell out of it.'

Freda spluttered incoherently at this new insult, and Babs pulled out a handkerchief to dab at her nose with it. 'Ted! Please! I can't stand much more of this.'

Ted glanced at her disdainfully. 'Oh, bloody hell? Don't start snivelling now, for God's sake. It's enough to drive a man to drink.'

'What about a new winter coat for our Barbara, eh?' Freda put in defiantly, ready to carry on with the war. 'It's a shabby man who makes a shabby wife.'

'No, no, Mam, it's a piano I want—'

'Babs had a new coat five years ago,' Ted interrupted. 'My old mam, God bless her soul, made her coats last ten or more. Never hounded my father for money, like some I could mention. Thrifty, my mam was, and a reasonable woman.'

'Thrifty, did you say, Ted?' Freda slapped her bony thigh with glee. 'I remember your mam, all right. Thin as a stick, but legs on her like hams. Water on the knee, it was. Spent most of her married life on all fours, scrubbing floors to keep your old man in beer and ciggies. She was bent double with rheumatics in the end.'

Ted sprang to his feet, lifting a hand threateningly. 'You poisonous old hag!'

Babs jumped up, too, and placed herself between husband and mother. 'Ted, don't!'

He stared at her, eyes glittering. Even in that moment of uncertainty and despair, part of Babs couldn't help admiring his looks: the straight, noble nose, carved lips like you see on those Greek statues, beautiful head of hair, and such a fine build. Lots of girls had been after him but he'd picked *her*.

He lowered his hand. 'I'm going out,' he said gruffly. 'Don't

65

know when I'll be back.' He stepped past her towards the door, grabbing for his coat and cap.

Babs turned to him, her hands clasped together. 'About the piano, Ted—'

'There'll be no piano and no coat, either,' he said, 'because I didn't get a rise.'

Babs's mouth dropped open. 'But you said . . .'

'I was having you on,' Ted said. There was a gleam of spite in his eyes.

'But why?'

'Because you're so stupid, woman, *twp*, daft as a brush. You'll believe anything. Stupid's your middle name.' He shook his head as though bewildered. 'How the hell I came to marry you, I'll never know.' With that parting shot, he left, slamming the front door after him.

'Well!' muttered Freda, breaking the brittle silence.

'Oh, shut up, Mam.' Babs flopped on to the chair Ted had vacated, hands covering her face. Such awful things he'd said, but he hadn't meant them. He was upset.

'Now do you believe me?' Freda asked in triumph.

'He's a good husband,' Babs cried. 'He doesn't drink and gamble his wages away. He gives me my housekeeping on the dot every Friday.'

'Pittance!' Freda spluttered.

Babs had to agree that the housekeeping allowance was slender. She could do with a few shillings more. She hated having to ask Ted for extra to buy shoes for the twins or even a pair of stockings for herself.

'What more proof do you want?' Freda asked.

Babs lifted her head wearily. 'What are you on about now, Mam?'

'He's gone out.'

'Don't I know it,' said Babs.

'Yes, but it's Sunday night, isn't it? No pubs or clubs open, no cafés. Dead, it is. As dead as last week's mutton. So where has Ted gone, eh?' Freda sat back, folding her arms across her narrow chest. 'I'm telling you, Barbara, Ted's got another table to put his feet under, and it's not too far from by here, either.'

Babs had had enough. 'Mam, shut up! Stop interfering in my marriage. I love Ted and, what's more, I *need* him.'

Freda hooted with laughter. 'Let me tell you a home truth, my girl. You need *him* like you need a carbuncle on your arse!'

Chapter Seven

Stella pulled her cardigan across her chest as she hurried down Victor Street towards home. The cruel whiplash of winter to come was in the wind that clutched at her hat and almost tore it off her head. Already she was regretting her impulsive visit to the pawnshop on Dillwyn Street in town.

It was a week since Eddie had turned up on her doorstep, and Griff had been led away by two policemen, but to Stella it felt like a decade. Having refused to bring charges against Griff, she'd heard nothing further from the police. Not knowing where he was and how he had fared made her nervous. Was he waiting to pounce on her as he had threatened?

But Griff's threats, real or imagined, were the least of her worries. It was Saturday again, and she was no nearer finding work than when Mrs Ridd had sacked her. Things were looking desperate.

As she approached her home, she saw Ted Thomas loitering on his doorstep. She had the impression that he was waiting for her and her heart lurched.

She walked past him, and rummaged in her handbag for her key.

'Hello, Stella, darling.'

She ignored him. Her fingers closed over the key, which she took out and tried to insert in the lock.

'Been waiting for you,' he went on. 'Thought you'd like to know about Griff.'

Stella paused. She had to summon all her willpower to look directly at him. He was wearing that smarmy smile, the one that made her feel cheap and dirty. 'What about him?' she faltered.

'Up before the magistrate last Monday, he was,' Ted answered. 'Two months, they gave him. How do you think he'll like clink?'

Stella was horrified. 'Two months in jail? They can't do that to Griff! He's a war hero.'

'You put him there, darling, remember.'

'But I didn't!' Stella flared. 'I told the police I wouldn't bring a charge against him.'

'They had enough without that,' Ted said. 'Assaulting a bobby, disturbing the peace. But it was *you* called the bobbies in the first place, and you can't deny it.' He guffawed. 'Griff'll love you for that.'

He took a step forward, and Stella backed away, trying to turn the key.

'Now you're really on your own,' he said. 'But you don't have to be lonely, Stella. Just give me the nod, any time, and I'll be in like a flash.'

Stella shivered with revulsion.

'I'll warm you up, soon have you sizzling.' Leering, he rolled his eyes, his mouth slackening. 'I got plenty to teach you, darling. Hot stuff you never got from Eddie.'

'You disgust me! Keep away!'

'Hey!' His tone hardened. 'You need a friend, mind. No job, no money coming in. Yes, sweetie, you need me, all right.'

Over Ted's shoulder Stella saw a group of people walking up the pavement from the park – Freda and Babs, with Rosie in her arms, and the three older children skipping along beside them. Relief flooded through her, and anger, too.

'I'd rather be locked up in a lunatic asylum, than be with you, Ted Thomas,' Stella grated. 'And you'd better get that dirty look off your face because your wife and kids are right behind you.'

Ted spun around to face his family. His twin daughters rushed past him into their house as if he wasn't there, screaming for their tea, with Freda following.

With a sideways glance at Stella, he went indoors, too. She felt relieved, yet drained. If Ted kept on pestering her like this, she might be forced to move. But where would they find another place now that money was so scarce? And why should she be deprived of Babs's friendship because of Ted's treachery?

'Hello, Stella,' Babs said cheerily as she approached, setting Rosie on her feet. 'I know it's a bit cold, but we took the kids down the park.' She winked. 'Anything to keep the peace between you-know-who.'

Danny ran to Stella, and she patted his head distractedly. He clutched at her hand, his face rosy and beaming. 'We saw the ducks, Mam, and I nearly caught one. Can we have a duck? I'll look after it and feed it. Can we, Mam?'

'Expect so, Danny,' Stella murmured absently.

Danny gave a wild whoop of joy. 'I'm going to have a duck! I'm going to have a duck!' He rushed into Bab's house to tell the twins.

'Tsk!' Stella chided herself. 'What have I done now? I don't know what I'm saying half the time, I'm that worried about everything.'

'You look worn out,' Babs said kindly. 'Perished, too. Where's your coat?'

'Left it with Mr Fingel in Dillwyn Street.'

'You pawned your coat?' Babs was startled. 'My God, Stella, how are you going to get through the winter without it? How much did he give you?'

'Two and six,' replied Stella. 'I was hoping for five bob, at least.'

'Come in and have a cup of tea,' Babs said kindly. 'We can have a chat before you take the kids home.'

Stella hesitated. She couldn't face Ted again. 'Don't want to disturb Ted having his tea,' she said.

'Oh, he'll have his, and go out again, now that we're home,'

Babs paused. 'He goes out a lot lately. Mam says . . .' She waved a hand. 'Oh, never mind. Come on, Stella, you'll catch your death.'

But Stella held back. She wanted the familiarity of her own home. And if she was there Ted might decide to hang around. The effort to be civil to him in front of Babs would be too much for her, tired as she was. Ted was to be avoided at all costs.

'Hold on, Babs. Let's go in my house, just you and me,' she suggested. 'Can Danny and Rosie stay in with Liz and Pat for a bit of tea? I've got a cheek, I know. Your mother'll watch them, won't she? She won't mind this once.'

Babs agreed, and they went inside together. Stella sat down before the range in the living-room, while Babs made the tea.

But no more than five minutes had gone by before Danny charged in with Rosie. Stella gave him a kiss, hesitated a moment, then patted Rosie's head, aware that Babs was observing her.

'When will I have the pet duck, Mam?'

'When its mother lays an egg.'

'When will that be?'

'When Nelson gets his eye back.'

'Aw, Mam!'

With a shrug of resignation, Danny settled himself on the mat at her feet. Any hope of a pet duck now sunk, he talked excitedly about the trip to Brynmill Park. Rosie, squatting beside him, said nothing, but stared fixedly at Stella as if afraid she might disappear.

'Thanks for taking them out, Babs,' Stella said. 'Must've been a handful, four kids let loose.'

'Enjoyed myself, I did,' Babs chuckled. 'I'm still a bit of a kid, myself.' She looked serious. 'You've heard about Griff, I suppose? Him being in jail?'

Stella nodded, but indicated the children. She didn't want anything said in front of them.

Babs looked down at Danny. 'Danny, love, take Rosie next

door to play with the twins for a bit. Your mammy and me want a little talk.'

Obediently, Danny got to his feet, pulling Rosie up too. 'What about?' he asked. 'Is it about Mrs Benson's fat tummy?'

Stella and Babs exchanged a startled glance and both nearly laughed, but Stella kept her face straight. 'No, love. It's about ladies' dresses, hats and shoes.'

'Oh!' Danny grimaced. 'That's boring!'

He and Rosie disappeared then, skipping across the backyard, and both young women gave themselves up to a fit of the giggles.

'He's fascinated by Mrs Benson,' Stella said, when she'd calmed down. 'He told me he can't understand why she's got such a fat tummy when the rest of her is so thin. I could write a book about his funny sayings.'

'Yes, he's a one, is your Danny,' Babs agreed. 'Rosie's a pretty little thing, and he thinks the world of her, you know,' she went on. 'Held her hand all the time we were in the park. It's as if he knows she's his sister.'

Stella fidgeted. 'I don't want him told just yet. When Eddie comes back, Rosie'll be gone from our lives.'

Doubt moulded Babs's mouth into a sceptical fold. 'You've got to face facts, love,' she said earnestly. 'Eddie may never come back. Anything could happen to him over there. I think you can make up your mind that Rosie's here to stay.' She nodded emphatically. 'And things will turn really nasty when Griff gets out of prison.'

'Yes,' Stella said miserably. 'He hates me, Babs, now I'm harbouring Eddie's child. But I won't let him hurt Rosie. I promised her father.'

She remembered the look on Griff's face as the policemen had led him away. He had been burning for revenge. Sometimes she woke in the night mortally afraid.

At least for the next two months she could rest easy in her bed, she thought. If only she could reason with Griff.

'Perhaps I should try to smooth things out between us.' She nibbled at her fingernail thoughtfully. 'I'm afraid, Babs, and not only for Rosie but for Danny, too. Do you think I should visit him in prison?'

'Go all the way to Cardiff? You can't afford it.'

Stella was dismayed. 'I thought he was in Swansea jail. He really doesn't deserve this, and it upsets me to know I had a hand in it.'

'Don't be daft, Stella,' Babs said impatiently. 'He was destroying your home. He might be planning to destroy you, too . . . Stella, love, I don't think Griff's quite right in the head.'

Stella said nothing, but in her heart she had to agree. Griff had changed so much – and if his mind had gone he might do anything to harm them. Her blood ran cold.

'Don't worry about him,' Babs advised. 'You'll be hard pressed to find enough money to feed Danny and Rosie.' A look of curiosity stole across her face. 'How are you coping with having Rose's child about the house?'

'I'm so ashamed of my lack of feelings towards little Rosie, Babs, but I can't help it.'

She put down her cup and saucer. She knew that no one in their right mind could do anything but love such a pretty child, yet every time she set eyes on Rosie Stella was reminded of Eddie's betrayal.

'Don't misunderstand me, Babs,' she said. 'I'll do my utmost to make sure she wants for nothing – she and Danny will be treated exactly the same – but I can't love her. All I can see is her mother and what she took from me.' She looked at her friend apprehensively. 'Have I shocked you, Babs?'

Babs gave a wan smile. 'I'm not easily shocked, kid. Anyway it's understandable after what you've been through. And it's only a week, mind, since she was dumped on you. You may feel differently a month from now.'

'Maybe, but I doubt it.' Stella sighed. 'I'll be glad when I hear from Eddie. How long does it take to get to Australia?'

'Weeks, maybe months. Do you remember the Wilsons from number seventeen? It was three months before their granny heard from them.'

Three months! They might all starve in that time. Stella thought over the mess she was in. An extra mouth to feed and no money coming in. She couldn't let her son or any child starve. Desperate situations needed desperate remedies. Was she desperate enough yet to follow Griff's suggestion? God forbid that it should come to that!

Familiar footsteps were hurrying across the backyard. 'Cooee! It's only me!'

Babs groaned. 'Oh, Gawd! Can't I have five minutes to myself?'

Freda fluttered into the living room, her eyes darting here and there, taking in everything. 'Oh, there you are, Barbara,' she said to her daughter. 'Thought I'd find you in by here.'

'You haven't left the children alone, Mam?' Babs said. 'If the twins get hold of the matches, our house could go up in smoke.'

'Ted's there,' Freda said testily. 'He's got a cob on, and there's a jib on him like he's lost a pound and found a brass farthing, and you were gone so long I thought you'd emanated to Australia or run off with the milkman.'

'Huh! Chance is a fine thing,' Babs muttered. She put her hand on her heart dramatically. 'Oh, if only a tall handsome stranger would take me away from all this!'

Freda flopped on to a chair. 'Well, while you're waiting for him,' she said, 'the firewood needs chopping for tomorrow. Ted wouldn't even answer me when I asked him to see to it. Me hands are that painful with rheumatics.'

She changed the subject neatly. 'Any luck with a job, Stella?'

'No. I'm thinking of taking in washing.' It was a feeble attempt at a joke.

'No shame in that,' Freda replied gravely. 'Done it myself when Barbara's father died. Had to. You think times are hard now,' she sniffed loudly, 'but you should have tried bringing up a family in those days.'

'For heaven's sake, Mam,' Babs said, 'Stella wants cheering up, not made more miserable. Taking in washing, indeed! No need to go that far.'

Freda fingered her chin thoughtfully. 'What you need, Stella, is lodgers.'

'Oh, I couldn't!'

'Oh, hoity-toity, missus!' Freda tossed her head so erratically that her hat nearly fell off. 'Taking in lodgers is good enough for the rest of the Sandfields, so what's so special about you, eh? Too posh, is it?'

'No, of course not—'

'Right, then! A quiet, steady, respectable tradesman and his wife.' Freda nodded wisely.

Stella couldn't bear the idea of another woman fussing about in her kitchen. 'This house is too small for two women.'

'A middle-aged man, then, set in his ways. You need someone, my girl.' Freda's expression was cunning as she looked into Stella's face. 'With Griff gone, you're on your own by here. Don't do for a young married woman to be alone. Gives some men ideas. Know what I mean, Stella?'

Suddenly Stella's cheeks were flaming with embarrassment and fear. 'Babs,' she said quickly, 'put the kettle on again, will you, please? I could do with another cuppa. Cold's gone right through my bones.'

As soon as her friend was in the scullery, out of earshot, Stella whispered urgently to Freda, 'I don't know what stories you've heard about me, Freda, but it's all lies.'

'I know what I heard going on right in this very room' Freda retorted in a husky voice. 'I'm not saying it's all your fault, God knows, but you wants to be careful, my girl.'

Babs returned then, and Stella felt guilty at having secrets from her best friend. Had it been any other man than Ted, she'd have told Babs about it. But Babs thought the sun shone out of Ted's nether regions, and Stella couldn't bring herself to shatter Babs's illusions.

Besides, if it came to a showdown, Babs wouldn't believe anything shameful about him. Ted could twist her round his little finger. Babs would believe him, not Stella, and she would be the poorer for having lost a good friendship.

'I'll put a card in the window of the corner shop,' Stella told them. 'See what turns up.'

But with *her* luck, an inner voice taunted her, the only thing that would turn up was trouble.

Chapter Eight

Babs lent Stella the money to get her coat back from Mr Fingel. She also offered to look after Rosie while Stella walked into town on Monday afternoon to fetch it. It was good to feel the warmth of the old coat around her again.

She didn't like borrowing from her friend and would repay her as soon as she could. She could've used some of Eddie's money, but he'd meant it for Rosie's upkeep. It wouldn't be right to spend it on anything that didn't benefit the child directly.

The only sure way to repay Babs was to take in a lodger. As soon as Stella got home she took a postcard to Mrs Gomer at the small corner shop on Gorslas Terrace. She would display cards in her window for a penny a week.

Mrs Gomer peered at the card short-sightedly. 'Lodger, you want, is it? Had a man in here earlier looking for a room to rent. Wants a respectable place, like.' Mrs Gomer studied at Stella, clearly assessing her respectability.

Stella's cheeks burned. With all these lies flying around, she hardly knew how to look people in the eye these days. 'What's he like?' she ventured.

Mrs Gomer shrugged. 'Young . . . nice suit, mind. Funny-looking overcoat, though. Some kind of fur,' Mrs Gomer gave a chesty laugh, 'but off no animal I ever saw. Shall I send him round if he calls again?'

Stella panicked. 'Heavens, no!' Then she remembered that she had to get some money, and quickly. She added, 'Thinking, I was, more of an older, working man, you know, staid in his ways, like. I'm on my own, see, Mrs Gomer.' Someone she could trust was what she meant. Someone who wouldn't get ideas about her being a woman on her own.

Mrs Gomer seemed to understand. 'Oh, well, he looks respectable enough, mind. Educated – speaks lovely, very posh. English, he is, I think. Looks like he can afford a good rent, too. Snap him up before somebody else does, I would.'

'Would you?'

Mrs Gomer nodded. 'Looks like a gentleman to me, not that I've met many.' She sighed heavily. 'It's usually the other sort I end up with.'

Stella reconsidered. A well-spoken English gentleman – a university student, perhaps? He sounded well above her class, so surely she'd be safe with him. She made up her mind. Yes, Mrs Gomer could send him round – yet, at the same time, Stella rather hoped he wouldn't come.

Nevertheless, when she got home she cleaned the house from top to bottom. Shabby and knocked-about her furniture might be, but no one could say she kept a dirty house. She looked regretfully at the stained wallpaper in the living room and the broken scullery window, still nailed over with plywood – it made the place so dark. She'd asked the rent man if the landlord would get it repaired, but he'd hinted she'd have to pay for it herself as the damage had been caused by a domestic quarrel. Looks like it'll never be mended then, Stella thought sadly.

She glanced at the clock. Danny would be home from school soon. Babs had agreed to fetch him and the twins, taking Rosie along for the walk. How good and generous her friend was, Stella reflected. If only there was some way she could show her appreciation.

She had just washed her face and changed her pinafore, when she heard the latch of the back door lift.

'Come on in, Babs,' she called from the living room as she put a few extra lumps of coal on the range fire.

'You sound pleased with yourself, you stuck-up tart!'

Stella whirled round, appalled to see Ted standing in the scullery doorway, his features contorted with rage. 'Ted! What do you think you're doing, barging into my home? Get out!'

'Not till I teach you a lesson, you conniving slut.'

He strode purposefully into the centre of the room, a muscle jerking spasmodically in his jaw. His arms were held stiffly at his sides, hands balled into fists.

'I said, get out, Ted.' She willed her voice not to quaver, though her knees felt weak with the dread of what he might be intending to do to her. 'Babs'll be here with the kids in a minute.'

'No, she won't. Given her money, I have, to take them round to the chip shop straight from school. And bloody Freda's buggered off home. So, you see, there's plenty of time for me to do what I came for. No one's going to disturb us.'

'You've no right to be here, Ted.' She pointed to the door. 'Get out now.'

She had refused to take violence from her brother, and she certainly wouldn't tolerate it from the likes of Ted Thomas. But she knew that a showdown was coming.

'Shut your mouth, you cheap trollop. I'll do the talking, and I'll do what I want, too. Who's to stop me?'

He stepped closer. The heels of her shoes were against the brass fender, and she could feel the heat of the flames on the backs of her legs. The fire irons were in the hearth. She wondered if she'd have time to reach for one when he attacked her, for she was in no doubt that he'd try.

'Getting a lodger just to spite me, aren't you?' he snarled. 'What's the matter, Stella? Not good enough for you, am I?'

'What I do is none of your business, Ted,' Stella cried, 'but you know I need the money. It has nothing to do with you.'

'Oh, you don't fool me, Stella. I know what your game is,' Ted barked, spittle foaming at the corners of his mouth. 'Think you can bring in some other bloke you're knocking off, is it? Just to make me jealous, eh? Had me on a string all along, haven't you?'

'You're out of your mind,' Stella cried. 'I've never given you any encouragement.'

Ted lifted a fist menacingly. 'Belt you one, I'm going to,' he fumed. 'Spoil that pretty face of yours. Then your fancy man won't look twice at you – nor will anyone else, for that matter.'

'Don't you lay a finger on me, you maniac,' Stella screeched. 'Clear off, Ted, before I call somebody.'

He lowered his arm, a satisfied grin spreading across his face. 'Who're you going to call, eh? Your brother? He's locked up, remember?' He snorted mockingly. 'No one gives a damn about you, Stella. No one cares if you rot in hell.'

His words hit home. There was no one to defend her from Ted Thomas. But Babs was still her friend.

'Babs cares—' Stella began.

'Oh, yeah,' he interrupted. 'You go running to my wife, spilling the beans, see where it gets you. She'll laugh in your face. I've got the stupid cow exactly where I want her – right under my thumb. She don't pee unless I tell her she can.'

'The police—'

'Listen, you bloody little teaser,' Ted pushed his face closer to Stella's, 'the bobbies will believe *me* when I tell them you're on the game, and you've been trying to entice me into your bed all along. The landlord will boot you out of this house when he knows you're using his premises to ply your dirty trade.'

'Lies!' Stella shrieked. 'Why are you doing this, Ted? Why pick on me?'

His manner changed abruptly. His mouth slackened, and the expression in his eyes turned from rage to lust.

'Fancy you, I do, Stella.' Beads of sweat broke out above his top lip. 'Told you often enough, haven't I? All you've got to do is be nice to me.' His fingers went to his flies, and he stroked the stirrings that were clearly visible beneath his trousers. He moved forward a step, as though he might clutch at her. 'A bit of the other from you a couple of times a week is all I'm asking,' he said. 'You want it too, I know you do. Stands to reason. How about it, eh, darling?' He reached out to touch her breast.

Stella hit his hand away. 'Get away from me!' she yelled. 'You disgust me!'

With a roar of fury, he struck the side of her face with the full force of his hand. Her head cracked painfully against the mantelpiece, and she almost lost her footing. Stella screamed in terror as, forced backwards, she felt the heat from the metal bars of the grate. Another inch and she'd have an awful burn to her calf.

Before she could recover, he struck her again, mouthing obscenities. 'You filthy tramp,' he shouted. 'I'm going to fix you good and proper this time. I'll teach you to bugger me about.'

The terror of being burned gave her strength, and as the second blow struck home, she staggered sideways away from the fireplace. Regaining her balance, she lurched towards the passage, hoping to escape into the street. 'Oh, my God! Somebody help me!'

But he was too quick for her. 'Come here, you snivelling bitch!'

He grabbed her arm, and twisted her round. His eyes were gleaming, his features aglow with delight at the pain he was causing her. 'I'm not done with you yet,' he growled. 'Before I'm finished a pig wouldn't spit on your reputation. I'm going to ruin you.'

His fist rammed into her left cheekbone, and her head went back again with a sickening jolt. She thought she heard a bone crack. The pain was excruciating.

'You and your brats will be homeless. I'll put you in the workhouse, you whore!'

His fist smashed into her face again so savagely she thought her jaw was broken. This time she was knocked her off her feet and sprawled sideways on the linoleum. 'No more, please! Don't!'

'That's right. Get down where you belong.' His tone was

gleeful. 'In the dirt at my feet, begging for mercy. Beg! Go on, then! Beg, you treacherous bitch.' He raised his boot and aimed it at her abdomen. Instinctively, Stella curled into a ball, knees raised to protect herself, and took the vicious kick on the thigh. She cried out in pain.

'Yes, go on, yell like a stuck pig,' he said. 'No one can hear you. No one will come.'

'Ted! Stop this, for pity's sake! You're injuring me.'

'I'll injure you all right. I'll put a crimp in your style, you stinking tart!' Ted shouted. 'Give you a broken nose, I will – then see how many blokes you'll get after you. Take that, you bitch!'

Stella whimpered, using her hands as a shield.

'Cooee! It's only me!' At the sound of the all-too-familiar voice, Ted stood transfixed. The satanic pleasure left his face abruptly to be replaced with white-hot panic.

'Freda!' Stella screamed. 'Freda, I'm in by here.'

After a furtive glance towards the scullery, Ted bolted down the passage towards the front door, as if the hordes of Lucifer were at his heels. Stella heard the front door slam back against the passage wall as it was opened violently, and he was gone.

She was on her hands and knees when Freda scuttled into the living room.

'Stella!' Freda rushed over to help her get to her feet. '*Duw annwyl, bach!* What's happened?'

Stella tried to get up but her leg was so painful from the kick that she almost fell back to the floor. Eventually she groped for the back of the armchair and hauled herself up. 'Got to sit down, Freda.'

She fell into the chair, struggling not to pass out. Thank God, her prayer had been answered. But now she'd have to deal with Freda's insatiable curiosity. She must hide the truth, for Babs's sake.

Freda was fussing, wringing her hands. '*Duw! Duw!* Look at your face! It's a mess. What happened, for God's sake?'

Stella touched her cheekbone gingerly. Already it was

swelling, sure to develop into a black eye. Her jaw was aching, too. Judging by the expression on Freda's face Ted had done a lot of damage.

She searched for an explanation that would satisfy Freda but wouldn't involve Ted. No good would come of Freda knowing the truth. 'I fell down the stairs, Freda,' Stella murmured, through her pain. 'Bumped my face on the furniture.'

Freda's mouth stretched into a straight, uncompromising line. 'Oh, come off it! I wasn't born yesterday, mind,' she said tartly. 'There was somebody in by here with you. Heard a man's voice, I did. Bawling like a wild thing he was—'

'Oh, and that's why you came in, was it?' Stella interrupted, wincing at the pain of trying to talk. 'To get a better earful?'

'Hey!' Freda tossed her head, the dusty posy of imitation flowers in her hat quivering. 'There's no need to be funny with me. Old I may be, my girl, but I'm not *twp*! I know there's something going on, and I know who did this to you, too.'

'You don't!'

'Yes, I do. I'd know that bugger's voice anywhere.'

Stella was alarmed. 'Freda, leave things be, for goodness' sake,' she pleaded. 'You don't know what you're stirring up.'

'It was Ted, wasn't it?' Freda declared. 'You two have been carrying on.'

'I haven't!' Stella cried out. 'Ted Thomas is the last man—' She groaned as her injured face began to throb. 'Oh, my God! The pain . . . I think my teeth are loose.'

'Hold on,' Freda said, her tone softer. 'You wants to bathe that face, and quick. It's coming out all colours. Sit by there now, while I get the bowl of cold water and a towel. He wants locking up, that man.'

In a moment Freda was back. It was such a relief to feel the cold water on her damaged skin as Freda gently bathed it.

'If you and Ted are not carrying on,' she said, with a loud sniff, 'why are you protecting him? And don't deny it,' she dabbed delicately at the bruised cheekbone. 'Like I said, I'd know Ted's voice anywhere.'

Stella knew there was no fooling Freda, and she didn't have the energy to try. But she still hoped to keep Babs from finding out. It seemed more vitally important than ever, now that she had seen the violent side of Ted which she hadn't known existed. 'All right, it was Ted,' she admitted. 'Now let's forget it, Freda, for everyone's sake.'

'Not on your life!' Freda wrung out the towel, and placed it on Stella's cheek again. 'Ted's supposed to be off sick from work today, though he looked all right to me this morning.' She frowned. 'What was he doing in by here, anyway, Stella?'

'Don't want to talk about it.'

'Oh, aye! Perhaps not, if you've got something to hide, like dirty work in the bedroom,' Freda retorted. 'Looks suspicious, to me. Why did he beat you, if you're not mucking about with him?'

Stella sighed. It was no good. Freda would not be side-tracked. 'Because I won't do what he wants,' she admitted dispiritedly. 'He's been after me since Eddie left. Just hints and smutty remarks at first, but lately he's started demanding I . . . go to bed with him. This happened because I'm taking in a lodger. He thinks I'm doing it to make him jealous.'

'*Myn uffern i!*' Freda cried shrilly. 'The bugger wants seeing to. If I was a man I'd beat him black and blue. The swine! I still can't understand why you've protected him all along.'

Stella pushed the wet towel away. 'It's not Ted I'm protect-ing,' she said. 'It's Babs.'

'She should be told,' Freda insisted. 'She has a right to know. When she comes back from picking up the kids from school, I'm going to tell her. We'll have it out with him!'

'No, Freda, can't you see? That's the last thing you should do.'

Freda was incredulous. 'You mean, let him get away with it? No bloody fear! He's going to get what's coming to him.'

'Oh, yes?' Stella asked, unable to keep the scorn from her voice. 'And what's that exactly? What can Babs do? Or you or me? Is she going to leave him? How can she? How would she live, her and the twins?'

Freda looked dismayed and thoughtful. Stella, feeling as sorry for Freda as for herself, touched the older woman's bony arm. 'Listen, Freda, Babs dotes on Ted. If you start something she'll think you're just being difficult, trying to break up her marriage. She thinks he's perfect.'

Freda flung the towel into the bowl, splashing water everywhere. 'I've got to do something. She's my daughter. I've got to help her.'

'Look, suppose Babs does believe you – us? First, she might blame me, and I'll lose a good friend.'

'Don't give a damn about that, do I?'

'Suppose she challenges Ted? He might start knocking *her* about, like he did me. Think of that!'

Freda's face took on a pugilistic expression. 'He wouldn't dare!'

'Yes, he would. And the next step from clouting Babs is to start hitting the twins.'

'I'll kill him!' Freda screeched.

'Doesn't bear thinking about, does it?' Stella said gently. 'But there's plenty of men around here who knock their families about; think it's their right. They get away with it year in year out because there's no one to stop them. We've got to protect Babs for as long as we can.'

'What can we do?' Freda bleated, twisting her fingers in distress.

'I don't know, Freda, love,' Stella said gloomily. 'We have to be careful. Ted likes hurting people. I saw that today. He wants to dominate. He thinks he's got Babs under his thumb so she's safe at the moment, but as soon as she starts accusing him he could turn violent. He knows she can't afford to leave him, so he still has power over her. At least she's happy in her ignorance.'

'Oh, if only her father was alive,' Freda wailed, then gave an impatient shrug. 'What am I talking about? Barbara's father was as weak as gnat's water. He wouldn't do nothing to help. It's me that's always had to cope.'

'I'm sorry, Freda.' Stella wondered why she felt the need to apologise. None of this was her fault. Yet Freda looked so distraught, and suddenly older.

'I'd do anything for my girl, you know, Stella,' she said forlornly. 'I'd even swing for that Ted.'

Stella had to hide a wry smile. She was young and healthy, yet had been no match for Ted Thomas. Freda would probably be finished after the first blow, yet Stella didn't doubt her staunch spirit.

'The best thing you can do for Babs,' she said, 'is to back me up when I tell her I fell downstairs. I hate lying to her, but it's for the best.'

Chapter Nine

The next day Stella was dismayed at the appearance of her face. Her cheekbone was blackened with bruising, and her eye was bloodshot. There was ugly discolouration on her jawbone, too. She looked a fright! She'd planned to slip down to the corner shop for a loaf of bread and half a pound of butter, but she couldn't be seen dead outside the house looking like this.

There was a nasty bruise on her thigh, too, but at least that couldn't be seen. She winced at the soreness, and cursed Ted.

When someone knocked at the front door at about half past ten, Stella felt so ashamed of her face that she pretended to be out. But the knock came again, a persistent and jaunty rat-ta-tat-tat.

Before Stella could stop her, Rosie ran down the passage to the front door, calling, 'Daddy! Daddy!'

Stella hurried into the front room, and peered though the lace curtains at her caller.

A tall man, wearing a wide-brimmed white hat and a bulky fur coat, the hem swaying around his ankles, stood on the pavement. It must be her prospective lodger, Mrs Gomer's English student. But what an outlandish appearance! Not her idea of a lodger at all. She was glad she'd had the sense not to open the door.

'It's not Daddy,' she whispered to Rosie, index finger to her lips. 'Ssh!'

Rosie tiptoed to her, and they waited for him to give up and leave, but he knocked again, the sound resonating through the small house. Obviously he'd heard Rosie calling and wasn't about to take no for an answer.

Two small boys, sauntering down the street, stopped and stared open-mouthed at him. Then Mrs Siddons over the road came out on to her front step, and stood, staring, too, and Stella realised she couldn't let him remain there any longer.

Hastily, she slipped a scarf around her head, hoping to hide most of her damaged face, and went to open the door. 'Yes?'

'Mrs Evans?' He peered at her. 'I've come about the room. Might I see it, do you think?'

Mrs Gomer was right. His voice was musical and cultured, quite at odds with his strange clothes.

'I'm sorry,' Stella said, keeping her face averted. 'It's not convenient at the moment.' Then she spotted the suitcase standing on the pavement close to the house.

'Oh, I say!' His tone was despondent. 'How dashed awkward. I was hoping to take it right away.'

He was still trying to peer into her face. 'Is Mr Evans in, might I enquire?'

'My husband is . . . away at the moment,' Stella said.

She wondered if she'd been wise to admit that. He was such a strange-looking man. She began to close the door. 'I'm sorry,' she said, with finality, 'but it really isn't convenient.'

He gave a deep sigh. 'What a pity! But there we are. These little things are sent to try us, what?' He shuffled his feet. 'Might I beg a glass of water?'

Stella was flummoxed. It seemed so rude to close the door and leave him standing there on the pavement, but she didn't relish allowing him to come in. He must have sensed her dilemma, for he swept off the white hat and gave a low bow. A thick forelock of shining blond hair fell into his eyes. 'Do excuse me, my dear lady,' he said. 'How rude I am. My name is Courtney Maitland. Perhaps you've heard of me?'

'No.' Stella shook her head, bewildered and the scarf slipped.

'Oh, my word! That's a lovely shiner,' he exclaimed. 'Ran into a door, I take it?'

Stella gathered up the scarf hastily. 'Something like that,' she answered, annoyed that he, a stranger, should comment on it.

'Raw steak,' he said. 'That's what you need. Does it every time.'

'If I had a raw steak,' Stella retorted, 'I'd cook it and eat it, never mind slap it on my face.'

He chuckled, and Stella realised that as he'd seen the state of her face there was no point in hiding it any longer. She let the scarf fall around her shoulders.

'Do you have references, Mr Maitland?'

'Yes, indeed, my dear lady.' He folded back the front of the fur coat and took an envelope from the inside pocket of his blazer.

Meanwhile, the small boys had been joined by friends. One edged closer. 'Is that a bearskin, mister?'

'Raccoon, young feller,' the young man replied amiably. 'All the rage in the States, what.'

'Looks like next door's cat!' There was an outburst of giggles.

He grinned widely at them, not the least offended, and Stella changed her mind about him. He wasn't stuck up, and had a ready sense of humour. 'The references, Mr Maitland?'

He handed her the envelope. 'I don't want to seem pushy, Mrs Evans, but wouldn't it be better if I came indoors?'

Stella had to agree. They were causing a spectacle on the doorstep. 'Rosie, go and play in the backyard, there's a good girl,' Stella said. Then to her prospective lodger, 'Come in, Mr Maitland.'

Picking up his suitcase, he stepped inside, and she followed him down the passage to the living room, where he put down the case and threw his hat on to a chair. He looked around him, and Stella felt a twinge of shame at her battered furniture.

He was quite tall, clean-shaven and, without his hat, rather handsome. His plentiful hair was worn a little longer than was usual, but perhaps that was the way with students, she thought.

91

Feeling a little self-conscious, Stella read the character references, which were so fulsome that she wondered whether he'd written them himself. But his gaze was open and steady as he waited for her response.

'Well, Mr Maitland,' she began, 'the room might be too humble for you.'

'Dear lady,' he held up a hand, 'I've no doubt it'll be ideal. All I want is somewhere to lay my head, and a well-cooked meal each evening.'

Stella felt he was rushing her a bit, but she warmed to him. He was probably a year or two older than herself, and had a easy manner. 'About the rent, Mr Maitland—' she began.

'Please! Call me Arnie.'

Arnie? Stella was puzzled. 'I thought you said your first name was Courtney?'

'Ah! Yes, Courtney Maitland is my stage name. I'm an actor, don't you know?'

Stella lifted her hand to her throat, unsure again. 'An actor?'

This threw a new light on the situation. Her father had had very strong views about actors, claiming that with their Bohemian lifestyle they were not to be trusted. Free-thinking and amoral, they were a racy bunch, likely to lead silly young girls astray. That's why he had never let her go to see the shows at the Empire on a Saturday afternoon, or even the plays at the Grand Theatre. Now this flamboyant young man wanted to share her home.

She glanced at the references again, suspicious. 'I don't know . . .'

'I'm very respectable, Mrs Evans.' His expression was serious, but she thought she heard laughter in his voice. 'I don't drink, either. Yes, I know! That's hard to believe in an actor. I'm really quite a decent chap.'

Pushing aside the feeling that her father would disapprove, Stella stared into the young man's face, comparing him with Ted Thomas. Ted was a ordinary working man, but there was nothing decent about him: he was downright lecherous and evil. But when she gazed into the young man's steady blue eyes she felt no underlying threat, no sense that he was mentally undressing her as she did when Ted looked at her. She found, to her surprise, that she was comfortable with Courtney Maitland. He was like an older brother . . . like Griff might have been, perhaps, had fate not destroyed his life and changed him.

'I'm sure you are, Mr Maitland.'

'Arnie, please!' He coloured a little. 'Arnold Hepplethwaite.' He made a *moue*. 'Not the sort of name one might see up in lights in the West End, what?'

Stella had to smile, even though it hurt her face.

'I see your point. You'll want to see the room, I expect. This way, please.'

Stella waited at the foot of the stairs, while Arnie popped his head around the back-bedroom door. He came down immediately. 'I'll take it,' he said. 'Can I move in now?'

'Oh!' Despite the presence of the suitcase, Stella was taken aback.

'Ah! I understand, dear lady. We haven't talked about the rent yet.'

Stella flushed. 'I'll have to ask at least ten and six a week,' she said hesitantly. She knew she would barely manage on that even, what with rent and now extra food.

'And how much for food and laundry?' Arnie had taken charge. 'Look, shall we say an even guinea a week, with everything thrown in?'

Stella gave a little gasp. That was an awful lot of money. Had she misjudged him? What exactly did he expect for it?

'Do you mind if I take this damned coat off?' he said suddenly. 'It's heavy and it's warm indoors.'

He slipped out of it and laid it across the back of the armchair. 'Are we agreed, Mrs Evans?'

With a faltering smile, Stella nodded. 'I suppose so.' A guinea was not to be dismissed lightly.

'Good! My needs are minimal,' he explained. 'A light breakfast, no lunch, but a hearty meal each evening, around ten thirty when I return after the last performance.'

'Performance?'

'I'm with the Monty Fitzgerald Players. We're doing a season at the Grand Theatre in town,' Arnie said. '*The Importance of Being Earnest* this week.'

'Pardon?'

'Oscar Wilde?'

Stella had no idea who or what he was talking about. She felt uninformed and stupid.

'*The Second Mrs Tanqueray* next week.' Arnie adjusted his bow-tie with a flourish. 'Monty's letting me take the male lead for once.'

Stella bit her lip, out of her depth. Arnie sensed her embarrassment. 'Er . . . will cooking in the late evening be a chore for you, Mrs Evans?'

'No, certainly not, Mr . . . Arnie,' Stella assured him, glad they were back on known ground. She was a good cook and no one could say differently. 'Just let me know the sort of food you like.'

'Plenty of red meat will be the ticket,' Arnie said. 'I'm a great believer in the roast beef of Old England, don't you know? Red meat and green vegetables, and you can't go wrong.'

He took out his pocket watch and glanced at it. 'I'm running late for rehearsals. Monty's given me an hour to find new lodgings and he'll be champing at the bit. I'd best be off. I'll pop back this afternoon for a nap, if that's all right?'

Stella was confused by the speed with which everything was happening. *New* lodgings, he had said. Why had he left his old ones?

He fumbled in the pocket of his waistcoat and took out a crumpled pound note and a shilling. 'There you are, Mrs E, my first week's rent. My mouth's already in shape for beef suet pudding tonight. All right? Good!'

He shook her hand heartily, then grabbed his case and raced upstairs with it. Within seconds he was back again. He shrugged into his fur coat, and retrieved his hat. 'Farewell for now, dear lady.'

While he was upstairs Stella had taken Griff's front-door key from the little china jug on the sideboard, the only ornament he'd not broken in his rampage. It seemed dangerous somehow to hand it over to a stranger, but she had accepted his money so everything was settled. She'd have to see how things went, and pray she hadn't been taken in by his charming manner.

He smiled as she handed him the key. 'How thoughtful. I just know we're going to get along famously, Mrs E.' He moved towards the passage, then turned back. 'Oh, and get some steak for that eye!'

The night before, Arnie had said he'd take toast and a poached egg for breakfast, and Stella got up extra early to get the fire going. She decided to do his breakfast first, before seeing to the children. He'd probably want to be off to the theatre first thing.

Still dead tired from not getting to bed until the early hours, she yawned as she pierced a slice of bread with the toasting fork, and held it close to the hot coals. Last night, Arnie had enjoyed her beef suet pudding, and they'd sat talking for ages. Stella learned that his family were quite well-to-do, owning a string of fashionable gentlemen's outfitters in the West End of London. 'Father wants me to take over the business eventually,' Arnie had confided, puffing at a large cigar, 'but I haven't finished sowing my wild oats yet.'

'Wild oats?' That had sounded alarming. Stella thought of her father again and felt guilty. Despite herself, though, she was overawed by the excitement and glamour that surrounded her new lodger.

'Figuratively speaking, Mrs E.' Arnie grinned, reassuringly. 'I want my share of freedom and frivolity before I chain myself to an office for the rest of my days. At the moment I'm enjoying strutting the boards.'

'Must be exciting,' Stella agreed.

'I was in the States for six months, trying moving pictures.'

Arnie wrinkled his nose. 'Didn't like it. Repeating one's lines over and over again, while some asinine chap in a cloth cap worn backwards yells, "Cut." In my opinion, moving pictures will never amount to anything. Nothing can replace live theatre.'

Stella ventured the question she'd wanted to ask all day. 'Where were you lodging before you came here?'

'Opposite the gasworks. Good digs, too.'

'Then why did you leave?'

Arnie shifted uncomfortably in his chair. 'Bit embarrassing, what?' He smiled ruefully and pushed back a gleaming lock of hair that had fallen into his eyes. 'Fact is, Charlotte Tempest, that's our leading lady, is taking too much of an amorous interest in yours truly. Her husband, Monty, thought it best I take myself out of harm's way.'

Stella was shocked. It seemed her father had been right. 'Does that sort of thing happen often in the theatre?'

Arnie had grinned broadly. 'Well, not to me, dear lady.'

Stella was brought back to the present with a jolt with the smell of burning toast. Drat! She'd have to eat it herself, charcoal and all. Waste not, want not.

With the toast finally ready, the butter on the table, and the egg poaching nicely in the saucepan of water and vinegar, Stella hurried upstairs. It was coming up to half past seven. Arnie was oversleeping and he'd be late for the theatre.

She tapped lightly at his bedroom door. 'Mr Hepplethwaite . . . er . . . Arnie. It's getting late.'

There was no reply, so Stella tapped again louder. 'Arnie, breakfast's ready.'

She was about to plunge into the room when the door opened and a tousled head was thrust out. 'I say! What's happening? Where's the fire?'

'Breakfast's ready, Arnie. You'll be late for work.'

He stood swaying, blinking at her in the doorway. With his shoulder-length mane of golden hair and his long white night-shirt, Stella was reminded of a bewildered angel, and almost laughed.

96

'Work?' Arnie repeated, obviously still half asleep. 'What time is it?'

'Gone seven thirty.'

'*What?*' Suddenly he was wide awake. 'My God, woman! It's still practically the middle of the night. Rehearsals start at ten. I don't rise till nine. Kindly remember that.'

With a whirl of the nightshirt, he retreated, slamming the door.

Stella was mortified. On only her second day as landlady she'd offended her lodger. She couldn't blame him if he packed and left, asking for his money back. And she'd spent most of it.

She ate the egg and toast herself, then got the children up, washed and fed them. Later she took a large china pitcher of hot water upstairs for Arnie to wash and shave, leaving it outside his door.

Babs had already promised that if Stella found a lodger, she would take Danny to school each morning with the twins. Just before eight thirty she tapped at the back door and let herself in, the girls crowding in with her.

Suddenly the house was filled with giggling as Danny chased the twins and little Rosie round and about the furniture. 'Ssh!' Stella begged. 'Make them stop, Babs, for goodness sake. They'll disturb Mr Hepplethwaite and I've already blotted my copy-book once this morning.'

Babs shepherded the children into the backyard. When she returned, her eyes were bright with curiosity. 'What's he like, then, this lodger of yours?'

'Bit unusual,' Stella confided. 'He doesn't get up until nine o'clock, mind. What'd you think of that? And he wants a big cooked meal last thing at night. He's an actor, you see.'

Babs's mouth fell open. 'Never!' She gave Stella a nudge. 'An actor! Oh, Stell, you'll have the neighbours talking about you.'

Stella had an uncomfortable feeling that she was right.

'Whatever's the matter with your face?' Babs asked this sharply. 'Looks like bruises. Hey! That lodger isn't knocking you about, is he?'

'Of course not!' Stella put up a hand quickly to hide her cheek. 'I fell downstairs on Monday, didn't I? Your mother was here. She saw it. Ask her if you don't believe me.'

Babs laughed, but looked perplexed. 'All right, all right! Don't get shirty. Why wouldn't I believe you?' She frowned. 'I wonder why she didn't mention it.'

'I'm sorry, Babs. Take no notice of me, will you? I'm nervous. I upset Arnie . . . Mr Hepplethwaite this morning. I wouldn't be surprised if he's packing to leave. I felt a right fool.'

'Oh, it's Arnie already, is it?' Babs teased. 'Getting proper chummy, then?'

Footsteps drummed down the stairs and at the next moment Arnie was there, white hat in hand, fur coat slung over one arm. His presence filled the room. 'I say, Mrs E,' he began, 'I'm dashed sorry about my behaviour this morning.' He sounded truly contrite. 'I do apologise—' On seeing Babs he stopped. 'Oh, I beg your pardon.'

Relieved that he was not on the point of giving notice, Stella hastily made introductions. 'Babs, this is Arnie, otherwise known as Mr Courtney Maitland, currently appearing at the Grand Theatre. Arnie, this is my best friend and neighbour, Barbara Thomas.'

Arnie stepped forward, his eyes on Babs's face. He took the hand that she extended towards him, but instead of shaking it, he bent his head and lifted it to his lips. 'I am honoured to meet you, dear lady,' he said. His voice had a thrilling note in it. 'Consider me your most humble servant.'

Stella couldn't suppress a smile at Babs's awed face. Her cheeks were pink, and Stella guessed her friend was impressed by the new lodger.

'Oh, Mr Courtney . . . Arnie,' Babs breathed, 'I've never met an actor before.'

'And I have never met such a one as yourself, Barbara. May I call you Barbara? A vision, indeed. You take my breath away.'

They stood close, Arnie's golden head bent towards Babs, whose upturned face was glowing. No wonder Miss Charlotte

Tempest showed too much amorous interest in him if he carried on like that, Stella thought wryly.

She gave a little cough. 'Babs, it's time for the children to get to school and Arnie wants his breakfast.'

'What? Oh! Right!'

Stella had never seen Babs look so flustered.

Arnie stepped back, gave Stella an apologetic glance, reached into his waistcoat pocket and took out two tickets. 'For the matinée performance next Saturday afternoon,' he said. 'Please accept them with my compliments and sincere apologies, dear lady.'

Babs took the tickets eagerly from him, and examined them excitedly. 'The dress circle! There's posh!' She was bouncing on her feet like a little child. 'Oh, Stell, isn't it thrilling? What shall we wear?'

Stella was dumbfounded. A visit to a theatre? Her father would be spinning in his grave. And, besides, she had nothing decent to wear. She couldn't possibly go. But she didn't want to appear churlish or ungrateful in front of her new lodger, so she smiled as graciously as she could and thanked him.

He sat at the table, rubbing his hands, obviously ravenously hungry. Stella hurried to fetch his egg from the scullery. When she returned Babs was standing in the middle of the room, chatting with Arnie, her cheeks still glowing.

'The school bell will be ringing soon, Babs,' she reminded her friend.

Babs took the hint. 'We'll be off then,' she said. 'See you later, Stell.' She dimpled prettily. 'You, too, Arnie.'

'I look forward to that, Barbara.'

When the others had gone, Rosie came and sat at the table, too, sucking her thumb, and watching Arnie.

Stella wondered suddenly what the child was making of her new life. Evidently she missed her father, who'd left her without even saying goodbye. She was with strangers in a strange place. Suddenly, despite her animosity towards the little girl's mother, Stella felt a shaft of pity strike through her, and then a flood of tenderness for the child.

When Arnie offered Rosie a piece of his toast, she took it shyly, and Stella experienced a vivid premonition. Her life was about to take a new turn. But as to whether it would be a turn for the better, she did not know.

Chapter Ten

Stella dithered for days before she decided not to go with Babs to see the play on Saturday afternoon. The truth was, she had nothing suitable to wear, and wasn't prepared to sit in the posh seats looking like Cinderella.

Babs was more than disappointed. 'But we'll have a bit of fun,' she insisted. 'Oh, come on, Stella, mun! No one's going to look at us.'

Stella was adamant. 'Take your mother,' she suggested. 'She hasn't had a day out for years, has she? The twins can play in by here until you come home.'

Stella gave the children the freedom of the house, except Arnie's bedroom. Sad that she was missing the treat, she sat in the living room, doors securely locked against an invasion by Ted, trying to ignore the din and flurry of boisterous children at play. She sewed patches on Danny's trousers and darned holes in the elbows of his jumpers, wondering if there'd ever be another opportunity to go to the theatre. She'd save a shilling a week out of Arnie's rent until there was enough to buy a length of material, and get something made up. Mrs Pugh at number forty-four did a bit of dressmaking and her prices were reasonable.

She felt excited at the prospect. Her life was very dull and lonely. Why shouldn't she have a bit of fun, get out and about and meet people? It was time to forget Eddie, even though she couldn't imagine being in love with anyone else.

That evening Babs popped in for a cup of tea and a chat after the children were in bed. 'Oh, it was good, Stella,' Babs said, her eyes shining. 'Mam and me felt like gentry, sitting in the circle. You should've been there, kid.'

'Was there singing and dancing, with girls kicking up their legs for all to see?' Stella asked, thinking of her father.

Babs laughed. 'Of course, not, silly. It's a play about a baby being abandoned in a handbag.'

'Oh, how sad.'

'No, no, it's a comedy, really. People were laughing anyway. Mam and me enjoyed ourselves. Arnie was good too, and he looked so handsome. He came to talk to us during the interval and bought us a tot of port and lemon each.'

'Drinks in the middle of the afternoon?' Stella was shocked.

'There's no harm in it. It's the thing to do when you're at the theatre,' she added knowledgeably.

'I wouldn't!' Stella declared. 'It's . . . decadent.'

Babs looked mystified. 'What's that?'

Stella didn't really know. It was something her father used to say. 'Theatre people are, well . . . loose,' she said lamely.

'Arnie isn't,' Babs said tartly. Her expression softened. 'Oh, he's lovely, isn't he, Stell? Such a gentleman.'

Stella had to agree that Arnie wasn't at all decadent, whatever it was. She liked him. When he was at home the house was filled with movement and sound.

'What was he doing jigging about out the backyard this morning?' Babs asked.

'Practising his tap dancing. He sings, too, but he needs music, he tells me.' Stella looked glum. 'They had a gramophone *and* a piano at his old digs.'

When Arnie came home after the evening performance Stella had his meal ready: roast beef, roast potatoes, Yorkshire pudding, and tender Savoy cabbage, with as much rich gravy as he wanted. Arnie liked plenty of gravy. He had arrived with a bulky brown paper parcel, which looked quite heavy. 'What-ho, Mrs E!'

He put the parcel on the floor, took off his fur coat, tossed aside his hat, and sat down, rubbing his hands. 'Something smells good. I'm ravenous.' Later, he sat back. 'You're a dashed good cook, Mrs E. I'd marry you if you weren't already married.'

Stella laughed. 'What, marry an actor? No fear!'

'Very wise, dear old thing.' Arnie nodded sagely, blond forelock falling engagingly into his eyes. 'We're an unsavoury bunch.'

Stella's eyes were on the parcel.

'Tell me, Mrs E,' Arnie went on, 'what sort of chap is Barbara's husband?'

Stella was startled. It had been a casual question, yet there was a tremor in his voice, and she lost interest in the parcel. 'Ordinary,' she replied cautiously. 'I mean, she thinks the world of him. He's teetotal and doesn't gamble the rent away.'

Arnie stroked his chin thoughtfully. 'I ask because Freda made some unflattering remarks about him. I wondered . . .' Arnie studied his fingernails. 'Is she happy, do you think?'

'She's happy in her ignorance,' Stella said, and bit her lip, annoyed with herself for speaking out of turn.

Arnie sat forward. 'There is something. I knew it!'

She shouldn't be telling him, but felt she could trust him to keep it to himself. And it would be a relief to pour it all out into a sympathetic ear.

'I'm afraid of Ted,' Stella began hesitantly. 'That black eye I had the other week, Ted did it.'

Arnie looked shocked, and Stella explained about Ted's demands, how she'd done nothing to encourage his attentions, quite the reverse.

'The swine!' Arnie sprang up. 'I've a dashed good mind to go next door, drag him out of bed and beat the living daylights out of him.'

'You mustn't do anything,' Stella said. 'The longer Babs stays in ignorance, the safer for her. Ted's a dangerous, violent man.'

Arnie clenched his fists. 'I wonder if he'd like to take on

somebody his own size. If I thought he'd laid a finger on her, I'd—'

'She's safe as long as she doesn't challenge him,' Stella said. 'That's why I don't want her to know.'

But Arnie looked restless and agitated. 'I know I've no right to say this, Mrs E,' he said quietly, 'Babs and I have only just met, but each time I see her, the house lights go up, if you know what I mean. I could fall in love with her very easily.'

Stella was troubled. 'I wouldn't want her to be hurt, Arnie,' she said. While Babs was no longer an innocent girl likely to be led astray, she needed to be wanted and loved. Stella doubted that Babs had much affection from Ted, and Arnie might turn her head. Wasn't she always singing his praises since they'd met?

'Babs is like me,' she went on. 'We're unsophisticated, straightforward, not used to blarney and charm in men. I hope you don't mind me saying this, Arnie, but as an actor you're a man who's here today and gone tomorrow.'

Arnie grinned. 'You've been reading my mail, as they say in the States.'

Stella was alarmed. 'Oh, no, no, I haven't!'

Arnie laughed, throwing his head back. 'You're priceless, Mrs E.' He touched her hand gently. 'Don't worry. I'll admire her from afar . . . for the present.'

'What does that mean?'

He sighed. 'It means I don't think I can help falling in love with Babs. I feel I've been hit by lightning. Do you know what I mean, Mrs E?'

Stella didn't, and she was distrustful of such hasty feelings. 'You've known her only a week or two,' she reminded him. 'How can real love grow so quickly?'

'I know what I feel, Mrs E,' he said. 'You must believe I'd never do her any harm. And heaven help that swine if he ever raises his hand against her.'

Suddenly Stella was weary. 'I'll go up now, if you don't mind, Arnie. Turn off the gas before you come up.'

'Do hold on a minute, Mrs E,' he said, and reached for the

parcel and hefted it on to the table. 'Look! I've got a surprise.'
He unwrapped it to reveal a gramophone and three or four large
black shiny discs inside brown paper sleeves. He lifted the lid.
'Shall we put on a record, Mrs E?' He sounded as excited as she
felt.

'It's very late,' she said uncertainly, but she was longing to
hear the machine play. 'How does it work?'

'One winds it up, like this, you see.' Arnie turned the handle
vigorously, then chose a record and placed it on the revolving
turntable.

'We mustn't have it too loud,' Stella murmured a warning.
'The children are in bed.'

'Don't worry,' Arnie assured her, and lowered the needle on
to the record.

Music flowed into the room, subdued, yet swirling against
the walls and ceiling, sweeping over her, too. She swayed to the
lilting rhythm, wanting to dance, but she didn't know how.
'Oh, that's beautiful, Arnie. What's it called?'

'It's called "Always". It's the hit song this year.'

A man's voice began to sing the words, sweet and sentimental. Suddenly the living room seemed a magical place, no
longer a shabby little room in a back-street.

'I wish I knew how to dance.'

'Nothing to it. Look here, Mrs E, I'll teach you.' He took her
hand and put an arm around her waist. 'You have a natural sense
of rhythm. Just follow me.'

Stella felt quite cheerful when she was tackling the piles of extra
washing on Monday morning. The weekend had gone happily,
with Babs coming in to spend Sunday evening with them,
listening to the records, and even dancing with Arnie. He was an
interesting man and, young as he was, had travelled a bit. He'd
delighted them with tales of his time in America.

Whenever she was in his company, Babs hung on Arnie's
every word, and Stella had moments of anxiety during the

evening. Was her friend too taken with Arnie? He'd spoken of love, but Stella didn't believe love could come so fast. And he was an actor, here today, gone tomorrow. She wanted to tell Babs to be careful, but didn't know how.

Stella lifted the hot galvanised bucket, heavy with white cotton underclothing, off the gas-ring and lugged it out to the backyard where a tin bath of cold water waited. She tilted the bucket on the flagstones so that the steaming sudsy water poured into the drain, then tipped the clothes into the cold water, and began to dolly it vigorously. She'd be at this for most of the day, but somehow it didn't seem so arduous as usual.

Rosie came running out to her, and before Stella could stop her, had jabbed a dirty stick into the water amid the clean cotton.

'Oh, Rosie!'

'I help, Mammy,' Rosie said, looking up at her.

A sharp retort was on the tip of Stella's tongue: *Don't call me Mammy, your mammy is dead*. But she couldn't voice it.

Instead Stella handed her the wooden tongs. 'Use this then, Rosie, and be careful not to get your dress wet.'

Rosie prodded away happily, as Stella watched, marvelling at how quickly children adapted. Then she set to work again, pummelling with the dolly. She was just about to go and fetch the mangle, when she saw someone standing at the back gate. It was Ted, in his park-keeper's uniform. The look of cold malevolence on his face frightened her.

'Got the poor little bastard skivvying for you, have you?' he sneered. 'You're not fit to be in charge of kids, you're not. I've a good mind to have a word with the authorities about your immoral goings-on, and have your kids taken away.'

'Why are you spying on me?' Stella asked. 'You should be in work.'

'Don't you tell me what to do, you brazen slut,' he grated and took a few steps into the yard. Stella quailed: the memory of last week's beating was clear and painful.

'Stay out of my yard, Ted.' She tried to still the rising panic in her voice. 'You're trespassing. I haven't invited you in.'

'Why not? You invite every other man in, you cheap whore.' His face twisted in fury. 'Do you think I couldn't hear what was going on in here Saturday night between you and that toffee-nosed beanpole you call a lodger?'

'How dare you?'

'Don't deny it, you hard-faced bitch! Trying to rub my nose in it, weren't you? You're a tease, you are, and somebody should see to you, good and proper.'

'Get out of my backyard, Ted,' Stella said, more angry than frightened now.

'Carrying on in here for all the neighbours to hear, for *me* to hear,' he went on, as though she'd not spoken. 'Playing that wild music. I know what was going on. He was giving you one, wasn't he?'

'I'm a decent married woman, as well you know, Ted Thomas,' Stella cried. 'And Arnie is a respectable man. Don't you go spreading your vicious lies about us.'

'Arnie!' Ted's lip curled. 'Him and his cut-glass talk. He don't fool me. I know what he's after with you. And he's getting it, too. I can tell by the way he struts about smirking, like a cat who got the cream.'

'You're a foul-minded pig!' Stella shouted, then checked herself when Rosie started to grizzle. 'You're scaring the child,' she said, and lifted Rosie into her arms. The child clung to her, both arms around her neck, staring at Ted, her bottom lip quivering.

'Huh! I bet the kid's seen plenty to scare her in this house.' His face creased in a suggestive grin. 'Do you and him do it in front of her, then? Or maybe your precious Arnie likes little girls, does he?'

Stella held Rosie tightly to her breast. 'You disgust me, Ted Thomas,' she said. 'When Eddie comes back, I'm going to tell him what you've been saying. You'll have to answer to him.'

'He's not coming back!' Ted snarled. 'He's glad to be rid of a two-timing trollop like you. I'm going to spread the word about you. You're not fit to live by here, among us decent people.'

'You leave me and mine alone,' Stella yelled. 'Keep away!'

'Oh, we'll keep away, don't you worry,' Ted sneered. 'I don't want you or your dirty pervert of a lodger contaminating my family. And you steer clear of my wife, too. She's no friend of yours any longer. I'll see to that.'

'Babs has more sense than to believe your lies.'

'She does exactly what I say.' He jerked a thumb towards his chest. 'She'd better, or she'll get a thumping. It's time I knocked some sense into her thick head.'

Stella choked back a retort. If he did raise his hand against Babs, she'd tell her friend everything she knew against him, even if it meant that Babs turned her back on their friendship.

With Rosie in her arms, Stella backed away, keeping her eyes on him. When she reached the back door, she darted in, slammed it shut, and slid the bolt into place.

After a moment she heard him turn out of the gate. He was whistling, and the sound sent shivers up her spine.

Babs had come to take Danny to school as usual next morning, though Stella had half expected not to see her after the things Ted had said. She searched her friend's face for signs of distress, some indication that Ted had been laying down the law, but Babs looked much as normal. In fact, there was a flush to her cheeks and a little gleam of satisfaction in her eyes.

'You look cheerful, Babs,' Stella said, as she pulled Danny's cap straight.

Babs's cheeks turned pink. 'Well, kid, you remember I was telling you a couple of weeks ago that Ted and me hadn't . . . you know. Well, last Saturday night he practically jumped on me.' She glanced at the children to see that they weren't listening. 'And every night since, kid,' she went on, almost giggling, Stella could see. 'I thought he'd stopped fancying me.

Well, as a matter of fact, I thought he'd stopped loving me, but everything's all right now.'

Stella turned away to wrap Danny's scarf more closely around his neck. Perhaps Ted had sensed Babs's interest in Arnie, and was making sure of her.

After her midday meal Stella decided she needed a few more provisions. Arnie was a hearty eater, and the larder was almost bare. She always dealt at the general stores at the bottom of Tegwyn Street, and often stayed to chat with Mrs Rogers, who served behind the counter, and whose son was in the same class as Danny.

She pushed open the door of the shop, heard the *ping* of the bell, and walked in. Mrs Rogers was behind the counter, talking with a woman who lived on the corner of Victor Street.

Stella smiled and nodded to them. 'Afternoon. Getting colder, isn't it?'

There was no response. The woman from Victor Street, a Mrs Avery, turned her head away, while Mrs Rogers stared at Stella stonily, then resumed her conversation.

Stella was perplexed. Usually Mrs Rogers had plenty to say, mostly about her son. However, the look on the woman's face worried Stella more. It was hostile. There was no other word to describe it.

Stella stood for a moment, feeling as though she were invisible. There was a bentwood chair nearby for customers to sit while waiting to be served. Stella sat down, prepared to wait. Mrs Rogers addressed her. 'What do you want in here?'

Stella got up, clutching her bag. 'Well, a pound of best butter, please. And cut me a half pound of Cheddar.' She glanced apologetically at Mrs Avery. 'You're before me, though, aren't you? I don't mind waiting to be served, Mrs Rogers.'

Immediately, and without a word, Mrs Avery moved away, her stiffened back turned to Stella.

Mrs Rogers's face was a mask of stone. 'Your custom is not wanted here.'

'Pardon?'

'You heard what I said. You're not welcome. We don't want your dirty money.'

Stella could only stare back, open-mouthed. She didn't know how to respond.

'Are you deaf or what?' Mrs Rogers asked. 'Close the door behind you, all right?'

'No! It's not all right,' Stella snapped. 'I'd like to know what you think you're playing at, Mrs Rogers. How dare you speak to me like that? I've dealt in this shop for years, paying my way as I go, like my parents before me.'

'Oh, yes, and they must be turning in their graves, poor dabs.' This was from Mrs Avery.

Stella gave her the merest glance. It was Mrs Rogers she was concentrating on. Who was she to tell long-standing customers that they were no longer welcome? Anyone would think she owned the place. Stella decided she wouldn't waste any more time on a counter hand who obviously didn't know her own job. She'd have it out with the owner.

'Now, look here, Mrs Rogers, I don't owe a penny to this shop, so I demand to know what's going on,' she said. 'I want to speak to Mr Peters to make a complaint.'

'Complaint, be buggered!' Mrs Avery exclaimed. 'He'll sling you out on your arse, as good as look at you. And I don't blame him, either.'

Mrs Rogers muttered in agreement, and Stella glared at Mrs Avery. 'Keep your long nose out, missus,' she said shortly. 'What's it got to do with you?'

'I'll tell you.' Mrs Avery bristled. 'It's every decent woman's duty to be on the watch out for immorality and stamp it out.'

'Well said, Mrs Avery,' Mrs Rogers butted in. 'Chucked in the Tawe, she ought to be, the dirty bitch. That might cool her off.'

Stella knew without being told that Ted was behind this, and was seized with panic that he had reported her to the authorities, as he'd threatened. Could they take Danny and Rosie away from her on the strength of a jealous man's lies? Something told her it *would* be that easy, and she'd be helpless to stop it.

'We won't tolerate the likes of you around here.' Mrs Avery's voice quivered with self-righteousness. 'Contaminating our families and corrupting our children. I've told my old man that if I catch him anywhere near your house he'll go without for six months.'

'You don't know what you're talking about,' Stella said. 'Someone has been spreading lies about me. You mustn't believe them.'

The two women exchanged a knowing glance, and Mrs Rogers's top lip curled. 'Huh, she's a cool one, isn't she? Butter wouldn't melt, eh?'

'You're a disgrace to the Sandfields, you are,' Mrs Avery said. 'Keeping a disorderly house smack-dab in the middle of respectable family homes. Carrying on with actors and goodness knows who else. You've got the cheek of the devil to show your face.'

'Orgies! That's what I've been told, and by more than one person, too,' Mrs Rogers declared quickly, not giving Stella a chance to defend herself. 'Neighbours have had to stuff their kids' ears with cotton wool at night to stop them hearing the disgusting noises coming from your upstairs. Call the police, I would, if I was one of them poor souls.'

'This is madness!' Stella cried. 'How can you believe such rubbish?' She clamped her lips together, giving both of them looks so bleak they held their tongues. 'But you *want* to believe it, don't you?' she went on savagely. 'Every bit of smutty gossip warms the cockles of your hearts, makes you feel superior.' She pushed her handbag firmly under her arm. 'I will take my custom elsewhere and gladly. I'll never set foot over this thresh-old again.'

She stalked to the door, then stopped. 'You're a pair of stupid women,' she cried angrily. 'Perhaps even more wicked than the person who is spreading these lies.' Lifting her chin high, she turned and walked out.

She kept walking, so upset she hardly knew where she was going, until at last she found herself outside Victoria Park across the road from the beach. She went through the gates and found a seat in a quiet spot, away from prying eyes, then gave way to her pent-up feelings, letting the tears run freely down her cheeks.

She was fast becoming an outcast in her own locality through no fault of her own, simply because she wouldn't let an unscrupulous man use her. Suppose her landlord heard these lies? She would lose the tenancy. What would she and the children do then?

By the time she had pulled herself together, and found a shop to buy the provisions she needed, it was past the time that Danny would be home from school. She dreaded going back to Victor Street, certain that everyone she passed was looking at her and pointing an accusing finger behind her back.

She guessed the telltale signs of her weeping still ravaged her face, so avoided meeting up with Babs. She'd been home only a few minutes when Danny, followed by Rosie, came in through the back door. There was a deep cut above his right eyebrow, and his lip was split.

'Danny!' Stella hugged him close. 'What happened, *cariad*?'

He struggled in her embrace. 'It was Mickey Rogers. He said something bad about you.'

Stella swallowed. How much more must she bear? And now her darling child was affected too. 'What did he say?' She dreaded to hear the words.

'I'm not sure. But I know it was bad because all the other boys laughed. So I hit him.'

Stella knelt on the floor, holding him tight, only dimly aware that Rosie stood nearby, her thumb in her mouth. She couldn't help crying again, and berated herself silently for her weakness.

'Don't cry, Mam,' Danny said, and put his arms around her neck. 'I thumped him good. His nose bled all over his jumper. Serves him right, anyway. He's always picking it.'

Chapter Eleven

October

Stella buttered the thick slices of toast for Arnie's breakfast, feeling a pall of gloom descend on her at the thought of the coming winter and Griff's release next month from prison.

Scarcely a night went by without her dreaming about him, reliving the moment before the policemen took him away, his face so full of hatred she'd hardly dared look at him. He'd come after her, sure enough, she felt it in her bones, and there was no escape from him. The presence of another man in the house wouldn't stop him taking his revenge. Something warned her he was beyond reason.

Stella put the kettle on the gas-ring to boil water for Arnie's morning shave, which he had to do by candlelight. If only she could get some extra money to have the scullery window mended. It was weeks since she'd tried to find work, but she'd have to try again until she found something – anything. Her lodger's guinea just wasn't enough.

Arnie was always cheerful in the mornings, but this morning his brightness depressed her even more. She sat at the table with him, hands clasped around her teacup, hardly hearing his chatter.

'I say, Mrs E, what's the matter?' He put down his cup. 'That blighter next door hasn't been bothering you again, has he?'

'No, thank heavens.' Stella sighed. 'Sorry to have such a long face, Arnie. It's nothing you need worry about. I need a job.'

Arnie took another slice of toast from the rack, smearing it with butter. 'What kind of job?'

'Anything I can get.'

Anything – except what Griff wanted her to do. She'd rather spend the rest of her life scrubbing floors or cleaning public lavatories.

Arnie looked thoughtful. 'I might know of something, but it would mean working unsociable hours. And, of course, you have the children to think of.'

Stella frowned. 'What are unsociable hours?'

'Times when other people are resting or out enjoying themselves.'

'Haven't the money to enjoy myself, have I? So I might as well be working. What's this job, then?'

'It's at the theatre,' Arnie said, surprising her. 'Charlotte Tempest's dresser has left. Poor old Mildred was with her for years. She says she's gone to nurse a sick relative, but I think they had a bust-up. Lottie took advantage once too often.'

'Dresser? But I know nothing about that work. I've never seen a play or set foot inside a theatre.'

'You can learn, Mrs E. It's common sense, really.'

Stella felt doubtful. 'What does a dresser do?'

'Assists Gertie, our wardrobe mistress, and helps Lottie with costume changes during the performance.'

'What's a wardrobe mistress?'

'Gertie looks after the wardrobe – the company's costumes. Sponges down garments and darns them, runs up the odd costume. She's in charge of the props too. The dresser assists.' Arnie gave a crooked smile. 'She also runs to fetch Lottie the odd bottle of gin.'

'She drinks?' Stella was scandalised.

'No more than the next leading lady. Doesn't affect her performance on stage.' He paused, smiling again. 'Don't let it put you off. You can do it. And the money's pretty good.

Monty's not stingy, I'll say that for him. Thirty-five shillings a week.'

Stella was astonished.

'You'd earn it, don't worry,' Arnie added, nodding sagely. 'It's non-stop backstage.'

'But that's almost double what I was getting from Mrs Ridd,' she exclaimed. 'Oh, Arnie, do you really think I could do it?' Doubt set in. 'Surely, for that money, they'll want someone with years of experience?'

'I'll put in a good word for you, but I'm not saying it's a permanent job. Monty's pleased with the audiences we're getting, and the theatre's full most nights, so the season might last until next spring. Then we'll be moving on.'

Stella felt her spirits lift. 'It would tide me over, and see us through Christmas. Oh, if only I could get it.'

Arnie wiped his mouth on a napkin, and rose from the table. 'Be at the stage door at about a quarter to twelve today, Mrs E,' he said. 'I'll introduce you to Monty.'

'What shall I wear? I haven't anything smart.'

'Whatever you wear you'll look splendid.' Then looked serious. 'Mrs E, I think I should warn you about a few things.'

Stella waited, hanging on his every word, eager to learn all she could. This job could be heaven sent. She *had* to get it!

'Never lend Lottie any money. You'll never see it again.'

'I don't think that's likely, seeing as I've hardly any myself.'

'Oh, our Miss Charlotte is a crafty one.' He adopted a high-pitched voice. '*Run and get me a bottle of gin, darling. I'll pay you when you get back.*' He shook his head. 'Don't fall for it.'

Stella giggled, pushing down a twinge of uncertainty.

'And whatever you do,' he went on, 'don't let her know you're my landlady.' He grinned sheepishly. 'You're too pretty. She'll be jealous and throw a spanner in the works. We'll say your husband is a friend of mine.'

'I don't like deceiving people, Arnie.'

She thought of her father again, and his views on theatre people. It seemed a strange world, fraught with intrigue.

'You do want this job, Mrs E, don't you?'

'Yes, of course . . .' Did she have a choice?

'One last piece of advice.' He looked rather uncomfortable. 'Never let Monty Fitzgerald catch you alone.'

She told Babs the news. Her friend's eyes were like saucers. 'Oh, Stella, I wish it was me. I'd love to do something like that. Mam says a little job would give me a bit of independence, but Ted won't hear of it.'

Of course not, Stella thought. He wants you totally dependent on him.

'I've been through my clothes,' Stella went on, pushing down the uncomfortable thoughts. 'All I can find that's half-way decent is that grey gabardine I bought the year Eddie left. The only good thing I can say about it is that it's clean.'

'Borrow my red suit,' Babs suggested. 'The colour will go well with your hair.'

Exactly at quarter to twelve Stella was at the stage door, feeling intimidated, wishing she hadn't worn Babs's suit. The skirt was too loose around the waist and kept sliding down over her hips. Remembering she had a safety-pin in her handbag, Stella stood just inside the door, attempting a hasty adjustment.

'What you want, miss?'

The voice made her jump and the safety-pin stabbed her finger painfully.

Through a hatch in the wall of a cubby-hole near the door, a middle-aged man, wearing a cloth cap and a muffler, peered at her over the top of a pair of spectacles. This must be Sid the doorman. Arnie had told her about him.

'I'm Mrs Evans.' She took a deep breath. 'Arnie . . . I mean, Mr Courtney Maitland is expecting me.'

'Oh, aye, you're after that job with her ladyship. Watch your back, *cariad*. She's a nasty piece is Miss Tempest.'

Stella was surprised at the bitterness in his voice, and annoyed, too, that her business here appeared to be common knowledge. She'd have a word with Arnie about that. She'd had enough of being talked about. But, then, it was best to make no comment, she decided. Least said, soonest mended.

Resisting the urge to hitch up her skirt, she asked, 'Where is Mr Maitland?'

'Might still be on stage.' Sid took a large watch from the pocket of his stained waistcoat and glanced at it. 'You can wait for him, if you like.' He jerked his thumb vaguely over his shoulder. 'Down the passage by there, turn left, then up the stairs, turn right, and Mr Maitland's dressing room is second on the left.'

With one last appraising glance he withdrew from sight, and Stella felt very alone. She walked hesitantly down the passage, the heels of her shoes clipping on bare floorboards, which looked as though they hadn't been scrubbed for weeks.

At the top of the stairs she paused to get her bearings. There was a damp, musty smell about the place, and a pungent odour that reminded her of mice, or even rats.

Shivering at the idea, Stella hurried forward, peering at a door. Second on the right Sid had said. When she reached it, she tapped, and waited, but there was only an uncanny silence. Suddenly, she had second thoughts about the whole thing, but just then her skirt slid off her hips. She clutched at it frantically, grasped the doorknob with her other hand and pushed. It opened and she stepped inside.

Daylight struggled feebly through the unwashed panes of a small window, which overlooked the backyards of houses in mean little streets behind the theatre. Stella could well imagine rats roaming there. The room was small, and stank of stale tobacco and perspiration, making her want to cough.

Dominating one wall, and surrounded by electric light-bulbs, was a large mirror above a dressing-table strewn with a mess of pots, bottles and brushes. Against the opposite wall was an ancient horsehair sofa that had lost most of its stuffing. However, it looked reasonably clean and she slipped off her coat, folded it neatly and laid it there.

She'd pin up her skirt properly, then leave without seeing Arnie. She'd make some excuse later. It was kind of him to think of her for the job, but she'd be out of place here.

The skirt proved difficult to pin while she was still inside it, so she took it off. There was a small screen near the head of the sofa. If Arnie came in while she was undressed, she could slip behind that.

The safety-pin was small and blunt and wouldn't pierce the material. Stella took it to the window to see better.

Without warning the door burst open behind her. 'I say, Maitland, old man, have you a fiver I could . . .'

Stella whirled, mouth open, and stared in dismay at the tall, broad-shouldered man in the doorway, dressed immaculately in a black blazer and grey trousers.

She didn't know whether to struggle into her skirt in front of the stranger, or make a dash for the screen. Instead she froze with embarrassment.

'I say! Well, well, what have we here?' He came into the room and closed the door behind him. 'Maitland is a sly dog, keeping a lovely little thing like you to himself.'

Stella didn't like the suggestive tone of his cultured voice, or his weak-looking chin. In fact, she didn't like anything about him.

The room shrank to even smaller proportions and she clutched at the skirt, holding it protectively in front of her.

'What's your name, sweetie?'

He was smiling beneath his moustache, but the smile didn't touch his eyes, which were bleary and dulled, curiously without light.

'Why haven't we met before?'

Stella was still speechless.

'Ah!' he exclaimed. 'You're overwhelmed at meeting me. Women usually are, my dear.' He smoothed a hand over his thick hair, which was dark and rather theatrically waved. 'Monty Fitzgerald at your . . . ahem! . . . service.'

Where was Arnie? Why didn't he come and rescue her?

He took a step closer, reaching out a hand for the skirt. 'Here, let me help you with that, sweetie.'

Stella flinched. 'Don't touch me!'

He raised thick eyebrows. 'Look here!' There was a sharp edge to his voice. 'I don't mind Maitland bringing his dollies backstage for a bit of slap and tickle once in a while, but share and share alike, that's what I say, what?'

'How dare you?' Stella cried outraged. 'I'm not Arnie's dolly, thank you very much!'

'Arnie?' He frowned. 'Oh, you mean Maitland.'

She edged towards the screen, intent on getting her skirt on and leaving this place. But he blocked her path. Stella felt desperate. He was so tall and strong. She'd stand no chance if he assaulted her. Would anyone hear if she screamed? Would anyone care?

'I'm a respectable woman looking for work,' she said sharply. 'Arnie said there was a job going as dresser to Miss Tempest.'

'Oh, he did, did he? Well, now, sweetie, I'm the man who hires and fires around here.' He fingered his chin thoughtfully. 'So you want to work for me, eh? That can be arranged very easily.' He smiled broadly. 'But I like to know my people well, especially the attractive ladies.'

He ran another penetrating glance over her. 'Nice figure. You're a striking-looking young woman,' he said languidly. 'But you know that, of course. That hair . . . my God! It's beautiful. You'd be wasted as a dresser. You belong on the stage.' He took another step closer. 'I can make you a star of the theatre, my dear, if you play your cards right.'

'All I want to do is leave this place,' Stella answered. 'Now please turn your back while I put on my skirt.'

He threw back his head and laughed loudly. 'No fear! The view is much too good.'

'You're no gentleman, Mr Fitzgerald,' Stella said shakily.

'What's your name?'

'Mrs Evans. Mr Maitland is a friend of my husband,' she prevaricated. 'My husband will be angry that I've been humiliated like this, and he's not a man to be trifled with.'

'I see.' Monty stroked his chin again, then smiled. 'Need your husband know? I mean, there isn't a wife alive who hasn't some secrets. No, forget your husband, my dear, I certainly shall.'

His smile was self-assured and relaxed. Obviously, he wasn't used to women refusing him. Stella eyed the distance to the door, wondering if she could catch him unawares and make a dash for it. But he was more canny than she thought.

'Job or no job, you're not leaving here, sweetie, until I've had at least one little kiss, I think.'

He stepped forward purposefully, and took her in his arms, his face flushed with anticipation. Stella opened her mouth to scream, but at that instant the door opened and Arnie stood there.

'Mrs E! Monty! What the hell's going on?'

'Arnie, please help me!' Stella shouted, struggling in Monty's arms.

'Get out, Maitland!' Monty roared. 'This is a private party.'

'No, Arnie! Don't go! Don't leave me here with him. Help me!'

Arnie marched in and gripped Monty's shoulder to pull him off her. 'Let her go, Monty, for God's sake!' he growled. 'What are you doing, man? Mrs E isn't some cheap doxy you can pick up. Damn it! She's – she's my landlady, a decent woman.'

'Oh, come off it, Maitland!' Monty thundered. 'If she's so pure, why was she waiting for you with her skirt off?'

Stella stepped back, breathless, freeing herself from Monty's hands.

'He didn't give me a chance to explain, Arnie,' she quavered. 'This is a borrowed skirt, and it's too big for me. I was trying to pin it up when he burst in here, and – and—'

She couldn't go on. It was too humiliating. With a frightened glance from one man to the other, she dashed behind the screen, stepped into the skirt, and pinned it to her petticoat.

The two men had not exchanged a word while she was out of sight, but when she came from behind the screen she saw that

Arnie was still furious, but that Monty had relaxed. He took a cigarette case, with a lighter, from an inside pocket and lit a cigarette, blowing smoke towards the ceiling. 'Looks like old Monty's been a bit rash,' he said amicably. 'You should've explained, my dear.'

'Would you've wanted to listen, Mr Fitzgerald?' she replied acidly. She reached for her coat on the sofa and slipped into it. 'I'm going now, Arnie,' she said, with all the dignity she could muster. 'It was kind of you to want to help me find a job. This is not the one.'

'Wait!' Monty exclaimed. He waved his cigarette. 'Now, don't be too hasty . . . What *is* your name – I mean your first name?'

Stella gave him a withering glance, and without bothering to reply, she marched towards the door.

He reached forward and caught her arm.

Arnie stepped forward and wrenched it free. 'That's enough, Monty. Mrs E's a friend of mine. I don't want her manhandled.'

'Simmer down, Maitland,' Monty said impatiently, and he waved a hand as though dismissing the younger man's concerns. 'No one's going to manhandle her, unless she wants them to. You don't know women as I do. Always saying no when they mean yes.'

Stella glared at him. Ted had said that too. He and Monty Fitzgerald were tarred with the same brush. She wanted no truck with either of them. 'Well, that does it!' she declared. 'Sorry you've been put in this position with your employer, Arnie.' She glared at Monty again. 'It was none of *my* doing.'

Monty shrugged. 'No harm has been done as far as I'm concerned,' he said casually. 'Merely a misunderstanding. Look, please, let's start again. You want a job. I like the look of you . . .' He raised a hand as Stella opened her mouth to protest. 'All right! Bad choice of words. You appear suitable for the position of dresser. I'm willing to take you on for the season. Thirty-five shillings a week suit you?'

Stella held her head high. 'No, thank you,' she said. 'I've

been humiliated and insulted. I wouldn't work in this – this flea-pit if you paid me forty shillings a week.'

'Righto!' said Monty promptly. 'Forty-five it is. You drive a hard bargain.'

'I say, Monty! Steady on!' Arnie exclaimed, disconcerted. 'Forty-five shillings? What are you up to?'

'Up to, Maitland?' Monty lifted his heavy eyebrows, as though hurt. 'I don't know what you mean, old man.'

Stella could only stare, her mouth open. When she found her tongue, she stuttered, 'You're willing to p-pay me t-two pounds, five shillings a week?' Most of the working men she knew got little more. She could certainly do with the money.

Arnie put his hand on her arm protectively. 'Come on, Mrs E, I'll see you to the stage door, and I'm awfully sorry.'

'No, wait a minute, Arnie.' She gazed keenly at Monty Fitzgerald, thinking of the scullery window and the coming winter. They'd need coal too, warm clothing for the children and good food. 'Will you treat me with respect in future, Mr Fitzgerald?' she asked.

'My dear, this was all a mistake. It won't happen again, I assure you. Besides, the company really needs you. Since old Mildred ran off Lottie has been impossible. When can you start?'

Arnie cleared his throat. 'Shouldn't Lottie be consulted first? And Gertie, too. I mean, Gertie doesn't get forty-five shillings a week and she's wardrobe mistress.'

Monty blustered. 'I'm running this outfit, Maitland. Both of them will do as I say and like it.'

Arnie looked doubtful, but said no more.

Anxiety assailed Stella. Perhaps it was too good to be true. She could see Arnie was troubled by the turn of events. And Monty Fitzgerald seemed too keen to employ her. Could she really trust him?

But forty-five shillings a week! It was a fortune! How could she turn it down? She'd have to risk it. As Arnie had warned her, she'd make sure she was never alone with Monty again.

'Now, my dear, I refuse to call you Mrs E.'

'My name is Stella,' she answered reluctantly.

'Lovely name for a lovely lady.' He grinned when she frowned. 'Force of habit! In the theatre, my dear, compliments are thrown about like confetti. Usually they mean nothing. You must bear with my odd little ways.'

'I hope you're being sincere, Monty,' Arnie said. 'Mrs E is under my protection, you understand. I shall have to take steps if—'

'For God's sake, Maitland!' Monty interrupted, blustering again. 'I've given my word as a gentleman.'

He turned to Stella with a smile, his voice softening. 'You'll want to know what's what,' he said genially, and Stella marvelled at the way he could change mood in an instant, but he was an actor, and perhaps didn't know the meaning of the word sincerity.

'The job is assistant to Gertie Peach, our wardrobe mistress, who oversees everything to do with dressers, costumes and props.' He gave an embarrassed little cough. 'No need to mention how much I'm paying you, my dear.'

'How many other dressers are there, Mr Fitzgerald?'

'Call me Monty, my dear. Mildred was our only dresser. She did for Lottie – Miss Tempest to you, of course, and for myself.'

Stella was startled and frowned at him. 'I'd be *your* dresser, too. Is that . . . proper?'

Monty waved a hand airily. 'The slightest duties in that area, my dear. A mere nothing. Seeing that my costume is intact and any extra props are to hand before I go on stage, all under Gertie's supervision, of course.'

It seemed reasonable. She'd be a fool to be oversensitive.

'Well? Are you still interested in the job?' Monty asked impatiently.

'Yes.'

'Righto. Start tomorrow. You can meet the company then. Mornings are spent rehearsing next week's production. We assemble at ten, sharp.'

'I'll be here on the dot, Mr Fitzgerald.'

'Oh, do call me Monty, my dear.'

'Thank you, but I shall call you Mr Fitzgerald, so there'll be no further misunderstanding.'

His lips twitched and she realised that, despite everything, he had a sense of humour.

'So I start tomorrow,' Stella said, as she pushed a steaming cup of tea across the table to Babs. 'I can hardly believe it. Forty-five shillings!'

During the afternoon she'd been repeating it to herself, almost afraid to believe it was true, yet considering all the things she'd be able to do with the money. But there were problems to overcome, and she hoped Babs would help her.

'Oh, kid! You're so lucky. Hey! What's he like in real life, this Monty Fitzgerald?'

Stella had decided not to tell her friend about the embarrassing incident with the skirt.

Babs didn't wait for an answer. 'I saw him in a play at the Grand once, years ago.' She put her elbows on the table and rested her chin on her hands, a far-off look in her eyes. 'With Minnie Foster, I went. Remember her, Stell? Her mother kept that chip shop bottom of Market Street. She gave us tickets. Oh! I'll never forget it. He's so handsome and dashing. Did you meet him?'

'Briefly,' Stella replied, tongue in cheek, handing Freda a cup of tea. 'A bit worn around the edges now, I'd say.'

'Well,' said Freda, after taking a noisy sip. 'I think you wants your head read. You with two young children to look after, staying out practically all night working. It's not decent for a married woman.'

'Oh, Mam! Don't be so old-fashioned,' Babs scolded.

Stella took a sip from her own cup. She'd been worrying about this. How would she manage if Babs didn't offer to help?

'And it's no problem,' Babs went on swiftly, as though reading her mind. 'I'll see to Danny and Rosie. They can sleep at our house until you come home.'

'No,' Stella said swiftly. It didn't seem right or sensible to break the children's rest. 'I don't want Danny's sleep disturbed. He's got school in the morning.'

Babs slapped a hand on the table. 'I've got it! Mam, you could stay in by here minding the kids when they're in bed, couldn't you?'

Freda looked startled. 'Me? Oh, I dunno, Barbara.'

'Yes, you could. You're always complaining you don't want to go home to your cold house.'

'Will you, Freda, please?' Stella put in her own plea. 'Until I come home to make Arnie's evening meal.'

'I'll do that, too,' Babs volunteered eagerly. 'Just tell me what he wants before you go to work, and I'll have it all cooked and ready. Mam can stay in by here during early evening, then when I come to do Arnie's meal, she can go and sit in our house. We'll manage it, won't we, Mam?'

Freda sniffed, though Stella thought she looked pleased to be needed. 'Looks like I haven't got much choice, don't it?'

Stella felt a lump in her throat at such kindness. 'I can't ask it all of you, Babs. You're doing so much for me already.'

'Listen, kid,' Babs said, leaning forward, 'you're my best friend and, besides, I'd love to be in your shoes, working in the theatre. It's so glamorous.'

Stella had a vision of peeling paintwork, dirty floorboards, and the odour of vermin.

'I can't be part of that,' Babs went on, 'so let me have the next best thing – you and Arnie telling me all about it. Oh, please, Stell!'

'What will Ted say?' Stella was certain he'd object, even if it was just to spite her.

'He won't know, mun,' Babs replied. 'He's out after tea every night, isn't he, Mam?'

Freda's jaw tightened, but she held her tongue.

'And you can make yourself comfy in by here, Freda,' Stella said. 'There'll be plenty of coal, and you can have what you want from the larder.'

Freda's expression brightened. 'Couldn't run to a bottle of stout, could you?' she asked. 'I like a drop of stout now and then.'

On forty-five shillings a week plus Arnie's guinea, Stella felt she could run to any luxury. 'It's a deal, Freda.'

Freda raised her teacup. 'Here's to it, then. Your new job in the theatre.' She blinked at Stella. 'I hope you won't regret it, my girl.'

Chapter Twelve

The next morning Arnie looked at his pocket-watch as he ushered Stella through the stage door. 'They'll all be on stage wondering where the devil I am,' he said. 'Come on, Mrs E. This way.'

Stella clutched at his arm, suddenly consumed by doubt. 'Oh, Arnie, am I doing the right thing, taking this job?'

'Mrs E!' He was on pins. 'Doesn't it all depend on how much you need the money?'

That was just it. Her head had been turned by the generous wage Monty Fitzgerald was to pay. Now she wondered if she were about to step on to a new path to disaster, and all for the sake of forty-five shillings a week.

Arnie pulled at her arm, but Stella held back.

'Forewarned is forearmed,' he said quickly. 'You're clever enough to avoid Monty from now on, and think of what you could do with the money. Repaper the living room for a start.'

Then, Arnie was leading her on towards a brightly lit stage. 'This place, just off-stage, is called the wings,' he explained.

Two tall young women, chattering in unmodulated voices, were coming into the wings from the stage area. As they pushed past, Stella stared at the way they were dressed. Both wore jap silk blouses in varying hues, pushed into the waists of wide-legged slacks of fine-weave white linen. She'd never seen women in trousers before.

'Are they chorus-girls?'

Arnie chuckled nervously. 'Whatever you do, Mrs E, don't let Elsie and Flo hear you call them chorus-girls. They're actresses, and take themselves *very* seriously.'

He pushed her forward on to the stage. Overawed, Stella glanced upwards. There seemed to be no proper ceiling: the shadowy space above her head, criss-crossed by beams and joists, went on for ever. All manner of curious structures were suspended there in mid-air.

She looked past Arnie's shoulder and out into the auditorium, and had another surprise. By the light of several enormous chandeliers hanging from a decorative ceiling, the auditorium glittered and sparkled like the inside of a fairy palace, with row after row of red plush seats awaiting an audience. Several figures were moving about among the seats, dusting and brushing. Even in the midst of her confusion, Stella wondered why they didn't take as much trouble with the parts of the theatre unseen by the public.

Arnie was urging her forward. Now that she was coming to terms with the strangeness of her surroundings, Stella steeled herself to meet the people she would work for.

A small table had been placed in the centre of an otherwise bare stage and several chairs were scattered around it, a couple obviously just vacated by the two young actresses.

Stella immediately recognised Monty, perched on the edge of the table nearest to her. Two women and another man sat nearby. The older woman was knitting what appeared to be a long scarf, her needles going at a furious pace. She didn't glance up as Arnie shepherded Stella forward, but Monty spotted them.

'Ah, Stella,' he boomed. 'Thought you'd changed your mind, my dear.'

'Sorry we're late for rehearsal,' said Arnie.

'Courtney!' The plaintive cry came from the younger woman sitting at an angle to the table at the far end. 'I thought you'd deserted poor little me!'

Arnie squeezed Stella's arm reassuringly, then moved towards the woman who'd spoken. 'Lottie, darling.' Arnie's ringing tones were ingratiating. 'You know that's impossible. You're never out of my thoughts, dear heart.'

Stella stared after him in bewilderment. He didn't sound like himself at all, and she eyed the woman whose hand he was holding. A white fur stole was draped around her shoulders, accentuating her classic features, while golden curls peeped out from under a close-fitting white hat. She resembled a Persian cat, sleek and exotic, her long legs crossed elegantly before her.

'You promised to take me to lunch at the Baltic Lounge, Courtney, darling,' Charlotte Tempest went on, in a plummy accent so vibrant that her voice must carry to the very rafters of the theatre. 'It's the only decent place to dine in this *awful* little town.'

Awful little town, indeed! Stella's hackles rose.

'Let me introduce you to the rest of the troupe,' Monty said to Stella. He put his hand under her elbow, and exerted more pressure than was necessary. 'This is Oliver Brent-Saunders, renowned for his Shakespearean roles. Oliver, meet Stella. She's Gertie's new assistant.'

Stella dragged her gaze away from Charlotte Tempest as the man rose to his feet. Dapper in a brocade waistcoat and pinstripe trousers, Oliver Brent-Saunders was older than Monty and shorter in stature. His smile was pleasant, if somewhat weary. 'My dear young lady.' He reached for her hand and brought her fingers to his lips, giving a showy little bow and clicking his heels. 'How delightful to meet you.'

'Ollie! Sit down!' The thunderous voice came from the woman who was knitting. 'She's only a dresser, *not* the Queen of Sheba.'

Oliver flopped back on to his chair, looking crestfallen.

'This is Evelyn Desmond,' Monty said, indicating the knitter, 'Oliver's lady wife, and celebrated star of the West End, aren't you, Eve, darling?' In an undertone he added, 'About thirty years ago.'

'I heard that, Monty,' Evelyn said peevishly.

She had an abundance of hair piled on top of her head; it must have been dyed for it was darker than was possible for a woman of her age. Short and stoutish, she held herself as upright as a ramrod; her impressive frontage, the envy of any duchess, was bedecked with several strings of colourful beads.

Evelyn treated Stella to an arrogant stare. 'I hardly require introduction to a mere dresser,' she said, with such contempt that Stella flushed. She opened her mouth to protest, but Monty swung her round to face Charlotte again.

'Lottie, darling, meet Stella, your dresser.'

For the first time Charlotte Tempest condescended to give Stella her attention. Her appraisal now was shrewd and thorough, taking in Stella's features and hair, the contours of her body. Her expression as she glanced away was dismissive, but her classic features hardened as though with anger. Stella was mystified.

'She's far too young for a dresser's position, Monty.' Her tone was edgy and brittle with suspicion. 'Are you planning to groom her for stardom? Is she to be *my* replacement, perhaps?'

'What nonsense, Lottie, darling,' he remonstrated. 'Who could possibly replace the sublime Charlotte Tempest? I'd be a fool to try.'

Charlotte's lips thinned as though she suspected him of mocking her. Then she looked at Stella again. 'What experience do you have as a dresser?'

Stella wanted to make the best impression despite her growing dislike of the woman. 'Well, none, really, Miss Tempest, but I—'

'Huh! I thought as much.' Charlotte chortled. 'What has Monty promised you, eh? Did he say he'd make you a star, now poor old Lottie's past her best?'

'Miss Tempest, I assure you I've no wish to go on the stage,' Stella stammered. 'To earn an honest living is all I want.'

Charlotte threw up her hands in a theatrical gesture. 'Oh, it's too, too absurd, Monty!' she cried shrilly. 'The poor creature will be underfoot and *totally* useless.' She averted her face and waved a white-gloved hand as though shooing away a worrisome fly. 'It's out of the question. Besides, Millie will be back soon. I want Millie.'

'Oh, for God's sake, Lottie!' Evelyn exploded, with impatience. 'Mildred's not coming back. Face up to it. You took advantage of her once too often. You take advantage of everyone.'

'Be quiet, you bloated old harridan!' Charlotte hissed.

Stella was reminded of a cat about to sink its claws into an adversary.

'I will not, you gin-soaked ham!' screeched Evelyn.

'Ladies, ladies!' Monty thundered. 'Please!' He seemed to strike a pose. 'I'm not asking you, Lottie, I'm telling you. Stella's your new dresser and assistant wardrobe mistress.'

Charlotte held up her chin archly and looked down her nose at Stella. 'Whose mistress, did you say?'

'Now that's enough, Lottie.' Monty looked furious. 'It's about time we got on with rehearsals. Where are those damned girls?'

He marched towards the wings, shouting their names, leaving Stella standing before the assembled troupe, feeling like a butterfly pinned to a board. She gazed at Arnie, but he avoided her eyes, his hand still clutched by Charlotte. Stella knew she'd get no help from that quarter. Evelyn Desmond also seemed waspish and unapproachable. What a thoroughly unpleasant pair! Doubt rose again, and Stella had never felt less sure of herself.

But I'm no quitter, she decided. She'd see it through, and not only for the money. She was indignant at the way both women had talked down to her, as though she were the lowest of the low.

Stella gave a final defiant look around the table. Arnie was studying what appeared to be a script. Only Oliver had a fleeting watery smile for her before he glanced away, under Evelyn's watchful eye.

Stella realised she'd have to battle on alone. Head high, she walked towards the wings. Monty, returning to the stage, passed her without a word, his arms around the shoulders of Elsie and Flo, all three laughing at some joke.

Stella stared after them in consternation. Well, she didn't need their help, she told herself. She had a tongue, she could ask. The first thing was to find Gertie.

She wandered around backstage until a man in overalls passed, pencil behind his ear, with a length of wood on his shoulder.

'Excuse me,' Stella said, 'do you know where I can find Gertie?'

'Seamstress's room is upstairs, love.'

In the corridor she passed Arnie's dressing room, and several others. The last door stood open and Stella could hear the whir of a treadle sewing-machine.

Tentatively, she tapped at the door and walked in. The air stank of stale tobacco, and something else. Mothballs? An old woman sat at an ancient sewing-machine. In a thin, lined face, dark, gypsy-like eyes squinted at Stella through a haze of smoke, a cigarette clinging precariously to her bottom lip.

'Wotcher, ducks?' The cigarette bobbed up and down but miraculously stayed put. 'You're the new dresser, eh?'

Stella nodded.

The woman stood up and shuffled towards her, tall and thin in a shapeless woollen cardigan and a narrow skirt that brushed her ankles. 'Me name's Gertie Peach.' She grinned, showing nicotine-stained false teeth, and held out a bony hand in greeting. 'And what's your moniker, then?'

'Stella Evans.'

'Okay, Stella, me ducks.'

Her voice was gruff but cheerful, and despite her rather rough exterior, Stella liked her.

'This here's wardrobe. See them trunks and baskets?'

She pointed to where several large trunks stood up-ended against a wall. Beside them, huge wicker baskets with lids were stacked one on top of another.

'We keep the company's costumes in them,' Gertie went on.

'The ones needed for the week's production are hung in the dressing room each Monday morning.' She grinned again. 'That's your job, ducks.'

Stella felt a surge of panic. 'How do I know which costume belongs where? Suppose I get it wrong and Miss Tempest . . . ?'

Gertie wrinkled her nose and the cigarette danced. 'You follow the cue sheets I give you, ducks. They'll tell you everything you want to know.'

She looked Stella up and down, her dark eyes sharp. 'You seem like you got a bit of sense about you, my girl. You'll learn fast. Any problems and I'll deal with Lottie.'

There was a gleam in Gertie's eyes. Stella felt reassured, and was eager to learn all she could. 'I promise I'll do my best, Mrs Peach.'

Gertie gave a hoot of laughter.

'Just plain Gertie, ducks. Never trusted any man enough to get hitched. Never sorry, neither. Men! They'll do the dirty on you as soon as look at you.'

Stella felt a pang. How true! And wasn't she the living proof?

'After each evening's performance, and twice on Saturday,' Gertie went on, 'make sure each player's costume is in good condition. Any damaged garment you bring to me. That silly cow Lottie often puts her heel though a hem, especially when she's had a couple.'

Charlotte Tempest sounded more and more like an ogre, and Stella wondered if she'd survive the first week.

'Cover each costume with a dust sheet,' said Gertie, seeming not to notice Stella's nervousness. 'At the end of the week, when the run of the play is over, we pack them away, and get out the next lot ready for the following week.'

Gertie smiled at her. 'On top of all that, you wait on Lottie hand and foot. Dressing, hair. Booze! You'll have to assist Monty now and again, too.'

'Why doesn't Mr Fitzgerald have his own dresser?'

'Money, ducks. The company scrapes by with enough to settle bills and pay wages, but there's nothing left for luxuries.

Elsie and Flo are only waiting to get better offers, then they'll be off.' Gertie gave a deep sigh of regret. 'The Monty Fitzgerald Players Touring Company don't attract the quality talent like it used to. Just a lot of has-beens and fly-by-nights.' Her smile widened into a grin. 'Still and all, it's not such a bad life in the theatre, ducks. I've done it for thirty years. You'll be all right. You'll catch on.' She tapped the side of her nose. 'But one word of advice. Watch out for Monty. He likes 'em tender, like you.'

Gertie pushed up the sleeves of her cardigan in a workman-like manner. 'Right! Dress parade tomorrow morning for next week's production, and full dress rehearsal Friday. There's plenty to do, so come on, ducks, help me with these trunks.'

'Well!' Babs pulled out a chair from under the table and sat down, reaching for the cup of tea Stella put before her. 'How did it go? Did you meet the players? Are they glamorous?'

'Let her get a word in, then, will you?' Freda exclaimed impatiently.

Back in her own living room, her morning at the theatre now seemed like a dream, or was it a nightmare? Stella wasn't sure.

'Well,' she said cautiously, 'they're not like us.' She went on to give an account of her first encounter with the Monty Fitzgerald Players, particularly Charlotte and Evelyn.

'Stuck-up lot!' Freda pronounced scathingly. 'All fur coat and no knickers, them actresses are, and all tarred with the same brush.'

'Gertie Peach, the wardrobe mistress, is all right, though,' Stella added. 'She's like us, you know, genuine. I'll learn a lot from her.'

'What for, I don't know,' opined Freda. 'It isn't a proper job.'

'Tsk!' Babs was irritated. 'I suppose scrubbing floors would be a proper job, would it? Getting housemaid's knee to show for it.' She turned to Stella. 'Oh, you are lucky, Stell,' she said, with a faraway look in her eyes. 'Finding a glamorous job like that.'

Stella said nothing. Glamorous was hardly the word she would have used. But she was lucky to be working at all. 'It's October already,' she said, changing the subject, 'and not a word from Eddie. He must've got to Australia by now. You'd think he'd drop me a line, just to ask about Rosie.'

'You'll never hear from him again,' Freda said, with conviction. 'Artful Dodg'em, he is, and he's dumped his unwanted doings on you.'

'I'm not giving up hope,' Stella answered quickly. 'Eddie's not a bad person, and he's not irresponsible. He'll turn up again, you mark my words.'

Arnie hadn't been back to Victor Street after rehearsals, and Stella presumed he'd taken Charlotte Tempest to lunch after all. She wondered if he felt guilty at having thrown her into the deep end to let her sink or swim.

She was quivering with nerves when she arrived at the stage door an hour before the start of the performance. A man she hadn't seen before was chatting to the doorman. When their glances met he took the pipe out of his mouth and smiled at her. 'I'm only guessing,' he said, 'but are you Mrs Evans, the new dresser?'

Stella nodded and he held out a hand. 'I'm Roland Telford, theatre manager,' he said, then replaced the pipe between his teeth.

Of medium height, he wore a comfortable-looking tweed jacket. Stella liked his clean-shaven, rather plain face. His accent showed he was a local man, and she was relieved to meet one of her own kind among these strange people.

'Has Gertie introduced you to the stage manager, Bill Reynolds, and Phyllis, his assistant and prompt? Good. They're part of Monty's company, of course. I'll introduce you to the stage hands later. They're employed by the theatre-owners, as I am. You'll find yourself fitting in in no time, and don't forget, any problems Gertie can't handle, don't hesitate to ask Bill Reynolds, or the DSM.'

'DSM?'

'Deputy stage manager. That's Phyllis again. In fact, she's the touring company's general dogsbody.' He patted her arm. 'Don't look so worried,' he said. 'Worse things happen at sea.'

Then he was striding away. Stella went about her business: Gertie had given her the cue sheets earlier, instructing her to study them, so she knew exactly what was expected of her. She was to report to Charlotte's dressing room straight away.

Squaring her shoulders, Stella turned her steps in that direction. Forty-five shillings a week was not to be taken lightly and, besides, hadn't she already decided to show those two snooty women she was just as able as the absent Mildred?

She tapped on the leading lady's door, and pushed it open. Charlotte was sitting in front of her mirror, still wearing her hat and fur stole.

She was finishing the contents of a glass tumbler, taking the last drop as though her life depended on it. Dark shadows under her eyes marred her striking features, and she looked older. When she caught Stella's reflection in the mirror, she swung around and, with a mewling cry, flung the tumbler fiercely at Stella's head. It missed narrowly, and crashed into the wall, fragments of glass flying in all directions. 'Get out!' she yelled. 'How dare you burst in here, you spying bitch? I know your game.' Stella got out. Was forty-five shillings a week enough to put up with this? She had just taken a few steps away when the door was thrown open and Charlotte looked out, her face flushed. 'Here! You! What's your name?' She beckoned imperiously to Stella. 'Help me dress for the first act. Come on!' she commanded. 'You should've been here half an hour ago. And where's the wig, girl? Oh, for God's sake, don't stand there gawping. Oh, really! Useless!'

Charlotte retreated and Stella followed her. The dressing room was scandalously untidy, discarded clothing flung everywhere. There was a pungent yet sickly-sweet smell about the place that Stella couldn't identify, but she was reminded of cheap eau-de-Cologne.

Under a cotton dust-sheet, a garment was hanging behind the door. Stella got it down and, with trembling fingers, undid the buttons. Charlotte snaked into it, and as Stella buttoned her up, the older woman regarded her in the mirror with a poker face.

'What's your name?'

'Just call me Evans,' Stella said. She couldn't bear to be on first-name terms with this dreadful woman.

'You understand this is only temporary,' Charlotte said brusquely. 'Mildred will be back soon, then you're out. I've still to be convinced that Monty's not got an ulterior motive in getting you in.' Her eyes glittered. 'Remember, I'll be watching you.'

Stella said nothing. She wouldn't give this woman an excuse to get her sacked.

Charlotte flattened her blonde curls with hairpins, slapping away Stella's hands when she tried to help. 'You clumsy fool, Evans! You almost drew blood then.'

She stabbed a finger at a bust on which hung a wig of black hair arranged in an elaborate Edwardian style. Stella was already reaching for it. 'The wig, you fool!' Charlotte snapped. 'Come on! They'll be calling soon. Oh, you're useless, Evans. You won't last five minutes in this job. I shall complain to Monty.'

Chapter Thirteen

Monty didn't turn away from the mirror when Courtney Maitland came into his dressing room before the performance one evening mid-week. The young actor looked agitated, and Monty wondered if Lottie had been chasing him too vigorously. Had she finally got him into her bed? He knew how voracious she could be, especially with a couple of gins inside her.

'Lottie's cutting up rough again, Monty,' Maitland said. 'She's got it in for Mrs E for some reason. Give her a chance, what? She's trying to do her best, but she's got problems, you know.'

'Haven't we all?' Monty replied laconically, as he applied shadow to his eyelids. He'd heard Lottie's raised voice earlier and had half expected his wife to come into his dressing room to complain about something. She was always complaining, these days. In fact, Monty mused, Lottie was becoming a bore. Nothing would give him greater pleasure than to replace her in the company with someone young, luscious . . .

'Just because Mrs E has been abandoned by her husband,' Maitland went on bitterly, 'some men think they can take what they want from her.' He struck a fist forcefully into the palm of his other hand. 'The swine!'

'Abandoned?' Monty swung round from the dressing-table, his interest stirred. 'You mean, Stella's a married woman without a man?' My God! What a gift! He wasn't quick enough to conceal his lascivious thoughts, and the young actor glared at him, visibly hot under the collar.

'Look here, Monty! Keep your distance from Mrs E, what? She's not like Elsie and the others. She's decent.'

Monty looked at him keenly, wondering what was behind this defence of Stella. He felt a flash of jealousy, recalling that Maitland and Stella shared a house. 'Anyone would think you had the hots for her yourself,' he said. 'You and she are not . . . sharing the sheets, are you?'

'That's a damnable thing to ask! If you were a younger man, Monty, I'd knock you down!'

'Save the passion for the boards, Maitland.' Monty turned back to the mirror. 'You might see yourself as her guardian angel, but Stella may have other ideas. She might welcome a gentleman's appreciation. And don't do me an injustice. I know she's different.'

Different and utterly desirable, he reflected.

In the following days he found himself obsessed with Stella, and jealousy flared whenever he thought of her and Maitland alone together at night. He couldn't believe the young actor wasn't taking advantage of the situation. He'd have to be a bloody saint!

When she was backstage Monty watched Stella avidly. She was luscious and ripe, ready for the picking. He wanted her badly. He planned and schemed how he could catch her alone, but she eluded him. He wouldn't let himself believe she was deliberately avoiding him. After all, the old charm had never failed him yet.

After the matinée on the following Saturday, when Stella had been with the troupe a week, Monty was ready to make his move. But he wouldn't rush at it this time, bull at a gate, as he had with others. Stella *was* a different proposition from the young women he was used to, gullible young actresses eager to make a name for themselves, not being too fussy how they did it.

Monty wiped away the last of the greasepaint, thinking of

the camp bed he kept in the small locked room behind the stage. It had seen plenty of action in countless theatres over the years. He combed his hair back from his face, revelling in its abundance. He was still a handsome man, vigorous.

Although he yearned for Stella, a man's needs had to be met, and Elsie had stepped willingly into that small room only last night. He wanted Stella to be willing, too, but something told him he'd not get her into that room, not of her own free will, anyway. But he had never needed to force a woman to yield to him. He didn't doubt that, with a bit of patience, he'd have Stella eating out of his hand.

He reached for his blazer behind the door and put it on, checking his appearance in the mirror, being extra-critical. He couldn't help a satisfied smile at what he saw. He was a fine figure of a man. Stella would be impressed.

He'd ask her out to supper tonight after the evening performance. He'd be old-fashioned about it, polite and gentlemanly. He wouldn't rush things, just dine her well, and pile on the old charm. In a week, or two, when he finally had that lovely body writhing under his, it would be all the sweeter for the waiting.

He was just about to leave his dressing room when the door was thrown open. 'Monty! You must get rid of her, now, this afternoon. I want the bitch out,' Lottie said.

Her voice grated on his nerves, dispelling the warm sensation he'd felt at the thought of Stella and her yielding body. 'For God's sake, Lottie, must you behave like a fishwife?'

He could smell the gin from where she stood in the doorway. Her hair was pinned close to her head, as though she'd just taken off her wig. She still wore makeup and her costume, a tight-waisted garment that thrust her breasts cleverly into display. But Monty wasn't impressed by her fading charms, not any more.

Once Lottie had been young and fresh, like Stella. Not that she couldn't still turn a man's head, but he was no longer jealous of her paramours. Now she irritated him like sand between the toes.

'Get those togs off,' he said curtly, 'or you'll have Gertie on the warpath again. I thought you were seeing Maitland after the matinée?'

'Did you hear me, Monty?' Lottie's brittle tones vibrated. 'I don't want Evans anywhere near me again. I'll refuse to go on if she remains. The woman is deliberately trying to undermine me. And I know why. It's jealousy.'

Monty turned away from her.

'She wants to replace me, Monty,' Lottie cried. 'You've promised her that, haven't you? Promised she'd be a star?'

'Don't be difficult, Lottie,' he said evenly, realising suddenly just how much his dislike of her had grown. God! What wouldn't he give to be free of her? But they'd made their reputation in the theatre, such as it was, as a team, and they could still strike sparks off each other on stage, which was what the public paid to see. He didn't relish breaking in a new stage partner, despite Lottie's suspicions.

'You're too much of a trouper to refuse to go on, Lottie.' He picked his words carefully. It was no good antagonising her when she was in this mood. 'You're a professional through and through, while Stella's an amateur at her job. You can't expect her to know all your . . . our little ways as old Mildred did. Give her another chance.'

'Give *that* one a chance, and she'll take everything. I'm warning you, Monty.'

'Lottie, be reasonable.' He glanced at his pocket watch. Stella might still be in the theatre. He might catch her. He'd had enough of Lottie and her gin-soaked tantrums.

'Your suspicions are groundless, Lottie,' he said. 'And, what's more, you're being unfair to the girl.'

'Unfair? Is that all you have to say, when the little minx is obviously after my position in the company?' Lottie cried passionately. 'Not to mention chasing Courtney Maitland for all she's worth.'

She was giving one of her best performances, Monty noted idly, and the remark about Maitland explained a good deal about

Lottie's aversion to Stella. It also sent a shaft of jealousy through him.

'Instead of doing her job,' Lottie went on, her voice rising, 'she's cornering him every other minute. He can't move for her.' She sniffed loudly. 'Not that Courtney would ever look at such a common little upstart.'

Jealousy stabbed him through like a sword blade, and anger followed – anger with Lottie for making him doubt his own powers. 'That's bloody nonsense!' he burst out heatedly. 'Stella is Maitland's landlady. He lodges at her house. There's nothing between them. I've asked him.'

There was silence for a moment as they looked at each other.

'You old fool!' Lottie hissed at last. 'As if he'd admit it.'

With a screech of rage and a sudden wild swing of her arm, Lottie swept the dressing-table clear of brushes, bottles and greasepaint, sending them crashing to the floor. 'His landlady, indeed! Damn her to hell!' she shouted furiously. 'Of course they're lovers. Right under my nose. The little whore!' She swung round, eyes sparking like a cat's when it scents prey. 'Now will you get rid of her? And you must insist Courtney returns to our lodgings. She's poison, Monty. She'll be the end of this company, mark my words.'

Monty was thinking clearly again. Stella wasn't cheap or a minx. She was tender and lovely, a prize worth scheming for. He wanted her more than he'd wanted any other woman, and he wouldn't see his plans for her spoiled by Lottie.

'No, I won't,' he stated. 'Because it's not true. Stella stays.'

Lottie stared at him for a moment. 'Oh, I understand now,' she said. 'Not only does she have aspirations for a glorious stage career, she's one of *your* tarts. Accommodating, is she, in that room behind the stage? You pathetic old ram!'

'That's enough!'

'Oh, no!' Lottie was outraged. 'You'll not get another performance from me until she is out of this theatre for good. Do you hear me? Either she goes or I do.'

Monty wanted to strike her, but held himself in check. 'You

go on stage, Lottie, and behave in the normal way,' he said slowly, 'or you're finished with this touring company.'

Lottie laughed contemptuously. 'I *am* the company!'

'Don't delude yourself,' Monty retorted. 'You're not Mrs Patrick Campbell. You were nothing when I met you. I *made* you, Lottie. I taught you everything, and don't you forget it. And I can end it. You *can* be replaced. Elsie isn't your understudy for nothing. She's coming on well. She could step into your part this week, like that.' Monty snapped his fingers in her face. 'So, you go, Lottie, if you like, but Stella stays.'

Babs glanced at the clock on the mantelpiece. Half five. Ted would be home for his tea any time. Knowing their noisiness often upset him, she'd sent the twins across to their grandmother, so he could have some peace while he ate. It was only fair. Besides, they never seemed to have time alone together any more.

She stood at the cooker, flipping over the succulent pieces of liver in the pan, the smell of the onions making her mouth water. Ted's favourite meal. He'd be pleased with her, sure to be.

She stirred the pan idly, preoccupied. Apart from the other week, when he'd wanted her every night, he hadn't touched her for ages. Cold and distant, he hardly spoke a civil word to her now, had nothing but complaints.

In one way it was a relief. The prospect of another pregnancy haunted her. The twins were enough to cope with. But what did his neglect mean? Was it true what Mam was always telling her, that Ted had a fancy piece?

No! She couldn't believe it. Ted didn't drink or smoke. He didn't throw money away on horses. He didn't have any vices, except perhaps that he was a bit tight with his money. But that was just thrift. He always said he never wanted to be like his parents, without two pennies to scratch their arses.

Perhaps it was her. Was she was growing fat and ugly? She

wasn't very bright, she knew that. Ted was always complaining about her stupidity.

The back door opened and Ted came in, slinging his haversack on the floor under the sink. He took off his cap and coat, then hung them behind the back door.

'Hello, Ted, love,' Babs greeted him, determined to make an extra effort to please. 'You timed it right. Tea's ready.'

Without a word, he strode to the stone sink, rolled up his sleeves and, started to wash his hands.

Babs viewed his stiff back uncertainly. 'I got your favourite by here, liver and onions,' she said.

He grabbed a towel, dried his hands, and looked at her for the first time. 'Not burning it, are you? I don't want bloody burnt offerings.'

Babs was abashed. She was a good cook. Even Mam had to admit that Babs was the best cook in the family. Ted had no call to say that. 'I've never burnt a meal yet, Ted Thomas, as well you know.' Her tone verged on truculence.

'Well, you're a dimwit at everything else, aren't you?' he said. 'Can't even keep your own kids in order. Run wild, they do.'

Babs felt tears prickle behind her eyes at his unfairness. She watched him stride towards the living room where the table was laid for his meal, suddenly desperate: their marriage was falling apart and she didn't know why.

'Ted, what's wrong? What's going on?'

He swung round and glared at her. 'What the hell do you mean by that? You've got a bloody nerve questioning me, you stupid woman.'

'I – I only wondered why you're angry with me all the time,' Babs said, her heart giving a little jump at the fierce light in his eyes. 'Sit down, love. I'll bring your food in.'

Quickly Babs put fluffy boiled potatoes on a dinner plate, and spooned over the simmering gravy, liver and onions. Plate in hand, she followed him into the living room, but he turned towards the kitchen table. 'What's this?' He pointed at a pie-dish filled with meat and vegetables, and the oval of pastry Babs had been rolling out.

'I'm making a steak and kidney pie for Stella and her lodger. She's working till all hours at the theatre. He likes a late cooked meal, so to save Stella I said I'd do it for her.'

'*What?*' Ted's face turned brick red with wrath. 'Are you mad, woman?'

'No, it's all right, Ted,' Babs said soothingly, standing there with his plate of food in her hand. 'It didn't cost us anything. Stella paid for the meat and everything. She wanted to give me something towards the gas as well, but I told her not to be *twp*.'

Ted's eyes narrowed. 'Do you mean to tell me that, even after I warned you about her filthy goings-on, you're still friendly with her?'

'Stella and me have been friends for years, Ted.' Babs frowned at him. 'I can't see anything wrong with her. You've been listening to gossip from that horrible Mrs Ridd. She's a menace, that woman.'

Ted pointed an index finger at her, his jaw jutting aggressively. 'You stay away from her next door, do you hear me? She's a slut, and I don't want it rubbing off on you.'

'But it doesn't make sense, Ted. I *know* Stella—'

'Don't be a lame-brained fool!' Ted bellowed. 'What do you think she's doing with that walking clothes-horse she calls a lodger? What do you think they get up to every night, the pair of them?'

He took a few steps towards her, his eyes blazing. 'Filth!' he shouted. 'That's what she's doing with him. I can hear them at night, right through the wall, rubbing my – our noses in it.'

Ted took a huge gulp of air, and Babs was alarmed to see a vein in his temple throbbing.

'Ted? Sit down.'

'Deliberately flaunting it, she is.' He shouted her down. 'Laughing at – us. They stoned women like her in the Bible, and she *needs* the dirt beaten out of her.' His fists clenched convulsively. 'I'd like to strip her naked and take my belt buckle to her, the stinking whore!'

'Ted!' Babs was shocked at his words and the wild look in his eyes. 'Please! Don't say such terrible things. Don't get upset.'

'Upset?' Ted roared. 'You stupid fat cow! Look at you!'

Babs felt as though he'd stabbed her through the heart.

'What man would want to fondle you, eh?' he went on harshly. 'Certainly not me. Just looking at you makes me sick, never mind touching you. And there's her next door, giving it away to any man but m—' He was overcome with a terrible rage that Babs didn't understand.

She was trembling with shock and hurt. 'But, Ted, I'm your wife!'

'You're nothing!' With a lunge he knocked the plate from her hands. It splintered into pieces on the stone floor of the scullery, china shards and food flying everywhere. Babs screamed. 'Shut up!' He lifted a hand, threatening to strike her too, and she cringed.

'Now, I'm warning you, Barbara,' he said, 'you stay away from that bitch, Stella. You don't bother with her or her kid. Understand me?'

'But, Ted, little Danny is innocent—'

'Do you want a thumping, woman?' he snarled. 'Well, then, you'd better do as I tell you, or else I'll teach you a lesson you won't forget. Got that?'

He strode to the back door and took down his cap and coat. 'I'm getting out of this pigsty,' he said. 'I want some decent food. Get on and clean up that mess, you useless article.'

Babs came in through the back door just as Stella was putting on her hat. She had missed the mirror over the fireplace since Griff had smashed it. If there was any bad luck due, she hoped it wouldn't come her way now that things were going well for her.

'Is my hat on straight, Babs?' she asked. 'First thing I'm going to buy when I get my pay is a mirror. I saw a good one in that second-hand shop on St Helen's Road.'

She glanced at Babs, and was concerned to see how white her face was: it was usually rosy with health and good-nature. 'What's wrong, love? Are you ill?'

Babs gave a ghostly smile, which made her seem all the more wan. 'Yes, that's it,' she said. 'It's my monthlies, you know. Always troublesome. I'll have a drop of gin and hot water later. That'll ease it.' She looked around. 'Where's Arnie?'

'He's gone on,' Stella said, picking up her handbag from the table. 'Wanted to have a word with Mr Fitzgerald about something. He looked a bit worried, I thought.' She sighed. 'I hope the company's not packing up just when I've landed this job.'

'It's the end of your first week, then,' Babs said. 'Looking forward to your pay, I expect.'

Stella made a face. 'Got to work a week in hand, worse luck. Never mind. Roll on next week, isn't it?'

'How are you coping?' Babs asked.

Her tone sounded hollow, and Stella looked at her keenly before replying. 'Barely,' she admitted. 'Oh, it's not the work, it's that Charlotte Tempest. I can't do anything right for her. She yells at me all the time. I think I'll have a word with Mr Fitzgerald myself. I mean, why should I put up with it?'

Her attention came back to Babs, who was standing quite still, hand on the mantelpiece, staring into the fire. She looked drawn. Stella had never seen her friend so fraught before, and wished she wasn't in such a hurry. 'Babs, what is it?'

Babs gave a little smile, but it seemed strained. 'Mam will be here in a minute to look after the children, and I've got a lovely steak and kidney pie for Arnie's supper,' she said. 'It'll be ready when you come home.'

On impulse, and because she was overcome by Babs's kindness, Stella hugged her, and kissed her cheek. 'Bless you, Babs, you're a godsend.'

'You'd better go,' Babs said, 'or that Miss Tempest will be whipping up a storm.'

Her laugh was brittle, and Stella thought her friend sounded near to tears. Reluctantly she said goodbye and hurried to catch the tram to work.

Chapter Fourteen

Charlotte's dressing room was a mess after Wednesday's matinée performance, dresses, shoes, underwear strewn carelessly around. There was even an empty gin bottle under the chair.

As she reached down for it something bright and sparkling, almost hidden from view against the skirting-board, caught her eye. As she retrieved it, Stella saw it was Lottie's treasured emerald and diamond spray brooch, presented to her by none other than Edward, Prince of Wales – or so she boasted.

Stella felt a little thrill at the thought of holding something that might once have known a royal touch, and fingered it in awe.

On impulse she held the brooch against the dark bodice of her dress, and looked at herself in the mirror, admiring the way the precious stones twinkled.

With a sigh, she was about to put it into Charlotte's jewellery box when the door burst open behind her and Charlotte stood poised on the threshold, Gertie behind her. Startled, Stella jumped back from the dressing-table.

Charlotte's sharp gaze took in the brooch in Stella's fingers, and with a shriek of rage, she sprang forward and snatched it from Stella's hand. Stella winced with pain as the pin stabbed her finger, drawing blood.

'Caught you red-handed, you sneak-thief,' Charlotte shrilled, a gleam of triumph in her eyes. 'I knew you'd come unstuck, eventually. Gertie! Send for a policeman.'

Stella took her bleeding finger out of her mouth. 'But I haven't done anything, Miss Tempest.'

'What?' Charlotte's eyes flashed. 'I catch you pilfering my brooch and you have the gall to deny it,' she cried. 'Ooh! What bare-faced effrontery!'

'Steady on, Lottie, old girl.' Gertie edged her way in. 'Let's hear what Stella has to say.'

Stella was thankful for Gertie's presence. 'Thank you, Gertie,' she said gratefully. 'I found the brooch on the floor at the side of the dressing-table, where you must have dropped it, Miss Tempest.'

'Liar!' Charlotte shouted. 'You were stealing it, just the way you're trying to steal my position in the company. You fancy yourself as an actress.'

'I don't!' Stella was angry now. 'I wouldn't live your immoral life for the world!'

Charlotte stared open-mouthed at Gertie, as if for support.

'Now, now, Stella, me ducks,' Gertie said soothingly, 'let's not get personal.'

'Personal?' Stella hooted. 'She's just called me a thief. How personal do you call that?'

'I can see right through you,' Charlotte said. 'You'd like to see the back of me, wouldn't you? Step into my shoes.'

She flounced to the dressing-table, opened a cigarette box, took one out, and put it to her lips, reaching for the gold cigarette lighter nearby.

'No, I would not, Miss Tempest.' Stella was in despair. Would nothing ever go right for her?

Charlotte couldn't make the lighter work and, with an unladylike oath, she flung it and the cigarette into the corner of the room, rounding on Stella with renewed fury. 'I know what Monty's paying you, and it's not a dresser's wages. He thinks he can groom you to take my place, but you'll never be an actress. You're as common as muck, no talent, no polish. So, you've cheapened yourself for nothing!'

Gertie clicked her tongue. 'Steady on, Lottie.'

Charlotte ignored her. 'You covet my career, my jewellery, even my admirer, Courtney Maitland. You're a gold-digger as well as a thief.'

Monty appeared at the open door, his face dark with anger. 'What's all this screaming, Lottie? I can hear you from the stage.'

Charlotte flung up a hand dramatically and pointed a long bony finger at Stella. 'It's that vile creature, your protégée, Monty,' she hissed. 'She's a common thief. We caught her pilfering my emerald brooch, didn't we, Gertie?'

'It's not true!' Stella spoke up. 'The brooch was on the floor. I was putting it back in the box.'

'A likely story!' Charlotte bellowed. 'Monty! I demand you send for a policeman. This – this *person* must be arrested. She's a thief, I tell you!'

Monty gave Stella a long look, his expression softening. She glanced at the other two women, worried that they'd noticed his partiality. She didn't want Charlotte getting any more outrageous notions.

'I don't believe it, Lottie,' he said. 'You're hysterical again.'

He turned to the seamstress. 'Come on, Gertie, what really happened?'

'Well . . .' Gertie sighed deeply. 'I've known Lottie a long time, and Stella's new to me, but I trust her. I believe her when she says she found the brooch and was putting it back.'

'You imbeciles!' Charlotte stormed. 'How can you be so blind? Especially you, Gertie. I thought you were a better judge of character.'

'Lottie, be reasonable,' Monty said heavily. 'A scandal is the last thing we want.'

'Oh, I thought any publicity was good publicity,' Charlotte returned sharply. 'Why are you protecting her?' Her eyes narrowed. 'Are you carrying on with her as well as Elsie?'

'Miss Tempest!' Stella was livid. The actress had gone too far.

'Enough!' Monty put his foot down. 'I warn you, Lottie, I'll not put up with your tantrums much longer.'

'My God!' Charlotte screamed. 'Why have you all turned

against me? Is my artistry to count for nothing?' She flung a poisonous stare at Stella, then tried to elbow her way past her husband.

'Courtney!' she called out loudly. 'Courtney, rescue me, I implore you!'

Monty grabbed her by the shoulders. 'Stop these histrionics, Lottie, for pity's sake. You're not fooling anyone. Pull yourself together, woman. Go to the lodgings, get some rest. We've still got the evening performance to get through.'

'Take your hands off me! I'm not one of your loose pieces.'

'Listen to me,' he said harshly, 'I want to see a leading lady on that stage this evening, not some worn-out hag.'

Stella knew she'd have to give up the job. She couldn't take much more of Charlotte Tempest, and being branded a thief was the last straw. But if she failed to turn up for the performance, Charlotte would proclaim it proof of her guilt. Stella wouldn't give her that satisfaction. Still, it took all her will-power to return to the theatre that evening. She knew it wouldn't be any picnic with Charlotte out for her blood.

Avoiding Charlotte's glare of hatred in the mirror, Stella stood behind her fumbling with the pins as she attempted to secure her curls.

'You clumsy bitch!' Charlotte shrieked. 'You stuck that hairpin in my scalp on purpose.'

'I'm sorry!'

Stella's fingers were awkward with tension. 'It was an accident, Miss Tempest.'

'Don't take me for a fool,' Charlotte shouted. 'You're out to do me an injury, you vicious minx.' She looked demented, Stella thought, shocked at the violence in her tone. It was unnerving to be the object of such hatred.

'Miss Tempest, please!'

'Don't interrupt me,' the older woman snapped. 'I've

warned Evelyn to keep her jewellery under lock and key, away from your sticky fingers. Oh, yes! I've made sure the whole company knows what a thieving guttersnipe you are.'

Stella dropped the hairpins on the floor. Charlotte had humiliated her in public. 'This is monstrous!' she spluttered. 'I've done nothing wrong.'

'Nothing wrong? Huh! You're a wrong one, through and through. I saw that as soon as I set eyes on you.' She pointed at the floor imperiously. 'Pick up those pins.'

Stella wanted to run from the room, defeated, but she held her ground. She was determined to stay and fight – not for the money, but for her good name.

It took a great effort of will, but obediently, she stooped and collected up the hair pins. She could feel the malignancy of Charlotte's gaze on her bent head, and knew the actress would do all she could to break her spirit.

'Keep away from Courtney Maitland,' she warned spitefully. 'You may have fooled him for now, but he'll soon come to his senses. And so will Monty. They'll see you for what you are.'

Stella kept her lips firmly clamped together. A throbbing headache was starting, but she wouldn't give Charlotte the satisfaction of seeing her weep. She tried to put in another hairpin, but Charlotte slapped away her hands. 'Get away from me!' she flared. 'Pass that wig to me.'

Stella did as she was asked, then stood back, her resolve to fight eroding under Charlotte's pitiless verbal assault.

'What Courtney sees in you, I'll never know,' she rasped. 'But, then, why do some men lower themselves with prostitutes?'

Stella couldn't let this insinuation go unchallenged. 'Now, just a minute,' she said, 'how dare you insult me? Arnie and I—'

'Don't try to bamboozle me,' Charlotte interrupted, while pulling on the wig. 'His so-called landlady. Huh! I have another word for what *you* are and it's something unmentionable in polite society.'

'Now, look here, Miss Tempest, I don't *have* to stay here and take your insults.'

'Then why don't you quit?' Charlotte snapped. 'Everyone knows you're untrustworthy, and you're useless as a dresser, anyway. You're only here to see what you can filch.'

'That's slander!'

'Only if it's not true,' Charlotte retorted. 'You can't deny I caught you sniffing around my jewellery box.'

'I *do* deny it!'

Charlotte stood up abruptly, adjusting the neckline of her costume. She cut an impressive figure. 'I've seen the likes of you come and go,' she said haughtily, over her shoulder. 'You're not the first to try to oust me from the top of the tree. Elsie thinks she can do it, but I'll see her in hell first.' She preened before the mirror. 'What class! What style!' she proclaimed. 'I was born with it. But you . . . You're a fly-by-night, Evans. What the Americans call a floozy.'

'You've no right to speak to me like this,' Stella seethed. 'I'm only trying to earn an honest living.'

'You're a thief, and a common guttersnipe,' Charlotte scoffed. 'I can guess how *you* earn your living – on your back, legs spread.' She tossed her head. 'Go and ply your trade elsewhere.'

'How dare you?' Stella was beside herself with rage, her palm itching to smack Charlotte's smug face. 'This is outrageous. I'm a decent woman, while you—'

'Decent? Don't make me laugh!'

There was tension in Charlotte's stance, and momentarily Stella was frightened: she know the actress wasn't above striking her and, involuntarily, took a step backwards, out of reach.

Charlotte's smile was tigerish. 'How many nights this week have you been with Monty in that room behind the stage?' she asked contemptuously. 'How much did he pay you?'

Stella couldn't believe her ears.

'Oh, don't look so innocent, Evans. I know he keeps a camp bed in there, where the likes of you entertain him. You disgust me!'

Stella's jaw tightened. Gertie had warned her about the room behind the stage and Monty's voracious appetite for younger women. That Charlotte could accuse her of such loose goings-on was too much.

'I won't put up with this a minute longer, Miss Tempest,' Stella declared. 'I'll complain to Mr Fitzgerald about your treatment of me.'

'Go ahead!' Charlotte stalked to the door. 'Just because you're his latest floozy, don't think he won't sack you on *my* say-so. I'm his wife, the star of this company, while your kind are two a penny. He can pick the next one up on any street corner.'

With that she flounced out.

Overpowering rage rendered Stella immobile. Charlotte Tempest was the most obnoxious woman she had ever met, even worse than Mrs Ridd, and that was saying something. She would well understand why Mildred, the former dresser, had left the actress flat, and felt like doing the same. But why should she let Charlotte win?

Stella decided to tackle Monty Fitzgerald straight after the last curtain. She must clear the air and put a stop to the woman's malicious ravings.

Another week's production over, and good audiences, too, Monty thought. It was proving an excellent season. *East Lynne* next week. That play always packed them in.

Standing bare-chested before an enamel bowl on a side table, he splashed his face and neck with water and was annoyed to find it cool instead of comfortably warm. Stella had brought it to the dressing room too early. She *was* avoiding him. Gertie had been talking too much. Damn her!

Yes, the season was going well, yet he was conscious of a shadow of discontent that had nothing to do with his professional life. It centred around Stella, because he wanted her and she was out of his reach. He tried to comfort himself with the thought that there was always another little dolly waiting in the wings, willing to be accommodating to the great Monty Fitzgerald.

But he wasn't comforted. Like a callow youth, he hungered for Stella. His pride wouldn't accept that she was unobtainable. He was disconcerted to realise suddenly that damn little else mattered to him except possessing *her*.

Monty glimpsed his reflection in the mirror as he towelled his face and neck, and caught something in his expression that he hadn't seen in years, decades even. Uncertainty and vulnerability.

Ridiculous, in a man of his age. It was laughable! Or pitiful.

Monty felt a tightening in his chest. Had he become a pathetic old ram, as Lottie had called him?

He sat before the mirror, staring into his own eyes. There was only one cure for this self-doubt. He *must* have Stella, by fair means or foul. Then the craving would leave him.

His thoughts were scattered by a tap at the door. 'Come in.'

The door opened and Stella stood there. Monty jumped up, forgetting he was bare to the waist. Immediately her face flamed scarlet and she turned away.

'Wait!'

'I'm sorry, Mr Fitzgerald.' She kept her face averted. 'I didn't know you were still dressing.'

'Wait, Stella, please.'

Hurriedly he reached for his shirt, put it on and buttoned it. He didn't know why she was here – maybe the old charm was working after all. 'Sorry about that, my dear,' he said, as casually as he could, while his blood pumped powerfully through his veins. 'I wasn't expecting anyone.'

Her cheeks were still flushed when she turned back to him and a spasm of desire surged through his body, so strong it almost made him groan aloud, but he quelled it.

'What can I do for you, Stella, my dear?'

She stood in the doorway, reluctant to step into his domain. 'It's Miss Tempest,' Stella began. 'I get on with most people, Mr Fitzgerald, but she's . . .' She hesitated.

Wisps of black hair curled against her cheek and he longed to touch it, to bury his fingers in it, to capture those thick shiny locks and draw her to him.

'Impossible?' Monty suggested, trying to keep himself under control. She mustn't suspect his feelings, not until the moment was right and he had her where he wanted her.

'Look, this is rather delicate, what?' he went on. 'You'd better come in and close the door. We don't want to be overheard.'

Stella did as he said, and Monty tried to steady his uneven breathing. They were alone. A thrill of excitement went through him. The chase was on!

'Lottie's impossible,' he said, 'but she can't help herself, my dear. It's the artistic temperament, common to most performers, not to be taken too seriously.' He gave a little laugh. 'I've been known to suffer from it myself.'

'I can't help but take it seriously, Mr Fitzgerald.' Her voice quivered, and he realised that she was more than put out: she was really upset.

'Miss Tempest insults me at every opportunity. She calls me bad names and makes terrible accusations. I'm not a thief or a loose woman.' Tears glistened in her lovely eyes, and he almost forgot himself in his desire to embrace her.

'Humour her, my dear,' he suggested. 'Lottie has never been able to tolerate beauty in other women. She feels threatened by it. Mildred was as plain as a pikestaff.'

The flowered wrap-around pinafore Stella wore couldn't hide the rise and fall of her pert breasts, and Monty almost burst with longing. The theatre would be empty soon. If only he could keep her here just a little longer . . .

'Humour her?' Stella repeated. 'No, Mr Fitzgerald, I won't. She's making my life a misery with her outrageous accusations about my morals. I don't *want* to give up my job, but I can't continue as Miss Tempest's dresser.'

Monty was alarmed, but tried to hide it. She mustn't leave, not while he was enmeshed in this agonising need for her.

'Don't be hasty, Stella. I'll have a word with her.'

'It'll do no good,' she said, flushing again.

'What has she been saying?'

She twisted her fingers, embarrassed – and irresistible. 'I'd rather not repeat it.'

'Come along, Stella, my dear, I'm your friend as well as your employer. I have to know if I'm to challenge her.'

'Well, she's accusing me of – of carrying on with Arnie. And if that isn't bad enough . . . with you, too. She's ranting about a camp bed and a locked room.'

Monty felt a towering rage. Damn Lottie to hell! She'd ruin everything for him, and it would please her to do it. 'Look, Stella,' Monty said, almost frantically, 'Gertie speaks highly of you, and I'm very pleased with your work. It would be a shame to give up now. Will you let Lottie's jealousy deprive you of a good wage?'

'I need the money, Mr Fitzgerald,' Stella said, uncertainly, 'and, despite Miss Tempest, I like the work, and Gertie, too – well, I get on with everyone except your wife.'

Monty ventured to step closer. There was a natural fragrance about Stella he'd noticed before, a scent that stirred him powerfully. With a sudden insight he realised it was purity, that rare quality, and felt himself burn to taste it.

'You mustn't let Lottie get under your skin. She's jealous because you're young and lovely . . .' A telltale huskiness crept into his voice, and he curbed it quickly. 'She's under strain, you know,' he cajoled her. 'She misses Mildred. They were together a long time, and it's been a busy season.'

'That's no excuse for the terrible things she says to me,' Stella answered. 'She wants me sacked.'

Her dark eyes flashed, and Monty's breath caught in his throat. She was truly lovely . . . a woman without a man. He imagined the fire within her, waiting for *him* to ignite it . . .

A surge of desire made his tongue cleave to the roof of his mouth. 'No, I'm sure that's not true,' he managed.

A more experienced woman would've already spotted that he was losing control. But she looked so vulnerable that he struggled not to lay hands on her.

'I can see you're upset, Stella, my dear, but don't be rash, eh? Wait until next week. I'll talk to Lottie over the weekend. She'll see reason.'

'All right, Mr Fitzgerald,' Stella said. 'I want to keep my job, if possible.'

She turned to leave, but Monty put a hand on her arm lightly. 'Look,' he said quickly, 'let me make it up to you, my dear, to show there's no ill-feeling.'

'I don't understand, Mr Fitzgerald.'

'Well, it's been a long week. We've both worked hard. Now we deserve some enjoyment. Get your coat and hat and I'll take you to supper. Have you ever dined at the Baltic Lounge in Castle Street?'

'You're very kind, Mr Fitzgerald, but I don't think so. It's late. I must get home.'

His hand tightened on her arm. 'Stella, you must relax, have some fun. A little supper, a little conversation. I hardly know anything of you. Please dine with me tonight.'

To his consternation she drew back nervously, trying to pull her arm free. Experience told him he should stand back now, but that tantalising scent was in his nostrils, and he might never have this chance again.

'Stella!' He grasped both her arms and tried to draw her closer. 'You're the loveliest woman I've ever met. Dine with me, please. An hour in my company wouldn't be so bad, would it? I'll take you anywhere you like. We'll drink champagne . . .'

It would be so easy to overpower her, take what he wanted. He'd never done that before but he was sorely tempted now.

She struggled, her face distorted with fright. 'Mr Fitzgerald! Please let me go!'

'Listen, my dear, you mustn't be afraid of me,' he said raggedly. 'I mean you no harm. I thought we might spend a little time together, that's all, get to know each other?'

'I want to leave this room.' Stella pushed her hands against his chest. 'You can't keep me here. Let me go!'

'Stella, listen!' he cried hoarsely. 'Maitland is just a boy. He knows nothing of women. I understand you, understand your needs.'

She gave another frightened cry but he held her firmly.

'I know how it is with you,' he persisted, hearing the pleading in his voice, and despising himself. 'Your man has left you, but that doesn't stop you yearning for what you once had. I know how to satisfy that need, Stella—'

'How dare you say these things?' she cried.

She beat at his chest impotently, and he shook her. Just enough to bring her to her senses, he told himself.

'Stop fighting me, Stella.' He was tempted to hit her in frustration. 'Why Maitland?' he asked angrily. 'Why not me? I'm not old, and I'm twice the man he is.'

'Help! Help me, someone!'

'Be quiet, damn you, or else I'll—'

Good God! He'd never resorted to violence before. Appalled by his behaviour, he released her.

'I just want us to be . . . friends,' he said. 'You're on your own, so am I.'

'You're a married man!'

'Only in name,' Monty said hastily. 'Lottie means nothing to me, hasn't for years. She has lovers—'

'I don't want to know, Mr Fitzgerald,' Stella cried. 'Please stand away from the door. I want to leave now.'

He could tell by the way her eyes darted about that she was waiting for a chance to escape, and he cursed himself. Now she'd always be on her guard – if he ever saw her again.

'Please, Stella,' he begged, 'I apologise for the way I behaved. Forgive me, and please don't hold it against me.'

He did step aside then, and she darted to the door and flung it open. She paused there for a moment, looking back at him.

'There's no need to throw in your job, Stella,' he said. 'It'll never happen again, I promise you.'

'You're right, Mr Fitzgerald,' she replied, 'because you'll never get the chance.'

Chapter Fifteen

Babs lifted the china basin containing a beef suet pudding out of the saucepan of boiling water and stood it on the draining-board. Then she untied the knotted muslin. Done to a turn, and it smelt delicious. Cooking in another woman's kitchen wasn't easy, but she daren't do it in her own, not after the way Ted had laid down the law.

And Arnie was so appreciative. Sometimes, she caught him looking at her in a way that gave her goose-pimples, those big eyes of his shining. Sometimes she could almost believe he fancied her. But, of course, that was her imagination. Arnie was an actor, and his eyes were part of his stock-in-trade. He probably looked at every woman like that.

Yet it amused her to wonder if Arnie *did* fancy her. Not that she'd ever be unfaithful to Ted, she told herself. He was a good husband, even though he'd lifted a hand to her more than once lately. Still, like most wives, she had to live with it. She set great store by the vows she'd made at the altar.

The latch lifted on the back door.

Arnie was here and she wasn't ready to dish up. Tsk! That's what comes of day-dreaming. She turned away from the gas-ring, reaching for the colander to drain the Brussels sprouts.

'Grub up any minute!' she called, as she looked towards the door, and almost dropped the saucepan.

Ted was there, his face thunderous. 'You treacherous cow!' he shouted. 'What's this? Defying me, are you?'

Babs put the saucepan of sprouts in the sink, thinking vaguely that they'd spoil if she didn't drain them. 'I didn't expect you back so early,' she said.

'I can bloody well see that, you bitch.' He was advancing into the scullery towards her. 'Going behind my back, is it? Well, I'll teach you a lesson you won't forget in a hurry.' He pointed at the back door. 'Now, get home!'

'I can't just now, Ted,' Babs said shakily, her palms moistening in panic. 'I'm doing Stella's supper. It'll spoil, mun.'

'Are you daring to argue with me, woman?' he shouted, lifting a hand threateningly. 'I'll spoil *you* if you don't get your fat arse through that door this minute.'

'But, Ted, listen—'

'I've done all the listening I'm going to.'

He grabbed a handful of her hair and wrenched back her head at a painful angle. Babs yelped with surprise and pain. 'Ted! You're hurting me!'

His mouth was close against her ear, and she felt his breath hot on her cheek.

'I'll hurt you a damn sight more if you defy me again. Now get moving, woman, back where you belong.'

He forced her towards the door, and Babs's eyes watered with pain.

'Don't, Ted! Please!'

'Shut your fat gob!' He gripped her upper arm with his free hand, squeezing hard, and shoved her towards the door.

Babs stumbled along as he pushed and shoved her, unable to believe what was happening. She'd seen him angry many times, and he'd cuffed her once or twice, but never before had he laid hands so roughly on her, and she was frightened.

They went through Stella's back entrance and into the lane behind the houses. Babs was relieved there was no one about to witness her humiliation. Within minutes Ted had pushed her through her own back door and into the scullery. He let go of her hair, and swung her round to face him. 'Now, then!' he began, in a hard voice. 'What do you mean by disobeying me, woman? What's your game?'

Babs expected her mother to come out of the living room to see what the rumpus was, but Freda didn't appear. Where was she? For the first time in her marriage Babs was afraid to be alone with her husband.

'I – I promised to help, Ted,' she said nervously. 'I don't see any harm in it.'

'No harm! You're more stupid than I thought.'

'Don't shout, Ted. You'll wake the twins.' She wouldn't want them to witness such a scene.

'I'll shout all I want in my own home.' He shook her violently.

Babs's teeth clattered together and she could hardly draw breath. Why was Ted behaving like this? She hardly recognised him for the man she'd married.

'Have you any idea of what you've been doing, you stupid bitch?' he asked wrathfully. 'Aiding and abetting a common tart in her filthy trade. Next thing, you'll be down the docks too, putting it about.'

'Ted!' Babs was shocked that he could speak to her like that. 'That's a terrible thing to say to me.'

'I say it because other people will think it,' Ted shouted. '*My* wife consorting with a whore! Your name will be mud and mine along with it.'

'But it's not true about Stella,' Babs ventured. 'It's all lies. That Mrs Ridd should be locked up.'

'It's true, and I can prove it,' Ted retorted. He sounded so sure of himself that Babs was confused.

'How?'

'Because – because Stella tried it on with me,' he said gruffly. 'Tried to entice me into her bed. Made it plain what she wanted.' Ted's face contorted with a strange emotion that Babs couldn't read.

Babs was dumbfounded. It couldn't be true. Not Stella.

She peered into his eyes, which shifted away from hers. That was enough for Babs. 'Ted, I don't believe you,' she declared. 'Why are you lying? What has Stella ever done to you?'

She was stunned when the back of his hand struck the side of her face. 'That's for defying me,' he stormed. 'And this—' He hit her across the face again, sending her staggering back against the stone sink. 'That's for calling me a liar in my own home.'

Afraid to utter another word, and fearing more blows, Babs lifted an arm to protect her face, whimpering, terrified. 'Now, you treacherous bitch,' he went on savagely, 'maybe you'll do as you're told in future. You set one foot next door, and I'll beat you black and blue. Got it?'

'I don't understand what—'

'Shut up! You haven't got brains enough to understand anything. If I find you've been consorting with that whore, taking her brat to school, or even talking to her over the garden wall, I'll kick you out of this house. You'll never see your kids again.'

'Ted, please, don't—'

He lifted a hand threateningly. 'Do you understand me, Barbara?'

She nodded numbly, staring into his twisted face.

'Now get up to bed,' he commanded.

Babs stumbled towards the living room. At that moment Freda appeared. 'What's all the shouting about?' she asked. 'I could hear you out on the pavement.'

She stared at Babs's swelling cheek.

'Barbara! *Myn uffern i!*' She dashed forward to her daughter's side and clutched her protectively. 'What's he done to you?'

'Get back to your own place, you old bag,' Ted shouted. 'You're not wanted here.'

Babs clutched at Freda's arm. 'You'd better go, Mam. Danny and Rosie are all by themselves next door—'

'Shut your face, Barbara! I've warned you, haven't I?' Ted roared. 'It's none of your business any more. And you bugger off home, Freda, or else.'

'Or else what?' Freda's eyes narrowed. 'Don't you threaten me, Ted Thomas. I'm not your missus. Touch me, and I'll have the bobbies on you before you can say rat-trap.'

She sounded brave, but Babs could see that her mother was trembling violently.

'Clear off, then,' he snarled.

'It's all right, Babs, love,' Freda said, to her daughter. 'I'll see to Stella's kids.'

'*I forbid it!*' Ted raised a fist.

'Forbid all you want,' Freda shouted back. 'You can't stop me.'

She stalked off towards the passage, then turned in the doorway. 'And if you strike my girl once more, Ted Thomas,' she warned, 'I'll swing for you. Twice over.'

Babs edged towards the door, too, aware of Ted close behind her. A new fear gripped her. The twins! How could she trust him not to lay hands on them?

'*You* put her up to that,' Ted accused her, 'and you'll pay for it. I'll take it out of your fat hide.' He pushed her violently towards the living room. 'I'm the master of this house, and don't you forget it. Now, get out of my sight!'

The streets of the town were all but deserted as Stella hurried home from the theatre, upset by Monty Fitzgerald's behaviour. She'd never go back there. No amount of money was worth the fright and humiliation. Then she remembered she'd worked a week in hand, and was owed a week's wages, so she'd have to face him again.

She let herself into the house, anxious to see Babs, tell her all that had happened, listen to her advice. As for a meal, she had no appetite left . . .

She was surprised to see Freda sitting at the table with Arnie. When they turned to her she could tell from their expressions that something had happened, and was alarmed. 'What is it? Is it one of the children?'

'No,' Freda said shortly. 'It's our Babs.' She swallowed hard before continuing. 'That bugger Ted has given her a good hiding.'

'Oh, no.' Stella flopped down at the table, still in her hat and coat. 'What set him off?'

'You,' Freda said shortly. There was an edge of bitterness in her voice. 'He found out she was still helping you, see, when he'd forbidden it.'

Arnie leaped to his feet. 'I'm going next door now,' he said, 'and I'm going to thrash him, the swine!'

Freda and Stella jumped up, too, and held his arms, feeling him shaking with rage.

'No, Arnie,' Freda said quickly. 'You'd make trouble for yourself, and things would be worse for Babs. She's got to live with Ted for the rest of her life, remember.'

'No!' Arnie said, in a strangled voice. 'She doesn't have to. I'll provide for her and the children.' He sat down again, his face in his hands.

Freda stared at him in astonishment. 'What's been going on between you?'

'Nothing,' Stella answered for him. 'Arnie's a gentleman.'

She felt guilty and responsible. She should have warned her friend about Ted's violence. 'Is Babs badly hurt?' she asked.

'Going all colours,' Freda answered. 'I'd like to take our bread-knife to that Ted.'

Stella took in the worry on her companions' faces and knew she would say nothing of her encounter with Monty Fitzgerald. Compared to what Babs had been through it paled into insignificance.

She wouldn't give up the job just yet, she decided, although staying out of Monty's way and bearing Lottie's insults wouldn't be easy. But she would miss Babs's help.

'Listen,' Freda said. 'Ted can't boss *me* about. Don't you worry, Stella, I'll carry on minding your little ones, and get a bit of grub ready of an evening for you.' She lifted her nose in the air. 'Unless you think my cooking isn't grand enough.'

Stella was touched. 'Oh, Freda! There's kind of you. But I don't want to make trouble for you with Ted.'

Freda's expression darkened. 'Put that bugger's lights out, I will, if he hurts my poor daughter again.'

Chapter Sixteen

Late November

Missed the last tram again! Stella bowed her head behind her umbrella as she hurried along Oxford Street, trying to protect herself against the driving rain.

Thank heavens it was Saturday! She could spend tomorrow quietly with Danny and Rosie. The little girl had such a loving nature, and Stella was growing more fond of her each day. When Rosie climbed on Stella's knee of an evening, and put her arms around her neck, Stella hugged her in return, finding her heart softening in tenderness. She had two children now, and she loved both dearly. She was ready to give her life to protect them.

Head down against the downpour, Stella breathed a sigh of relief, she turned the corner into Victor Street, thankful to be almost home.

As she passed the butcher's, she was taken off-guard when a tall figure lunged at her from the doorway and grabbed her arm, almost jerking her off her feet. The stench of liquor filled her nostrils, and Stella squealed.

'Quiet, damn it! It's me, Griff.'

Stella gasped. He was the last man she wanted to meet on this dark night. What did he mean to do to her?

'Griff! Let me go!'

The light from a street-lamp fell on his gaunt face. She hadn't given him a thought for weeks. 'I thought you were still in prison,' she said.

He tightened his grip on her arm. 'Hoped I was, more like it.' He flung out a coarse oath. 'You'd rather they'd locked me up for good and thrown away the key. Right? But no such luck for you, my girl. I'm back and I've a score to settle.'

'Not with me!'

Rain was buckling the brim of her hat and trickling down her neck. Her coat was damp around her shoulders and she shivered, but from fear of her brother rather than the cold.

'I've done nothing to you, Griff,' she said shakily. 'I'm family, your sister, remember?' Suddenly she was angry that he was threatening her. 'Why are you skulking about by here like a thief?'

He didn't answer but jerked her forward into the doorway. 'Sister or not, you grassed me up to the bobbies,' he rasped. 'You deserve a good hiding for it, or worse. I warned you I'd come looking for you, didn't I?'

'You were breaking up my home,' Stella said, her voice rising. 'What did you expect?'

'I expected you to stand by me,' he spat. 'Instead you threw me to the wolves.'

'I never wished jail on you, Griff,' she muttered. 'I'm only sorry you had to go through that.'

'Sorry, my arse!' he snarled. 'You were glad to see the back of me. We could've had a nice little racket going, with good money coming in.'

'No, we couldn't!' she cried defiantly. 'What you wanted me to do was disgusting.'

'You were giving it free to Ted Thomas.'

'Ted's lies!' Stella was close to tears. 'Why believe him instead of me?'

'Loyalty and a home, that's all I ever wanted from you,' he went on bitterly, as though she hadn't spoken. 'A bit of help from my own family, especially after your bloody husband stole my wife. Well, now it's my turn, Stella. I want what's owed me.'

'I owe you nothing, Griff,' she said. 'Now let me pass. The children are waiting for me.'

'So! You've still got Eddie's bastard, have you?'

'Don't call her that!' Stella said sharply, her growing love for Rosie making her angry at the slur. 'And it's none of your business, anyway.'

'Anything to do with Eddie Evans *is* my business after the way he ruined my life. I want that kid out of our house, do you hear me?'

'*My* house, Griff,' Stella reminded him. 'Rosie is part of my family now and she stays until Eddie comes back.'

'He's never coming back!'

So many months had gone by, and there'd been no word from Eddie. Perhaps Griff was right. Yet the night he'd called at their home, he'd shown so much love for Rosie. Could he really desert her . . . or had something happened to him?

'Eddie trusts me to take care of her,' Stella said, 'and I intend to, until he comes for her.'

'Take it from me,' Griff grated, 'you'll never see that husband of yours again. I can't bear the sight of the brat, so send her to the children's home.'

Stella blood boiled.

'It's you that doesn't belong any more, Griff,' she cried. 'I *did* try to help you, but you'd rather wallow in your own misery. You're no longer fit to be among decent people.'

'You treacherous slut!' Griff growled. 'I ought to finish you off now, like—'

Griff was mad, beyond all help, she thought. She'd have to box clever to get out of this.

'Let go of me, Griff,' she murmured. 'I'll do anything you want. Come round to the house tomorrow and we'll talk about it. Just let me go home now.'

'Liar! Do you think I'm *twp* or what?' Griff said. 'Don't try to be clever with me, Stella.'

'For God's sake, what do you want Griff?' she forced out.

'Money. I've got to have money,' he said desperately. 'I owe Charlie, and he's not a man who'll wait.'

There was fear in his eyes, but Stella could not feel pity for him.

'I don't have any money,' she said.

'Come off it! I know you've got a job at the Grand, *and* what it pays. Ted Thomas told me. You owe me, Stella. You promised Dad I'd never go without.'

'I owe you nothing! You can't bully me.'

'I can do anything I like. I could do you in now if I wanted to, and they couldn't get me for it because I've got friends.'

'Friends!' Stella was scornful. 'Thieves and murderers like Charlie. You're in debt to him and running scared.'

'Perhaps I am,' he said, 'but he won't grass me up.'

'No, slit your throat, more like.'

'Shut up!' he said aggressively, 'and hand over the money you've got in your bag. All of it, mind.'

Her week's wages were in it – she'd not had time to go to the corner shop. 'No, Griff! I need it for rent and food for the children.'

He snatched the bag roughly from her, then struggled to open it with his one hand. It fell to the ground. 'Pick it up,' he ordered her. 'Get the money out. Now!'

'You can't rob the children, Griff. They're innocent.'

'There won't be any children if you don't give me that money.'

Stella's breath caught in her throat and she stared at him wide-eyed.

'What do you mean?'

'The houses round here are old,' he said. 'No one would stand a chance if a fire broke out.'

Stella's hand flew to her mouth in horror at what he was implying.

'It could easily happen,' Griff growled. 'You and the kids in bed at night. The house would go up like a box of matches, and no one would get out alive. Do you understand me, Stella?'

'Oh, God, Griff! You wouldn't do that.'

'*I* don't have to do anything. My murdering friends would do it, though, if I asked them. Now, do I get that money or what?'

Stella knelt, scooped up her handbag, and fumbled with the clasp.

At that moment measured steps sounded, progressing along Victor Street, and Griff tensed.

The bobby on his beat! Now was her chance to escape, and Stella opened her mouth to scream, but before she could take a breath Griff clamped his hand firmly over her mouth. 'A copper!' he whispered hoarsely. 'Keep quiet.'

Stella struggled violently, feeling as if she were suffocating. Ignoring his curses and threats, she pushed his hand away long enough to draw in a deep breath and scream, 'Help! Help!'

Her voice echoed in the street, and the footsteps began to run towards them.

'You bitch!' Griff stepped away from her. 'I'll get you for this. I'll make you sorry you were born, you and Eddie's bloody kids.'

He was poised, ready to flee. 'Keep looking over your shoulder, you double-crossing trollop,' he snarled, 'because I'll be there, and *next* time you won't know what's hit you.'

He took to his heels, and she heard his footsteps fading into the distance. Next moment the policeman ran up as Stella staggered out on to the pavement. 'You all right, missus?'

'A bit shaken,' Stella replied. That was putting it mildly.

'Who was he?' the policeman panted. 'Someone you know?'

Stella hesitated. She could give Griff up now, bring a charge against him, put him in prison for a longer stretch. Her family would be safer with him inside. But he'd see it as further betrayal, and be even more determined to harm her. The policeman's intervention had saved her this time, but he couldn't be with her and the children constantly.

Surely Griff hadn't meant what he'd said about setting the house afire.

'No,' she said, making up her mind. 'He was a stranger. It was money he was after. Thank you, officer, for saving me.'

She was about to walk away, anxious not to answer any more awkward questions. 'Hey! Hold on a minute!' he exclaimed, putting out a hand to detain her. 'You can't just walk off, you know. A serious crime has been committed here. I'll have to report it.'

With an officious sniff, he took out a notebook and pencil. 'Now, then, missus,' he said, 'what's your name and where do you live?'

Chapter Seventeen

December

Another Saturday matinée was over. Just one more performance to go before the weekend, then they could all rest.

Stella didn't know how Gertie had kept going after slipping on that patch of ice on the pavement outside the stage door this morning. Her ankle had swollen up like a balloon, and would've put most people out of action straight away, but Gertie was a trouper and wouldn't give in.

Stella watched as, leaning heavily on a walking-stick, Gertie hobbled painfully into her domain, and flopped on to the chair in front of her sewing-machine. Her face was white and drawn, and Stella could tell she was in considerable pain. 'You should keep off that ankle, Gertie,' she advised.

'It *is* giving me gyp, ducks,' Gertie admitted, 'but the show must go on.'

'Listen, I can manage,' Stella assured her quickly. 'I know the ropes now. Why don't you get off to your digs and rest? I'll get Sid to call a cab.'

Gertie looked doubtful, but Stella saw that she could be persuaded. 'What can go wrong?' she asked, with more assurance than she felt. 'Phyllis will muck in, and I've got the cue sheets. The performance will go like a dream, believe me.'

That was Gertie's own favourite expression, and she grinned.

'All right, me ducks,' she agreed. 'Thank God it's you and not that Mildred. She was a dozy lump. I wouldn't have trusted her with a school concert.'

Stella was relieved that Gertie was being sensible, yet afraid, too. It *was* a big responsibility, but she was sure she could do it. After all, it was just the one performance.

She helped Gertie down the stairs and sat her in Sid's cubbyhole until the cab arrived. At the last minute Gertie seemed reluctant to leave. 'Don't forget next week's props have to be brought up from the basement,' she reminded Stella. 'I've left the list by the sewing-machine.'

'I'll see to it all.' Stella helped her into the cab.

'I'd start now,' Gertie said. 'Don't leave it all until tonight, ducks, or you'll never get home to those kids of yours.'

'Good idea.'

'And careful when you bring that big mirror up,' Gertie said, clutching her hand. 'It's vital for next week, and a real antique. We wouldn't be able to replace that at short notice. Get one of the stage hands to help you.'

'Leave it to me,' Stella said. 'You rest that ankle.' She watched the cab speed away and suddenly felt deserted.

By the time she'd collected the list from the seamstress's room and completed some of Gertie's unfinished chores, she found all the stage hands had left the theatre. The actors had gone, too, and so had Roland Telford. Only she and Sid were left.

When she suggested he might help her bring up the props from the basement, especially the large mirror, he pulled his cloth cap further down around his ears and looked at her askance. 'What! Do my back in? No fear, missus. Not my job it isn't. And you wants to be careful.'

'It's got to be done, Sid.'

'Leave it till after the performance tonight, when them stage hands can help,' he suggested, wrapping a muffler round his neck and buttoning his jacket.

But Stella didn't fancy that. She hated being in the theatre late at night. Look what had happened with Monty the last time she'd stayed behind. 'I'd rather see to it now,' she told him.

Sid shrugged. 'You'll be all alone,' he said solemnly. 'Keep a eye out for the ghost.'

'What ghost?' Stella was scornful.

'Well, some say it's the ghost of Madame Patti. I dunno, though.' Sid glanced around as though it might be listening. 'The chap who was doorman afore me, he seen it,' he went on confidentially. 'Turned his hair white overnight, it did.'

'You're not being very helpful, Sid.'

'Just trying to warn you, aren't I?' He grinned toothlessly. 'See you later, then, gal, I hope.'

The stage door slammed shut after him. Stella listened to the creaks and groans of the building. The theatre was old and had a long history. There probably was a ghost, she reflected, perhaps more than one, but she wasn't disturbed by the idea. She was more afraid of the mice, spiders and cockroaches, especially down in that dingy basement.

She pulled herself together, and rolled up her sleeves. There was so much to do, and she was determined not to let Gertie down. Working to the list she spent the next half-hour making several journeys between the basement and the seamstress's room. She left the mirror until last.

It leaned against the back wall of the basement, almost as tall as she was. She tried to manhandle it forward, but it was too heavy in its ornate gilt frame. Standing in front of it, hands on her hips, Stella doubted she could move it a yard, let alone get it up the basement steps.

She was still considering it when she heard a stealthy sound, as though something was edging closer to her.

Rats!

Stella spun round, peering along the length and vastness of the basement area. The electric light-bulbs gave only a weak light, and many corners were in deep shadow.

It was nothing, she told herself sternly. And as she could do nothing about the mirror, it was time to go.

She was about to re-cover the mirror with its dust-sheet when she glimpsed a furtive movement in the reflected shadows behind her.

Stella froze. That was no rat. Someone was there, in the shadows, watching her. But, except for herself, the building was empty.

She mustn't panic! Her fingers trembling, Stella rearranged the dust-sheet, trying to appear undisturbed. The basement steps were at the further end away from her. She tried to calculate the distance in her mind's eye.

She turned casually, rolling down her sleeves, brushing cobwebs from her skirt, trying to move unhurriedly towards the steps. After she'd gone a few paces, she broke into a run, but skidded to a halt as a tall, bulky figure stepped out from behind some stacked props skips, barring her way.

Stella let out a squeak of fright. 'Mr Fitzgerald!'

He looked dishevelled in his shirt-sleeves, standing before her, legs apart, swaying. His face was ruddy and his skin was bathed in sweat.

'What are you doing here, Mr Fitzgerald?' she bleated. 'I thought you'd gone with the others.'

'Did you, Stella? Did you think I'd wait for ever?'

'I don't understand.'

'I think you do.'

He'd obviously been drinking. She hardly recognised him as the confident man who'd agreed to employ her all those weeks ago. As she looked at his staring eyes, Stella judged him to be in a dangerous and unpredictable mood. Instinct told her to be careful. She searched for a way to talk him out of whatever was on his mind. She thought she knew exactly what he wanted of her, and shivered with revulsion.

'Mr Fitzgerald, you're not well,' she began. 'You have another performance tonight. You should lie down.'

'Lie down with me, Stella.' His voice rang out as though he were on stage giving a performance, and he held out a hand. 'Come with me to my little sanctum behind the stage.

Give yourself up to me, body and soul, as I know you want to.'

Stella drew back. 'Mr Fitzgerald, please! You don't know what you're saying.'

'And you don't know how much I want you.' He took another step towards her. 'I must have you, Stella.'

Caught alone in the basement with a drunken, lust-crazed man, Stella was more frightened than she'd ever been of Ted Thomas. If only she could distract him.

'Oh, Stella!' he cried theatrically. 'I think only of you. I can't sleep, I can't work. You don't know what you're doing to me, you beautiful witch.'

Suddenly his mood darkened. 'But perhaps you do,' he rasped. 'Perhaps you enjoy playing games with men. Jezebel!'

She might have laughed at the absurdity of him and the situation, but his expression told her he was in deadly earnest.

'You're ill,' she said, as persuasively as her chattering teeth would allow. 'You should go to your digs and perhaps see a doctor.' She took a sideways step, hoping to slip past. 'I'll go and call a cab, Mr Fitzgerald.'

'No! You can't leave me now. I won't let you.' He moved closer, and Stella's heart leaped into her throat. 'You want me, too, Stella.' His voice took on the ringing tone again, and Stella wondered if the drink had sent him out of his mind. 'I know you do, my raven-haired darling. Don't fight it, Stella. We were meant to be together.'

He sounded as though he was repeating lines from a play. He'd lost touch with reality, and she was only too aware of the danger she was in.

'This is silly, Mr Fitzgerald,' she rapped out. 'You're being foolish.'

'I can't help it! You drive me to it,' he exclaimed.

'You swore you'd never behave like this again,' Stella said. 'You promised as a gentleman, Mr Fitzgerald.'

'Damn it, Stella! Don't call me that! Don't keep pushing me away. Call me Monty.'

'Look . . . Monty,' she decided it was better to humour him than make him angry, 'I don't know what kind of woman you think I am—'

'I've waited,' he interrupted. 'Now I can wait no longer. I *must* have you.'

'You insult me by behaving in this way,' Stella burst out. 'I don't want *you*, don't you understand? Stand aside, please.'

Anger flashed across his face. 'No woman has ever refused Monty Fitzgerald.'

She could see he was losing what little self-control he had left. He was a big man, powerful, and she was no match for him. He might be capable of anything in his present state.

'Mr Fitzgerald!' she shouted, hoping to bring him to his senses. 'You're not on stage now. There's no audience watching. You're making a fool of yourself. Now, let me pass.'

'I've waited patiently all these months. I can't wait any longer. If you won't give me what I want willingly, then, by thunder, I'll take it!'

He lunged for her, pinned her arms to her sides and pulled her to him. His large sweating face was close to hers and she could smell the liquor on his breath.

She screamed wildly, only too aware that there was no one to hear her.

'Kiss me!' he demanded, panting.

His wet mouth clamped down on hers, and Stella struggled, revolted. She squirmed against him, feeling as if she was in some nightmare, yet knowing that worse would follow if she couldn't escape him.

Twisting her head she freed her mouth and let out a piercing scream. 'Let me go! Let me go!'

'It doesn't have to be this way, Stella,' he panted, his arms enfolding her in a bear-hug. 'Come upstairs with me. I swear I'll be good to you. I'll make you happy.'

As he spoke he forced her back against the mirror. Stella knew that in a moment she'd fall on to the filthy basement floor, and would be helpless to prevent him violating her.

She stopped struggling and went limp in his arms.

'All right, Monty,' she said. 'But not here. Take me to the room behind the stage, where you take Elsie.'

He gave a choking sigh. 'I knew you'd see reason. You want me, too,' he said ecstatically. 'Oh, Stella! You won't regret it, I promise you.'

The pressure of his body on hers eased a little, and she was able to step away from the mirror, but he didn't release her altogether. He held her close to him, so that they were hip to hip, and began to walk her towards the steps. He kept talking to her in a soothing, wheedling tone, but she hardly heard what he said.

Once up the steps, she'd make a run for it, or find a way to delay the inevitable. Someone was sure to come in soon to get ready for the evening performance.

When they were at the foot of the steps, he said, 'I've locked and bolted the stage door, Stella, so don't think you can trick me.'

So she couldn't get out. Then she remembered the scene dock, and prayed he'd forgotten to lock that.

She hung back deliberately, showing reluctance to climb the steps and, as she'd hoped, he pushed her in front of him.

'There's no need to be afraid of me, Stella,' he said, as they climbed the stairs. 'All I want is to love you. I've dreamed about it for so long.'

'I'm flattered,' Stella lied.

'Of course you are, my lovely,' he said, in vibrant tones. 'No woman refuses Monty Fitzgerald.'

They neared the top of the steps, and he stretched out a hand to turn the doorknob.

Seizing her chance, Stella kicked him viciously. He let out a yell of pain, and let go of her wrist.

Stella was through the door in a flash and running. Instinctively she made for the stairs leading to the first floor, intent on getting into Gertie's room and locking herself in. Half-way there she remembered that the door had no lock.

Sobbing with terror and panic, she ran downstairs just as

Monty staggered though the basement door, clutching his groin. 'You cunning bitch!' he roared. 'You won't get away from me again. I mean to have you, Stella, one way or another.'

'Keep away, Monty. You sicken me.'

'You little teaser! I've never used force on a woman in my life but you're driving me to it. Maybe that's the way you like it, eh?'

'You won't get away with it,' Stella quavered. 'Touch me and you'll go to prison.'

'Do you think anyone would take your word over mine? I'm Monty Fitzgerald, celebrated gentleman of the theatre.'

'You whisky-soaked has-been!' Stella was stung to recklessness at his words. 'You're not so great. Your own company laughs at you behind your back. Even your wife despises you.'

Growling wrathfully, he faced her in a crouch as though he was about to spring at her.

'Stay back, I tell you!'

Stella watched him warily but, has-been or not, Monty wasn't an actor for nothing. There was no warning in his eyes before he lunged at her and she was taken off-guard.

With one hand he caught her wrist and the other wrenched at the neckline of her dress. It tore loose, exposing her body, which was now covered only by her slip. 'Let's see what you've got, my back-street beauty,' he said, gleefully.

Instinct took over, and Stella fought back. With a cry, she raked his cheek savagely with her fingernails.

He recoiled, and she pulled herself free. Then she ran, not caring in which direction, just trying to put distance between them.

Panting, near exhaustion, she was on the stage, and looked around frantically. She spotted an iron ladder bolted to the opposite wall. The electricians used it to reach the overhead lights. Above her head, stretching from one side of the stage to the other, was the catwalk. It looked a narrow flimsy structure, but Stella was glad of that. Monty wouldn't dare follow her there.

She scrambled on to the ladder, and started to climb. She glanced down once to see if he was following and felt dizzy. Please don't let me fall!

His heavy footsteps sounded nearby and he called her name. Terror spurred her on and she continued to climb. She was less than half-way up when Monty appeared on-stage.

Watching her, he gave a roar of drunken laughter. 'There's no place to hide, you silly girl. Come down.' His voice was coaxing. 'Stella, stop acting like a coy schoolgirl.'

Don't look down! a voice in her head ordered. She would keep her eyes on the narrow fly platform at the nearest end of the catwalk.

'Stella!' He sounded angry again as he stood at the foot of the ladder looking up. 'Stop being a bloody little fool. You'll fall and break your pretty neck.'

With relief, Stella climbed on to the fly gallery. She mustn't look down, just sit where she was until help came. She managed to get into a squatting position on the narrow fly-floor, and felt a little safer.

Monty had stopped shouting. Had he gone away? Clinging to the rail for support, Stella ventured a glance down. He was on the ladder, climbing towards her.

This was lunacy! Apart from anything else, there was room for only one person on the fly-floor. He was putting both their lives at risk.

'What are you doing?' she called down. 'Are you mad, Monty? Go down, for pity's sake.'

He leaned away from the ladder at an alarming angle, and the hairs stood up on the back of Stella's neck.

'I'm coming for you, my lovely Stella. You won't get away from me. You'll be mine tonight. I've ached for you long enough.'

'No!' Stella screamed. 'Go back. It's not safe. You'll kill us both.'

But he kept climbing.

Stella looked along the length of the catwalk. There was no

fly-floor at the other end, and even if there had been, there was no way to climb down on that side of the stage.

'Monty!' she called desperately. 'I'm coming down to you. Please go back down to the stage and wait for me there. I promise I won't run away again.'

'I don't trust you, my lovely.'

An any moment his head would appear above the platform. There was no way Stella could stop him joining her without endangering his life — both their lives.

With her heart in her mouth, Stella stepped out on to the catwalk, a series of wooden slats lashed together with plaited rope. More rope acted as a flimsy safety-rail at hip height. It was adequate for an electrician tending the overhead spotlights, but would it bear the weight of two people?

Before Monty could step on to the platform, Stella had ventured half-way across the catwalk, well out of his reach. She endeavoured to keep as still as she could, since the slats swayed like a hammock with her every movement.

Now Monty was standing on the platform, holding out his arms to her.

'Come on, Stella. I know you're frightened. I've come to rescue you.'

'Go down, Monty. Leave me be!'

She took a hasty step back and the catwalk tilted alarmingly. She clutched frantically at the safety-rail.

Monty laughed. 'You're afraid of heights, but I'm not,' he said, and held out a hand. 'Come on. Don't be a silly girl. I'll help you down.'

'Leave me alone, Monty,' Stella begged.

'Now, you know I won't do that. I've waited too long to have you, and have you I will.'

'How can you talk like that when we're both in such danger?'

'Danger? The bridge is as safe as houses.'

With these words he stepped out on to the catwalk and took a few steps towards her, making it shudder and swing.

Stella screamed hysterically. 'Oh, God! You'll kill us!'

'Come down,' Monty said, moving towards her again, 'or I'll shake you down.' He leaned rhythmically from side to side, giving momentum to the catwalk's sway.

'Stop it!' Stella screamed. 'You're mad!'

'Will you come down?'

'Yes!'

'Now you're being sensible.' Monty took another step forward. 'Give me your hand, Stella. I'll help you.'

But Stella couldn't move. Her muscles were locked.

'You lying minx!' Monty snarled. 'You're playing games with me again. I'll teach you a lesson.'

With that he swayed wildly from side to side, so that the catwalk twisted and bucked high above the stage. Then suddenly, without warning, his foot slipped on a slat and he lost his balance. His arms flailed as he tried to regain it, but the catwalk's erratic movements thwarted him. His hands clutched wildly at . . . nothing.

There was the briefest moment when the earth stood still and they stared at each other in silence. The horror that filled Stella was etched on Monty's face.

Then, with a terrible cry, he toppled over the rope rail, to fall headlong to the stage below. There was a resounding thud that echoed through the theatre, then silence.

Stella began to scream, and went on screaming, unable to stop, unable to believe what had just happened. She knelt where she was, eyes squeezed shut, trying to obliterate her last sight of Monty's face as he realised he was falling to his death.

Her eyes snapped open. Suppose he wasn't dead. He might be badly injured and needing her help. Stella drew breath that turned into a sob of terror. She must climb down to him.

She got up gingerly and, taking one faltering step after another, she negotiated the catwalk and stepped on to the solid fly platform. Now she must climb down the ladder.

It proved an easier descent then she had imagined. When she

reached the stage, she stood still, afraid to turn round, afraid of what she would see.

Monty hadn't made a sound since he'd fallen, but he might be unconscious, she told herself. If he was injured every moment counted.

Slowly, she turned and looked at him. He lay in a twisted mound, limbs at all angles. She moved towards him. The first thing she look in, which filled her with renewed horror, was a red stain spreading over the boards.

She went a few steps nearer and knelt down. Without touching him she knew the truth. His head was at an unnatural angle to his twisted body. He couldn't possibly be alive.

She had seen death before, first her mother and then her father, but never like this; never in such a dreadful form. Suddenly, she was filled with pity and remorse. Had she brought him to this? Would others blame her? Accuse her?

All at once Stella was terrified. The authorities might not believe her explanation. They might accuse her of pushing him to his death. Already her reputation was unsavoury, thanks to Ted Thomas. And she had a jailbird for a brother. She might go to prison! She might be hanged!

What would happen to Danny and Rosie if she were taken away?

Stella got up and stepped away from Monty's crumpled body. She must leave the theatre now, pretend to be ignorant of the tragedy. Go now, an inner voice warned her, before someone comes to prepare for the evening performance, before you're trapped.

Mesmerised, she stared down at his still form. But there'd be no performance now. For once, the show wouldn't go on.

Pulling herself together, she forced herself to think clearly. She must behave as normal, leave now and return at her usual time. No one must suspect she was involved.

She turned to flee, then heard a sound that turned her blood to ice-water.

Somewhere in the theatre a door banged.

Stella was uncertain from which direction the sound had come. She called out wildly, 'Who's there?'

But there was no reply, nothing except a deadening silence. Stella stared through the proscenium arch, feeling as though a thousand eyes were on her, yet instinct told her she was alone.

But someone had been in the theatre earlier, had witnessed all that had occurred. Why hadn't they come to her aid when Monty had assaulted her? Why hadn't they shown themselves when he'd fallen?

Suddenly, Stella was mortally afraid. Someone knew she was involved in Monty's death. That person now had power over her. Who was it? And how did they mean to use their terrible knowledge?

Hurrying cautiously from the theatre on legs that would barely take her weight, Stella was too frightened to conjecture. All she knew was that some unknown enemy was determined to bring her to harm.

Chapter Eighteen

It seemed no time at all before Stella was making her way back to the theatre. She had to time her arrival just right. Too early, and the dreadful experience of 'finding' Monty's body would overwhelm her. Never late as a rule, to be late today would appear suspicious. She must steel herself to act as though the death was shocking news. Fearful, she stumbled as she walked, knowing she was no actress, and must give herself away.

As she went along Singleton Street, passed the theatre's box-office entrance, she saw two policemen ahead, standing on the corner near the bus station.

Bracing herself, she walked past them on the other side of the street, and round the corner. Feeling their eyes linger on her, she approached the stage door. One called out to her, making her jump. 'Just a minute, there, miss!'

Stella held her breath, as the policeman strode unhurriedly towards her.

'You're going into the theatre, are you?'

Stella could only nod, her mouth too dry to speak.

'What's your business there?'

Stella cleared her throat, praying her face and voice wouldn't reveal her guilty knowledge. 'I work for the repertory company. Is – is anything wrong?'

'I'm afraid there's been an accident,' the policeman said.

'An accident?'

'A fatal one.'

'Oh, I see.'

The policeman cocked his head to one side, looking at her keenly. 'Don't you want to know the details?' he asked sharply. 'Most people do.'

'Yes, of course,' Stella answered promptly. 'I – I was shocked.' She tried to pull herself together. 'What's happened, officer?'

'Not permitted to say, am I?'

'Perhaps I shouldn't go in, then?' Stella asked hopefully, half turning to move away. 'I can go home again, if—'

'No,' he said quickly. 'Inspector Edwards wants to question all employees. Give your name to the constable at the stage-door office.'

Stella identified herself as instructed, and was told that Inspector Edwards would see all employees eventually in Mr Fitzgerald's dressing room. In the meantime, she was not to leave the theatre without permission.

She made her way to the seamstress's room where she found Gertie in a flood of tears, tended by Phyllis.

'What are you doing here, Gertie?' Stella asked, surprised to see her. 'I thought you were at your digs.'

'I couldn't rest,' Gertie sobbed. 'I've been in this job all these years and never once missed a performance.' She let out a wail before covering her mouth with a rumpled handkerchief.

'She found him, you know, her and Sid,' Phyllis volunteered. 'Out there on stage, dead as mutton.'

Gertie wailed again.

Stella decided to take charge. 'Go and make her a cup of tea, Phyllis, please.'

Phyllis looked rebellious, not liking the idea of being told what to do by the lowly assistant dresser.

'Please?'

Phyllis went reluctantly.

'It was a terrible shock.' Gertie sobbed. 'I've known Monty for thirty years. At one time we were very close, if you get my

192

meaning.' Her tone was regretful. 'That was before he set up this company and met Lottie.'

Even Gertie! Was there no limit to Monty's philandering? Stella reminded herself quickly that she shouldn't think ill of the dead.

She was still comforting Gertie when a constable came to tell her Inspector Edwards wanted to speak with her.

Stella was all of a tremble as she entered the dressing-room to see a big man sitting in the chair before the mirror. It made her shiver to see someone sitting in Monty's place, so she concentrated instead on the black bowler hat resting on the dressing-table.

Inspector Edwards glanced up briefly as she entered. His face was lined and worn, but intelligence showed in his shrewd eyes.

A difficult man to fool, Stella guessed. She knew she'd have to lie through her teeth while looking him straight in the face.

He indicated a chair. 'Sit down.'

His tone was terse and businesslike, and she found relief in that. He glanced at a sheet of paper in his hand, and Stella wondered what was written on it.

'You are Mrs Stella Evans?'

Stella nodded.

'Mrs Evans, I understand from the doorman, Sid, that you remained alone in the theatre after the matinée?'

Stella nodded again. It was no good denying it. 'Yes, for about half an hour.'

'Why?'

She felt on safe ground for the moment. 'Gertie, that's the wardrobe mistress, twisted her ankle and went to her digs to rest it. I offered to get the props out of the basement for next week's production.'

'And did you?'

'Most of them,' she said. 'I couldn't move the heavy mirror on my own, so I . . .' She swallowed convulsively. '. . . I left it and went home.'

'Did you see Mr Fitzgerald?'

Something was sticking in her throat, making it difficult to speak. It was guilt. She struggled to answer calmly, without a tremor. 'No,' she lied. 'The theatre was empty.'

'You're certain of that?'

Suddenly she thought of the person who'd witnessed the drama. Had they spoken up? Was this policeman setting a trap for her? She had no time to think it through, and could do nothing but carry on with her story. 'Yes.'

Inspector Edwards sniffed thoughtfully.

'Mrs Evans, had Mr Fitzgerald shown any sign or reason why he should commit suicide?'

Stella was shocked. 'He didn't kill himself!' she burst out, without thinking. 'It was an accident!'

The Inspector stared at her. 'You sound very positive, Mrs Evans,' he said at last, 'as though you witnessed it.'

Stella shook her head vehemently, cursing herself for being so naïve. 'I . . . what I meant was that Mr Fitzgerald didn't seem the type. I'm sure his wife will say the same.'

The Inspector ignored her words. 'You're certain, are you, Mrs Evans, that the theatre was empty while you were here?' he asked slowly. 'Think carefully, now. The presence of another person could throw a different light on the tragedy, especially if that person fails to speak up. Highly suspicious, that.'

Stella averted her eyes from his piercing glance.

'You heard and saw nothing?' he persisted.

Stella took a deep breath to steady her nerves. 'Nothing, Inspector,' she murmured.

When the policeman spoke again it was in an almost confidential tone. 'As a matter of fact, Miss Tempest agrees with you,' he said softly.

Stella was startled. 'What?'

'Yes, she's adamant her husband wouldn't have committed suicide, and I'm not at all convinced of it myself.' His voice was stern. 'Nor am I happy with the accident theory, Mrs Evans.'

Stella tried not to flinch under his gaze.

'He fell from the catwalk,' he went on gravely, bringing the terrible picture of Monty's stricken face into her mind once again. 'What was he doing up there, Mrs Evans? Can you answer me that?'

Stella mumbled a denial, fumbling in her handbag for a handkerchief, praying the interview would soon be over. If the police refused to accept suicide or an accident, that left only foul play, and she was in grave danger.

'Very well, Mrs Evans. That'll be all,' he said suddenly.

Stella stood up. 'Can I go home?'

'Yes,' he replied briefly, and scribbled in a notebook. 'The sergeant has your address, Mrs Evans,' he went on, startling her. 'We may be in touch again. There's a lot unexplained here, and I don't like it.'

Feeling as though she were suffocating, Stella stumbled out of the room and went to find Gertie before she left. She was worried about what was to happen next. Surely, without Monty, the company would be finished, and she'd be out of a job. It was callous to think of herself, with Monty lying dead in some cold mortuary, but she had the children to think of. If the actors disbanded, Arnie would leave, too. Without his rent, and without a job, money would be dangerously short.

Gertie's eyes and nose were still red from weeping, but she'd recovered sufficiently to think of the company's interests. 'Tonight's performance has been cancelled, of course,' she told Stella sadly, as she hobbled about her domain. 'As for next week, it all depends on whether Bill Reynolds can find a replacement for Monty over the weekend. He's ringing all his professional contacts up in the Smoke.'

Stella was scandalised at the cold-bloodedness of it. 'A replacement? So soon?'

'The show must go on, ducks,' Gertie said seriously. 'Our livelihoods are at stake. Monty would do the same.'

'But how can a newcomer learn his lines in time?'

'Probably won't need to,' Gertie said. 'Veterans of the boards have a repertoire, ducks. They've performed these plays so often over the years they know them by heart.' She sniffed. 'Lines are not the problem. It's clash of personalities that can ruin a production, you know, old feuds and jealousies. The cast has to work together in reasonable harmony, otherwise we'll sink.' She lowered her voice. 'Of course,' she went on, 'Ollie thinks he should step into Monty's shoes and take the leading roles, but frankly he's not up to it. I can see trouble brewing.'

Phyllis appeared in the doorway briefly. 'Stella, Lottie wants to see you in her dressing room, pronto.'

Stella's insides twisted. She'd had little to do with Charlotte Tempest recently. To be summoned now seemed to spell trouble.

She was sitting in front of the mirror, dabbing her face with a powder puff when Stella opened the door. Her expression as she turned to Stella was as cold and lifeless as that of a wax mask. There was no outward sign that she'd wept for her dead husband or that she was distressed. 'Have the police spoken to you?' Charlotte asked, in a haughty tone.

'Yes. They've given me permission to go home.'

'Have they, indeed?' She raised arched painted brows. 'Do they know you were Monty's latest flibbertigibbet, eh?'

'That's not true!' Stella declared. 'How dare you say that?'

She was angry, yet she trembled inside. Had Charlotte been skulking about the theatre earlier, and was she now preparing to denounce her?

'Because he more or less admitted it to me,' Charlotte snapped. 'I wouldn't be surprised if you and he were cavorting in his love-nest behind the stage after the matinée. Did a naughty game go wrong? Is that it?'

'This is monstrous!' Stella burst out. Charlotte's outrageous assertion was too near the truth to be comfortable. If she repeated it to the police there would be further questions, and Stella knew she didn't have the wit to parry them.

'Well,' Charlotte said, 'it makes no difference now. With Monty dead the company is mine, and I can do what I want. Hire and fire whoever I like.' She glanced at Stella, her eyes glittering with spite. 'I wanted Monty to get rid of you,' she went on. 'He wouldn't, and we know why, don't we? Monty changed his women as often as he changed his shirt. You wouldn't have lasted, of course. You back-street girls age quickly. He'd have tossed you aside like an old worn-out glove'

Stella remained silent. It was futile to argue with this woman. 'I won't stand here listening to your ravings,' she said at last. 'I'm going home.'

She turned to the door, but Charlotte rapped, 'Wait! I haven't finished with you.'

'Haven't you said enough?' Stella demanded.

'Oh, don't worry, Evans,' Charlotte sneered. 'This is the last time we'll speak together because you're sacked. Bill Reynolds has whatever money is owed you – and at the proper rate! Pick it up and get out! I don't want to see your face around here again.'

It was no more than she'd expected. Without another word Stella turned and left, slamming the dressing-room door behind her. She went in search of Bill, the stage manager, and found him using the telephone in Roland Telford's office.

When she tapped at the open door both men looked up. Bill waved her in, even though he was on the telephone, his weathered face wreathed in smiles.

'Can yer get 'im on the Paddington train tonight? Yer can? Cor blimey, Smithy, me old china! Yer've saved me bacon. I owe you one. Cheers!' With that he hung up the receiver.

'We've done it!' he declared gleefully. 'Chesney Winslow hisself. Bit long in the tooth, but he'll do. Her ladyship should be pleased.' He grinned then winked. 'She and Chesney are old shipmates, so to speak.' He glanced at Stella and his smile faded. 'Oh, sorry, gal. Given you the elbow, has she?' He fished in his trouser pocket and brought out a crumpled brown envelope. 'There yer are, gal. Sorry and all. Best o' luck to yer.'

With that he jumped up and scuttled out.

Just like that! Sacked and paid off just weeks before Christmas! What could she do now? One thing was certain: it wouldn't be such a happy Christmas as she'd hoped for.

Now that Bill Reynolds had vacated the seat behind the

desk, Roland Telford moved to sit at it. Stella was embarrassed that he had witnessed her summary dismissal. She managed a faint smile. 'Well, that's that.'

'Perhaps you were working on the wrong side of the footlights,' Roland suggested, giving her a speculative look.

Although his glance wasn't offensive, not like the calculating looks Ted Thomas and Monty had given her, he appeared to be weighing her up.

'I think you're right,' she agreed, determined to make light of her situation in front of him. 'Oh, well! Best get home, I suppose, put on my walking shoes and start looking for another job.'

'Not much hope, eh?'

Stella shook her head, recalling the weeks of fruitless search before Arnie had spoken up for her at the theatre. It looked as though she was back where she started.

'Losing your job just before Christmas is no joke,' Roland went on. 'I've watched you, Stella. You're a good worker. What did Miss Tempest have against you?'

Stella bit her lip. 'Clash of personalities,' she answered evasively. She couldn't tell him the real reason. Roland Telford was shrewd enough, though, and might already think he knew, jumping to conclusions like so many other people did.

'I think you've been hard done by.' He leaned back in his chair. 'From what I've seen these past weeks, Charlotte Tempest is a virago.'

That was putting it mildly, Stella thought. 'It's water under the bridge now,' she said, 'but thanks, Mr Telford, for all the help you gave me backstage.'

'Hold on! Look, I'm thinking of taking on another usherette. The theatre's booked solid for the next few weeks with the Christmas rush and all.'

'Mr Telford, are you offering me a job?' Stella asked. Had her luck changed?

'It's not as glamorous as working backstage, of course.' He looked uncomfortable. 'I know what Fitzgerald was paying you, Stella – a man's wage, really, and I don't want to know why.'

Stella was stung. 'I can assure you, Mr Telford,' she said, a little crossly, 'there was never anything improper between me and Mr Fitzgerald.'

'Well,' he went on, rearranging papers on his desk, 'it's none of my business, anyway.' He looked up at her seriously. 'I can't offer you that kind of money, nowhere near it, but if you want the job at the usual pay it's yours.'

'I'll take it!' Stella cried. 'When can I start?'

'Monday. See the wages clerk, Mrs Benson. She supervises the usherettes, and she'll explain your duties.'

He stood up and held out a hand in a gentlemanly manner. 'Welcome aboard, Stella.'

Chapter Nineteen

With the arrival of Monty's replacement, the following week's production went ahead. Stella was glad she was no longer part of the uneasy company, and felt she might find real happiness – if only she could stop reliving the part she had played in Monty's death.

Her new job suited her down to the ground. The other usherettes were a friendly bunch, and Mrs Benson was good-natured, happy for the girls to leave as soon as the second interval was over. It meant Stella was always in time for the tram home.

It meant, too, that she could see to Arnie's meal herself, and not involve Freda more than was necessary. She saw nothing of Babs and missed her a great deal. But, as Freda told her, Ted was still cutting up rough and making her daughter's life a misery.

The only cloud on Stella's horizon was the coming inquest into Monty's death. Until that was over she couldn't rest easy. She still worried about the mysterious witness, but with the police having departed from the theatre, and nothing further said about the circumstances of his death, she began to believe it might have been just her imagination that awful night. Perhaps there never had been a witness at all.

The inquest was held a week after she had started her new job. The verdict was reported in the *Cambrian Leader*: accidental death. The news buzzed around the changing room where the usherettes slipped into their smart uniforms. She was relieved there had been no mention of foul play, and despite what he'd tried to do to her, Stella was glad his name had not been besmirched with the stigma of suicide. Monty could rest in peace with his reputation intact.

It was over at last. Perhaps now she could forget it ever happened.

When Arnie came home after the performance that Monday night Stella noticed a change in him. He threw his fur coat on to a chair, his hat after it, looking done in, not his usual exuberant self. 'Mrs E, we've come to the parting of the ways, I'm afraid,' he said, as he took his place at the table.

Stella was bringing in a plate of steaming food to put before him. 'Oh, no! I am sorry, Arnie,' she said. 'What's happened? Is it . . .' her lips trembled with dread '. . . something about Monty's death?'

Arnie looked down at the meal before him without his usual enthusiasm. 'No. It's Lottie,' he said. 'Now the company's hers she's antagonising everyone. She had a terrible bust-up with Eve and Ollie. Their last performance is next Saturday night, then they're off.'

'Clash of personalities.' Stella nodded knowledgeably. 'Gertie said it could happen.'

'And Elsie's had an offer from a repertory company in Liverpool. If Monty were here he'd have talked her out of it, held things together, but she finishes on Saturday, too.'

He pushed away the plate of food untouched. 'You know, Mrs E, Monty dying like that has upset everyone, and it was a dashed awful shock to me, too,' he said gravely. 'It's soured everything.'

'But it was an accident,' Stella pointed out. 'The coroner said so.'

'Yes, I know,' he replied despondently. 'But nothing will ever be the same again. Suddenly it all irks me – the backbiting, the in-fighting, the jealousies, not to mention predatory females.'

Stella looked at him askance, not sure what he meant. He

gave a thin smile. 'No, Mrs E. Lottie never got me into her bed, and she's starting to hate my guts for that.'

'What will you do?' she asked quietly.

He straightened up, as though pulling himself together. 'I'm giving up the theatre,' he said. 'I'm going home. I've sown enough wild oats. I'll join my father in the business, settle down.' He grinned sheepishly at her. 'Earn an honest living.'

'Are you disappointed?' Stella asked. 'Never again to see your name up there in lights?'

'There are more important things,' Arnie said quietly. 'Like love, for instance.'

Stella smiled. 'I couldn't agree more. It's finding it, that's the trouble.'

'But I have found it!' he told her eagerly. 'I'm in love with Barbara. I'm going to ask her to come away with me – the children, too.'

Stella was poleaxed. She'd no idea of his true feelings. 'Arnie, you can't do that!'

'Why not?' he demanded. 'I love her. I must get her away from that swine, Ted. I can provide a home, comfort, everything she could possibly want.'

'Does she love you?'

Arnie thought. 'I think she might,' he said eventually. 'I pray she does.'

'Arnie,' Stella said carefully, 'I don't want to interfere between you and Babs, but think what you're proposing. Yes, she'd be better off without Ted. He's a beast. But . . .' She didn't know how to put what she meant into words without disparaging Babs. 'Arnie, your family has wealth and power. You belong to a class that's a world above Babs and me. How would your family feel if you brought home a married woman with two children? And would she divorce Ted? Think of the scandal. Your family wouldn't accept her, and she'd be lonely and miserable.'

'Then I won't go home,' Arnie said fiercely. 'I'll stay in Swansea, get a job.'

'Doing what?' Stella couldn't keep scorn out of her voice. 'Serve behind the counter in some tailor's shop? Dig ditches as a labourer?'

She sat down near him, and laid a friendly hand on his forearm. 'Arnie, you have no trade, no skills. Life is hard down here among us poor folk. Money's scarce. You have a career waiting for you in your father's business. It's your duty to follow that, your destiny.'

'But I love Barbara, dash it! Why shouldn't we be happy?'

'If you love her you'll want what's best for her.'

His shoulders slumped. 'I've waited patiently, but a man can take only so much, Mrs E. I can't go on without her.' To her distress, he looked close to tears. 'I can think of no one but her, the two of us together for the rest of our lives.'

'Look,' Stella said, 'go home to your family. Wait a few weeks while you think it through. You'll have plenty to occupy you with learning the business. Don't rush into anything. If you do, you'll not only hurt yourself, you'll hurt Babs, too. Sleep on it.'

Arnie stood up and reached for his coat and hat. 'I know you mean well, Mrs E,' he said softly. 'You're a good woman. I'll go up now, but I doubt I shall sleep.'

Arnie didn't mention his feelings for Babs again, and Stella wondered if she'd been wise to interfere. Perhaps her friend was in love with Arnie, too, and was longing for him to speak out. Perhaps she'd spoiled the lives of two people of whom she was fond.

The Monty Fitzgerald Players gave their final performance on Saturday and, without speaking his heart, Arnie said his goodbyes on Wednesday the following week, two days before Christmas Eve.

Stella wished he could have stayed with them over the holiday – she'd saved enough for a goose. But he was going home to his family, who were waiting to welcome him. She'd miss his company and his friendship. Without him, the house would be empty and her life the poorer.

Generously, Arnie had given her the gramophone, to re-member him by, he said. As if she'd ever forget Arnold Hepplethwaite!

Right up until the last minute Stella hoped there'd be a Christmas card from Eddie, but Christmas Eve arrived and there was still no word. She found it hard to understand his disregard for his little daughter, who obviously still missed her father, and mentioned him frequently.

Stella was up late that evening, waiting for two excited children to fall asleep. She had a train-set for Danny that had cost more than she could afford, and a doll for Rosie – one that said, 'Mamma,' when it was tipped upside down, with some picture books they could share.

When she crept into the bedroom in the still of the night they were fast asleep in the double bed. Stella put the toys at the foot of the bed, wishing she could have bought lots more for them. As she gazed at their serene sleeping faces, she noticed how alike they were, Eddie's children. *Her* children, now, Stella thought, realising how much she loved them both.

But she had to admit that. Eddie *had* washed his hands of them. He was never coming back for Rosie.

'Bubble and squeak, and cold goose for dinner,' Babs announced wearily on Boxing Day to anyone who'd listen. 'I'll scrape down the carcass later.'

'Will Ted be back, d'you think?' Freda asked, giving her daughter a sidelong glance, as she wiped the breakfast plates.

Babs shrugged despondently. She had no idea what her husband's plans were, although he'd made it plain that Freda had better keep away as long as she persisted in helping Stella. Freda continued to do as she pleased, and Babs was glad, even though Ted took it out on her, lashing her with his tongue if not his fists. He hadn't struck her again, but the threat was always there, and the least little thing set him off – the twins screaming, a careless word. She was afraid to ask him anything these days.

Babs threw the dishcloth into the bowl of water. It'd been the most miserable Christmas she'd ever known, and she was glad it was over. Ted was to start work again tomorrow. Perhaps he'd be better-tempered then.

Babs flopped on to a chair in front of the range, warming her toes on the fender. She'd nursed a hope that Ted would offer to take her out this afternoon. No buses were running, but they could have strolled on the Prom.

But he'd gone off without a word. Where was he? Nothing was open Boxing Day, except the pub, but he despised drink. Perhaps he'd gone to a pal's house. It hurt her that he'd rather be with someone other than his family at Christmas time.

Babs gave another sigh. There was nothing to look forward to any more. Everything had changed and she didn't know why.

Freda came in from the scullery, wiping her wet hands on the tea-towel.

'Listen, why don't you pop next door?' she suggested. 'You haven't had a chat with Stella for weeks. She must be lonely, now her lodger's gone.'

'Suppose Ted comes back?' Babs asked anxiously.

'You needn't stay long,' Freda said, 'and I'll knock on the wall if there's a sign of him coming up the street.'

Babs hesitated.

'Go on,' her mother urged, 'it'll do you good. And besides, are you going to let him keep you a prisoner?'

'I'm not a prisoner, Mam,' Babs retorted. 'Don't exaggerate.' But she stood up ready to take a chance.

Hurrying through the back entrances, she tapped on Stella's door, and replied to her friend's challenge. Then she heard the key turn and the bolt drawn back. What was Stella afraid of?

Her friend's delight made her glad she'd taken the risk. 'Oh, there's lovely to see you, Babs,' Stella said joyfully, giving her a hug. 'How did Christmas go?'

'I've had better,' Babs admitted, aware that Stella was scrutinising her face. 'How about you?'

'The kids and me enjoyed ourselves. Plenty to eat, like.' Stella sighed. 'We miss Arnie.'

'Sorry, I was, not to say goodbye to him,' Babs said regretfully. 'I liked him. He was good fun.'

Stella turned from the gas ring, a strange expression on her face. 'What did you think of Arnie really? I mean, did you get fond of him?'

'Fond! Hey! I'm a married woman. Fond, indeed!'

Stella opened her mouth again, about to say something more, then turned away.

They were both avoiding the real issue, Babs knew. It was no good skirting around it: Stella was her best friend. She should have no secrets from her. 'I suppose Mam told you about Ted giving me a couple of fourpenny ones to be going on with?' She tried to keep her tone light, but was unable to shake off the sense of shame, as though she'd brought his violence on herself.

'Oh, Babs, I'm so sorry!' Stella grasped her in a tight hug. 'I was afraid . . . I wouldn't have had it happen for the world.'

Babs was taken aback. 'No need for you to apologise, Stell.'

'But it *is* because of me, I know it is,' Stella insisted. 'I wanted to tell you, Babs, many times, but I was afraid you'd believe it was my fault. I know you think the world of Ted . . .'

'What are you going on about?' Babs asked, mystified. 'Tell me what?'

'About Ted and me.'

'*What?*'

A chill went through Babs, right to her bones. 'What about you and my husband?' she asked. Then looking at Stella's expression, she thought she knew, and was thunderstruck. 'Stella! Are you telling me you've been carrying on with him behind my back?'

'It isn't like that,' Stella cried. 'Ted is a liar, Babs. You must listen to my side—'

'Your side, indeed!' Babs was furious. 'After all the years we've been friends, after all I've done to help you.' She gave a cry of despair and was staggered by an overwhelming sense of betrayal. 'It was *you* who turned him against me!' she wailed. 'Made him hate and despise me. Oh, Stella, how could you?'

'No! You've got it wrong,' Stella howled. 'It isn't true, I swear it, no matter what he's told you.'

'You've betrayed me,' Babs exclaimed wildly. 'You stabbed me in the back.'

'I'm the one who's been betrayed,' Stella cried, 'by Ted's vicious lies. He pestered me, Babs, pestered me for . . . favours . . . and when I wouldn't give in, he blackened my name.'

'You're putting it all on him, and I don't believe it!' Babs shouted. 'Ted said you'd turned into a slut. He's a model husband. He doesn't drink, smoke or gamble—'

'No!' Stella cried out passionately. 'He only beats his wife black and blue!'

The scullery was filling with steam from the kettle, forgotten, on the hob. Stella reached out automatically and turned off the gas.

Babs could hardly believe that Stella was standing there as bold as brass, confessing to this treachery. So much for their friendship. It obviously meant nothing to her.

A great lump of misery rose in her breast. How could she bear to look at either Ted or Stella again, knowing how they'd fooled her? They must've laughed their heads off each time they were together. She didn't like the images that came into her mind.

Then, she was startled by a loud knock on the front door, and nearly jumped out of her skin. She thought it was a warning from Freda, and edged towards the back door.

'Babs, please don't go yet.' Stella took a step towards her. 'We've got to talk. We can't leave it like this.'

'I never want speak to you again, you husband-snatcher!' Babs burst out.

There was another knock.

'You've got the wrong end of the stick, Babs.'

The knock interrupted them again.

'Stay here while I answer the door,' Stella said. 'Let me explain properly – please.' She darted away.

Babs's heart was filled with pain and despair. She was about to turn away to leave when the voices in the passage stopped her.

'Mrs E! I've come back. I had to!'

'Arnie!'

Curiosity got the better of Babs. She walked into the living room just as Arnie and Stella emerged. He had on his fur coat and the white wide-brimmed hat that Babs admired so much. It made him look so debonair and handsome, like a star of the moving pictures.

Arnie pulled up short at the sight of her. 'Barbara!'

'Hello, Arnie.'

'I didn't expect to find you here,' he went on, blinking in confusion, 'but I'm glad you are.'

She managed a smile, though it was an effort. He was a friend, and she wanted to know what had brought him back, until a new thought struck her. Had Stella been carrying on with him, too, as Ted had said?

'I'm just going,' Babs said shortly, throwing Stella an angry glance. 'I don't want to play gooseberry at a lovers' reunion!'

'No, please!' Stella and Arnie chorused.

Arnie threw his coat over a chair. 'I *had* to come back,' he said earnestly.

'If you think you're the only man in her life, you'll be disappointed,' Babs blurted. 'I've only just found out she's carrying on with Ted.'

'Oh, Babs!' Stella cried. 'Please listen!'

'I didn't come back to see Mrs E, fond of her though I am,' Arnie said. 'I came back for you, Barbara.'

'Oh, what nonsense are you talking?' She was impatient, caught up in her own misery and humiliation. 'I know what's been going on in this house.'

'Barbara, I . . .' He glanced at Stella. 'Mrs E, I wonder if you'd mind leaving us alone, what?'

Stella looked agitated. 'Arnie, I know what's in your mind, but I don't think this is the right time—'

'Dash it! Of course it is,' he replied firmly. 'Please, Mrs E?'

With a helpless glance at Babs, Stella left the room and Babs heard her footsteps on the stairs.

'Let's sit down,' Arnie suggested.

Babs didn't move, but he grasped her arm, led her to a chair and pushed her on to it. He sat, too.

'I won't stay in this house any longer,' Babs told him sullenly. 'My world's just been turned upside-down by the person I trusted most. I don't feel like chatting, Arnie.'

'You can start a new life with me.'

Babs stared. 'What?'

'I love you, Barbara.' He leaned forward, looking into her face. 'I love you dearly, and I want you to be my wife.'

Babs was angry and hurt at his insensitivity. 'Is this a joke? Has *she* put you up to it?' she demanded. 'Not funny, it isn't! Not everyone has *her* low morals.'

'I've never been more serious in my life, Barbara. And you're wrong about Mrs E. She's the best friend you've got.'

'Oh, yes – I don't think,' snapped Babs.

'Listen, what I'm saying has nothing to do with Mrs E,' he said. 'I've felt this way about you for a long time. Mrs E thought I shouldn't speak of it, but I *must* know how you feel.'

Babs lifted a shaking hand to her brow. Stella, whom she would once have trusted with her life, had betrayed her. Ted, the husband she'd loved and obeyed, had deceived her. And here was Arnie babbling on about love, as if he didn't know the bottom had fallen out of her life. 'My best friend has stolen my husband,' she blurted. 'How you think I feel?'

'It isn't Stella's fault.'

'Oh! I should've known you'd defend her.' Babs leaped to her feet. 'She's got you on a string as well.'

Arnie stood up and grasped her shoulders. 'Barbara, someone has to make you see the truth,' he said. 'Your husband is a lecherous swine. He's tormented Mrs E with his unwanted attentions ever since her husband left her. She kept it from you because she wanted to protect you.'

'So she says!'

'A few months back she told you she'd fallen downstairs, remember?' Arnie persisted. 'That was Ted's doing. He beat her mercilessly because she wouldn't give in to him. Now he's doing the same to you. How long before he starts on your children?'

Babs stared up into his face. His gaze was so clear and steady that she was almost persuaded, but she shook her head. 'You're lying. I don't know why, but you are.'

'Barbara, it's the truth. I wouldn't lie to you, I love you too much. I want you to come away with me, and the children, too.'

'Stop! You're confusing me,' Babs cried, struggling out of his grasp. 'Stella practically confessed—'

'Mrs E is innocent,' Arnie said. 'She did nothing to encourage him. But other women are less scrupulous . . .'

'What do you mean?'

'I've been concerned about you for a long time, Barbara,' he said gently. 'Many times I've wanted to knock Ted into the middle of next week for the way he treats you. And I've been watching him, too, whenever I can—'

'You had no right!' Babs burst out.

'Love gives me the right,' he asserted strongly. 'I love you and I want to protect you, if only you'll let me.'

'I don't want to hear any more,' Babs said, distressed. 'I'm going home. I wish I'd listened to Ted and not bothered with Stella.'

'Ted! Ted!' Arnie raised his voice angrily. 'Don't you understand yet? He's deceiving you over and over again. Where do you think he goes every evening? There's a young widow living on Carogwen Terrace—'

'I don't want to know!' Babs shouted. 'Don't you understand? Without Ted I have nothing. No home, no money, no life . . .'

'You have me,' he answered simply. 'I can give you all those things, and more. I promise you, Barbara, you'll want for nothing. Come away with me, I beg you.' His gaze was beseeching. 'I'll take care of you and the children. My family has money . . .'

Babs stepped back, staring at him. The truth was sinking in. Or perhaps she'd known it all along and wouldn't face it. But now she had to. 'No, Arnie. It won't do.' She lifted a hand when he tried to interrupt her. 'I like you, Arnie, a lot, but I'm not in love with you.'

'You thought you loved Ted,' he reminded her, 'but you're no happier for it.'

'I did love him!' Babs countered quickly. 'I do love him! He may be betraying me, like you say, and he has turned against me, that's true, but he's still my husband. I'm still a married woman. Only death can change that.'

'You can divorce him.'

'Divorce!' Babs was profoundly shocked. 'Shame my family, my children?' She lifted her chin. 'Perhaps that's all right for toffs like you, Arnie, but not for the likes of me.'

'There's no shame—'

'In my mind there'd be shame enough,' Babs retorted. 'I made my marriage vows in good faith, and I intend to keep them, even if Ted doesn't.'

'Barbara, please!'

Arnie tried to pull her to him, but she resisted. 'Please don't turn me away,' he blurted. 'I can't go on without you. Have pity on me, Barbara.'

'I thought you were a gentleman, Arnie,' she said tremulously, 'but you're trying to take advantage of me. How could you?'

She wrenched free, and darted towards the back door, ignoring his calls to wait.

Freda was in their scullery, putting the kettle on when Babs burst into her home, slamming the back door behind her. She leaned against it for a moment, out of breath and almost out of her mind.

In her heart she knew Arnie had spoken the truth, and Ted's abuse was proof that he no longer cared for her. She remembered his self-righteousness when he had spoken so disparagingly of Stella – all the time he'd been lusting after her. How could she bear him to touch her ever again, knowing what she did?

And if Arnie and Stella knew of Ted's disgraceful behaviour, so did others. Everyone must be sniggering behind her back, thinking what a fool she was not to see it.

Babs gave a little moan of pain, and Freda looked round.

'Oh, there you are!' she said impatiently. 'You were gone so long I thought you'd migrated to Australia.' She paused, staring at Babs keenly. 'Well, what's the matter with you, then?' she asked shortly. 'Looks like you lost a pound and found four-pence.'

Babs stared at her mother wordlessly, her mind a swirling mass of doubts and fears. What was she to do now? Go on as though nothing had happened? Take all the punishment Ted dished out?

But to finish with her so-called marriage would leave her without a roof, without money, without security. The thought frightened her more than Ted's fists.

Stella had faced the same difficulties with courage and determination, an inner voice taunted her.

But what about the twins? She must protect them, no matter what it cost her.

'What're you waiting for?' Freda asked impatiently. 'You said you'd strip the carcass when you came back from Stella's. I hate that job.'

Babs tried to smother the dread rising in her breast. Every-thing had changed. Her whole world had come crashing down. Now her home seemed an alien place, where she didn't belong.

'I want to ask you something, Mam,' she began shakily. 'Something very important.'

'Well, go on then. I'm all ears.'

'Supposing . . .' A sob rose in her throat. 'Supposing a woman found out her husband was seeing other women,' she managed. 'Would she be in the right to leave him?'

Freda folded her arms across her thin chest, and Babs knew she'd have to explain everything. She walked into the living room on legs that felt as heavy as lead. She pulled a chair from under the table and flopped on to it.

Within seconds Freda was by her side. 'What's happened, Barbara?'

Babs didn't reply straight away, feeling that to voice the words made them irrevocably true.

'Mam, Ted has been unfaithful to me.'

'Tussh!' Freda's exclamation expressed disappointment. 'I told you that months, years ago, didn't I?' she said impatiently. 'But you wouldn't listen, would you? Oh, no! The sun shone out of his arse, didn't it? Well, now you know better.'

'He's been pestering Stella for . . . well, you know what.' Babs raised a hand to her throat. 'Oh, God! I can hardly believe it. My Ted!'

'Oh, I can!' Freda spat out the words. 'He gave her a belting, too. The dirty coward!'

'You *knew* about that?'

'She wouldn't let me say anything.'

'There's a young widow in Carogwen Terrace, too, who doesn't turn him away, apparently.'

Freda folded her lips angrily.

A sob constricted Babs's throat. 'Mam! You knew about *her* as well, and you never said!'

Freda's eyes sparked, on the defensive. 'Huh! You'd have told me to mind my own business,' she said sharply. 'That's all the thanks I'd get.'

'I can't go on, Mam,' Babs said tearfully. 'I can't pretend any more. I'm going to leave him. But where will we go, me and the children?'

'Come and live with me,' Freda said quickly.

'But that's just across the road. I need to get away from him, far away.'

It was on the tip of her tongue to tell her mother about Arnie wanting her to go away with him, but she decided it was best forgotten. She wasn't even tempted, and didn't need her mother to tell her that would be a bad mistake.

'There's nowhere else, Barbara, love,' Freda said gently. 'I can take care of the girls during the day, because you'll have to find work, won't you?'

'But I don't know anything except housework,' Babs wailed, laying her arms on the table and resting her head on them.

Freda put her arm around Babs's shoulders in a rare gesture of sympathy. 'We'll scrape by,' she said. 'The main thing is you can get away from that brute.'

'I dread setting eyes on him,' Babs confessed.

She'd told Arnie she still loved Ted, but she couldn't rid her mind of the images of Ted with another woman. She could easily hate him now, she thought.

'Say nothing,' Freda warned sharply. 'Act daft. When he goes to work tomorrow, we'll move you and the kids over the road. Stella will help us.'

'What will he do when he knows I've left him?' Babs grasped her mother's hand. 'Mam, I'm afraid!'

'If he starts any rough stuff,' Freda said grimly, 'we'll have the law on him.'

Chapter Twenty

Stella was making toast soldiers for the children's breakfast early next morning when Babs put her head round the back door. 'Can I come in, Stell?'

'Of course!' Stella was delighted to see her. She'd spent a sleepless night wondering if their friendship was over because of a no-good, faithless husband. 'I thought you weren't talking to me any more.'

Babs came in and leaned against the stone sink. There were dark smudges under her eyes, suggesting she, too, had found sleep impossible. 'Sorry, Stell.' Her tone was unsure. 'I didn't know what to think at first. It was such a shock.'

Stella regarded her friend keenly. 'Was it really? Didn't you suspect?'

Babs shook her head, a bleak look in her eyes. 'No more than you suspected Eddie and Rose,' she said, and Stella looked away. It was true. She'd been fooled completely.

'I should've guessed something was wrong when his attitude changed. Nothing I did pleased him,' Babs observed, with a sigh.

'You loved him, trusted him,' Stella said softly. 'Besides,' she went on, 'Ted's clever. Look at the evil lies he's told about me, and people who should know better have believed him, even my own brother.'

'Oh, Stella, I'm so sorry!'

'You mustn't reproach yourself, Babs. You're a victim, like me.'

'Not any more,' Babs said. 'I'm leaving him today. That's why I've called in. Will you help me, Stella?'

Stella dropped the butter-knife on the bread-board, went to her friend and put an arm around her shoulders. 'Do anything I can, you know that.'

'We're staying with Mam. It's all arranged. I couldn't stand another night under his roof. Last night I pretended the twins were ill and I slept in their room to keep out of his way.'

As Babs was speaking Stella heard Arnie's feet on the stairs. When he came into the scullery her friend looked dismayed. 'I thought you'd gone,' she began.

'I didn't want to leave without seeing you again, Barbara,' he said, with a tremor in his voice. 'I don't want to part in acrimony. I couldn't bear it.'

'There's no more to say . . . except, thank you for opening my eyes,' Babs said.

Arnie's head was bowed. He was overcome, Stella thought, and her heart went out to him, for she knew he was true and sincere. But she knew, too, that Babs had made a wise decision. Their worlds would never meld.

As soon as the children had had breakfast Stella went next door to help in the move. Arnie volunteered his muscle-power, too. 'It's a relief to know she's getting away from that swine,' he whispered to Stella.

A small crowd of neighbours from along the street gathered to watch the proceedings, as the twins' bed and their clothes were carried across to Freda's home. There were pitifully few things for Babs, Stella noticed.

'Take only the bare essentials, I will,' Babs told them at the start. 'I'll not have him say I robbed him.'

By midday the move was complete, and Stella got on with preparing a bit of dinner. Afterwards, Arnie made no move to leave. She was in no hurry to see him go, but was worried about him. He'd been a good friend to her and Babs, but Stella knew

Babs would never change her mind, and there'd be only heartache for Arnie as long as he hung around hoping.

She decided to speak frankly. It was for his own good. 'What train are you catching?' she asked casually, removing his empty plate.

He glanced up at her, his smile strained. 'Glad to see the back of me, what?'

'You know that's not true.'

'Sorry I sound bitter,' he said, 'but Barbara's refusal is a blow to my pride as well as my heart.'

Stella placed a sisterly hand on his shoulder. 'The sooner you go home and start making a new life for yourself the better,' she said.

'Yes, I know, but I'm not leaving here until late this evening. When Ted Thomas realises Barbara has left him he might make trouble for you.'

'But it's nothing to do with me!'

'He'll blame you, mark my words. And I want to be around when he does.' Arnie stood up and took a thick wad of folded banknotes from an inside pocket of his jacket.

'Here's a hundred pounds, Mrs E. It's for Barbara.'

Stella was astonished. 'She'll never accept it.'

'I know. That's why I'm leaving the money in your hands. Without work she'll be in want in months to come. Perhaps she'll accept a loan from you, her friend. She need never know from whom the money came.'

'It's such a large sum! The responsibility! I can't accept it – I mean, where on earth would I hide it in this house?'

'Open a bank account,' he suggested blithely.

Bank account? She knew nothing of such things, wouldn't know where to begin. 'No, no, Arnie, I can't do it. Don't ask me.'

'Please, Mrs E? Do this one thing for me.'

With deep misgivings, Stella allowed him to put the money in her hand. Suddenly, she felt as though a great weight had landed on her shoulders.

'That's settled,' he said, almost cheerfully. 'Now, I'll take the children for a walk in the park, if you're willing to trust them to me. I'm dashed fond of them, you know, Mrs E, and I'm going to miss them. We'll be back before tea time, I promise.'

When they'd gone Stella moved about the house in a quandary. Where to hide the money? Where would it be safe?

Eventually, she stuffed the notes into an old stocking and tucked it under the mattress of the double bed.

She wanted to slip across the road to Freda's to chat with Babs, but was afraid to leave the house empty. No one could possibly know, she told herself, yet the thought of all that money weighed on her like a ton of bricks.

At tea time, when her one-time lodger had disappeared again on business of his own, the children sat at the table, full of chatter about their walk in the park with Uncle Arnie. She knew it would be difficult to explain why he was leaving and why they'd probably never see him again, and decided to put it off until later.

Stella was just pouring herself a second cup of tea when, without warning, the back door crashed open, and Ted Thomas stormed into the living room, his face livid with fury.

Stella leaped to her feet, putting herself between him and the children. 'You bitch!' he bellowed. 'Where is she? I demand to know the meaning of this.'

He was holding out a sheet of paper torn from a child's exercise book. Stella had no doubt it was a note Babs had left for him. She lifted an arm and pointed to the door.

'Get out of this house, Ted. You've no right to be here.'

Behind her the children were whimpering. She must get them upstairs and out of harm's way.

'I want to see my wife,' Ted yelled. 'Get the stupid bitch down here. I know she's hiding upstairs.'

'Babs isn't here. Now get out!'

Ted took a few steps towards her, and Stella backed away. The children shouldn't have to witness what might happen next.

'Don't play me for a fool, Stella,' he growled, his face taut with fury. 'I won't stand for it. You're behind this.'

'You're mad!' Stella cried. 'Whatever Babs has done, it's nothing to do with me.'

'Liar!' he shouted. 'You know full well what she's done. You put her up to it. She wouldn't have the guts or the brains to do this by herself. But I'll make you pay, you cheap tart, if I have to beat you black and blue.'

'Keep back!' Stella warned, half turning to ward off any blows. 'You lay a finger on me and I'll yell for a bobby. I couldn't before because of Babs, but now she knows everything about you, it's a different story.'

He lifted a fist and Stella cringed.

'Have you up for assault, I will, Ted. I promise you.'

'Don't make me laugh, Stella.' He was scornful. 'Who'd believe you – an unfit mother? Selling your own kids for whores, for all we know. I'll report you for it.'

Stella's mouth fell open. Of all the lies he'd told about her that was the worst. 'How dare you accuse me of such a monstrous thing?'

'I can say what I like and do as I like,' Ted jeered. 'I'm respected around here. A decent working man. I'm not a sot, like some, and I don't throw my money away on the dogs and horses. People around here know me for an honest man.'

'Honest man!' It was Stella's turn to be scornful. 'You don't know the meaning of the word. What honest man beats his wife and keeps another woman? Wicked, you are, Ted Thomas, and Babs is well rid of you.'

'Shut your mouth or I'll shut it for you. Permanently!'

'Perhaps you'd like to try that on me, what?'

Ted whirled to face Arnie, who was standing motionless in the scullery doorway, shirt-sleeves rolled up, his hands at his sides encased in boxing gloves.

Stella stared at him in astonishment, and even Ted looked bewildered.

'What's *he* doing here?' he asked Stella belligerently. 'Thought your fancy man had buggered off and left you.'

Eyeing Arnie's tense face, Stella turned to Danny. 'Get upstairs, and take Rosie. Stay up there until I tell you to come down.' Danny, his little face white with fright, grabbed Rosie's hand and pulled her away towards the passage. 'I just want Ted to leave,' Stella said to Arnie. 'I don't want any trouble.'

'Don't worry, Mrs E. We'll play by the Queensberry Rules.'

Ted was scowling at Arnie. 'What've *you* got to do with my wife?'

'Not as much as I'd like,' Arnie said provocatively. 'Not half as much.' He lifted the gloves. 'Now, put them up!'

To Stella's astonishment, Arnie darted into the living room and began dancing around on his toes, the boxing gloves raised in front of his face.

'Come on, you lily-livered beater of women,' he yelled mockingly to Ted. 'Let's see how you face up to someone your own size.'

He danced closer to the other man, making short jabs with open gloves towards Ted's head.

'Arnie, be careful!' She said. No one knew better than Stella how hard and viciously Ted could strike with his fists, and although he was shorter than Arnie, he was heavier.

'Yes, you'd better listen to her,' Ted said. 'Don't want to spoil that pretty face of yours, do you?'

'You're not so bad-looking yourself, Thomas,' Arnie said, 'but I intend to alter that.'

'Arnie, please,' Stella begged. 'Stop this now.'

'It's too late for that,' Arnie said grimly. 'Besides, I've been wanting to do this for a long time.'

He lowered his head behind the gloves again, still prancing on his toes. 'Have no fear, Mrs E,' he went on. 'I won the junior boxing championship at my school three years running. I know exactly what I'm doing. I'll teach this bully a lesson he won't forget.'

Arnie circled his quarry in the confined space of the living room, his feet making complex patterns on the linoleum. 'Come on, you low-down scum,' he crooned. 'Let's see what you're really made of.'

A growl rose from Ted's chest as he turned and turned, keeping wary eyes on his agile adversary.

'Arnie, if you must do this, please go outside,' Stella begged. 'This is my home.'

'We don't want onlookers,' he said, continuing to circle. 'No witnesses.'

'Who does this sissy think he's frightening?' Ted asked.

Arnie chose that moment to let fly a real punch. His right fist streaked out with the speed of a cobra, and Ted reeled back towards the fireplace, clutching his jaw, looking dazed.

'That one's for Mrs E's black eye!' Arnie capered on his toes. 'How do you like it, eh?'

'You bastard!' Ted yelled. 'I'll bloody flatten you, smash your teeth down your throat, I will.'

'Brave words!' Arnie taunted. 'Come on, then, coward.'

With a snarl of rage, Ted rushed forward, arms flailing wildly, and Stella screamed, expecting Arnie to go down under the rain of blows, but the younger man danced out of range to the other side of the table. 'I say! Is that the best you can do, Thomas? Poor show! You fight like a woman.'

Ted charged again, head down, only to meet Arnie's fist, which struck him full force on the bridge of his nose. 'That one's for Barbara,' Arnie said wrathfully. 'I'll teach you to lay hands on the woman I love.'

Blood spurted from Ted's nose, spraying the front of his shirt, and he staggered back, shaking his head, causing flecks of blood to fly on to the tablecloth nearby.

'Arnie, for God's sake, that's enough!' Stella shrieked.

'Not half enough, Mrs E,' he shouted. 'I'll teach this swine a lesson he won't forget.'

He lowered his head behind the gloves again, a dark expression on his face that Stella had never seen before. She'd heard of blood lust, and wondered, in fright, if she were witnessing it now. Was there a savage streak in all men?

'Arnie!'

But Ted had recovered. 'I'll kill you, you bloody pansy!' he roared, beside himself with rage. 'I'll tear you limb from limb.'

Arms outstretched, he tried to grapple Arnie, but his adversary side-stepped, and threw another well-aimed punch, with the full force of his shoulder behind it.

The glove hit Ted squarely in the mouth, and he yelled in pain then sank to his knees on the mat in front of the hearth.

'What ho! To hell with Queensberry!' yelled Arnie triumphantly, and with a upward swing struck another blow at Ted's face as he knelt there, sending him sprawling backwards to lie still.

'You've killed him!' Stella whimpered.

'No such luck,' Arnie panted, standing legs astride over him. 'But I wish he'd get up – I haven't finished with him yet.'

'Yes, you have!' Stella said, and pulled him away. She glanced down at the prostrate form on the mat before the fireplace.

'Oh, my God! Look at his face – the blood! This is awful.'

'Don't feel sorry for *him*,' Arnie growled. 'Remember what he did to you and Barbara. I *could* kill him for that.'

Stella wrung her hands. 'We can't leave him lying there. He'll bleed to death.'

'Nonsense!' Arnie looked down contemptuously at his defeated foe. 'But you're right, Mrs E,' he agreed. 'He's making the place look untidy.'

He stooped, gripped his opponent under the armpits and began to drag him towards the back door. Ted's bloodied head lolled grotesquely to one side.

'What're you doing?' Stella cried, her knuckle in her mouth.

'Throwing the blighter out,' Arnie growled. 'I'll put him in the back lane. He can come to there.'

'But it's freezing cold,' Stella said. 'He might die.'

'Not him!' Arnie said shortly. 'The devil looks after his own.'

Stella was in no position to argue. Ted would wake up soon, and it would be better if he was nowhere near her or her children.

There was blood on the mat as well as the tablecloth. Stella put them in the tin bath in the backyard, intending to wash them through the next day. By the time she'd done that, Arnie was back. He pulled at the strings of the boxing gloves with his teeth, then took them off. 'I do feel better for that exercise,' he said. 'It's good to know I haven't lost my touch.'

'I can't be pleased with what you've done, Arnie,' Stella said severely. 'You might have made things worse. Ted's a vengeful man. He won't let it rest. It's a good thing you're leaving tonight.'

'No, I'm not leaving tonight,' announced Arnie firmly. 'He'll be like a bear with a sore head when he wakes up. He might come back. He's fool enough. I'm staying the night, if you don't mind?'

'I do mind, Arnie. I want you to go.'

'I say, Mrs E,' he was astounded, 'you can't mean it!'

'I do. This is my home, and you've turned it into a boxing ring. Blood's been spilled. It was bad enough when my brother was here but I never expected such behaviour from you.'

'But the blighter needed to be taught a lesson,' Arnie argued. 'I did it for you and Barbara.'

'Did you? Or maybe you did it because Babs refused to go away with you.'

'That's unfair, Mrs E.'

'Things have gone too far,' Stella said. 'I never thought I'd say this to you of all people, Arnie, but I want you to leave, tonight, as you planned.'

'I see,' he said shortly, and turned away, but Stella caught at his arm.

'This is my home, Arnie. It's all I have left.'

He was icy-cold, racked with pain, and couldn't see properly in the pitch darkness. What had happened? Where was he? Somewhere outside, on the cold, hard ground.

It was an effort to sit up, and pain throbbed in his face. He licked his lips, wincing at the raw soreness. They were swollen, and tasted salty.

Blood!

Then he remembered. Stella's bloody fancy man had used him as a punchbag, and *she* had egged him on.

Ted felt a swell of rage against her. He'd pay her back, he vowed, in like coin and in full.

With a groan he got on to his hands and knees. His head felt heavy, as though it had grown to twice its normal size, and a stabbing pain shot through his nose when he tried to stand upright.

Gripping the rough stones of the garden wall he managed to pull himself up, and leaned against it until his legs felt stronger, and he had his bearings.

Now that he was above the deep shadows of the wall he was aware of shapes outlined against the crisp winter moonlight: the roof of the lavatory in his backyard, the gate swinging open in the icy night breeze. Staggering, he reached the door, and almost fell into the scullery.

He lit the gas-light, looked in the shaving-mirror hanging on a nail behind the door, and was even more enraged by what met his gaze. His top lip was split open, and bruises were already turning purple along his jaw line. What frightened him most was the damage to his nose: it was twice its normal size and looked displaced. It was broken! He lifted a shaking hand to touch it, but hesitated, afraid of the pain.

Stella would pay for this! She'd pay for contaminating Barbara with her filth. He'd spoil Stella's pretty looks for her. By the time he'd finished with *her*, she'd not be able to show her face in daylight.

Images of how he'd pay her back crowded his mind as he bathed his face in cold water, but even with some of the dried blood washed away, it looked no better and he felt even worse.

How could he go to work tomorrow, face his workmates, looking as though he'd been hit by an express train? How could he explain it away? They'd laugh at him. *Him*, Ted Thomas, whose wife had taken him for a chump, made him look a fool. She'd turned him into a laughing-stock. No woman could be allowed to get away with that.

Staring at the damage, he burned to take his revenge. And not only on Stella. Barbara was responsible for this! And, by God, she'd pay for it. He'd break *her* bloody nose.

Where was she, the fat cow?

If she wasn't at Stella's, she was over the road at her mother's. She had no right to walk out on him. Who did she think she was, anyway? She was fit only to cook his food and wash his clothes. He owned her.

He'd fetch her back, now, tonight, drag her if necessary. Let the neighbours see him do it, too. Shame her in front of them. No one could blame a wronged husband for punishing a runaway wife. It was his right.

And once he got her here, he'd give her a good hiding, show her who was boss, once and for all.

He felt a thrill run through him at the thought. He'd enjoy it, too, as he'd enjoyed beating Stella. He remembered the look of terror on Stella's face. He wanted to see it on Barbara's, wanted to hear her plead for mercy. But there'd be no mercy for her.

Chapter Twenty-One

Babs came in from the backyard of her mother's house, empty coal-scuttle in her hand and a frown on her face. 'Mam, there's nothing but small coal out the coal-house, and not much of that.'

'Huh!' Freda was standing at the sink, a dripping dish-cloth in hand. 'My pension doesn't run to a full coal-house, Barbara. Paying for a bit of food, rent and gas is all I can manage most weeks.'

'Why didn't you tell me you were short, Mam? I could've loaned you something. Tsk! To think you've been going without a fire . . .'

'You had enough on your plate, my girl, with that Ted,' Freda answered. 'It makes my blood boil to think of the way he's treated you, chasing other women.'

'Well, that's in the past now,' Babs said quietly, taking the empty coal-scuttle back into the living room, 'over and done with.'

'Is it?' Freda asked, 'I don't think so, my girl.'

'We'll have to get some coal,' Babs said quickly, trying to change the subject. 'I'll go over to Stella's later. She'll lend us a bucketful until I can find a coal-man tomorrow.'

'Oh, aye! Tomorrow!' Freda said. 'Maybe you'll be back with Ted tomorrow. He crooks his finger and you'll go running.'

'I'm not going back!' Babs said strongly. 'I'm finished with him. This is it, Mam. I've left him, and it's for good.'

Freda gave a deep sigh. 'It's like waiting for the other shoe to drop, isn't it?'

'What is?'

'Waiting to see what he'll do about it.'

She glanced at the old grandmother clock ticking loudly on the wall. Babs followed her eyes. It was coming up to eight o'clock. Ted usually got home from work at about six. He'd have read her note by now. Why had there been no reaction from him?

Perhaps he was glad she'd gone, and was already with his fancy woman down in Carogwen Terrace. Somehow, she doubted it. She knew Ted well. He'd have to retaliate.

'I'll pop over to Stella's now for some coal,' she suggested.

Perhaps Stella had heard something. She might've even seen Ted.

'No! Don't go out!' Freda said quickly. 'He might be out there – waiting.'

'I can't stay trapped by here for ever, Mam,' Babs said bluntly. 'I'll have to start looking for work tomorrow. Scrub floors, I will, until my knuckles bleed rather than go back to him.'

'Brave words!'

'What's the matter, Mam?' Babs asked crossly. 'Sorry, are you, letting us come under your roof? If you are, we can just as easy get out.'

'Don't be soft!' Freda said sharply. 'Of course I'm not sorry. I'm your mother. Where else would you go? No, it's *you* I'm worried about, Barbara. That ruddy Ted is liable to do any- thing.'

Babs regretted her crankiness. She didn't dare show it, but she was not a little frightened at what she'd done, abandoning home and husband. She wasn't even sure it had been the right thing to do, as far as her children were concerned anyway. She was depriving them of their father, and what he could provide for them.

'It's me that's sorry,' she said. 'I'm causing you worry, and you're not getting any younger, are you, Mam?'

'Here, let's have a cuppa,' Freda suggested, and bustled into the scullery to put the kettle on.

Babs pulled out a chair and sat down. She could understand her mother's nervousness. Until she faced Ted and his inevitable outburst, she'd be on pins herself.

Freda was just bringing the cups and saucers from the scullery when there was a loud banging on the front door. Although she'd been expecting it for hours, the sound made Babs jump almost out of her skin.

Ted's furious voice shouted through the letter-box: 'Barbara! Open this bloody door, now!'

The women looked at each other, and Babs saw a flicker of panic in Freda's eyes. 'It's all right, Mam,' she said, shakily. 'He'll get fed up and go away in a minute.'

Only she knew he wouldn't, not in his present mood, and the knocking and shouting went on. Obviously Ted was so angry he didn't mind drawing a crowd. Well, that was up to him, if he wanted to make a side-show of himself.

Babs was worried about the twins and forced herself to slip into the passage and up the stairs. The two girls were already at the bedroom door. 'Go back to bed, you two,' Babs said, as calmly as she could. 'It's only Dad.'

When she went down to the living room again, Freda was standing near the table, her face taut and white.

'He's kicking my front door, Babs,' she said tensely. 'He'll kick it in, in a minute, and if he causes damage the landlord will have *me* for it.'

Before Babs could stop her she darted down the passage. 'I'm going to answer the door and give him a piece of my mind.'

'No, Mam! For God's sake, don't do that!'

But her warning was too late. The key was turned and the bolt pulled before Babs could reach her. The door slammed open against the passage wall, almost knocking Freda off her feet.

'Stop that kicking!' Freda screeched, as Ted barged into the passage. 'Get out!'

Ignoring her, he pushed her aside roughly, and advanced further into the passage towards Babs, who was standing in the living-room doorway.

'Oh, so there you are, you bloated cow,' he shouted, and she cringed, terrified at the sight of him, and the rage in his face. 'Hiding behind your mother as usual.'

'Don't you touch her, you devil!' Freda yelled. 'I'll call a bobby to you.'

'Get your things,' he commanded Babs. 'You're coming home, now!'

Babs could only stand and stare with her mouth open. Ted was almost unrecognisable, with his swollen nose and bruised face.

'What do you think you're looking at?' he barked.

'What happened to your face, Ted?'

'As if you don't know!' he snarled. 'You put him up to it, didn't you? You and that slut across the road.'

'What?'

He advanced towards her, and Babs retreated into the living room.

'He was waiting for me,' he grated. 'He's a bloody boxing champion, for God's sake! I didn't stand a chance.' He jerked his thumb towards his face. 'This is down to you, and I'm going to give you a taste of the same.'

'Keep away from her, I tell you!' Freda ranted.

'Shut up, you skinny old crow, and get out of my way,' he put a hand against Freda's chest and shoved, 'or you'll get the same. I've had enough of the pair of you.'

'Don't you manhandle my mother!' Babs cried. 'I won't stand for it, Ted.'

'You'll stand for anything I dish out and like it! You've let that tart, Stella, contaminate you with her filth.'

'Ted! Don't say such things. I'm your wife!'

'Wife?' His tone was scathing. 'You've been carrying on with that bloody actor, haven't you? Making a fool of me.'

'None of this is true, Ted,' Babs wailed. What had Arnie been saying?

He lifted a fist. 'Don't bother denying it,' he rasped. 'He practically admitted as much when he used me as a punch-bag.'

Babs took refuge on the other side of the table, her eyes on his fist, expecting to feel the full force of it on her face at any moment.

'I've done nothing wrong, Ted, I swear it,' she said. 'I wouldn't break my marriage vows. Not like . . . not like you.'

He scowled, but lowered his fist. 'What's that you said?'

Suddenly Babs felt bolder. She'd left him. She was no longer his skivvy. They were finished, and he could do no more to her. 'You've been pestering Stella for months – years.' She spoke up clearly. 'She told me all about it and about the vicious beating you gave her—'

'She's scum and a liar!' Ted bellowed. 'Nobody'll believe what a prostitute says—'

'She's not a prostitute,' Babs shouted. 'That's a base lie you've been spreading about her, because she wouldn't—' The words stuck in her throat. 'Because she wouldn't go to bed with you.'

'You pig!' Freda screeched. 'Strung up from a lamp-post, you ought to be. If I was a man—'

'I told you to shut up, you old hag!' Ted bawled at her.

'What about that piece you've been seeing in Carogwen Terrace?' Freda blustered. 'You ought to be ashamed of yourself.'

'Shut up, you old cow, or I'll do you in!'

Babs was at the end of her rope. How much longer must she listen to this yelling? Even though she'd left Ted, it still went on.

'Ted!' She clasped her hands in front of her breasts in an effort to defuse the situation. 'How could you betray me like that? I've been a good wife to you, haven't I?'

'Are you calling me a liar, Barbara?' he asked ominously.

'Yes, I am!' she declared. 'You're the one who's been carrying on. I suppose you believe it's all right for a man to betray his wife and children and knock them about when he feels like it. You're despicable!'

'What *you* think doesn't count,' he said harshly. 'Now, get your things and come with me.'

'The children—'

'They can stay here for now,' he said. 'But you're coming home.'

'I'm not,' Babs said defiantly. 'I'll never set foot in that house again. Nor will the children. We're all better off without you, Ted.'

'Oh, defy me, would you?' Ted yelled. He grabbed a handful of her hair and dragged her towards the passage and the front door.

With a howl, Freda went for him, beating ineffectually at him with her bony, distorted fists.

Still holding Babs captive by her hair, Ted shouted a coarse oath and lashed out at his mother-in-law, striking a heavy blow to her upturned face.

She was knocked flying, and as she fell, her head hit the corner of the sideboard. With a strange little choking groan she sank on to the linoleum and lay in a heap, blood oozing from a gash in her temple.

Babs screamed, and stared down at her mother's prone motionless body.

'Mam! Mam! Oh, my God, you've killed her, Ted.'

'It's her own bloody fault.' Ted pushed her towards the passage again. 'Come on, get going.'

'No! Let me go! I have to see to my mother. She needs help.'

'Let the poisonous old hag die,' Ted snarled. 'The world will be better off without her. Now, do as I tell you, or I'll slap you silly right here and now.'

'Leave me be!' Babs screamed. 'My mother needs me.' With a supreme effort she shook herself free of him, darted to Freda and fell to her knees beside her, hands hovering over her, afraid to touch her.

'Keep away from her, I said,' Ted shouted. 'The old

scarecrow deserves everything she gets! I should've done it years ago.'

'My mother's dying, you callous brute,' Babs sobbed. 'I hate you, Ted. I wish *you* were dead!'

At that moment Babs saw the twins standing in the living-room doorway. They were staring in terror at their grand-mother's body, and crying.

Ted rounded on them. 'Get upstairs, the pair of you, now, or you'll both get a hammering you won't forget.'

It was too much for Babs. She felt a terrible fury rise in her breast, and with the desperate cry of a mother defending her young, she sprang to her feet, throwing herself at him, heedless of any danger to herself.

'I'll never forgive you for this, Ted. I'll see you in prison for it.'

She clawed at his face, until a heavy blow sent her staggering back against the table.

'Take that, you treacherous bitch!' he yelled. 'I'll break every bone in your body, if you try that again.'

But Babs was too incensed with hatred to heed any warning. Resolutely, she pitched herself towards him again, her small fists flying, aiming instinctively for his already injured nose. She caught him a lucky blow on the bridge and he screamed in pain.

'How do you like it, Ted?' she shrilled. 'You can dish it out, but can you take it? I wish Arnie had killed you.'

He stepped away from her, his hand raised to protect his injuries, and stared at her. His eyes were cold as ice and without feeling. 'A lesson, you need, you fat ugly lump,' he said slowly. 'And I'm going to teach it to you now. You've been asking for it for a long time.'

His hands went to his belt and he loosened the buckle. Taking it from his waist, he wrapped the end around his palm, then began to swing it back and forth. The large brass buckle flashed in the gas-light, making a swishing sound as it sliced through the air. 'Wait until you feel this cut through your skin,' he grated. 'That'll take the fight out of you.'

Babs recoiled. 'You wouldn't dare, Ted,' she gasped. 'Not even *you* would do that.'

'Forty lashes you're getting, my girl.' He grinned, swinging the belt. 'A bit of blood-letting and a bit of pain. That'll clean away the filth you've picked up from that Stella.'

She was about to plead, when Freda moaned, and Babs turned to her, thankful that her mother was still alive.

The next moment she screamed in agony as the belt slashed across her shoulders, the buckle cutting into her flesh. The pain was excruciating, and she thought she would faint at the power of it.

Ted raised the belt again. 'That's one,' he said. 'Thirty-nine to go.'

The buckle whistled towards her head, and with a cry, she raised her arm to protect her face. The buckle hit her upper arm, and Babs screamed again – and went on screaming mindlessly.

She heard the swish of the belt and waited for the next blow, but it didn't come. Instead there was a commotion near the front door and heavy footsteps tramped down the passage.

'Here! What's going on?' A large policeman appeared in the living-room doorway. 'What's all the screaming about, missus?'

He took in the sight of Babs on her knees beside Freda's inert body, and Ted's raised hand wielding the belt.

'Stop that!' the policeman ordered him. 'Put that down.'

'She's my wife,' Ted shouted. 'I've got a right to chastise her.'

Eyeing him warily, the policeman moved nearer to Babs, and withdrew his truncheon from his belt. 'Now look, mister, I don't want no trouble with you, see,' he said evenly to Ted. 'Put that belt down.'

'The bitch deserves it, I tell you,' Ted shouted. 'I *own* her, and I can do as I like with my own property.'

'Put it down!'

Perversely, Ted swung the belt around his head with even more force than before, letting fly at Babs's upturned face. She screamed in terror. But the buckle didn't find her flesh this time.

Instead, it caught the policeman across the face. He roared with pain and fury. He clapped a hand to the reddening weal that appeared across his cheek, then looked at the blood on his fingers. 'Righto, boyo!' he bellowed. 'Now you've bloody done it! Wants to play rough, do you? Well! Take that!'

The heavy truncheon struck Ted on the top of his head, and he yelled in pain and shock, his knees buckling. Regaining his balance, he sprang at the policeman, shouting, 'You bloody fool! It's her that needs the stick, not me.'

The truncheon was knocked from the policeman's hand, and he and Ted closed in a grapple. As they swayed about amid the furniture, Babs was too frightened to get to her feet, but remained crouched over her mother, trying to protect her from the heavy boots.

She was relieved when the policeman manoeuvred Ted into a half-nelson, found his whistle and blew it enthusiastically.

'You're under arrest, boyo,' the policeman gasped, but Ted was still fighting to shake off his assailant.

'I got my rights as a husband, damn it!' he yelled. 'It's her that wants arresting. Let me go!'

Babs thought he looked as though he'd gone completely insane.

There was the sound of more heavy boots pounding down the passage, and another policeman appeared. He sized up the situation immediately and got out some handcuffs. Between them, Ted was overpowered but still he protested. 'You've got this all wrong, you simpletons!' he stormed, struggling against his bonds. 'She's been messing about with other men. I've a god-given right to punish a wayward wife. Any court in the land will uphold that.'

'I dunno nothing about that,' one of his captors said, 'but you attacked and wounded a policeman, so you're for the high-jump, boyo.'

With difficulty Babs got to her feet, ignoring the pain in her shoulders and arm. 'He attacked my mother, too,' she wailed. 'She may be dying. Do something!' She pointed a finger accusingly at Ted. 'He did it deliberately,' she went on, trying to keep a sob from her voice. 'He tried to murder her.'

'Settle down, missus,' an officer replied calmly. 'Send for a doctor.'

'But my mother's badly hurt,' Babs insisted.

'The doctor'll see to that, missus,' a policeman said. 'Meanwhile, we've got to get this maniac to the station to charge him with assault on a police officer. He's in serious trouble, believe me.'

'What about my mother?' Babs cried out. 'He's got to answer for that, too. If she dies I want him strung up. Do you hear me? Strung up!'

'You bitch!' Ted yelled back. 'This is all your fault.'

Babs dropped to her knees again beside Freda, as the policemen bundled Ted out, his protests ringing in her ears.

As soon as they'd gone, Stella appeared in the living-room doorway. Babs was never so glad to see anyone in her life.

'Oh, Stella, help me!'

Straight away Stella was on her knees beside her, gently touching Freda's throat. 'She's still alive. I can feel her pulse. No, don't try to move her,' she warned, as Babs attempted to lift her mother's head on to her lap. 'Just cover her with a blanket. I've sent for the doctor.'

Babs rushed to the airing cupboard next to the fireplace for a blanket. It seemed like hours since Freda had been struck down, and Babs felt as though her mother's life was seeping away. She was old and frail, and couldn't withstand such injury.

Carefully, she covered the inert figure, praying that her mother would survive.

'He'll be here soon,' Stella said. 'I sent Mrs Lippert's eldest boy on his butcher's bike to get him. When I saw Ted had got in here, I knew someone would be hurt. I was afraid for the children.'

'Thank God for you, Stella,' Babs sobbed.

'You should let the doctor look at your shoulder and arm, too,' Stella said. 'You're bleeding.'

'It doesn't matter,' Babs replied dully. 'I suppose there was a crowd outside, gawking?'

She hoped they'd had a good view of Ted, the supposedly model husband, being led away in disgrace by the police. He deserved to be humiliated. And she didn't care if the neighbours were gossiping. All that mattered was Freda.

'Who sent for the police?' she asked.

'I did,' Stella said. 'I'd been keeping my eye out for trouble, and when I saw Ted kicking Freda's door, I ran up to the corner and got a bobby.'

'Poor Mam! She tried to protect me, and she ended up hurt. Oh, Stella, if my mother dies because of Ted's wickedness, he'll pay for it!'

At that moment a voice called a hello from the front door, and Babs breathed a sigh of relief as a tall man in a pinstripe suit and camel hair overcoat walked into the living room carrying a black Gladstone bag.

Stella went out into the passage as the doctor began to examine Freda, and Babs followed her. 'I must get back home now,' Stella said quietly. 'I had to leave the children on their own. Danny's a sensible boy, but I'm worried about them. They'll be frightened alone.'

'Oh, Stella,' Babs pleaded, 'take the twins with you. I'll have to stay with Mam.'

The doctor came out into the passage pushing a stethoscope into his bag. He looked at both women enquiringly. 'Which of you is the daughter?'

'I am,' Babs said. 'How is she, Doctor?'

'Deeply unconscious, I'm afraid,' he replied gravely. 'She has sustained a serious head injury, and I'm worried.'

His gaze slid away, and Babs raised a hand to her mouth. He was trying to tell her that Freda might not recover.

'I'll go back to the surgery and ring for St John's Ambulance from there,' the doctor went on. 'You've probably got an hour to get her things ready. Meanwhile, keep her warm, but don't attempt to move her. Leave that to the ambulance men.'

'Thank you, Doctor,' Babs said, and he strode towards the front door.

'You see to Freda,' Stella said, when he had gone. 'I'll deal with the girls. Don't worry about them. They'll be safe with me.'

With that Stella ran upstairs, and Babs went back to the living room. She knelt again at her mother's side and eased a cushion under her head. Tears welled in her eyes as she looked down at Freda's white, pinched face. She was a good mother for all her criticising, and Babs wished she'd been kinder to her. If Freda died now, she'd never know how much her daughter loved her.

'Don't die, Mam,' she whispered. 'I love you and I need you. Please don't die!'

Chapter Twenty-Two

Babs pressed a key to Freda's house into Stella's hand. 'Heaven only knows how long I'll be at the hospital,' she said, lines of strain showing in her face. 'Take the key, then you can slip back for anything the girls want.'

Stella hated leaving Babs alone to face whatever might happen next, but her own children needed her, too, so she gathered the twins to her and took her leave.

Bundled into their coats, hats and scarves, the girls clung together, giggling, as Stella shepherded them across the street to her home. She could understand their near-hysteria. Already keyed up by their father's violence, they were out in the dark without their mother, and with the prospect of sleeping in someone else's bed.

'Quiet, girls,' she admonished them gently.

Her own home was still in darkness, as she had expected, but as she took out her key to open the front door she realised, with a jolt, that it was standing ajar. Her heart almost stopped beating.

Something was wrong.

Pushing the twins behind her, with another urgent warning to be quiet, Stella stepped cautiously into the passage, pausing to listen intently.

Before she went to fetch the policeman she'd warned Danny that on no account was he to come downstairs, much less open the front door. He was to stay in bed and look after Rosie until she returned.

Stella strained to hear the slightest sound, but the house was silent. A wave of dread flowed over her, and fear tightened her throat.

Her mind raced. What had possessed her to leave the children alone? If anything had happened to Danny and Rosie, her own life would be over.

A new and terrifying thought struck her. Whoever had got into the house might still be there, waiting to pounce.

She opened the door of the front room and peered inside. Everything seemed normal, as far as she could tell in the faint glimmer from the street-lamp, which showed through the lace curtains at the window.

'Stay in here, girls,' she whispered. 'I'll come back in a minute.'

'What's wrong, Auntie Stell?' one of the twins piped up.

'Ssh!' Stella hissed. 'Stay by here and be quiet.'

She crept upstairs, pausing on every stair to listen. Finally she eased herself through the door into the front bedroom. The double bed was empty, the bedclothes in disarray, and fear swelled in her heart.

Oh, God! Where were they?

Stella stood there helplessly, wringing her hands. Then a thought struck her. They might be hiding in the living room, too afraid to make a sound. She almost fell down the stairs in her hurry to find them. The room was in darkness, and Stella stumbled to the mantelpiece where she found the stub of a candle and some matches. As the candle flared into life, crazy shadows danced around the room.

'Danny!' Stella screamed. 'Danny! Rosie!' She thought she heard a faint cry, and rushed into the passage, holding the candle high. 'Danny! Where are you?' The cry came again, close by, but muffled. Suddenly, there was the sound of a feeble knocking from the small cupboard under the stairs.

It took her a moment to turn the small brass knob and open

the door. Kneeling down, she looked inside the confined space. In the candlelight two tearstained faces peered back at her.

'Danny!' Stella was overjoyed to see him. 'Rosie! What on earth happened?'

She pulled them out and held them tightly, kissing their damp faces. They clung to her, and Stella realised how much she loved them both. Rosie was as much her daughter as Danny was her son.

'It was Uncle Griff.' Danny rubbed his eyes with his knuckles.

'Uncle Griff?' Stella's blood turned to ice-water. 'He was here?'

'Rosie thirsty!'

While Stella was desperate to learn what her half-brother had been up to, she knew that the children's needs were paramount. All four had had a harrowing time and must be exhausted. She gathered the twins from the front room, lit the gas-mantle in the living room, and herded the four children in there. She poured each a glass of milk and gave them some biscuits.

Rosie was asleep before she'd finished her milk, so Stella carried her upstairs and placed her in the double bed, then told the twins to get in too and settle down. They were already asleep when Stella joined Danny in the back bedroom, in the single bed.

'How did Uncle Griff get in, Danny?' she asked him, as he snuggled close to her.

'Dunno, Mam,' Danny mumbled sleepily. 'Me and Rosie were in bed, like you told us, when Uncle Griff came in and started shouting and swearing at us. I thought he was going to kill us, so I grabbed Rosie and we ran downstairs and hid in the cupboard.'

'Did he come after you?' Stella asked, sick at the thought.

'He was stamping about for ages,' Danny said, 'but Rosie and me kept as quiet as mice.'

'How long was he here?'

'Dunno,' Danny answered, with a wide yawn. 'When he

went away we tried to get out of the cupboard but we couldn't 'cos there's no doorknob inside.'

Griff had probably been drunk, Stella thought, and certainly out of his mind to do such a thing. How often had he been in her home without her knowing about it? They weren't safe in their beds any more.

Arnie's money!

Stella sat bolt upright.

But Griff couldn't know about the money. More likely he was on the look-out for anything he could find. Had he found the stocking under the mattress? She had to know. Babs would need that money more than ever now, especially if Freda had to stay in hospital for any length of time. And if Freda died, Babs would be in dire straits.

Stella slipped into the front room quietly. The three girls were peacefully asleep. Trying not to disturb them, Stella slid a hand under the mattress and felt around.

The stocking had gone.

She crawled round to the other side of the bed, and pushed her hand under the mattress. Nothing. Arnie's hundred pounds had been stolen.

Stella sank on to her haunches, despair in her heart. She'd been robbed by her own brother.

The cold evening breeze was making her shiver but Babs hovered as the men lifted the stretcher into the ambulance. 'You coming with us, missus?' one man asked kindly.

She nodded dumbly, too distraught to speak.

'Up you go then, love.' He took her arm and helped her in. 'Casualty, Bert,' he said to his companion, 'and we'll have the bell on. Them tram drivers are as blind as bats after dark.'

Babs followed the ambulance men as they carried Freda up the steep wooden-floored corridor to Casualty, where a tall big-boned woman, wearing a dark blue dress, starched apron and cap, came forward to give Freda a cursory inspection before waving the stretcher into an adjacent room. As Babs tried to follow, the woman treated her to a cautionary frown. 'You wait there,' she instructed, pointing to wooden benches arranged in rows, 'until a nurse has time to get the patient's details from you.'

It was a long time before a young woman in a mustard-coloured uniform approached and asked questions about Freda. Babs told her everything she could, except Ted's part in the tragedy. She didn't know why she kept that back. It wasn't for Ted's sake. 'How is my mother?' she asked tearfully, as the young nurse turned to go. 'Why doesn't someone tell me?'

The girl put a comforting hand briefly on her arm. 'We're doing everything we can,' she said. 'When we're ready to explain, either Doctor or Sister Bowen will come and talk to you.' She was about to walk away then paused. 'Would you like a cup of tea?'

A little later, when Babs had drunk the tea, she felt more hopeful. Freda would pull through, she told herself, and tried to believe it. Her mother was stronger than she looked.

But what if she didn't?

The prospect of losing Freda horrified her. She'd relied on her mother more than she cared to admit. Freda had always been at her side, ready to give advice, support, and stand up for her youngest daughter in the face of violence. And look where it had got her. In hospital, with a broken head. If anything happened to Freda Babs would be alone, except for the twins. She couldn't imagine how she'd cope single-handed . . .

Babs didn't realise she'd dozed off, her head sunk on to her chest, until someone touched her arm, and she looked up, startled, to see the young nurse again. 'Your mother's been taken up to Ward Ten,' the girl said. 'You can go up now. Doctor will see you there to explain matters.' She pointed to a door. 'Go through there. It leads to the main corridor.'

Babs glanced at the clock on the wall. It was gone midnight. In the main part of the hospital the lights were dimmed; no one was about at this hour and a great hush had fallen over the building. She felt as though she were in a nightmare world.

She found Ward Ten at last, after negotiating many twisting corridors, and entered timidly, aware of the sleeping patients. A nurse bustled forward. 'My mother, Freda Price, has just been admitted,' Babs said, in a low voice. 'Can I see her?'

'We've put her in a side room,' the nurse told her, in an undertone. 'You can see her, but please be quiet. Patients are sleeping.'

Freda was pale, and looked small and frail lying in the bed under spotless sheets. Her head was bandaged, but loose hair straggled on the pillow, making her look like a child, Babs thought, with a lump in her throat.

She pulled a chair forward and sat, taking Freda's hand in hers. Her mother's flesh felt cold and dry, and Babs was filled with foreboding. Let Mam open her eyes, she prayed, in anguish. If only I can tell her I love her. Let it not be too late, let there be a second chance.

There was a soft footfall behind her. She turned her head. 'Mrs Thomas?' the nurse asked in a whisper. 'Doctor would like to speak with you in Sister's room.'

With a heavy heart, Babs followed her.

'Take a seat, Mrs Thomas. I'm Dr Mitcham.'

The doctor was young – hardly out of short trousers, it seemed to Babs.

'How is my mother, Doctor? How soon before she re-covers?' She clutched her handbag nervously, watching his face as he leaned back in the chair, toying with a pencil on the desk.

'Mrs Price's condition is serious,' he said, in a low voice. 'Apart from an extremely severe laceration of her temple, her skull is fractured. She has lapsed into a coma.'

'Oh, no! When will she wake up?'

Dr Mitcham paused, as though weighing his words.

'It's not a matter of when,' he said slowly, 'but of if, I'm afraid.'

A little cry of distress escaped Babs. Dr Mitcham leaned

towards her sympathetically. 'I wish I had better news,' he said, 'but I can hold out little hope. Her age is against her, you see.'

Although Babs struggled to control them, tears trickled down her cheeks, and she fumbled in her handbag for a handkerchief.

It couldn't be true. Not Mam.

'But she mustn't die!' she said desperately. 'Are you sure, Doctor?'

'I'm sorry, Mrs Thomas,' he said, and she knew he meant it. 'Of course, we're keeping the police informed.'

Babs gasped. 'The police?'

'Well, as I understand it,' he said soberly, 'she was attacked by your husband.'

'How did you know?' Babs asked, with a flutter of fear in her stomach. 'I didn't tell that to the nurse.'

'The police themselves and the doctor who saw Mrs Price at the scene of the attack gave us all the details.' His expression reflected surprise that she didn't understand. 'If Mrs Price does not survive,' Dr Mitcham went on, 'your husband will be in very serious trouble. He will be charged with manslaughter, at the very least.'

'Oh my God!' Babs whispered. 'To think it has come to this.'

'Mrs Thomas, why don't you go home?' Dr Mitcham suggested.

'No!' Babs was agitated. 'I must stay here and keep watch.'

'You can do no good here,' he said firmly. 'You've had a terrible shock, and should rest. And you must have a family who need you.'

'My children . . .' she murmured.

'Well, there you are. Go home,' Dr Mitcham urged, and stood up. Babs rose to her feet. 'Try to sleep,' he went on. 'Telephone tomorrow morning to find out how your mother is doing, but you must be prepared for the worst.'

Babs couldn't leave without trying one last time for a glimmer of a chance. Leaving now would be like deserting her mother. 'Is there no hope?'

'Mrs Price is in good hands,' he assured her earnestly, 'but there's nothing you can do for her yourself, believe me.'

The hours of upset were telling on Babs, and she knew she must be sensible for the sake of the twins.

The darkened streets outside the hospital were deserted, and Babs walked wearily across Hospital Square towards the Sand-fields, conscious of the hollow sound of her own footsteps on the paving-stones.

It was as though she was the only person left alive in an empty world. This is what loneliness is like, she thought. If Freda died life would be lonely, now that her family had broken up. The night was giving her a taste of what was to come.

When she reached Freda's house on Victor Street, she put the key into the lock, dreading the moment when she'd have to step into the cold, empty house. She glanced across at Stella's home.

It was in darkness, of course, and it wouldn't be fair to wake her and the children now. Stella had been in this position for almost five years and had borne the loneliness without com-plaint, Babs reminded herself. She must find the same courage.

Babs sank, exhausted, into the armchair near the lifeless range. She couldn't face going up to bed: it didn't seem right.

Pulling her coat over her shoulders, she laid her head back, and offered up a little prayer that, come morning, Freda would be awake and battling towards recovery.

A strong easterly wind, with a taste of snow in it, was blowing as Stella crossed the street to Freda's house. She opened the door, stepped inside and shivered. It was almost as cold indoors as it was out, and she wondered if she should light a fire so that the house would be warmer when Babs came home. But the twins needed clean underclothes, and she decided she must see to them first.

About to climb the stairs, she glanced through the open living-room door and was startled to see a still figure huddled in the armchair.

'Babs!' Stella ran to her friend. 'Babs, are you all right?'

Babs opened her eyes and stared up as though perplexed.

'Babs! You haven't been sitting here all night, have you?'

'What time is it?' Babs sat up with difficulty, as though her joints had seized up, then pulled the coat around herself, shivering. 'Ooh! I didn't realise how cold I'd got.'

'You should've come over to me as soon as you got back from the hospital,' Stella scolded. 'You've had nothing to eat or drink, I'll bet.'

'I didn't want to disturb anyone,' Babs replied, rubbing her arms.

'You could catch your death in this cold house,' Stella said. The moment she said the words she could've bitten off her tongue.

Babs looked towards the mantelpiece where the old clock ticked away the seconds. 'What *is* the time? I have to telephone the hospital to see how Mam is.' She stood up shakily and struggled into her coat.

'I'm going up to the telephone box in Park Street. I've got to know what's happening to her.'

'You'll sit right down again.' Stella took hold of her and forced her down into the armchair. 'I'm going to make you a cup of tea.'

'Stella, you don't understand,' Babs cried. 'My mother's in a serious condition. I've got to know.'

'You can't go out in this icy weather without food and a hot drink inside you,' Stella argued doggedly.

But seeing the misery in Babs's face, even the way she was hunched over in the chair, she understood her friend's distress. She'd gone through the same anguish with her own parents. 'Look,' she went on quickly. 'I'll go and telephone for you, if you'll go straight over to my place to stay with the children. Get some hot tea inside you and something to eat. There's plenty in the larder.'

'I should be the one to telephone,' Babs insisted, her eyes glistening. 'It's my duty. I owe it to Mam.'

'Now be sensible, Babs!' Stella exclaimed. The dark circles under Babs's eyes emphasised her exhaustion. She looked fit to drop. 'You're near breaking point, admit it,' she went on firmly.

'They won't tell you anything,' Babs persisted. 'You're not family.'

'I'll pretend I'm you,' Stella said. 'Now get across the road. It's warm there. I banked the fire up last night. The children were asleep when I popped out, but they might be up and about now. When they see I'm missing they'll be frightened after what happened with Griff . . .'

Stella was reluctant to say any more about her brother and the theft of Arnie's money. She had the feeling Babs would be angry with her for accepting the money in the first place, and she needed to choose her moment to explain.

'Griff? What's he done now?'

'I'll explain later,' Stella dismissed the matter quickly, and Babs didn't pursue it. 'Have you got some coppers for the telephone?'

Babs gave her some pennies, repeated the telephone number of the hospital twice, and Stella hurried out into the late December morning, whispering it to herself so that she did not forget it.

Within days the New Year would be upon them, but there was little to be joyous about, Stella reflected, especially for Babs with her mother in hospital and her husband in prison.

Unused to the telephone, Stella was nervous as she lifted the heavy receiver, pushed two pennies into the slot and waited for the operator's voice. 'Number, please!' a plummy voice asked.

In that split second Stella's mind went blank. 'Forgotten it, haven't I?' she said.

There was a haughty sniff at the other end. 'Press button B and clear the line, please.'

'I want the hospital!' Stella shouted. 'It's a matter of life and death!'

'Oh, all right, then.' The voice sounded more human. 'Putting you through, caller.'

The ringing was answered, but confusion almost defeated her when she couldn't make herself heard until she remembered Babs's instruction to push button A. More pennies had to be inserted before she was speaking to someone on Ward Ten. 'I'm enquiring about Freda Price . . .' Stella began.

There was silence, then murmuring at the other end of the line.

'Just a minute,' a woman's voice said clearly at last. 'Doctor wants a word with you.'

'But I'm only enquiring—' Stella said, panicking.

'Hello, Mrs Thomas,' a man's voice said. 'This is Dr Mitcham. We spoke earlier. I hope you took my advice.'

Stella decided to bluff her way through. 'Yes, indeed,' she fibbed.

'I'm glad,' he went on, 'because I have sad news for you. I'm afraid your mother died in the early hours of this morning, not an hour after you left. I'm so sorry.'

'Oh, no! It can't be true!' Stella leaned against the wall of the telephone box, trying to come to terms with the news.

Freda was gone? So quickly? It was unbelievable. How was she to tell Babs?

'I did warn you this might happen, Mrs Thomas,' Dr Mitcham went on, 'and I'm so very sorry.'

At that moment the pips sounded and Stella hastily pushed another two pennies into the box. 'Thank you,' she said.

'You can inform the undertaker,' he went on. 'However, with the unusual circumstances of your mother's death, I can't issue a death certificate until after the post-mortem and inquest.'

'Post mortem? Inquest?' Stella's voice rose in panic. 'But why?'

'We talked about this, Mrs Thomas,' Dr Mitcham said patiently. 'Your mother died from injuries sustained in an attack by your husband. This is a police matter now. The coroner's officer will be in touch with you about the formalities. The undertaker can help you with this.'

After more words of vague thanks Stella replaced the

receiver, feeling drained. What she'd feared for a long time had finally happened. Ted's violence had led him to take someone's life, and poor Babs was left to suffer the agony of it.

She was thankful it was she who'd received the terrible news, and not her friend. It would be difficult enough telling Babs of the tragedy, but at least she could do it gently, and be on hand to offer comfort.

Her friend would need more than comfort, though. Warm-hearted Babs would blame herself for this, even though Ted was responsible.

Stella's feet dragged as she walked back to Victor Street, dreading the moment when she would have to face Babs.

She let herself into her home and walked slowly into the living room, glad that the children were still upstairs.

'Is that you, Stell?' Babs dashed out of the scullery, looking eager and hopeful. 'How's Mam? Has she come out of the coma?'

'Sit down, Babs, love,' Stella said quietly. 'I've got some bad news.'

Babs's face drained of colour. 'No! Don't say it, Stell. I can't bear it.'

Stella went to her and took her in her arms.

'Come on, Babs.' She led her to the armchair. 'Sit down by here.'

Like a child, Babs allowed herself to be taken to the chair. She was shaking uncontrollably. Stella knelt on the mat beside her, holding her cold hands.

'You've been through so much these last few weeks.' She felt her heart twist in her breast at the sight of grief on her friend's on her face. 'I'm sorry to be the one to tell you this, but your mam passed away in the early hours this morning.'

'Oh, God, no. Say it isn't true.'

Stella swallowed hard. 'There's more, Babs. Brace yourself, love.'

'What?'

'There has to be a post-mortem and an inquest.'

Babs shook her head.

'The police will insist,' Stella went on. 'Freda died because of what Ted did to her. He's in big trouble now. There'll be gossip and scandal.'

She knew the power of gossip. It could tear an innocent person to shreds. Ted's wrongdoing might reflect on Babs and the children. They might be pilloried by association. People could be so cruel.

'You've got to prepare yourself for it, Babs. If only you could get away from the Sandfields for a while.'

Babs bowed her head. 'I don't give a damn about gossips,' she murmured. 'And I don't give a damn about Ted, either. He killed my mam. I hope he hangs, and may his bones rot!'

'Babs! Think of the twins.'

Babs began to weep. 'I can only think of my mam, now. I loved her, Stell. I know I was always grumbling about her, but I really loved her.'

'I know you did. And she loved you, too.'

'What time . . . did she die?'

'Less than an hour after you left.'

'I should've stayed!' Babs moaned. 'I'll never forgive myself for deserting her.'

'She wouldn't have known you were there,' Stella said. 'She never woke up.'

'But *I* know!' Babs cried. 'It's all my fault. If I hadn't left Ted this would never have happened and Mam would be alive. Oh, God, what have I done!'

'Babs, don't torture yourself like this,' Stella pleaded. 'You couldn't stay with Ted. If you had it'd be you lying dead in the mortuary sooner or later. Then what would happen to the twins?' Stella felt a great swell of sympathy. 'It's a terrible blow, kid, I know,' she said gently, 'but you've got to go on, and I'll help you.' After a minute or two, she went on, 'Poor Freda, she always did her best, and only wanted you to have a better life than she had, better than you've had so far, married to Ted. That's why you mustn't blame yourself, but move on.'

Babs pressed her lips together, trying hard to curb the tears. 'I don't know how I'll manage without her, Stell.'

Stella ran her tongue nervously over her lips before asking carefully, 'How are you going to pay for the funeral?'

Babs swallowed, straining for control. 'Mam had a penny insurance policy,' she said. 'She's been paying into it for years. Let's hope it's enough.'

Stella rose from her knees to stand near the mantelpiece. The time had come to confess about Arnie's money. Babs seemed to sense her unease because she looked up sharply, her tear-stained face white. 'Babs, there's something I have to tell you.'

'Something more about Mam, is it?'

'No, love. It's about Arnie.'

'Don't mention him at a time like this,' Babs said impatiently. 'If you're suggesting I take him up on his offer, Stella, forget it. I won't make a mockery of my vows.' Her face crumpled. 'Even if my husband is a murderer.'

'It's not that,' Stella assured her. 'The fact is, Arnie left some money with me, a hundred pounds, just in case you're short, like. He knew you wouldn't take it from him.'

Babs gaped, then recovered herself and dabbed at her reddened nose with a handkerchief. 'He's right!' she exclaimed. 'Send it back to him, Stella. I don't want it – and you had no right to accept it.'

Stella twisted her hands together. 'I can't send it back, Babs. It's been stolen . . . by Griff.'

'What?' Babs jumped up. 'My God, Stella! Why must you interfere in my life? Haven't you done enough? If you hadn't flirted with Ted in the first place, none of this would've happened. I'd still have my marriage, and Mam would be alive.'

'Babs!' Hardly able to believe what she'd just heard, Stella was wounded to the heart. 'What a terrible thing to say! And you don't believe a word of it.'

'Yes, I do,' Babs said feverishly.

'No!' Despite her sympathy for her friend Stella felt like

shaking some sense into her. 'I gave Ted no encouragement. He didn't need any. Ask *her* down in Carogwen Terrace.'

Babs recoiled, and Stella was filled with regret for raking that up. They shouldn't be quarrelling at a time like this. 'I'm sorry, Babs, so sorry, but I've been through hell too,' she said. 'I'm no more to blame than you are.'

Babs stared at her for a moment, then flung herself into the chair, hiding her face in her hands. 'Stell, I'm sorry.' She sobbed bitterly, hunched over in the chair. 'I don't know what I'm saying, I'm that upset. Mam's been killed, my marriage is over, my life is falling apart. Someone's to blame, so it *must* be me.'

Stella went to her, put an arm around her shoulders, and tried to ease the great sobs that racked her. 'Perhaps it's not even Ted's fault,' she said. 'It's just fate, playing havoc with our lives.'

She let Babs cry for a while, knowing the grief had to be released somehow. After a while she patted her friend's shoulder. 'Come on,' she said. 'I've got a drop of port put away. We'll have half a glass each now. We both need it. Besides, we've a lot to talk about.'

'Port! At this time of the morning?' Babs wiped her nose. 'You're living high off the hog, aren't you?' She was clearly trying to sound more herself.

'Christmas present from Arnie, bless him,' Stella said. 'It'll be there until next Christmas if we don't drink it.'

She went to fetch the bottle, and poured two measures. Babs lifted her glass to her lips then hesitated. 'Stell, we shouldn't drink this before breakfast. We'll be squiffy.'

'First time for everything,' Stella said philosophically. 'Let's drink to Freda, God bless her.'

There were fresh tears in Babs's eyes as she raised her glass again.

'You can't stay in your mam's house now,' Stella remarked later, as they washed up the breakfast things, with the children playing in the living room.

'Why not?'

'It's unlikely the landlord will make over the tenancy to you since you've been there only a day.'

'Oh, my God! What am I going to do, Stell? Me and the kids are homeless!'

'You can move back in next door.'

The plate Babs was wiping slipped from her fingers and clattered on to the draining-board. 'I'll never live there with him again!' she said heatedly. 'I'd rather go up Mount Pleasant to the workhouse.'

'Ted'll never come back to that house,' Stella said. 'If he isn't charged with murder, then it'll be manslaughter. So it's either prison for a long stretch or he'll be hanged.'

'I want to see him hanged!' Babs said vehemently. 'Perhaps it's wicked to say that, but I can't help it.'

She leaned against the draining-board, her eyes closed, as though shutting out a terrible image. 'I never thought I'd feel such loathing for the father of my children.'

Stella thought about Eddie then. Even though he'd deserted her, and saddled her with his unwanted responsibility, she didn't hate him for it. Instead she was aware of a growing indifference to him. With a shock she realised she no longer loved him, and if he returned tomorrow, pleading to come back to her, she'd refuse him without a second's hesitation.

Despite the sadness of the moment, Stella experienced a lightening of her heart and a sense of freedom at the knowledge that Eddie no longer mattered. Love was strange, she reflected. It came and went, and sometimes you weren't even aware of it.

She knew one thing for sure: she'd be wary of love in the future.

'Next door is yours, Babs,' she went on. 'The landlord doesn't know you've left Ted. Move back in straight away, then perhaps the tenancy will pass automatically to you. You'll have to show you can pay the rent, mind, so find a job soon.'

Get a job! Giving that advice was easy enough, Stella reflected, but it could take weeks. Without Arnie's money to help out, Babs and the children would be thrown out on the streets, homeless in the cruel winter weather.

Grimly, Stella made up her mind that she couldn't let it happen. She'd find Griff, wherever he was, confront him with his thievery and force him to give back the money. She'd threatened him with the police many times, but now if he refused she was determined to give him up.

Chapter Twenty-Three

Everyone knew Griff Stroud was trouble of the worst kind, and finding him proved more difficult than Stella had anticipated, yet she was certain he was in the area.

She enquired of the husbands of several neighbours along Victor Street, and even knocked on a few doors along Carogwen Terrace, only to be met with harsh words and doors slammed in her face. No one wanted truck with Griff Stroud or any of his family.

The weather was getting colder, with snow threatening. Earlier she'd helped Babs and the twins return next door, and had lent her friend enough to pay a week's rent. Gossip had probably already informed the rent man that Ted was in prison but a week's money might persuade him that Babs was a viable tenant in his stead. Stella fervently hoped so.

She said nothing to Babs of searching for Griff, to get back the money, or what was left of it. Her friend would only remind her of how foolhardy her mission was, and Stella was well aware of the dangers in confronting her half-brother with his criminal pals. But she was riddled with guilt that her carelessness had made Babs destitute.

After an hour or two of fruitless search that afternoon, she was tempted to return home to her tea. Then she remembered something Mrs Ridd had told her, that Griff was friendly with one particular criminal, Tommy Parsons. If her memory served her right, he lived on Ysbyty Street, in a maze of drab alleys that stretched as far as the prison.

Stella quailed at the idea of walking in that area by daylight, never mind after dark, but she was no more than ten minutes away from it, her conscience reminded her, and it was her brother's thievery that might condemn Babs to the workhouse.

There seemed to be a pub on every corner, and they were already busy. Stella passed them with her heart in her mouth, unnerved by the raucous laughter and singing. Sounds couldn't hurt her, she told herself sternly. She should be more wary of shadowy figures lurking in shop doorways.

A street-lamp illuminated a dingy sign on the side of a house, and she realised she'd found Ysbyty Street. The houses were overshadowed by the high grim walls of the prison.

Stella walked slowly along, at a loss to know which was the right house.

A fat woman, wearing a shapeless coat, emerged suddenly from an open door, dragging a wailing youngster by the hand. 'Stop howling, you little perisher,' the woman shouted, at the top of her voice, 'or I'll clout you again.'

Stella seized her chance. 'Excuse me,' she began.

'Eh?' The woman stopped short, peering at her in the lamplight. She wasn't that much older than Stella, but her features were bloated, and she looked unkempt and worn. 'What you want?' the woman asked belligerently.

'I'm looking for Tommy Parsons,' Stella said. 'Do you know him?'

The woman pulled in her quivering chin, a challenging look in her eyes. 'I might do. What you want him for, then?'

'That's my business,' Stella said. 'Do you know him or not?'

The woman wiped her knuckle across her squat nose, then down the front of her coat.

'No need to get stroppy,' she said. 'Course, I know him, you stupid cow. I'm his wife, aren't I? Now, then, what do you want with my hubby?'

Stella was too surprised to reply for a moment, and Tommy's

wife found that suspicious. 'Now, look here,' she blustered, 'not one of his flipping working girls, are you?' She scowled. 'Cos if you are, you can bugger off from by here. Tommy knows better than to bring home any of his women.'

Stella grasped her meaning. 'No, I am not!' she cried. 'Anyway, it's not your husband I want to see. I'm looking for my brother, Griff Stroud.'

Tommy's wife took a step back. 'Griff? That madman?'

'Where is he?' Stella interrupted, her stomach turning over at the look of fear on the woman's face.

Tommy's wife was looking at her suspiciously again. 'What do you want to know for? Did the bobbies send you?'

'Don't be daft!' Stella exclaimed. 'I'm not interested in what he and Tommy get up to. I just want to talk him. Family business. Where is he?'

Tommy's wife glanced furtively over her shoulder towards the house from which she'd just come out. Stella was suddenly alert.

'Er . . . down the Archer's pub,' Tommy's wife said belligerently. 'You know, down by the docks. There for hours they'll be, so you'd better clear off, missus.'

'You're lying!' Stella said. 'He's in here, isn't he? Is that where you live?'

Without waiting for an answer, Stella stepped round the woman and the child, and strode to the door. She hesitated on the step. A dank smell of damp and dry rot, but mostly neglect, wafted towards her along the dark passage. It was far from inviting.

'Hey! Wait a minute!' Tommy's wife shouted. 'You got no right barging in by here, you haven't. Now bugger off!'

'I must see Griff,' Stella insisted, trying to force her way past the stout woman. Desperately, she shouted down the passage, 'Griff! It's Stella.'

A short, heavy-shouldered man of stocky build lumbered into sight, faintly illuminated by gas-light from the back room. A couple of days' growth of bristles covered his cheeks, and his small piggy eyes glinted. 'What's all this shouting, Maisie?'

Maisie Parsons hooked a stubby thumb towards Stella.

'It's her, mun, Tommy. I told her to push off, but she won't. Wants to see Griff.'

'He's not here,' Tommy Parsons said tersely, 'so sling your hook, missus.' He disappeared into a back room.

'You heard him,' Maisie said, trying to force Stella back on to the pavement. 'Push off.'

But Stella resisted: having come this far she was determined not to budge. Babs needed that money and it was her duty to get it back.

'Griff!' Stella yelled, forcing her way past Maisie and into the passage. 'I'll call the bobbies, if you don't face me.'

A storm of cursing issued from the back room, and Tommy Parsons came out again, barring Stella's way. Close to, he was an unpleasant figure: under the bristles, his face was red with rage, and Stella's knees trembled at the vicious look in his eyes. All the stories she'd heard about Charlie Pendle and his murdering cronies came to mind.

'Get out!' shouted Tommy.

'I want to see my brother.' Stella stood her ground. 'You can't stop me.'

'I'll stop you, all right, stop you for good,' Tommy threatened.

Stella didn't move but braced herself to turn and run if he attacked her.

Her stubbornness enraged him. '*Myn uffern i!*' he growled. 'You're asking for it, you are, and you're going to get it.'

He raised an arm, fist clenched. But the blow was not struck. There was a swift movement behind him, and his arm was forced down. 'If there's any bashing to be done, Tommy,' Griff said savagely, 'I'll do it myself.'

He looked even rougher and more unkempt than she remembered. Evidently he hadn't spent the money on himself. In her heart she held little hope that he'd return the money, but she had to try. She owed it to Babs, and besides she was determined to challenge him for stealing from her. Yet, she quailed, realising the danger she was in.

'She's going to call the bobbies,' Tommy snarled.

'She's all talk,' Griff said. 'Leave this to me.'

He turned his gaze on Stella. 'Now, what are you doing here?'

'I think you know, Griff,' she said. 'You took . . .' She tailed off, aware of Tommy and Maisie standing by, taking in every word. 'You took something from my house last night while I was out. I want it back. It doesn't belong to me.'

Griff laughed scornfully. 'You think I'm *twp* enough to fall for that one?'

'What's she on about, Griff?' Tommy asked, looking from brother to sister.

Griff's expression hardened. 'I dunno,' he said offhandedly. 'Talking through the back of her neck, as usual. I wasn't anywhere near her house last night.'

'Griff!' There was a warning note in Tommy's voice. 'You haven't been working on the side, have you? You know what Charlie does to blokes who double-cross him.'

'I don't know what she's talking about, I tell you!' Griff grated. 'Now clear off, Tommy, and take that useless fat piece with you. I want to talk to my sister in private.' Griff's glare was so malevolent, that Tommy clearly thought better of arguing with him. He gave Maisie a rough push towards the back room, and they both disappeared, the grizzling child following in their wake.

Stella was about to speak again, but Griff silenced her with a warning shake of his head. He took out a key, unlocked the door of what in any other house would have been the parlour, and shepherded her inside. Match-light flared briefly to ignite the gas-mantle, then Griff closed the door.

There was no furniture in the room, while a blanket covered the window. Tea-chests were stacked around the walls on all sides, leaving just a small area in the middle to stand. Stella felt claustrophobic. 'What kind of a place is this? What've you got in those tea-chests?'

'Mind your own business!' Griff said brusquely. 'You'll forget you saw this, if you know what's good for you. I mean it, Stella. Forget you were ever here. Got that?'

'Wouldn't be here at all, would I, if you hadn't stolen that money from me?' she said. 'How could you rob your own sister?'

'Keep your voice down. Tommy'd slit my throat in a minute for that kind of moolah.'

Stella shivered, and looked around with distaste. 'This house is filthy, disgusting! How can you live here?'

'What choice did you leave me?' he answered sharply. 'You kicked me out, remember.'

'Do you wonder?' Stella flashed back. 'The kind of people you associate with, the way you carried on, smashing up the only bit of home I've got.'

'You'd better go,' he said, pushing her towards the door. 'It's not healthy for the likes of you around here.'

'No! I came to get the money back, and I'm not going until I do.'

'Listen, you silly bitch, I didn't take any money. I wasn't there.'

'You were, you liar!' Stella cried out. 'You frightened the children half to death.'

Griff's lips thinned. 'I told you to get rid of Eddie's bastard, didn't I?'

'Rosie's none of your concern,' Stella said. 'And your wasting time, Griff. Give me the money, now.'

He turned away, unperturbed, and began rummaging in one of the tea-chests. Again Stella wondered what was hidden there: probably stolen goods or some other ill-gotten gains.

'The money, Griff. It belongs to Babs. A . . . friend left it for her. She needs it now Ted's in prison. You must've heard Freda died because of Ted Thomas.'

He turned back to her, wearing an unpleasant smirk. 'You can earn more,' he said. 'There's plenty where that came from.'

264

'I didn't earn it, I tell you,' Stella answered impatiently. 'How could I? I don't get much of a wage as an usherette.'

'Usherette? That's a new name for it.'

'Griff, Babs needs that money to live,' Stella persisted. 'She's desperate.'

'Then let her earn it flat on her back, same as you did,'

'What?'

'There's only one way a woman can get hold of so much money,' he barked at her, 'so don't try to kid me, Stella.'

'Listen, Griff,' she snapped, 'the money was given into my keeping by Arnie, my lodger, for Babs, because he knew she'd be in need some day. Now your thieving will put her and her kids in the workhouse.'

'You must think I'm daft to believe a story like that,' he said scornfully. 'No one gives that kind of money away for nothing.'

'Arnie's a gentleman,' Stella retorted. 'But that's like the man-in-the-moon to *your* kind, isn't it?'

Griff gave a bitter chuckle. 'Gentleman, my arse! All men are after one thing, and that bloody actor of yours is no different.'

'You've lived among scum like Tommy so long,' Stella blurted out, 'you've forgotten there are some decent people in the world.' Then, suddenly, she fell sorry for him. She stepped closer to him, laid a hand against his chest. 'Oh, Griff, look where you've fallen – into the gutter.'

Griff knocked away her hand, his features like granite. 'Whose fault is that?' he snarled. 'You did me down, Stella, cheated me. That money is mine. You owe me.'

Her pity evaporated, and anger bubbled in her breast. She'd get nowhere arguing with him. And if she didn't best him now he'd think he could come to her house whenever he liked and take whatever he wanted. Neither she nor the children would be safe in their own home. 'Fed up with this, I am, Griff,' she cried. 'If you don't hand over Babs's money now, this minute, I'll go up to the police station in Alexandra Road first thing tomorrow and give you over.'

GWEN MADOC

He dipped his head, looking at her through his eyelashes. He said nothing. He didn't need to. His expression said it all.

Stella bristled at his indifference. 'Oh, yes, I know! Threatened that more than once, haven't I? This time I mean it, Griff. I swear on . . . on Dad's grave that I'll give you up for a thief.'

The smile was wiped from his lips at the mention of their father. 'Black treachery, that is,' he snarled. 'You're a hard bitch to do that to your own brother.'

'Call me any name you like, Griff,' Stella lifted her chin bravely, 'it doesn't change anything. You believe I owe you a life, but I don't. It wasn't me who crippled you or made Rose leave you.'

'Why, you—' Griff lifted his one arm, fist clenched. 'I ought to smash you one for that.'

'Well, go ahead, then! Assault as well as thieving. You'll get ten years next time.'

They stared at each other, but before either could speak again the door burst open and Tommy Parsons stood there, his fat wife peering wide-eyed over his shoulder. 'Are you out of your mind, Griff, showing her this?' Tommy bellowed, sweeping a hand around at the tea-chests. 'She'll gab to the coppers and we'll all be done for. You bloody fool, Charlie'll kill us – stick us, like pigs!'

'Get out, Tommy!' Griff shouted back. 'This is none of your business. She's not telling nobody nothing.'

'Too right, she's not,' Tommy yelled, and plunged forward into the narrow confines of the room, ''cos I'm going to do for her good and proper, so don't try to stop me.'

Without warning, and with lightning speed, Griff smashed his fist into Tommy's face, sending him reeling back into the passage to land heavily on his rump, while Maisie fled, screaming.

Tommy sat on the floor, his hand to his face. Dazed, he stared up at Griff, his eyes watering.

'Warned you before, haven't I, Tommy?' Griff snarled. 'Keep your nose out of my business. You'll live longer.'

266

'She'll blab!' Tommy bleated plaintively. 'Got to shut her up.'

'She won't blab,' Griff said confidently. 'She won't dare, because I've got the goods on her, see.' He kicked at Tommy's outstretched leg. 'Now, make yourself scarce, Tommy, before I forget we're pals.'

Griff shut the door as Tommy scrambled to his feet. Stella heard him lumbering down the passage to the back room, shouting for Maisie. Stella hoped the woman had the sense to disappear until her husband had calmed down.

'How can you live with these people?' she asked. 'The squalor and violence. Dad would be so ashamed of you, Griff.'

'Shut up!' Griff growled. 'Don't mention our father to me. He's dead and out of it.' He struck his chest with a closed fist. 'I'm alive and have to go on living somehow, any way I can. And that won't be for much longer unless I can square Charlie.'

'Not with Babs's money,' Stella said stubbornly. 'I meant what I said, Griff. I *will* give you up to the police if you don't hand it over.'

He grabbed her wrist, twisting her arm, and Stella cried out in pain. 'Griff! You're hurting me.'

'Hurt?' he snarled. 'You don't know what hurt is, but you'll find out if you don't keep your mouth shut about that money.'

With a grunt he let her go, and Stella rubbed her wrist, reddened by the pressure of his fingers. 'I don't know you any more,' she said, in a half-whisper, afraid of him. 'You're like some wild animal. What's happened to you, Griff?'

'Don't be so bloody stupid,' he growled. 'I live among wolves so I have to be one. I didn't ask for this.' He indicated his empty sleeve. 'I do what I must.'

'Even if it means robbing your own sister? I'm not frightened of you. I'll do what I must, too.'

A single tea-chest stood near the door. Griff sat on the edge of it, gazing at her with a smugness that made Stella shift uneasily from one foot to the other. She didn't like his sudden change of attitude, as though he'd already won the battle between them.

'You'll do nothing,' he said confidently. 'You've got too much to lose to get mixed up with the police – like your freedom, if not your life.'

Stella took a step back from him. He looked as if he really meant the threats.

'You're as bad as Tommy,' she said, a catch in her throat. 'Worse. I'm a stranger to him, but you're my brother.'

'Oh, *I* won't take your life. I'll leave that to the authorities. All nice and legal.'

'What do you mean?'

'I know what happened, Stella. I was there.'

'What?' Stella was puzzled.

'I was in the theatre the afternoon that flashy actor bloke died,' Griff went on, an unpleasant smile on his face. 'It was like watching a play.'

He lifted his arm, his hand making a sweeping downward motion, like a bird taking a dive. At the same time he made a whistling sound through his teeth. 'Then . . . splat!' He grimaced. 'Nasty!'

Stella stood perfectly still, unable to move. Her heart felt as heavy as stone. 'It was you all the time!' she muttered at last.

'Strewth,' Griff said chattily. 'You climbed that ladder like your arse was on fire. Why you bothered, I don't know. You could've made a mint out of him.'

'You saw him fall? Then you know it was an accident.'

Suddenly she was chilled right through and her teeth were chattering. She'd known someone had been there that afternoon, but she'd never dreamed it was Griff.

'What were you doing there, any way? Spying on me?'

'I needed money, what else,' he growled, 'I saw it all. If I get what I want, then it remains an accident as far as the bobbies are concerned. If not, well, I'll tell them I saw you push him. It was murder, cold-blooded and calculating.'

'The coroner declared it an accident at the inquest,' Stella responded quickly, trying to sound calm, but she could remember Inspector Edwards's suspicious questions.

'Yes, but I know that the bobbies aren't happy with that, because they couldn't account for his being on the catwalk. New information would probably reopen the case.'

'What new information?'

'A witness who saw you push him.' He smiled thinly. 'Whether they call it murder or manslaughter, it's curtains for you, Stella. And both your brats will end up in children's homes.'

'You wouldn't do that to me surely, Griff,' Stella cried out passionately. 'It's not human.'

Griff stood up abruptly.

'I want fifty per cent of what you make from your lucrative little sideline. I can even throw some trade your way. Charlie's got connections, businessmen, mind you, not trash, who'd like to meet someone like you. Be nice to them, show them a good time, and we could be rolling in it.'

'I'm not on the game, Griff, never have been and never will be!' Stella shouted. 'There's no pot of gold at the end of the rainbow.'

She stared at him defiantly, and finally his glance slid away from hers.

'You *know* full well it is not true,' Stella said triumphantly. 'You just wish it were. It would suit your purpose.'

'Don't defy me, Stella,' Griff retorted, rallying. 'On the game or not, you'll play it my way from now on, or the coppers will get your name. You'll lose your home, your kids and your life. Think about that.'

'Babs's money—'

'Get out!' Griff bellowed. He wrenched open the door, grabbed her arm and bundled her into the passage. 'Make the most of your freedom, Stella, because it won't last long unless you see reason. I'll be round your house day after tomorrow. There'd better be more money for me. Understand?' He shoved her out on to the pavement and slammed the door.

Stella ran as though for her life, tripping and stumbling over loosened paving stones in her haste to get away.

When she was clear of Ysbyty Street a wave of relief swept over her. When she was nearer the town centre, she'd feel safer still.

Hurrying along Morag Street, she was startled when a bulky figure suddenly stepped out of a shop doorway on to the pavement ahead. Just another drunk, she thought, trying to calm her jangling nerves, gone in there to relieve himself, but as the figure moved closer, Stella had a shock.

It was Tommy Parsons!

He stood in front of her, and Stella came to an abrupt stop. 'Let me pass, Tommy.'

'*Mr Parsons* to you,' he snarled. 'Thought you'd get away easy, did you?'

'What do you mean?'

Stella stepped into the gutter to dodge round him, but he moved too.

The skin all over her body prickled and instinct told her that Tommy Parsons was a dangerous man, perhaps even more dangerous than Griff.

'You know well enough,' he grated. 'You sly cat.'

Stella clutched her handbag to her chest. 'No, I don't know. What do you want?'

She couldn't keep the fear from her voice, and she knew that Tommy, like the animal he was, would hear it and act on it.

'Got an eyeful tonight, didn't you?' he said harshly, his eyes glittering in the evidence of her fear of him. 'Saw things you shouldn't.'

'I saw nothing!' Stella cried, in panic.

'You know too bloody much, and that's a fact. That brother of yours might trust you, but I don't, see.'

Stella's terror mounted. 'Tommy . . . Mr Parsons, I swear to you, I don't know what you're talking about. I had urgent family business with Griff, that's all. Please let me pass now.'

He snorted. 'You're going nowhere, missus. Blabbing to the coppers is a capital offence where I come from. Gets you a throat slit from ear to ear.'

Stella quelled a scream. She mustn't lose her nerve or she'd be done for. Tommy Parsons meant business. 'I haven't blabbed,' she said, through chattering teeth, 'and I won't.'

He took his hand out of his pocket. Something steely flashed in the faint light from a nearby street-lamp, and Stella's heart almost stopped. A knife. 'I won't blab, Mr Parsons!' She gibbered, eyeing the blade. 'I promise. Please believe me!'

'Too right, you won't, you mouthy piece,' he snarled. He grasped her arms, and Stella almost choked on the stench of neglect and liquor that rose from him. She struggled but he overpowered her easily. He tried to spin her round so that he'd be behind her, her throat exposed to the blade.

Stella fought wildly, hysteria rising. He really was going to kill her. He'd slit her throat, right here in the street, and she'd die in a filthy gutter.

Stella began to scream like a banshee, blood-curdling screams that began deep in her belly, powered by horror and fear. Frantically, she resisted his attempt to get behind her, beating at his face and chest with feeble fists. 'Let me go, you murdering beast!'

He cursed as he tried to subdue her. 'Finish you here and now, I will,' he snarled, his rancid breath making her feel sick. 'You copper's nark.'

He finally manoeuvred himself behind her, grabbed her hair and yanked her head back. The knife was poised to strike.

In one last desperate act of self-preservation, Stella kicked backwards with her remaining strength. The heel of her shoe caught him on one ankle.

He roared like a maddened bull, and dropped the knife. It clattered to the pavement, and spun into the gutter. Furious, he swung her round and slapped her face with the back of his hand, a stinging blow. 'Take that, you bitch!' he growled. 'And that's just for starters.'

Stella felt something slice into her cheek, and screamed hysterically, not knowing whether she'd been cut with a knife.

Terror like she'd never known before powered her, and she

screamed anew, with a final plea for deliverance. 'Help! Help! Murder!'

As though in answer to her prayer, a piercing police whistle sounded, then again, and heavy boots raced closer with each second that passed.

Tommy Parsons released her and looked furtively over his shoulder. 'You're lucky this time,' he snarled, 'but I'll get you.'

He glanced back again at the sound of running feet coming ever closer. 'Soon shake 'em off,' he said confidently. 'And don't forget, I know where you live, you and your kids.' He made a slashing gesture across his own throat with the inside edge of his hand, a malignant glitter in his eyes. 'Get at you, I can, all of you, any time I want to, see?'

Past his shoulder under a far street-lamp Stella saw the figure of a policeman skid around the corner into Morag Street. Another joined him from across the opposite corner, both charging forward.

'Help!' Stella yelled at the top of her voice, waving frantically at the pair racing towards her.

With an obscene curse, Tommy snatched up his knife and ran in the opposite direction as if all hell was after him.

Stella's knees were about to give way now that the danger had passed, so she staggered to the window-sill of a nearby house and perched there.

One policeman dashed past her, straining at top speed after Tommy Parsons, while the second pulled up sharply to look at her. 'Careful!' Stella managed to call out after the running man. 'He's got a knife.'

'Are you all right, missus?' the officer asked, still panting from effort. 'If you are, I'm going to help my mate.' He peered into her face. 'You're bleeding!'

'It hurts, too,' Stella said, almost in tears.

'Do you know who attacked you?'

She could expose Tommy, help to put him away where he couldn't hurt her or the children, but that would mean exposing her brother, and she knew she daren't do it. Griff wouldn't hesitate to implicate her in Monty's death if only out of revenge. 'No,' she said. 'Never saw him before. He was trying to rob me, I think.'

'I see,' the policeman said. 'A knife attack on a defenceless woman in an attempted robbery, eh? This is very serious, this is. Wait by here, missus,' he said, 'until we get back with our prisoner. We'll want all the details.' He ran off after his colleague.

Watching him go, Stella thought of the night Griff had accosted her. The police had taken her name and address then. They'd hardly believe it was a coincidence that she had been attacked a second time. They'd be suspicious. She mustn't be identified. If she was questioned again she might be linked with the death at the theatre. She couldn't risk it.

Besides, if Tommy gave the police the slip, and they didn't come to arrest him, he'd know she had been telling the truth and that she wasn't a copper's nark.

As soon as the policeman was out of sight, Stella jumped up, new fear propelling her legs. She ran though the streets, afraid to slow down, afraid even to look over her shoulder, and was exhausted by the time she reached Victor Street.

Babs was standing outside looking agitated. Stella almost fell through the door. 'Bolt the door, Babs!' she cried.

'Stella! Whatever's the matter?'

'Bolt the door! Quick!'

Babs did as she was asked, then stared at Stella wide-eyed. 'Where have you been, Stell? I've been worried sick. You've been gone for hours.'

'Danny and Rosie?' asked Stella, panting. 'Are they all right?'

'Course they are. In bed upstairs, aren't they?' Babs said. 'The twins, too. I didn't know what to do when you didn't come home. I thought it best.'

'You did right,' Stella said. 'We mustn't leave them alone for a moment.'

'What?'

Stella was struggling with her coat. Suddenly she felt weak.

She let Babs help her, then sank into the armchair. Her heart was still pounding, her mind in turmoil. She could hardly believe what had happened earlier.

'Stella!' Babs cried. 'Your cheek's bleeding!'

'Oh, Babs,' Stella sobbed, unable to catch her breath.

'What happened?' Babs asked, and sat down on a wooden chair near the fireplace.

Stella was reluctant now to reveal her foolhardiness. 'I went to find Griff, to get your money back.'

Babs's mouth tightened. 'I told you, Stella, it's not *my* money. I want no part of it. Why do you keep interfering?'

Stella felt angry at her friend's ingratitude, after all the horror she'd just gone through. 'There's stubborn you are, Babs,' she said sharply. 'And you can't afford to be proud. You're flat broke.'

'I'll manage.'

'Oh, will you?' Stella snapped. 'Ted's in prison. He can't help you even if he wanted to. You've got no job. You've got a roof over your head only by the skin of your teeth, and that's only for this week.'

'Something will turn up.'

'Let's pray it does, because Griff won't part with the money, denies he ever took it. He – threatened me.'

'Did he cut your cheek?'

'No, that was Tommy Parsons, Griff's crony,' she said carefully. 'He thinks I'll blab to the bobbies about him and Griff. He caught me in Morag Street and hit me but, thank God, the bobbies came and chased him away.'

Babs was looking frightened again. 'He won't come here, will he?'

Stella put shaking fingers to her mouth. 'I don't know, Babs. We'll have to be careful. Look, stay in by here tonight,' she said. 'We won't disturb the kids at this late hour. You can sleep in the back bedroom. I'll manage on the chair.'

She needed company tonight after what she'd been through, and looked at Babs appealingly.

'Good idea, Stell,' Babs said. 'Better bathe your cheek with some salt water, kid.'

The armchair wasn't very comfortable for a night's rest, but Stella drew the blanket over herself thankfully. She wasn't alone, thank heavens, and she was in her own home.

She could so easily be lying dead in a gutter with a gash in her throat. It was pure luck that she wasn't. Yet at this very moment Tommy Parsons could be somewhere nearby, watching, waiting for the right moment to attack.

Chapter Twenty-Four

On the day of Freda's funeral it rained heavily and chilling winds blew. It was a small gathering, just a few husbands and sons of close neighbours attending. Babs had wanted to go, even though women folk were not expected to do so. Funerals were the prerogative of men. Stella persuaded her against it, not only because attending would flout custom, but because she'd be wet through, chilled to the bone, and it might be too much for her. Freda's insurance policy had provided just enough to cover the funeral expenses, but not enough to pay another week's rent.

Stella sat in the living room of Babs's house with her friend, the table laid out with ham sandwiches and a few fairy cakes. It wasn't much of a send-off for poor old Freda, but it was all they could afford.

'The landlord's agent, Mr Perkins, said I must get rid of Mam's furniture by next Friday, and be out of her house,' Babs said tearfully. 'It'll break my heart, Stell.'

'I know,' Stella said sympathetically, 'but at least the furniture will bring in rent money for a few weeks more. You'll need to look for a job, Babs, love. You can't put it off much longer.'

'I know, but what can I do? I'm not good at anything.'

'You're a good cook,' Stella reminded her loyally. 'Why not do a bit of private cooking? You could advertise yourself as an occasional cook.'

Babs looked doubtful. 'Am I good enough?' She shrugged. 'Anyway, wouldn't know where to start, would I?'

'I've got an idea,' Stella said eagerly. 'Why not put a card in the window of a shop in the Uplands. Lots of posh houses up there, ladies having dinner parties, and all that. Go on, mun, try it.'

'I shouldn't be thinking of this now, not on the day of Mam's funeral,' Babs said.

'Listen,' Stella said, 'if Freda was here she'd be right at your elbow this minute, telling you not to be so *twp*.' Stella touched her friend's arm. 'Besides, Babs, she's gone, but you and the children are alive. You've got to soldier on.'

Babs gave a great sigh, and squared her shoulders. 'You're right, Stell. I'll go up the Uplands tomorrow morning, first thing.' She looked hesitantly at Stella. 'Could you lend me thru' pence to put the card in the window for a week?'

Stella took her purse off the sideboard. 'Here's sixpence, love,' she said. 'Put it in for a fortnight.'

Three or four mornings later when she was cleaning her parlour window Stella saw a large black motor-car moving slowly along Victor Street. It stopped outside Babs's house and, to Stella's astonishment, a man wearing a chauffeur's uniform got out and knocked at Babs's door.

Stella craned her neck, trying to see what was happening. Babs came out on to the pavement, hands smoothing her flowered pinafore. At the behest of the chauffeur, she tottered towards the car and spoke to someone through an open window.

Stella's mouth dropped open when the door swung open and Babs stepped inside. She was out of sight for a good ten minutes, and Stella was almost climbing the walls with curiosity.

Finally, she emerged and stood on the pavement, while the big black motor-car moved away down the street. When she turned towards Stella's house, she was beaming. Stella dashed down the passage to open the front door.

'Stell!' she screeched. 'You'll never guess what's happened.'

'What?'

'Did you see that motor-car? Wasn't it posh?'

'Well, who was it? Go on, mun, tell me!'

'Mrs Prosser-Watkins from Eaton Crescent, a really posh lady. Wants me to cook for her dinner parties, two evenings a week. Good plain food, she said, that's all she wants.'

'What's she paying?' Stella asked, determined to be practical.

Babs was ecstatic. 'Oh, Stell, I can hardly believe it. A guinea a time. Imagine that! And she said there might be more. Often her guests tip the cook if they've really enjoyed the meal.'

Stella threw her arms around her friend and hugged her. 'Babs! You're made! You'll get lots of engagements now, you'll see.'

Babs burst into tears and began to sob uncontrollably.

'Now, now!' Stella said, and led her to the living room. 'Let's have a cuppa to celebrate.'

When Babs's tears had subsided, Stella thought she should sound a note of caution. 'Babs, you must be prepared to face the consequences of Ted's trial over the coming weeks or months.'

'I don't care what happens to him, I tell you,' Babs declared bitterly. 'I never want to see him again.'

'Of course not, but you're his wife,' Stella pointed out, 'and mud sticks. Mrs Prosser-Watkins probably has lots of posh friends, and when they realise how good a cook you are, you'll be in demand. Don't let on that Ted Thomas is anything to do with you. Make out you're a widow.'

Babs's plump face fell. 'Hate telling lies, I do,' she murmured. 'They always come back to smack you in the face when you least expect it.'

'Yes, but something good is starting in your life, Babs. Don't let Ted ruin that for you, too.'

Babs sniffed, then nodded. 'You're right, Stell. Got to be sensible, I have. I can't afford principles, can I?'

Stella fingered her chin thoughtfully. They were both facing a much bigger problem now. Who would look after the children when they were both out at work in the evenings?

'We've got to organise something for the children,' Stella said. 'Babs, would you mind my kids sleeping in your house from now on?'

Babs looked puzzled. 'Of course not, but why?'

'Well, I'll be at the theatre and you'll be out cooking, and I'm still worried about Tommy Parsons,' Stella explained. 'With all the kids sleeping under one roof, we can share the cost of someone to mind them.'

'Oh, that's a good idea,' Babs said. 'But who?'

'Leave it to me,' Stella said, tapping the side of her nose. 'I've got an idea.'

The next morning, before she slipped down to the corner shop for a loaf, Stella went across the street and knocked on the door of number nine.

Mrs Siddons answered. Her wispy hair was done up in metal curlers, her head half covered by a scarf. There was a smudge of black-lead across her rather long nose. 'What you want? Oh, it's you, Stella.'

'Can I come in a minute?'

Mrs Siddons looked doubtful. Stella wasn't surprised: her neighbour was cannily close about her own doings, but poked her nose into other people's business readily enough. A nosy-parker, Freda had always called her, but Stella, in need, was willing to be charitable.

'You caught me black-leading my grate.'

'So I see,' Stella said. 'But I want to talk to you about a bit of work.' Standing on the doorstep, Stella looked left and right. 'It's a bit private, like,' she said, in an intriguing whisper.

Mrs Siddons's eyes sparked with interest, and she opened the door wider. 'Well, come in then, but don't look at the place 'cos it's upside-down.'

Stella followed the older woman through to the living room. Newspapers were spread out over the mat in front of the range where a tin of black-lead and a brush lay. Everything else was as neat as a new pin.

Mrs Siddons didn't suggest they sat down. 'How did the

funeral go?' she asked. 'How's Babs?'

'Bearing up,' Stella answered shortly.

Freda's funeral had taken place well over a week ago, Stella thought Mrs Siddons's enquiry was well overdue.

'Terrible thing, wasn't it?' Mrs Siddons cocked her head. 'What was it all about, then? Mind you, I could hear him shouting that night from in by here, but couldn't catch the words, like.'

Angered, Stella bit back a sharp retort, remembering her scheme and the part she hoped Mrs Siddons would play in it. 'About this work,' she said pointedly. 'Wondered if you'd like to earn a few extra shillings each week.'

'Doing what?' Mrs Siddons sounded suspicious. 'I do cleaning down the Cricketer's pub most mornings, see.'

'It's evening work,' Stella assured her. 'Child-minding, for me and Babs.'

Mrs Siddons's brow furrowed, and her tone was sharp and accusing.

'And what will you and her be doing while I'm minding your kids?'

Stella held her temper. She was in no doubt that her neighbours had heard the gossip Ted had spread about her last year, but Mrs Siddons had a clear view of her front door and must know that there were no shady comings and goings to support his lies.

'You know perfectly well that I'm an usherette down at the Grand Theatre,' she said sharply. 'That's evening work. Babs is setting herself up to do private cooking. That's evening work, too.' Of course, Babs might not be out cooking every night at first, but hopefully her reputation would grow and she'd be in demand. They needed to secure someone now. 'We must have someone to take care of our children,' Stella went on. 'What do you say?'

'Babs Thomas . . . Oh, I dunno.' Mrs Siddons made a face. 'A murderer for a husband! I wouldn't want to associate with people like that.'

Stella gritted her teeth, furious. But, then, the woman was

probably only repeating what others were saying. Babs could look forward to more of the same in the months to come. '*Babs* never killed anyone,' she said. 'She's as pure as the driven snow. She's on her beam end, and needs help.'

'Yes, but—'

'And *you* have nothing to boast about, have you?' Stella pressed on belligerently. 'Not with your Trevor up before the beak last year for stealing that bicycle. A month behind bars, he got, didn't he?'

'A miscarriage of justice!' Mrs Siddons was red in the face now. 'My boy's innocent. And, anyway, the blooming bike never had no brakes, neither. Nothing more than a death-trap!'

'Well, you didn't steal any bikes, Mrs Siddons,' Stella smiled sweetly, 'so Babs and me won't hold it against you. Now do you want the job or not?'

Mrs Siddons sniffed, smoothing her ruffled feathers. 'I'll have to think about it. How much?'

'Four and six a week, Monday to Saturday. It's money for jam, really, isn't it?' Stella asked persuasively. 'Sitting in Babs's cosy living-room, a good fire going, and all the tea you can drink.'

Mrs Siddons looked mollified. 'Well, if you put it like that . . . Five and six, mind, and not a penny less.'

Stella pursed her lips, then nodded in agreement. 'How about your Trevor?' Stella asked. 'Can he manage without you of an evening?'

Mrs Siddons looked a bit mournful. 'Never here, is he? Grabs a bite to eat tea time, then out with his pals. I don't see him again until breakfast. No comfort to me, he isn't.'

Fair play to Mrs Siddons, Stella thought a week later. She arrived promptly on time when Babs had engagements to cook on three consecutive evenings, and had even done Babs's ironing on one occasion. 'Well, I couldn't just sit there looking at it, could I?' she said, when Babs thanked her. An extra sixpence was added to her pay. Stella thought it was six shillings well spent, and Babs agreed.

Everything was working out well, Stella decided. Griff had not been in touch, and each day her fear of Tommy Parsons receded.

Mrs Prosser-Watkins was proving a useful contact, and Babs was kept busy most evenings. But for all that, her new happiness and prosperity were overshadowed by the coming trial. Ted's case was to be heard at Swansea Crown Court in February, and he would stand trial for manslaughter. The general opinion was that, if he was convicted, he would face at least fifteen years in prison.

Stella and Babs were sitting in her warm living room the following Sunday night, the four children safely in bed, when Babs looked up, her eyes glistening. 'Mam would be proud of me if she could see me cooking in those posh kitchens up in Eaton Road. Oh, Stell! How the other half live! I swear you can smell the money as soon as you step over the threshold.'

'Hey!' Stella said jokingly. 'You're not getting big ideas, are you?'

'Some hope!' Pain flitted briefly across Babs's face. 'Not with a convict for a husband.'

'Fifteen years is a long time,' Stella said thoughtfully.

'Yes, and I'm glad I'll never have to set eyes on him again,' Babs declared.

Stella thought of Eddie, wondered how long he'd stay in Australia and if she'd ever see him again. She and Babs were in the same boat, really. 'What will you do, Babs, if Ted's convicted? Divorce him?'

'Oh, no!' Babs shook her head. 'I'm devoting myself to my children, their future and my work. I want no man in my life again.'

'Nor I,' Stella agreed. Sometimes she felt empty and lonely, but that was better than the pain of rejection. It was best to put aside thoughts of love: she could never trust it to be true.

Chapter Twenty-Five

Two weeks after Freda's funeral, Stella was hurrying to catch her tram home from the theatre when she spotted a figure lounging under a lamp-post outside the ironmonger's on the corner of Oxford Street. Certain it was Tommy Parsons, her heart skipped a beat, and she stopped. Like a mesmerised rabbit, she froze on the pavement.

He didn't move, but stood as if he was basking in the lamp-light. There was arrogance in the way he leaned against the post, a cigarette dangling from one corner of his mouth.

Nowhere was safe from him, Stella thought. She'd been a fool to believe he'd give up so easily. His sort never did.

People were still about, and she looked around, hoping to see a familiar blue uniform, but there wasn't a spiked helmet in sight. When she glanced back fearfully towards the lamp-post the figure was gone. Panicking, Stella swung round, full circle. Where was he? She didn't know whether it was best to move forward or retreat. He could be anywhere, in any dark doorway, waiting to lash out with that knife.

She couldn't remember how she got home, and was still all of a tremble when she called in at Babs's to see how Danny and Rosie were, and have a final cup of tea before bedtime.

Babs was quick to pick up on her state of mind. 'Stella, you're as white as a sheet,' she said, as she put the tea before her.

'I saw Tommy Parsons on the way home,' she said, her voice

quivering. 'He was waiting for me. It was a warning, I know it was. I was so scared.'

'What are you going to do?'

'I dunno. He knows where I live and where I work. He can get to me any time.' She gulped. 'I'm half afraid to sleep in my own home tonight. Can I nap by here in the armchair?'

'Of course you can! I only wish I had a bed to offer you.'

'I'll manage tonight.'

'There'll be other nights, though, Stella,' Babs said. 'Isn't it time you took in another lodger?'

'Don't think so. Wouldn't find another like Arnie, would I?' she said. 'He was a good friend.' She squared her shoulders. 'Pull myself together, I must,' she said firmly. 'Can't live my life being frightened. I'll just have to keep my eyes open when I'm out and about at night.'

She tried to sound confident, but she wasn't fooling Babs any more than herself. 'Why don't you go and see the police?' Babs asked. 'Tell them what's been happening. They'll put Tommy Parsons where he can't hurt anyone.'

Stella glanced away, not wanting Babs to see the guilt that had seized her. Monty's death had been an accident, yet she still felt responsible. In giving Tommy up to the bobbies, she'd betray Griff, and he would give her up.

'Tommy's got pals who are just as bad,' she said lamely. 'My goose would be cooked if I talked to the police.'

Stella was on her knees scrubbing the front-door step in wintry sunshine the following morning when a long dark shadow fell across her.

With a frightened cry, she struggled to her feet, staring up, expecting . . . She didn't know what.

'Oh! Sorry, missus!' a deep voice said. 'Didn't mean to startle you, like.'

Stella squinted up at him into the sun, and lifted a hand to shade her eyes. A tall, well-built young man, in faded blue overalls under a dark donkey jacket, stood before her. In one hand he carried a large leather Gladstone bag, secured with a belt, and in the other, a wooden box, which looked like a tool chest. He made a burly figure, but he didn't look dangerous. Well . . . not really.

'Are you Mrs Evans?'

'Yes,' Stella replied cautiously. 'What do you want?'

'You've got a room to rent.' He held out a postcard. 'The lady from the corner shop gave me this.'

Stella took it from him. It was the card she'd left with Mrs Gomer advertising for a lodger. 'But that was months ago,' she said, astonished. She'd certainly had her money's worth for a penny a week. 'I'm sorry,' she went on hurriedly. 'The room's not available.'

'Oh, *Duw! Duw!*' He lifted his flat cap and scratched his head. His hair was short, brown and wiry, with a natural curl. 'And there's me hoping for a warm fire and a bed for the night, not to mention a cup of tea.' He sounded at a loss.

'I'm sorry Mr . . . er . . .'

'Walters,' he answered eagerly. 'Owen Walters. Plumber, I am, see. Starting at Nener's this morning – well, as soon as I find lodgings, like.'

His accent was strong. 'You're not from Swansea, Mr Walters?'

He smiled and lifted his cap again. 'Trehafod I'm from, see. Up the Rhondda. Got into Swansea last night, I did. Spent the night in the station waiting room. *Duw! Duw!* It's cold, mun.'

'Dear, dear!' Stella felt sorry for him. 'All night at the station? It couldn't have been very comfortable.'

Owen Walters smiled engagingly and Stella felt her own lips twitch in response. 'Well, what's a working man to do?' he said, philosophically. 'Got to go where the work is, see.'

Without making it obvious Stella studied him. He was well over six feet, broad of shoulder and not many years older than she was. He had a frank, open expression, and his hazel-coloured eyes held her gaze without faltering. It didn't seem fair that while she had a cosy room going begging he had to spend the night at the railway station.

'So, the room's gone, then,' he said.

'Well . . . it's not gone, exactly,' Stella said, deciding to be frank. 'The fact is, I'm not looking for a lodger at the moment.'

'Oh. There's a pity, isn't it?' He lifted the Gladstone bag to his shoulder. 'Well, best be on my way, then.' He half turned to leave, then looked back at her. 'Any other rooms to let around by here, Mrs Evans?'

'No. Sorry.'

'Oh, well!' His broad shoulders sagged tiredly as he turned away.

'Just a minute,' Stella called impulsively, 'would you like a cup of tea before you go on searching?'

'Oh, *Duw*! There's kind!' He gave her a happy smile, like a little boy who had just been offered a toffee apple, and Stella's heart did a somersault. Her face heated with confusion as Owen Walters followed her down the passage to the living room. He stood in the doorway respectfully as she bustled self-consciously into the scullery to put the kettle on. 'Take your coat off for a minute,' she called. 'Sit by the fire. It's a cold day, isn't it?'

'Not half as cold as it was on the station last night,' Owen told her. 'And those blasted seagulls – oh, pardon! Those blooming seagulls started squawking before it was even light.'

Stella put her head around the scullery door. 'Would you like a toasted teacake, Mr Walters?'

'Oh, there's kind of you.'

He was sitting on the wooden chair next to the range, hands held out to the fire. He dwarfed everything in the room.

Stella sliced a teacake in half, then toasted both sides over the gas-ring.

She must be mad inviting a stranger into her home. He *said* he was a plumber, but he could be anyone. It might be a trick. But she shouldn't let her fear of Tommy Parsons make her suspicious of everyone. Owen Walters looked a decent bloke.

Stella carried the tea-things into the living room. He stood up respectfully as she came in, and Stella was impressed by his manners. Not even Arnie had done that. 'Sit down, Mr Walters,' she said. 'How do you like your tea?'

'Strong as brown leather,' he replied.

She watched him wolf down the teacake, and wished she'd prepared two. He was on his second cup of tea when Stella ventured a probing question. 'So, you're starting with Nener's, then? Good firm to work for, I hear.'

'The best.' He wiped his mouth with a spotless handkerchief, and Stella wondered if he had a wife up in the valley. 'Now all I need is a good, respectable place to lodge.'

'I expect your wife's anxious about you being away from home, like?'

'Not married, I'm not, mun,' Owen said. 'Plenty of time for that when I've made a bit of headway in the . . . er, my profession.'

'Profession?'

Owen flushed. 'My trade, I mean.' He shifted uneasily on the chair. 'It's a man's duty to provide everything his family needs, isn't it? It's no good rushing into things too soon.'

Stella nodded in agreement. She liked what she had heard, and he was sincere, she could tell. She liked his direct gaze, and his respectful air. Instinctively, she knew he wasn't a man to take advantage of a woman on her own.

She thought of Tommy Parsons and Griff. They might think twice about breaking into her home if she had someone like Owen Walters under her roof. The back bedroom was going begging, and she could always use the extra money.

'Er . . . about the room, Mr Walters,' Stella began, diffidently, 'perhaps we can come to some arrangement after all.'

'Very tidy, I am, Mrs Evans,' Owen said, sitting forward eagerly. 'Keep the room spotless, I will. Don't smoke or drink, so you needn't worry there.' He gave her the benefit of his dazzling smile again. 'Sober as a judge, I am.'

Stella felt her breath catch a little, and wondered if she was rushing into something too quickly. It had been a long time since she'd found a man attractive enough to feel awkward, even shy, in his presence, but Owen Walters was having this effect on her.

She began to doubt her own motives in taking him in, and felt ashamed. But it was too late to withdraw her offer now and, besides, she didn't want to.

'The rent is . . . twelve and six a week,' Stella said – was this too much to ask? 'Meals included, of course, Mr Walters. Breakfast, dinner and early tea. I work evenings at the Grand Theatre, you see.'

'Rent's fair.' Owen fidgeted on his chair again. 'Working odd hours, I'll be, though,' he said, 'so don't worry about dinner and tea for me.'

Stella pushed a strand of hair self-consciously behind her ear. 'But you haven't seen the room yet. It might not be suitable.'

'I'm sure it will be.' He stood up and reached for his donkey jacket. Fishing in the inner pocket, he brought out some money, a pound note and two half-crowns, and handed them to her. 'There you are, Mrs Evans, two weeks' rent in advance.' He put on the jacket. 'Best be off to my employment now, then. I'll leave my bag here.'

Stella went to the small vase on the mantelpiece where she kept the spare front-door key. She held it out to him. 'You'd better have this, Mr Walters.'

As he took it from her he gazed penetratingly at her, as though he was sizing her up. Stella felt even more confused. Then that smile of his broke through. '*Diolch yn fawr*, Mrs Evans!'

He strode towards the passage and Stella followed in his wake. 'Expect me when you see me,' he said.

Then she was closing the door on his retreating figure. In the living room his Gladstone bag was still near the chair. She lugged it upstairs and put it in the back bedroom, then stood, mulling over her decision, striving to be honest with herself.

Her new lodger was nothing like the man she'd married, yet she felt a powerful attraction to him. She'd not experienced that with any man other than Eddie.

It was all on her side, of course, and very foolish. Even though her husband was thousands of miles away and she would probably never see him again, she was still a married woman. She felt a little resentful. These last few months she'd begun to accept that there could never be another man in her life, then along comes Owen Walters, stirring up feelings and longings she thought she'd buried for good.

She should've turned him away, not fallen into the trap. There could never be anything between them, not the way she'd want it anyway. And he'd already told her he didn't intend to settle down for a while.

Still, she was comforted. Owen Walters's presence in the house would make the nights less terrifying, and she could start to sleep easy in her bed.

With satisfaction, she fingered the crisp pound note and the silver coins in her apron pocket. The money would come in handy, too.

It took a few days for Stella to get used to having a man in the house again. That first morning she'd come downstairs to get the fire going, only to find it already lit and Owen at the stone sink in the scullery, stripped to the waist, having a wash-down. The magnificence of his muscled chest and shoulders made her face flame, and she felt like a gauche schoolgirl.

Owen was surprised when Danny and Rosie showed up at the breakfast table from next door, and Stella explained the arrangement she had with Babs.

Rosie was shy, but Danny and Owen hit it off immediately, for which Stella was thankful. Owen stood up manfully under the barrage of questions about his work with which Danny peppered him.

'So, you're going to be a plumber, too, then, when you grow up?' Owen asked Danny at breakfast a week later.

'No, I'm going to be a policeman,' Danny announced

decidedly, 'with a whistle, and a truncheon for bashing robbers over the head.'

'Is that right?' Owen sounded interested, putting down his fork for a moment. 'Was . . .' He glanced at Stella. 'Is your daddy a policeman?'

'My husband worked on the railway when he was . . . home, Mr Walters,' Stella explained, 'but he's in Australia at present.'

She laughed nervously. She went on, in a joking tone, 'Gone to find his fortune, I believe.' She couldn't bring herself to admit that her husband had left her. It made her seem inadequate.

Owen's smile was slow and thoughtful. 'Land of opportunity, so they say, but give me Wales any day.'

Stella had just sat down at the table after pouring a second cup of tea for Owen, when the back door was flung open.

'Stella!' Griff yelled. 'Come for my money, I have, so where is it?'

He barged in without ceremony, as dishevelled as ever. At the sight of him, Rosie squeaked in terror and ran to hide her face in Stella's lap. Danny's eyes were wide, his spoon poised half-way to his mouth, as though paralysed.

Stella felt paralysed, too, with consternation, wondering what Owen was making of the spectacle.

'I said, where's my money?' Griff surged forward, but stopped short when he saw the man sitting at the table.

Owen rose from his chair, and the two men stared at each other. Then Owen lowered himself back into his seat, eyes fixed on Griff.

'Huh!' Griff grunted. 'Giving your customers breakfast as well as bed, now, are you? Hope he's paying extra for that food.'

Stella put Rosie to one side and jumped up, her face burning with humiliation. 'Griff! How dare you talk like that? This is Mr Walters, my new lodger.'

'Lodger! That excuse is wearing a bit thin, Stella. You'll be telling me next he sleeps in the back bedroom.'

Owen leaped up now.

'That's enough of that,' he said. 'Who is this man, Mrs Evans?'

'Her brother,' Griff answered for her, 'if it's any business of yours, mate.'

'And you talk to her like that?'

'How else would you talk to a trollop?'

Stella was horrified. 'How could you?' she cried. 'In front of the children, too!'

'Phfff!' Griff smirked. 'They see and hear plenty in this house.'

'Do you want him to leave, Mrs Evans?' Owen asked. He took a step away from the table. 'Sling him out on his ear, I will, if you like.'

Griff eyed Owen's bulky shoulders, uncertain for the first time since he had come in.

'He better not try it, Stella,' he warned her, 'or I'll have something to tell the coppers about a certain gentleman who fell—'

'Griff!' Stella cried, in agitation, wondering just how much Owen was taking in. 'It's all right, Mr Walters. As you can see, my brother suffered in the war. He's not himself.'

There was bitterness in Griff's derisive hoot of laughter. He looked and sounded mad, Stella thought.

'You'd better get off to work, Mr Walters,' she added. 'We'll be all right.'

Owen didn't looked convinced. 'You're certain?'

Stella nodded, anxious for him to be gone before Griff said anything else.

'Yes, push off!' Griff said to him. 'You got what you came for.'

Owen turned a stony expression on Griff, and Stella wondered at the change in him. Suddenly, he looked a different man, and she felt uneasy. 'Please, Mr Walters,' she said. Without a word Owen strode into the passage, closing the living-room door behind him.

Stella was aware that Rosie was cringing into her skirt behind her, and that Danny's face was white and frightened. 'How dare you storm into my home like this, frightening my children, insulting me and my lodger?'

'Shut your trap!' Griff bellowed. 'Just give me the money you've earned on your back these last couple of weeks.'

'There *isn't* any money. Don't you understand?' Stella screeched in frustration. 'I'm *not* a streetwalker, as you well know in your heart, Griff. I know you are desperate for money, but you'll have to find it some other way.'

'I'm desperate, all right,' he said, with a mocking smile, 'desperate enough to do anything so, hand it over.'

'All I've got is my wages from the theatre,' Stella lied and tried to control the sob in her voice, afraid he'd see she was fibbing. 'Are you going to rob me again?'

'Rob you? You owe me, Stella. It's your fault Rose left me – yours and your bloody husband's.'

'You're always bleating about that,' Stella was overwrought, 'and I'm sick of it – sick of you. Why don't you face up to the truth, Griff? If it hadn't been Eddie, it would've been someone else. Rose was man mad, and *you* weren't man enough for her.'

His face whitened at her rash words, and suddenly she was fearful. But controlling himself with effort he held out his hand, palm up. 'The money, now.'

Stella took a pound note from her apron pocket, and handed it to him. He was crazy and dangerous, and antagonising him further was too risky. Griff's lips drew back from his yellowed teeth in an angry growl. 'Is that bloody all? You must think I'm soft in the head.' His bloodshot eyes were ablaze. 'Don't mess me about, Stella, or you'll be very sorry, I warn you.'

'Griff, for God's sake!' Stella felt she had to make a stand even though crossing him was perilous. 'We need the rest to live on, or has your decency died along with your self-respect?'

'Decency! That's a good one. I've got plenty on you, remember?' he warned, menacingly. 'One word from me and your brats'll be taken away.'

'The last man who threatened that is now in prison,' Stella

snapped. 'Ted'll probably spend the rest of his life there, and you're going the same way, Griff.'

'Wouldn't mention prison if I were you, Stella,' Griff said. 'The coppers still want to know what really happened to that actor bloke. But *I* know how he broke his neck. And who pushed him.'

'Go to the police, then!' Stella cried, at the end of her tether. 'They won't believe the lies of an ex-convict. You'll get no more money out of me, and if you come here again—'

A noise in the passage made her spin to face the door. Someone was just leaving the house.

Owen had heard everything of which Griff had accused her. Would he believe it?

Griff caught her expression. 'What is it?'

'We were overheard. My lodger must have been listening.'

'So what?' Griff's tone was scornful, but his eyes were wary. He pushed the pound note into his jacket pocket. 'I'll be back on Sunday morning, Stella,' he said, 'so you'd better have something for me.'

With a poisonous glance at Rosie, he loped out through the scullery. Stella raced after him, slammed the door shut and bolted it.

It was too late, of course. A stranger, living in her home knew her secret: her guilty knowledge of how Monty Fitzgerald had died.

By the time she left for work at the theatre that evening Owen had not come home. He was still out when she returned later that night, after checking with Babs that the children were all right.

She went to bed early, ashamed to see him face to face. It was almost midnight when she heard the key turn the lock of the front door, his soft footfalls on the stairs, his bedroom door closing quietly.

Next morning she had to screw up her courage to go down

and start breakfast. As usual, Owen had lit the fire, and the living room was warming up nicely.

Owen, shaved and washed, came out of the scullery carrying the teapot. He paused when he saw her, and Stella lowered her gaze. She wouldn't be surprised if he was about to give notice, and couldn't blame him either. He was a decent man, while Griff's lies painted a different picture of her.

'Morning, Mrs Evans.' Stella was surprised at the lightness of his tone, and her heart lifted. He put the teapot on the table. 'Look,' he went on apologetically, 'there's sorry I am, being so late coming home last night. Hope I didn't disturb you.'

'No, of course not,' Stella replied, relieved at his easy manner, as though nothing had changed. Perhaps he hadn't heard the awful things Griff had said.

'I'm sorry, too, about leaving you alone when your brother came yesterday,' he said. 'Didn't want to interfere in family matters, like. Afterwards I was worried. He seemed in a state.'

'It's the war, you know,' she replied hastily, yet felt herself relax at his words. 'It did terrible things to him.'

His tone was still respectful. If he *had* overheard the quarrel, surely his attitude would've changed? He wouldn't be able to hide it. Owen was as straight as an arrow, she'd stake her life on it.

Then Danny and Rosie came in from next door, and the peace of the morning was disrupted, blissfully, Stella thought. She missed tucking the children up in bed each night and always looked forward to breakfast with them.

This morning seemed extra special, because Owen was smiling at her.

Chapter Twenty-Six

Stella stepped off the tram at the stop in Hospital Square and into pelting rain that was turning to sleet. Berating herself for forgetting her umbrella, she dashed for cover in a shop doorway. Her coat was damp around the shoulders, and water ran off the brim of her hat down her collar, making her shiver. What a night!

Stamping her feet, she longed to get home and have a warming cup of tea. She peered out, hoping for a break in the downpour. The streets were shiny with water, and deserted. Another little shiver went though her, which had nothing to do with the rain. The more people about in the streets the safer she felt.

Her only comfort was that, despite his threat, Griff hadn't called at the house for weeks, and there'd been no sign of Tommy Parsons either. She put it down to the presence of Owen Walters. Her lodger was worth his weight in gold. He was a godsend.

Finally, the rain eased and Stella hurried away towards the Sandfields and Victor Street. But the break didn't last long. The downpour started again with a vengeance when she reached the corner of Carogwen Terrace, but there was nowhere to shelter so she pressed on.

As she passed the entrance to the back lane behind Howell's dairy, a figure jumped out at her. Before Stella could scream, someone dragged her into the lane.

Tommy Parsons! He'd got her.

But she wouldn't go down without a fight, and she was ready to let fly with her fists.

'Keep quiet! Don't scream, or else.'

Through her terror Stella recognised Griff's voice, and felt a measure of relief that it wasn't the murderous Tommy. 'Griff! What in God's name are you doing? Let me go!'

Rain was pouring down on them, she'd lost her hat and her hair was plastered to her head and face.

'Get in here.'

He shoved her through the open gates of the dairy's yard, then into an outbuilding. It was dark, and the stench of sour milk and horse manure hung in the air. Stella gagged on the stench.

'We shouldn't be in here, Griff,' she ventured. 'We're trespassing.'

Somewhere nearby the dairy's dray-horse shuffled about uneasily, as though sensing the presence of strangers. Stella had seen it about the streets many times: a huge beast, with heavy feathered feet.

'Stop whingeing, woman, and pipe down.'

The horse stamped its feet, and Stella imagined being trampled to death by its hoofs.

'Why have you brought me here?' She whimpered. 'What are you going to do to me?' Had Tommy sent him to do his dirty work? If so, she was at his mercy.

'We need to talk.' She tried to find comfort in the commonplace words, but couldn't bring herself to believe him.

'Talk?' Stella forced down her terror, trying to sound unruffled. 'Why didn't you come to the house, then?'

'Oh, yes, that's likely, isn't it?' Griff's tone was harsh. 'I walk right into your little trap. You'd like that, wouldn't you? You must think I'm proper *twp*. Lost an arm, I have, not my mind.'

'Trap? What are you talking about?'

'As if you don't know,' Griff grated angrily. 'You copper's nark!'

'You know better than that, Griff,' Stella replied. 'You

shouldn't listen to that Tommy Parsons. He belongs on the gallows.'

'He's right, though, isn't he?' Griff yelled. 'Coppers sleeping in your bloody house now. If that isn't narking, what is?'

'You're raving, Griff,' Stella cried.

At the sound of their voices the horse became even more restive, kicking at a wooden partition. Stella heard the wood splinter. She wanted to scream, but fear almost choked her. 'Let me out of here!' she cried. 'I'm afraid of it, and the stench is awful.'

'Shut up!' Griff grabbed the front of her coat, bunching up the material in his fist. Pressing at the base of her throat, he forced her back against the wall, almost lifting her off her feet. 'You're not going anywhere until I get the truth out of you. And maybe you'll never leave this shed if I don't like what I hear. Get me?'

Stella's legs were weak. 'Has Tommy sent you to kill me?' she asked. 'Think what you're doing, Griff, for God's sake. I'm your sister. Don't – don't push me under the horse's hoofs.'

Griff laughed. 'Now, that's a new one. Hadn't thought of it. Good idea, though. Must remember it.'

Her courage spurred by his laugh, Stella snapped, 'Perhaps you prefer slitting my throat, like Tommy tried to do.'

'What?' Griff eased away his fist.

'Oh, don't act so surprised, Griff,' Stella said scathingly. 'You must have sent him to do it.'

'Don't talk like a fool! What happened?'

'That night I came to see you,' Stella said, 'he accosted me on my way home. He had a knife and he tried to use it on me. He'd have done it too, if the bobbies hadn't come along.'

Griff muttered an oath. 'Not again! Tommy's becoming a dangerous liability,' he said grimly. 'Even though I'm in debt to Charlie, I'm still his number-one man, but Tommy would like to take my place. I'll have to do something about him.'

The menace in his voice made Stella quake. He hadn't said yet what he intended to do to her. If only she were out on the street she might have a chance of escape.

With a quick movement she tried to slip past his useless shoulder, but he grabbed her and hauled her back.

'Oh, no, you don't!'

'Let me go!'

'Shut up!'

'Oh, God! Tommy sent you to finish me off! You can't do it, Griff, you can't!'

'Save it! Not his lackey, am I?' Griff started. 'Tommy's days are numbered, but he still has his uses. He's been watching your house, seen that copper go in and out like he owns the place.'

'There's no copper. Tommy's lying, trying to make trouble,' Stella insisted. 'Turning you against me for his own ends. He wants you to do his dirty work.'

'Don't lie!' Griff thundered. 'Saw it with my own eyes, I did. A copper with his feet under your table, and in your bed too, for all I know.'

'What was he talking about? 'You don't mean Owen, surely?'

'Course I mean him,' Griff grated, through clenched teeth. 'Who else?'

'But you've got it wrong, Griff. Owen's not a policeman. You and Tommy see bobbies everywhere. Guilty consciences.'

'Don't get clever with me, Stella.'

'Owen's a plumber. He's only just down from the valleys. Do you think I wouldn't know if I had a policeman in the house? And he's *not* in my bed.'

'He's a detective constable,' Griff insisted. 'Tommy knows him, because Walters nicked him once.'

'I don't believe it!' Stella's heart was racing. 'Why would Owen lie? Why would he tell me he's a plumber?'

'Oh, use your head, woman!' Griff exploded. 'He's got his sights on somebody, hasn't he? Just waiting for the right minute to nick 'em.'

'It's not true. It can't be.'

But Griff's certainty made her uneasy, and remembering the odd hours Owen kept, she was filled with dread.

If Owen Walters was a policeman, living in *her* house, he

must be investigating *her* over the death of Monty Fitzgerald. That could be the only explanation.

But how did the police know she had been involved? Griff must have told them his lies, after all.

'It was *you*, Griff,' she accused him. 'You told them I was in the theatre that afternoon. You betrayed me!'

'Don't be a fool,' he said gruffly.

'Then how did they know?'

Griff stepped away. She could have made a run for it now, but she didn't move, just stood like a statue.

The police were waiting to pounce on her and it could happen any minute. Owen, pretending to be her friend, had set a trap for her. She'd lose Danny and Rosie, and perhaps spend the rest of her life in jail, all because of a man's lust.

'Help me, Griff!' she cried out desperately. 'Tell me what to do.'

'Get rid of Walters,' Griff replied. 'Tell him to bugger off, but don't let on you know he's a copper.'

'But that won't stop him! He could arrest me at any minute for Monty's death. What am I going to do?'

'He's not after you, you *llelo*.' Griff said, harshly impatient. 'He's after me.'

'*What?* But why?'

There was a heavy silence.

'Never mind! Just get shot of him.' Griff moved quickly, his silhouette caught in the doorway. 'Don't double-cross me, Stella, or you *will* get trampled.'

Then he was gone.

Stella leaned against the damp wall for support. After a few minutes, during which confused thoughts whirled through her befuddled mind, she slipped out of the door, and ran pell-mell in the pouring rain towards Victor Street.

Stella went to bed long before Owen came in. She had to think things through, still not convinced that Owen was after Griff rather than her. The police wouldn't go to all this trouble over petty theft.

She was shocked at her brother's revelation, and hurt. She had thought Owen a man she could trust, and had felt there might be more than friendship between them. Instead, she had been betrayed again by a man's lies. First Eddie, then Ted, now Owen. She was too trusting. Oh, what an idiot she was letting herself be taken in, letting her heart soften. She could've fallen in love with Owen.

He must be laughing at her behind her back, him and his superiors. The sooner Owen Walters was gone from her life the better. Doubtless, she'd not be free of police interest yet awhile, but at least she'd salvage some of her pride.

Stella had to force herself to confront him next morning, determined to tell him to leave immediately, not wanting him under her roof a day more. It was still early, so the children hadn't come in from next door, and Stella was thankful for that. She couldn't see this through in front of their innocent eyes. They thought so much of Owen, and wouldn't understand. A sob escaped her as she reached the bottom stair.

Owen was in the scullery, whistling a tune from one of the records Arnie had left. Stella's mouth tightened. He had accepted her hospitality, and in return was ready to send her to prison.

Stella took a deep breath and marched into the scullery. That was a mistake. There was hardly room for two people, and he filled the space. She felt intimidated.

'Oh, morning, Stella,' he said, easily enough. 'Ready for a cup of tea?'

Stella swallowed her rising anger, annoyed with herself for allowing him to use her first name. The nerve of him! Treating her like she was some dim-brain, unable to put two and two together. But she'd have gone on being fooled if it hadn't been for Griff. 'No, I don't want tea,' she snapped. 'Come into the living room, Ow – Mr Walters. I have something to say to you.'

Stella turned on her heel. He followed.

'Stella?'

'*Mrs Evans* to you, if you don't mind!'

'Pardon?'

'I'm giving you notice, Mr Walters, as from this minute,' she said resolutely. 'Pack up and get out.'

His jaw went slack in astonishment. 'What? Why?'

'I don't have to explain my reasons,' Stella said curtly. 'I want you gone from my home.'

'Stella, what's going on, mun?'

'Don't you pretend with me,' she said, unable to contain herself. 'I won't be made a fool of in my own home.'

Owen spread his hands wide in a gesture of mystification. 'Look, I don't know what the heck you're on about, Stella. Why are you kicking me out? Who's making a fool of you?'

'You are!' Stella was shaking wrath. 'Pretending to be a plumber, when all along you're a—'

Stella cut herself short. Griff had asked her not to reveal that she knew the truth about Owen's profession, but she couldn't do that now. She must have it out with him. She'd force him to honest with her.

'Go on.' His voice was hard and his expression wary.

She was unnerved at the change in his attitude. 'All right!' she said. 'You're no plumber. You're a policeman, and you're here investigating . . . someone.'

'Who says so?'

Stella stamped her foot in fury. 'Don't take me for a *llelo*, Owen,' she cried. 'You lied to me.'

'Who's been filling your head with this rubbish?'

'Stop it!' Stella screeched. 'You're a policeman. Have the decency to admit it, and that you've been deceiving me, living here under false pretences.'

He stared at her for a long moment, then drew out a chair and sat down. 'Have you got something against the police?' The question threw her off balance.

'Of course not!' Stella blurted. 'But I won't have a liar under my roof. I've had enough of them wrecking my life.'

'Sit down,' he said, in a tone so different from his usual affability that she felt afraid, but she wasn't cowed.

'Don't you order me about in my own house!'

'Sit, Stella! If you insist on knowing the truth I'll enlighten you.'

Shaking like a reed in a gale, Stella pulled out a chair opposite him and sat down. She clasped her hands together in her lap. His expression was so serious and official that he seemed a stranger. 'Your informant, whoever he is, is quite right,' he said. 'I am a policeman. You must tell me who it is.'

Stella wasn't about to make things easy for him. 'Never mind that,' she replied, with spirit. 'You owe me an explanation. I have a right to know what's going on in my own home.'

'I don't think my superiors would approve of me telling you anything, but . . . I am a policeman. I'm posing as a plumber in an undercover investigation.'

'Who are you investigating?'

He stared at her for a moment. 'You, Stella. I'm investigating you in connection with a death.'

Stella stared at him wide-eyed. Then she shook her head violently. 'But Monty's death was an accident,' she blurted out. On the edge of hysteria, the words tumbled out and tears with them. She couldn't stop either.

'I *was* there that afternoon,' she admitted. 'He tried to assault me. I climbed on to the catwalk to get away from him. He followed and . . . fell.' Stella half rose from her chair in near panic at what she was revealing. 'I didn't push him, Owen. I swear by God I didn't. It was an accident.'

Owen's brow furrowed. 'Who the hell is Monty?'

'Eh?'

Stella's thoughts were in turmoil. 'Monty Fitzgerald,' she said, at a loss. 'He died a few months ago, at the Grand Theatre. Fell and broke his neck.'

'I see. Withholding information.' Owen looked grave. 'You should've been straightforward with the police at the time, Stella. I may have to report this.'

She stared at him dismayed.

'Who would've believed me?' she whispered. 'The police are still suspicious or you wouldn't be here, would you?'

He fingered his chin thoughtfully. 'I remember the incident now, although I wasn't on the case. It's over, done with,' he said. 'The actor's death was an accident, pure and simple. That's not why I'm here.'

'What do you mean?'

'That's not the death I'm investigating,' he said.

'But you said you're investigating *me*,' Stella said. 'If it's not Monty then whose death?'

Owen was silent, regarding her intently. Eventually he said, 'Either you really don't know, or you're a damned clever actress yourself.'

Stella jumped up. 'I've had enough of this, Owen,' she said tensely. 'I demand to know why you're investigating me. Either be straightforward or get out now.'

Owen stood up too, towering above her, intimidating. 'I'm investigating murder, Stella,' he said slowly. 'The murder of your husband, Eddie Evans.'

Stella's jaw went slack. She was aware of a sound coming from her throat, but she couldn't form words. Her legs were wobbly and she swayed. Owen sprang forward and took her arm, easing her on to a chair. 'You all right, Stella?'

'Eddie, Eddie.' They were the only words she could manage.

'I'll get you some water,' Owen said, and strode into the scullery. He came back almost immediately with a tumbler. 'Drink this.'

Stella gulped at it. It went down the wrong way and she began to cough. Owen patted her back. 'Steady on, mun, Stella.'

She looked up at him pleadingly. This was a nightmare. He couldn't have said that Eddie had been murdered. It couldn't be true. 'Eddie's in Australia!' she said. 'He's not dead. He can't be!'

'He is, Stella.'

'No! You're playing games with me, Owen. Why?'

He said nothing, but stared at her stonily.

'He sent me a letter,' she insisted.

Owen was alert. 'What? When? Let me see it.'

She rose shakily to her feet, went to the sideboard and opened a drawer. Eddie's letter was on top. She'd reread it so many times, knew it off by heart. She handed it to Owen, and he scanned it quickly. 'This is dated September last year,' he said, looking up at her sharply. 'Four months ago. You haven't heard from him since. Didn't you think it strange?'

The shock was wearing off now. 'Strange?' she asked. 'My husband ran off with my sister-in-law and I heard nothing from him for four years. Then he dumped his unwanted child on me, and pushed off abroad . . . No, Owen, I didn't think it strange.'

'Stay calm, Stella.'

'Calm? You're telling me my husband has been murdered and I'm to stay calm. I don't believe Eddie's dead at all.'

'No good denying it, Stella. It won't go away.'

There was a glint of sympathy in his eyes. Far from being comforted by it, she felt irritated. 'Don't be so damned patronising, will you?' she cried. 'I won't believe it until I see his body.'

'Wouldn't advise that,' he said. 'As far as the police pathologist can tell, he died about four months ago.' He glanced at the letter again. 'About the time you received this.'

'How do they know it's Eddie?' Stella whimpered.

'Papers were found on . . . the body. Passport and a letter. There's no doubt, Stella, your husband was brutally murdered.'

She winced at the terrible truth. Then a monstrous thought struck her. 'Here! Wait a minute – you're investigating me. You think I killed my husband?'

Owen dropped the letter on to the table, then moved to the mantelpiece. 'You must understand, Stella, that although your brother, Griff Stroud, is well known to the police, you're not. We didn't know what kind of a woman you were. You might've been out of the same mould, and there were rumours . . .'

'Lies!' Stella wailed, dismayed to know that while Ted would bother her no more his lies lived on. 'I'm no cheap tart.'

'Still, there was talk . . . gossip that you were on the . . .'

Owen's expression was apologetic, but Stella didn't feel forgiving.

'On the game?' Stella shrieked. 'That was the sick imagining of another crazed killer, Ted Thomas.'

'My superiors suspected you and your . . . lover might be responsible,' he said. 'Getting rid of an unwanted husband. It's been done before.'

Stella was almost beside herself with rage. '*Lover!* How dare you? What kind of a woman do you think I am?'

Owen took a step towards her, his expression pleading. 'I know you're innocent, Stella. Not long after I came to live here I realised you were a decent, respectable woman.'

Stella glared up at him. 'If I'm innocent why did you stay on? Why go on nosing into my life?'

He moved closer, and Stella, anticipating that he might try to take her hand, backed out of reach. His shoulders slumped. 'Don't you know?' he said huskily. 'Thought I'd made it plain.' He ran his fingers though his hair. 'I stayed purely for personal reasons, and I think you know what they are, Stella. You've come to mean so much to me—'

Stella flinched at the words she had been longing to hear him speak for weeks. She couldn't bear it: he had concealed things from her, lied to her. He was probably lying now. 'Don't, Owen. Don't tell me more lies, not now.'

She walked over to stare through the living-room window into the backyard.

'Where did Eddie die?'

'We're not sure yet.'

'Where was he found?'

'On board a cargo vessel bound for South America.'

'What?'

'We're certain he didn't die aboard ship,' Owen told her matter-of-factly, as though discussing the price of bread. 'A member of the crew was caught trying to dump the body overboard in deep water.'

Stella gave a sob.

'The captain put in at the nearest port,' Owen went on, 'and the body was shipped back to Swansea. This was in October last.'

'I should've been told!' Stella sank on to a chair. 'The police had no right to keep it from me.'

True, she no longer loved Eddie but he had been the father of her child, Danny, and Rosie's father, too. She would mourn him, for the years they'd had together, some of which had been good.

'I'm sorry, Stella,' Owen said. 'I don't mean to sound callous. Do you still love him?'

Stella sniffed back the tears, and wiped her cheeks with the heel of her hand. 'No, not after the way he betrayed me . . . but he was my husband.'

'Stella, we've got to face facts. You had no hand in killing Eddie, but I believe Griff did.'

Stella was appalled. 'No! He's gone off the rails, I admit, but that's because of the war and what it did to him. He's no killer. Why would he do such a terrible thing?'

'Revenge,' Owen said. 'The oldest motive in the world. Eddie must've been killed near the docks. Griff and his cronies do a lot of shady business in that area. The cargo vessel was handy to hide the body. Either Eddie was lured there or it was a chance meeting.'

'I don't believe Griff had anything to do with it,' she insisted, then hesitated, dreading the answer to her next question. 'How did Eddie die?'

'You don't want to know that, Stella, believe me.'

'Please!'

'His throat was slit.'

Stella covered her face with her hands. And suddenly, in her mind's eye she was back on the street, fighting for her life, a knife at her throat. She was certain she knew the truth.

'Owen, listen!' She grabbed at his arm. 'Griff didn't kill Eddie, I'm sure of it. He never carries a knife or any weapon. It was Tommy Parsons.'

'Parsons?' Owen was sceptical. 'Eddie didn't know him. How could he have dealings with him when he'd been working in Bristol for four years? No, Parsons doesn't have a motive for murdering Eddie, but Griff does.'

'A man like Tommy Parsons doesn't need a motive,' Stella blurted impatiently. 'Once he waylaid me and tried to slit my throat.'

'*What?*' Owen darted forward and seized her by the upper arms. 'I need to know every detail, Stella.'

Telling it brought back all the horror of that night. She'd never forget it as long as she lived, and now, knowing the way Eddie had died, she guessed what nightmares lay ahead.

She was shivering uncontrollably after she'd told him everything. He put an arm around her shoulders, and she didn't pull away, needing to feel his warmth and strength.

Then she remembered his deceit, and his willingness to suspect her of a most foul deed, and struggled out of his grasp. 'This doesn't change anything, Owen,' she said. 'I want you to leave.'

'That's daft,' Owen argued. 'After what you've just told me, you need my protection even more. I'm staying.'

'No!' Stella drew away. 'Pack your things and go.'

'Stella, you can't be left alone here.'

'I'll be safer with you out of my home,' Stella retorted. 'I'm no copper's nark, and I have to prove that.'

Owen's face was white. 'Stella, I couldn't bear it if anything happened to you.'

She turned her back on him abruptly. 'I don't want to hear that, all right? Please go!'

'Don't have much choice, do I?' Owen replied, his voice unsteady. 'But with me out of the way, you're making it easy for them.'

She wouldn't look at him; couldn't bear to. Her heart ached for the way things had turned out, but she couldn't forgive his betrayal. Was there no man who'd be honest with her?

Chapter Twenty-Seven

Arriving home from work late in the evening, Stella saw that the gas-light in the passage was out. That was unusual. Babs always lit it so that there would be a welcoming glow when she got home from the theatre. Well, she couldn't expect her friend to remember every night: she had enough on her plate, what with her cooking work and the four children to feed at tea-time.

Stella turned the key in the lock and went in, then closed the door behind her and bolted it, mindful of the danger that lurked in the streets. At this minute, Tommy Parsons might be watching and waiting. She walked down the darkened passage, still wearing her hat and coat, and went into the living room.

Tapers were kept on the mantelpiece and, aided by the just discernible glow of the banked up fire, she put one into the heart of the coals. It flared into life, and she reached up to the gas-light at the side of the fireplace, lifted the glass funnel and lit the flame. It caught, and brightened slowly, throwing the room into a dim light.

Stella was about to slip out of her coat but instead let out a scream at the sight of a figure slumped in the armchair.

'Shut up,' Griff said, irate. 'We don't want Babs barging in.'

'Griff!' Fresh fear snaked through her to see him. 'What in heaven's name are you doing sitting here in the dark?'

'You got rid of the copper, then,' he said. 'Glad you're being sensible at last, Stella.'

Her panic evaporated. 'Answer me, Griff! What are you doing in my house when I'm not here? Stealing again, is it?' She tossed her head towards the door. 'Get out!'

'I'm your brother, Stella, and I'm here to stay. I'm moving back in tonight, so don't argue.'

'Oh, no, you're not!'

'You've got no say in it,' Griff rasped back. 'Now that copper's gone this is the last place the police will look for me.'

Stella wondered if Owen had already alerted his superiors to his suspicions about Griff. 'Why are they looking for you?'

Griff wiped his nose on his sleeve. 'Couple of houses up in Sketty broken into. They suspect I did 'em.' His grin was jeering. 'They'd be right, too. Me and Tommy.'

Stella whipped off her hat and coat, playing for time. She had to get rid of him somehow. 'You can't stay here, Griff,' she declared. 'I won't stand for it.'

He pushed himself to his feet. 'I told you, Stella, you got no bloody say in the matter. I'm taking charge. You'll do as I tell you from now on. I've got plans for you, my girl, big plans.'

Stella didn't bother to protest. What would be the use? Griff could no longer comprehend decency. One thing she was determined about: she had to get him out of the house tonight. He couldn't be allowed to come anywhere near Danny and Rosie.

'I don't want you here,' she blurted. 'We've been through this before, Griff. I don't want your filth contaminating my children.'

'Your children!' The venom in his tone made his voice coarse. 'That bloody little pale-haired bastard is no kin of ours. That's the first thing I'll do – send her to the orphanage where she belongs.'

'Leave Rosie alone!' Stella stormed. 'Haven't you taken enough from her already? If it wasn't for you, her father would still be alive—'

'What?' Griff barked.

Stella's mistake hit her like a blow to her chest. Before he'd left, Owen had warned her repeatedly to say nothing to Griff about Eddie's death. As far as his murderer knew, Eddie's body was in the deep waters of the Atlantic, never to be found.

Unlike Owen, she was convinced that Griff had not killed Eddie himself, but he was thick with Tommy Parsons, and that creature was capable of anything. But she knew where Griff's loyalties lay, with his criminal cronies, and by the look on his face now, she'd just put herself in grave danger.

'What was that you said, Stella?' he repeated ominously, and took a menacing step towards her. 'What do you know about Eddie Evans – and more to the point, what do the coppers know?'

'I know he's dead,' Stella wailed. 'Murdered, his throat slit. The police suspect you – revenge because of Rose. Tell me you didn't do it, Griff!'

He loomed over her. 'How did they find out?'

'Eddie's body was discovered and brought home. Oh, Griff, for pity's sake, in the memory of Mam and Dad, say you didn't do it.'

Griff's face contorted. 'You treacherous slut! You've been working with the coppers all along, sold me down the river. I ought to give you the same as Eddie got.'

'No, Griff, think of Danny.'

'Another of Eddie's tribe! I should do in the lot of you. You betrayed me, Stella.'

She'd expected him to deny the killing of Eddie, but he hadn't. He *was* guilty, as Owen had said. Her mind reeled. 'You betrayed yourself!' she said. 'Or maybe it was Tommy Parsons, trying to save his own neck. Think about that, Griff. How far can you trust *him*?'

Griff's eyes narrowed, and Stella knew she'd struck a raw spot. Perhaps Tommy Parsons knew too much.

'Tommy's been getting too big for his boots lately,' he said, as though he was speaking to himself. 'The time for a reckoning has finally come.' He moved away. 'Going out I am,' he said, 'but I'll be back, you can count on it.'

'If I were you, Griff,' Stella said, 'I wouldn't come back here. I'd get as far away from Swansea as possible. The police are sure you killed Eddie.' She hoped that would frighten him. 'They're just waiting to pounce. They could be outside at this minute.'

Griff swore.

'I mean it, Griff. Don't come back. I never want to set eyes on you again.'

'Oh, I'm not finished with you, Stella,' Griff assured her. 'Not by a long chalk. We've got some business to settle, and I need money. You'd better be prepared to play the game my way or your precious Danny will end up at the orphanage, too. I've got nothing to lose now.'

Fear clutched at her heart. 'Don't threaten me! If you killed my husband, I'll never forgive you, Griff. I'll see you hanged, for it.'

His expression was wild and she thought he would hit her but instead he strode into the scullery, and she heard the back door slam behind him.

As soon as she was alone, Stella fell to her knees on the hearth mat, all her feelings flooding out in bitter tears.

Her own brother was a murderer. He'd butchered Eddie. Stella resolved then that she'd do anything to protect Eddie's children against Griff. She had a good mind to go to the police in the morning, and tell them what she knew. It was either Griff or her, and she was determined to survive.

Next morning Stella was glad that it was Saturday and there was no school for Danny. She wanted to keep the children with her at every moment. She wouldn't go into work either, she decided. When the coast was clear, she'd slip up to the telephone box and call the theatre. She didn't care if it meant the sack.

Babs would be bringing Danny and Rosie in from next door at any moment so Stella put two eggs on to boil for their breakfast. She'd just lit the gas-ring, when the back-door knob rattled and someone tried to get in. Stella almost swallowed her tongue in fright, and was transfixed until Babs called, 'Stella, aren't you up yet?'

She unlocked the door and pulled back the bolt. The two children bounced over the threshold, 'Hello, Mam,' followed by Babs.

'What's wrong, Stella, love?'

Stella tried to pull herself together.

'Nothing. Just overslept, like.'

She couldn't bring herself to say that Eddie was dead, murdered by her brother. The horror of it swept over her again, and she could hardly take in what her friend was saying.

'Well, listen!' Babs said excitedly. 'I've got a surprise for you, something to cheer you up.'

'What?' Stella asked vaguely.

'An outing to Neath Market for the lot of us,' Babs bubbled. 'What do you think of that? And free of charge, as well!'

The children had rushed into the living room to take their seats at the table.

'You remember me telling you about that lady I cook for regular, Mrs Percival, who lives in Killay?' she said. 'Well, she's sending her car and chauffeur up to Neath today, to collect some furnishing materials. She said me and the kids can go along with him for the ride, do a bit of shopping if we like.'

'That's nice, Babs,' Stella agreed absent-mindedly. 'Have a good time.'

'You're coming too,' Babs said, with a grin. 'Asked if I could bring a friend, see. A day out on the cheap, mun! It'll be lovely. The car's coming about eleven, so be ready. Right?'

Stella fingered her cheek. 'I can't, Babs, love,' she said apologetically. 'Truth is –' She stopped, then went on, 'Truth is, Griff was round here last night, threatening to move back in. I managed to get rid of him, but I daren't leave the house in case he comes back.'

Babs looked crestfallen. 'Oh, there's a pity, Stell. I was looking forward to a trip, all of us, like old times. We haven't had a bit of fun for ages.'

'I know, and I'm sorry, Babs,' she said, 'but I daren't risk it.'

'Tsk!' Babs folded her arms across her chest dejectedly. 'He ought to be locked up, he did. Oh, Stell, you'll have to do something about him – tell the police, or something.'

Stella smiled thinly. She longed to tell Babs the truth but the less she knew, the better for her. There was no knowing what Griff was capable of in his present state of mind.

'You're right, kid,' she agreed. 'I must end it one way or another.'

Babs left reluctantly. 'If you change your mind, Stella, let me know.'

'Are we going to Neath, Mam?' Danny wanted to know, bouncing up and down on his chair.

'No.'

'Why?'

'Never mind!' Stella snapped. 'Eat your egg – you, too, Rosie. Here are some more toast soldiers.'

The children were just finishing their milk when Stella heard footsteps crossing the backyard.

Cursing herself for forgetting to lock the door after Babs left, she rushed into the scullery but it was too late. Griff was already standing there, his expression grim. 'I'm back like I said. For good. Get me some food.'

Stella only just smothered a cry of alarm. His eyes glittered feverishly, and some instinct warned her that he was teetering on the edge of violence. There were new, dark, crisp-looking stains glistening on the front of his jacket and sleeve. Stella couldn't take her eyes from them.

'Danny! Rosie!' she cried. 'Go upstairs this minute.'

'No!' Griff thundered. 'Those brats stay right where they are. Nobody's going anywhere.' He reached into his jacket pocket and brought out an object that, for a moment, Stella didn't recognise. Unreason simmered in his eyes as he lifted it and pointed it at the children. Stella's eyes popped and nausea rose. It was a gun.

'Griff!' she screamed. 'Put that damned thing away. Where did you get it?'

'Brought it home when I was invalided out of the Army,' he replied hoarsely. 'Thought I might need to use it on myself some time, if things got too much to bear.'

He gave a dry laugh, and Stella heard an undertone of near hysteria — maybe fear, too.

'Looks like that time might be here, doesn't it, Stella?' he said thickly. 'But I won't be going alone.'

He waved the gun.

'Be careful!' Stella wailed. 'It might go off.'

'It'll go off all right, when I want it to. Rose is dead, and there's nothing left, except revenge.'

'Revenge? On who?' Stella cried. She had to reason with him. 'Eddie's dead. No one's to blame, Griff, except maybe Rose.'

'Shut up!'

'It was her choice to leave,' Stella was defiant, despite her terror. 'You can't hold me or the children responsible.'

'I know what I have to do now,' he said. 'You're right, Stella. Eddie died because of me. I must wipe the slate clean.'

He pointed the gun at Rosie, who was trying to hide behind Danny. 'And when she's gone, the slate will be clean.'

'That's not Rose, your wife!' Stella howled. She took a step towards him, not knowing what she intended to do. 'That child is innocent. She never asked to be born, like you never asked to go to war. You don't want to do this terrible thing, Griff,' she implored him, unable to take her eyes off the gun. 'I know Rose's death was a shock, but you'd lost her long before that.'

Griff swung the gun on her. 'I told you to shut your mouth,' he yelled. 'She'd have come back to me if Eddie hadn't stopped her.'

'You're fooling yourself. You're ill, Griff. Let me help you.'

'Don't make me laugh. You're an inch from selling me out to the coppers, my own sister.' His eyes glowed with hatred at he stared at Rosie. '*She*'ll never betray a man. I'll see her dead first.'

'You can't do it,' Stella went on. 'Griff, open your eyes, for God's sake, and see the truth.'

317

'Truth? You wouldn't know the truth, Stella, if it upped and smacked you in the chops.'

'You can't kill a child, Griff!'

A strange smile twisted his lips. 'Child, man, what's the difference? I fixed Tommy Parsons for good,' he said with satisfaction. 'He won't split on anyone ever again.'

Stella stared at him, aghast. 'What are you saying? What have you done?'

'He had it coming.' Griff looked savage. 'Now keep quiet or it'll be your turn. You, and *both* those brats of Eddie's.'

Griff took a step towards the children, lifting the gun, and Stella dashed forward to shield them. 'You'll have to shoot me first, Griff,' she cried. 'And after the first shot the police will descend on this house like a pack of wolves. They're out there now, watching, waiting. I – I sent for them.'

'So Tommy was right. You did shop me.' Griff's lip curled with contempt. 'Let the coppers come, then. They'll be too late. I've got nothing to lose now.'

Stella took a step back, trying to herd the children towards the comparative safety of the passage. Perhaps, if she diverted Griff's attention, they could make a dash for freedom.

'They'll shoot you down, Griff.'

He smiled grimly.

'They'll do nothing as long as I have you and the kids as hostages.'

'Hostages! You wouldn't dare! You'll never get away with it.'

He waved the gun in a wide arc. 'Get going.'

'What?'

'I want the three of you in the front room. I need to keep an eye on the street. No tricks, Stella, or Danny gets the first bullet in his head.'

There was a knock at the back door. Then Babs's voice called, 'Stella, the car's here. Have you changed your mind?'

'What the hell does she want?' Griff muttered.

'We're going on a day trip with her this morning,' Stella lied.

'Day trip in January?'

'It's the truth, Griff,' Stella assured him. 'Her employer's giving us a cheap day out at Neath Market.'

'This is a trick!'

'No – but she'll get suspicious in a minute if I don't answer the door. Put the gun down, Griff. Let us go.'

'Not a chance! Get rid of her,' Griff commanded. 'And remember, I'm right behind you.'

Stella made her way to the back door. She unlocked it and held it ajar. 'Hello, Babs. Thanks all the same, but we won't be coming with you after all.'

'After all? I thought . . . ? Oh! I see. Well, there's a pity.'

Babs moved to step inside, but Stella kept the door half closed. 'Sorry, Babs, it's not convenient.'

Babs's smile faltered, and her eyes flickered towards the boarded-up kitchen window. 'Got other plans, is it?'

'Yes, we have to stay indoors. Danny's got a rash on his stomach,' Stella said carefully. 'I was up with him all night.'

'I understand, kid.' Babs nodded slowly. 'Fetch . . . something for it, I will,' she said. 'Don't worry, Stell. It'll be all right.'

With that Babs hurried off through the back gate. Stella closed the door, Griff at her shoulder.

'Glad you had the sense to keep your mouth shut,' he said, with satisfaction. 'Lock the door again, and give me the key. The front-door key, too.'

Reluctantly, Stella did as she was told, and Griff slipped the keys into his pocket.

'Okay,' Griff jerked his head towards the passage. 'Now get in the front room.'

There wasn't much in the way of furniture in the room, which was hardly ever used. An aspidistra stood on a small table in front of the window, while a second-hand horsehair sofa was placed against the wall opposite. A small multicoloured rag-rug, which Stella had made, lay on the linoleum before the empty cave of the fireplace.

'Sit down and keep quiet,' Griff commanded, indicating the sofa.

Stella sat, with an arm around each child. The room was perishing cold. She should ask for a blanket for the children, she thought vaguely, as she searched for a way they might escape.

Griff stood with his back against the wall beside the window, moving the curtain aside to peer down the street.

He'd left the door wide open, probably to allow him to hear any approach to the back of the house. Stella had a clear view of the passage and the lower part of the stairs, and eyed the distance to the passage speculatively; just a few short steps.

Could the children make it? If only she could divert him long enough for them to escape. But how could they get out with both doors locked? She thought of the boarded-up scullery window. Perhaps she could prise away the plywood somehow, just enough for both children to squeeze through.

She had to try something. Griff's face was white and strained – he must be building up to some final act of insane violence.

After what seemed like a lifetime of silence, Stella ventured to speak. 'Griff, this makes no sense, holding us prisoner, like this. I thought you loved Rose. She wouldn't want you to hurt her child.'

'Eddie's bastard!' Griff exploded.

Stella knew she must do something.

'I lied, Griff,' she burst out. 'I haven't called the police. They're not out there.'

He turned his gaze on her, and she saw fury in his eyes.

'You can still get away, Griff,' she hurried on. 'The police don't know you've . . . done for Tommy Parsons.'

'Charlie Pendle knows,' Griff said. Panic showed fleetingly in his eyes. 'I'm a marked man.'

'Then give yourself up,' she urged. The hopelessness in his dry laugh chilled her.

'Oh, yes – and hang by the neck?'

She could almost smell his desperation and defeat. 'You *can* escape,' she sobbed. 'I've got some money in my purse. It's not much, but it'll buy you a rail ticket to Cardiff. You can disappear.'

'This is the end of the line, Stella. For all of us.'

'Griff! For pity's sake—'

'Mam!' Danny piped up. 'I'm thirsty. I want some water.'

'Shut him up!' Griff roared. 'Or I will!'

'He can't help it!' Stella flared angrily. 'They're just children. They don't understand all this.'

She thought of the scullery window. There was an old screwdriver in a box under the sink. She could prise open the plywood with that. 'Let him go into the scullery for water, Griff. He can't do you any harm. I'll stay here.'

'Nobody goes anywhere,' Griff shouted. 'What do you think this is? A picnic?'

'Mam! I'm thirsty!' Danny wailed.

'Wee-wee!' Rosie squealed. 'Wee-wee, Mammy!'

'Bloody kids!' Griff took his gaze away from the street to glare furiously at them, as they both began to cry.

'*Myn uffern i!*' he bellowed, furious. 'All right, then! They can go in the scullery. But,' he pointed the gun at her, '*you* stay right where you are, Stella.'

'Danny, help Rosie wee-wee in the bucket under the sink,' Stella said, then whispered in his ear, 'Call Mammy to help turn on the tap.'

With cautious glances at Griff, the children went out into the passage, hand in hand.

Anxiously, Stella listened to the faint scuffling movements in the scullery.

'Hurry up, you kids!' Griff shouted. His patience was already running out.

'Mam! I can't reach the tap,' Danny called. Stella's heart ached at the tremor of fear in his voice. 'Come by here, Mam! Turn the tap on.'

Stella took a chance. 'Go and turn the tap on yourself, Griff, if you don't trust me.'

'I can't take my eyes off the bloody street, can I?' he said angrily. 'Oh, go on, then. But no dodges, mind, or I'll come out there shooting. Understand?'

'Yes, Griff.' Stella swallowed hard. 'You can trust me.'

'Huh!'

Stella hurried out to the scullery, turned on the tap full, and let the water run into the sink. The sound of it splashing down the plug-hole was somehow comforting: it might drown out other sounds.

She found the old tin box under the sink, and laid trembling fingers on the screwdriver. The plywood was held in place with only small tacks, and was surprisingly easy to ease open. She was opening one side as quietly as possible when Griff called from the front room, 'What's keeping you, Stella?'

'I'm swilling the bucket,' Stella shouted back, 'or it'll smell nasty.'

Her heart thumping like a kettle-drum against her ribcage, she attacked the bottom edge of the plywood, the screwdriver slipping and sliding in her trembling hands. The last tack burst free.

Stella lifted Rosie on to the draining board, and with both hands, forced the plywood backwards and upwards, giving enough space for a child to squeeze through.

'Quick, Rosie! Run to Auntie Babs's house.'

The child wriggled through and Stella heard her drop down on to the flagstones outside.

'Come on, Danny,' Stella urged, in a desperate whisper. 'Auntie Babs is waiting. Run!'

Danny was bigger, and Stella had to strain against the plywood to force it back. He was squirming, and whimpering with fright, as he got stuck half-way through. Suddenly there was another shout of fury from Griff.

'Stella! Get back in here now, and bring those brats with you.'

Danny was crying with terror, and desperately Stella gave one great heave at the plywood. It gave way under the pressure, cracking and snapping like a clap of thunder.

'What the hell was that?' shouted Griff in fury, rushing out of the front room.

With one tremendous push, Stella forced Danny through the gap, and stood defiantly with her back against the draining-board, shielding the window from Griff's view as he burst into sight.

'You *did* nark on me to the coppers,' he yelled wildly, his face suffused with blood. He waved the gun. 'I've just spotted one looking round the corner of Varteg Street.'

He stood still. 'Where are Eddie's brats?'

'Safe!' Stella shouted in triumph. 'You can do what you like to me, Griff, but Eddie's children are safe.'

The blood drained from his face, and his mouth hung slack. Then, deliberately, he put the gun down on the draining-board.

For a moment Stella thought he was giving up, but the next moment he hit her with such force that her head banged against the scullery wall. 'You'll pay for this with your life,' he said harshly.

Her legs gave way, and she would have slid to the floor, but Griff grabbed the front of her dress and held her upright. 'You'll meet up with that precious husband of yours sooner than you think,' he said. 'A bullet in your brain will do it.'

He let her go, and Stella staggered to regain her balance. He put the gun in his pocket, grasped her arm and propelled her into the front room. 'Come on! I want those coppers to see you.'

Stella stumbled before him, terror making her speechless. But, at least, she'd got the children to safety. That was what mattered. But all hope of getting out alive was fading fast, and she prayed for deliverance.

In the front room he sent her sprawling on to the sofa, then sprang to the window to peer out.

'There's another!' he shouted, strange excitement in his voice. 'Take a couple of coppers with me, damned if I don't.'

A frightened sob escaped Stella as she sat huddled against the arm of the sofa, straining to make herself as small as possible.

He spoke again. 'You're right, Stella — Eddie would be alive now, if it wasn't for me. Shall I tell you how it happened?'

'No!' Stella wailed.

'I'm going to tell you anyway, Stella, because you haven't suffered enough yet for what you, he and Rose did to me.'

Chapter Twenty-Eight

September 1926

Griff pushed the pint tankard across the table towards his companion, slouched opposite. It was still reasonably early of a Saturday evening, yet he had to raise his voice to make himself heard above the din in the smoke-filled saloon bar at the Archers pub. 'Get me another pint, Tommy.'

'Hey!' Tommy scowled. 'You've been gypping me for drinks all afternoon, mate. It's not my fault that sister of yours kicked you out without a penny piece to scratch your arse.'

Griff's lips drew back from his teeth in a snarl. 'Shurrup!'

He didn't want to be reminded of Stella's treachery. She'd gone back on her promise to Dad. Turned her back on him just when he needed her the most. She had a roof over her head and a family. He had nothing. And it was all her fault. Well, she wouldn't get away with kicking him out on the street. He'd see her in hell first.

With difficulty he focused on his companion's face. 'I said, get me another drink!'

Tommy looked mutinous. 'Fed up with this, I am.' He spat on the beer-stained floorboards. 'You wants to get up to Victor Street right now, have it out with her, give her a couple of smacks across her chops just to show you won't be buggered about. You can't let a woman treat you like that.'

In fury, Griff grabbed his tankard and slammed it on the table, making the slops spill. 'Another drink I want from you, Tommy, not a bloody lecture. Look, I'll pay you back.'

'Huh!' Tommy was scornful. 'When?'

Griff glanced around, making sure no one was close enough to hear what he said. 'We're doing that house up in Sketty tomorrow night,' he reminded his companion. 'Pay you back out of my share of the loot, I will.'

'Oh, all right, then.' Tommy rose reluctantly from his seat. 'But this is the last one, right?'

Slimy rat! Cursing under his breath, Griff watched Tommy shoulder his way to the bar. Bitterness and fury were choking him. Now he had no choice but to associate with such scum as Tommy. And that one needed watching. Slit a man's throat for fourpence, he would, mate or no mate.

But Tommy was right in one thing! Stella had treated him like dirt. All she cared about was herself and that brat of hers! Eddie Evans's kid!

Tommy returned with two brimming tankards. 'Make that last.' He dumped one in front of Griff. 'Get no more out of me tonight, you won't, boyo.'

'But it's not half nine yet.'

'Too bad. Go out and knock over a tobacconist's or something.'

Griff threw a good swallow of beer into the back of his throat. He'd have this then bugger off; go back to Victor Street and maybe knock some sense into Stella. The selfish bitch.

He finished the drink faster than he should have, then struggled to his feet. His legs were stiff after sitting for so long. Strewth! He'd had more than he thought. But he'd walk it off.

'Where you going?' Tommy half rose from his seat.

'Home,' Griff growled. 'In the mood to give somebody a good hiding, I am. Might as well be Stella.'

'Come with you, I will,' Tommy said eagerly. 'Give a hand.'

Griff looked down at him with distaste. Tommy's piggy eyes were shining feverishly, like a ferret's when it scented a rabbit.

He'd drunk measure for measure with Griff, and was looking for trouble. 'Don't need no help,' Griff replied gruffly.

Tommy pushed back his chair. 'No trouble, mate.'

Griff cursed. 'It's none of your business, Tommy, so keep clear. There's nothing in it for you.'

'She might have a bloke with her,' Tommy persisted. 'Could be a rough house, mun. You need me.'

'No, see you tomorrow, Tommy.'

Griff lurched away, pushing one-handedly through the drinkers crowding the saloon bar. Most men took one look at him and moved out of his way. One-armed man or not, he was feared, and that gave him a sense of satisfaction. They all knew Griff Stroud!

He stepped out of the pub and swayed on the pavement, regretting his decision to leave so early. Missing a good night's drinking, he was. He might've bullied a few more drinks out of Tommy or some other mug, but it was humbling having to cadge from the likes of them, and he was fed up with it. All because of Stella's meanness. She'd feel the back of his hand tonight, and no mistake.

The booze hoisting his resolve, Griff staggered away down the street. It was a good walk from here to the Sandfields, but he'd be the better for it. It would clear some of the spiders' webs from his mind.

He'd got no further than a couple of streets away from the Archers when, rounding the corner from Trawler Street, he noticed a man turn the opposite corner, and walk down the other side. There was something so familiar in the way he moved that Griff paused in his stride and peered hard through the dusk.

He knew that man, knew him well. He felt a stirring in his chest, as though unpleasant memories were about to surface. Was he a copper on the snoop?

When the man passed under the next street-lamp, shock hit Griff as though someone had punched him in the stomach.

Myn uffern i! Eddie Evans! It couldn't be! The drink was making him see things that weren't there.

But the man's echoing footsteps on the pavement were real enough. He was wearing a trilby and his coat collar was up against the sharpness of the night air. It *was* Eddie Evans.

Damn him to hell!

His thoughts in turmoil, Griff drew in a great gulp of air and felt dizzy.

If Eddie was back, then so was Rose. Both of them, right here in Swansea, where he could get at them – punish them for what they'd done to him. He must follow Eddie, find out where Rose was. He didn't know what he'd do when he found her, but at least he could face her down, show her what she'd brought him to.

Eddie was walking fairly quickly as though he had somewhere to go or someone to meet. Griff had difficulty keeping up with him, and cursed the drink.

What was Eddie doing in a run-down area like this? He couldn't have any business with the kind who lived around these parts, not unless he'd changed in the last four years. Law-abiding to a fault, except when it came to stealing another man's wife.

Rage mounted in Griff at the thought. It seemed to add strength to his legs. All the hatred that had festered inside him these last four years churned again, swelling until he thought his head would burst with it.

He tried to move faster to catch up with his quarry, yet not give himself away. They were moving towards the docks, the rows of terraced houses giving way to tall warehouse buildings and storage yards. Eddie stopped to light a cigarette in the shadows of high double gates, and Griff was undecided as to what to do next. He glanced around. There was no one about. A quick move now and he'd be on Eddie before the other man realised the danger. It had to be now. This chance would never come again.

Griff lurched forward as Eddie walked on. He caught up with him, grabbed his arm and hauled him round to face him. Eddie wouldn't escape this time.

'What the bloody hell—'

'Evans, you bastard!' Griff yelled. 'Where's my wife? Where's Rose?'

He was gratified to see fear flare in the other man's eyes. 'Griff! Where the hell did you spring from?'

'Where is she? I want to see her.'

'You can't.'

Enraged, Griff released Eddie's forearm, grabbed the lapels of his coat and yanked him forward so that they were eyeball to eyeball.

'You swine, Eddie!' Griff snarled. His heart was racing, and a red mist was gathering behind his eyes. 'You'll take me to Rose now, or I'll beat you to a pulp.'

'Get off me,' Eddie shouted, and, with a hefty shove, pushed him off. 'You'll never see Rose again. She's where you can't touch her.'

The red mist filled his head, and Griff clawed for Eddie's throat. But Eddie was too quick for him. His fist crashed into Griff's jaw, sending him reeling back. Somehow he stayed upright and stood poised to plunge forward at his assailant again.

'I don't want a fight, Griff,' Eddie yelled. 'There's nothing left to fight over.'

'You stole my wife, you bastard, and I'm going to kill you!'

'Don't be a fool,' Eddie called, and Griff heard mockery in his voice. 'You're getting old, mun. You wouldn't stand a chance against me.'

'I can take you single-handed,' Griff snarled, aware of the irony of his own words. He stumbled forward on trembling legs.

'Look at the state of you! You're a wreck, Griff.' Eddie guffawed. 'Huh! And you wonder why Rose left you. You're no man, mun, you're a living scarecrow.'

With a cry of rage Griff lurched forward, but his opponent side-stepped, and Griff's fist whistled through thin air. At the same time he felt a tremendous blow plough into his ribcage, knocking the breath from his body, and another into his face.

Griff crashed on to the pavement, where he lay face down, panting.

Eddie stepped back a pace. 'I could finish you off, if I wanted,' he said, 'but I hold no grudge against you, Griff. Rose loved me not you, and that's all that matters now.'

Griff strained to rise, but his legs wouldn't co-operate. He was so enraged that tears were welling in his eyes. 'I'll get you, Evans,' he was almost sobbing, 'if it's the last thing I do.'

'Don't be a *llelo*, Griff,' Eddie said. 'You're down. Stay down. You've had enough.'

Griff was kneeling now, but unable to rise to his feet without help. In impotent fury, he gazed up at Eddie's mocking face. 'You bloody swine! I could kill you.'

A stealthy movement in the shadows behind Eddie caught Griff's attention. Someone was watching him grovel here on the ground.

'I didn't steal Rose,' Eddie was saying. 'You lost her when you lost your arm. It was the war that took her away from you, not me.'

Griff couldn't take his gaze off the shadow as it moved into the lamp-light. Tommy Parsons was creeping silently towards Eddie. 'What the hell are *you* doing here?' Griff called to him.

'None of your business, Griff,' Eddie answered, misunderstanding. 'We won't meet again, I hope. And a word of warning. Leave Stella alone.'

Tommy reached into his pocket, and Griff saw the flash of steel. A wave of horror flooded through him and he lifted his arm in warning to Eddie. 'Look out, Evans! Behind you, man!'

But he was too late. Tommy leaped like a panther on to his target. With one arm he clasped Eddie across the chest and shoulders, and the hand holding the blade made a wide slicing motion across his victim's throat.

A horrible liquid scream issued from Eddie's mouth and, with a gurgle, he slumped. Tommy let the body fall to the ground, where it twitched and bucked for a few seconds before it lay still.

From where he knelt, Griff could see a pool of darkness forming under Eddie's head. 'You've killed him!'

'That's what you wanted, wasn't it?' Tommy said. 'I heard you say so.'

'No! I wanted him alive, to show me where my wife is,' Griff cried in anguish. 'Oh, Rose! Now I'll never find her. What have you done, you fool?'

'You're better off without her.' Tommy wiped the blood from the blade onto his sleeve. 'Cheap tart! Two a penny they are round here.'

'I'll kill you myself, Tommy, for what you've done,' Griff howled, still on his knees.

'Get up!' Tommy urged. 'We've got to get away from by here before somebody spots us.'

On his feet at last, Griff hung back. 'We can't leave him lying here.'

'Why not?'

Griff searched his mind. He felt numb with shock. He had always thought he wanted Eddie Evans dead, but not like this. Eddie had been his one hope of finding Rose, and getting her back. Now Tommy had taken that away. He'd pay him back one day, but not yet. Tommy was still useful.

'The coppers will think it was me,' Griff said. 'He's my brother-in-law.' His throat closed and he thought he'd gag on his own spittle.

'We'll get rid of the body, then,' Tommy said.

'How?'

Tommy's face had a crafty look. 'We'll hide it first, then we'll ship it out. A mate of mine is sailing on a vessel tomorrow, bound for Rio de Janeiro. He'll dump it in deep waters for the right price.'

'I've got no money.'

'Charlie will see to it.' Tommy grinned knowingly. 'You can owe him.'

Griff shuddered. From now on Charlie Pendle would own

him, body and soul. He'd never be able to clear the debt. He might as well be dead.

'Well, don't stand by there like a wet weekend, Griff, mun,' Tommy said, in a practical tone. 'You've got one good arm, so give us a hand with him.'

Chapter Twenty-Nine

'Don't tell me any more.' Stella was cold with revulsion. 'I can't bear to hear another word.' She rocked and moaned in anguish, shoulders hunched, her hands covering her face.

Eddie! To die like that!

Nothing could ever blot out the ghastly scene just described. He'd died a horrible death, and the images Griff had conjured would be with her for ever. 'Eddie would still be alive if it weren't for you. You're as guilty as Tommy. I hope they hang you, Griff,' she whispered. 'You deserve it.'

'They'll never get the chance,' he rasped. He abandoned his watch of the street for a moment to glance at her. 'Don't you get it yet?' he asked, in a voice raw with emotion. 'Neither of us will leave this house alive today. It's over for both of us.'

Stella saw that he was beyond feeling or reason, and hoped that when death came it would be quick. Her heart broke at the thought of Danny and Rosie alone in the world.

She glanced into the passage. If she had to die it might as well be in an attempt to escape. When Griff wasn't looking she'd make a dash for the door.

A movement on the staircase caught her eye. Her jaw dropped as, through the banisters, she saw a man's calves encased in navy serge trousers.

A policeman!

Stella gasped.

'What's the matter?' Griff snapped.

'Th – Thinking of Eddie, I am,' she stammered, raising her voice so that it could be heard in the passage, 'and how you let him die. You didn't try to save him from Tommy Parsons' knife.'

'Eddie had it coming,' Griff growled, and turned back to the window.

Stella was sorely tempted to look out into the passage again, but afraid to draw his attention.

The policeman didn't know Griff had a gun. She must warn him somehow.

'Put the gun down, Griff. Give yourself up,' she said loudly. Out of the corner of her eye, she saw the feet on the stairs hesitate, and knew that her warning had been noted.

She met Griff's eyes as he swung round to her, suspicion etched on his face. 'What are you up to?' he asked, staring at her. 'You're as white as a sheet. What's wrong?'

'What's wrong?' Stella heard the hysteria in her voice. 'You're going to kill me any minute. What do you *think*'s wrong?'

'Afraid to die, Stella? Don't you believe you'll see Eddie again?' He turned his attention back to the street, and Stella risked a glance into the passage. The feet were on the move again.

Griff held back the curtain with the gun barrel, craning his neck to peer left and right. 'I wonder how many of those coppers out there are afraid to die, too,' he said, with a hollow laugh.

Now Stella could see a uniformed figure in the passage, minus a helmet, standing just outside the door, back pressed hard against the wall. It was Owen Walters. He signalled to her to keep quiet.

'Take some of the buggers with me, I will, this very day,' Griff went on. 'The rest will remember Griff Stroud for a long time to come.'

Stella almost choked with terror. If Griff came towards her, he'd see Owen, and he'd shoot him instantly. She must do something! Unable to bear the suspense a moment longer, Stella got up and stumbled towards him. He swung round, pointing the gun at her. Stella almost fainted, believing that he was about to fire.

'Want some water, I do, Griff,' she bleated. 'And I want to go to the lavatory. Open the back door.'

'Won't fall for *that* trick again,' Griff bawled. He slipped the gun into his pocket, and pulled her to the window. He wrenched down the curtains and pressed her against the pane. Stella screamed. 'Let's see if the coppers will shoot you before I do,' he said, into her ear.

Someone grabbed Griff from behind, and he roared in fury, 'What the bloody hell!'

'You're under arrest, Stroud,' Owen shouted. 'Hand over that gun.'

Stella whirled away from the window, while Owen held Griff in a bear-hug. Griff struggled furiously to free himself, and reach the weapon in his pocket.

'Get the gun, Stella. Quick!' Owen bellowed.

Petrified, Stella hesitated, and leaped forward just as Griff snatched his arm free, and struck her across the face. Stella's knees buckled and she collapsed.

'I'll get you for this,' Griff stormed. 'I'll kill you both. Copper and his double-dealing nark.'

'You're done for, Stroud,' Owen panted. 'Give up! There's no point in fighting on, man.'

Griff's answer was another howl of rage.

Stella struggled to her feet just as Griff forced his hand into the pocket that held the gun. He raised it, jacket and all, in her direction.

'Now, you bitch!' he raved, foam at the corners of his mouth. 'You die now, and it's your own fault.'

'Run, Stella! Run for your life!' Owen shouted, trying to throw his opponent off-balance. 'I can't hold him much longer.'

Stella wrung her hands.

'I told you to go, Stella. Damn it!' Owen yelled

At that moment, Griff freed himself, and rounded on Owen with a shout of triumph, pointing the gun into Owen's face. But Owen threw a mighty punch and Griff went down to sprawl on the rag-rug before the fireplace. He was already battling to get up again, when Owen grabbed Stella's hand and dragged her to the door.

'Come on! Let's get you out of here!'

They dashed into the passage, Griff's curses ringing in their ears.

'Both doors are locked,' Stella cried. 'Griff has the keys.'

'Upstairs,' Owen ordered. 'The loft – that's where I came in. I'll hoist you up. Crawl through to next door.'

Stella had always been nervous that it was possible in these old houses to crawl the entire length of the terrace through the lofts, now she was thankful for it.

Stella stumbled up the narrow staircase, Owen right behind her. They'd never make it. Even if she had time to climb into the loft, Owen would be trapped.

On the small square landing at the top of the stairs, he prepared to lift Stella to freedom. 'Come on! I'll give you a leg up.'

'But what about you? You won't have time to get away.'

'I'm going back to arrest him.'

'You can't!' Stella shouted. 'He'll kill you. He's crazy!'

'Maybe, but it's my duty.'

'Owen, don't do it, for the love of heaven,' Stella begged. 'If anything happens to you I couldn't bear it.'

They heard heavy feet in the passage. 'Coming for you, I am, copper!' Griff shouted.

He appeared at the foot of the stairs, and saw them, trapped on the landing. He stood there, grinning, gun in hand. 'Sitting ducks, eh!'

Owen pushed Stella behind him.

'Stand still!' Griff ordered.

'Don't be a fool, Stroud,' Owen said evenly. 'Put the gun down. You're under arrest. It's over.'

Griff chuckled. 'It's over for you, copper, and for that devious witch with you.'

'Griff!' Stella shrieked. 'For pity's sake, don't shoot! I'll do anything you want. Anything!'

'Too late, my girl. You had your chance.'

Stella saw him lift the gun, and aim at Owen's head. 'Goodbye,' he said, and, squeezed the trigger.

Stella expected to hear the terrible roar of a bullet smashing into Owen's head, but there was just a dull metallic click.

The grin on Griff's face was wiped away. He glanced at the weapon, then pointed it towards them. The trigger clicked again.

Before he had time to try a third time, Owen had leaped down the stairs. With a roar of triumph, he threw himself at Griff. Both men went sprawling, but Griff hung on to the gun, trying to point it at his opponent, while Owen fought to shake it from his grasp.

Stella came down the stairs, crying helplessly, just as Griff struck out savagely with the barrel of the gun, catching Owen across a temple. Blood spurted from the gash, but Owen didn't go down, but still grappled his adversary around the waist. Griff struck Owen's head again.

'Stop it! You'll kill him!' Stella yelled, and took a step towards them.

'Stay where you are, Stella!' Owen ordered her breathlessly.

With a curse, Griff struck yet again, but this time the blow glanced off Owen's shoulder. Using Griff's body, the policeman hauled himself to his feet, and closed with his opponent.

Both men lurched through the frontroom door, locked in a deadly embrace. Stella couldn't see them from where she stood but she could hear their grunts and groans as each strove to master the other. Something fell to the floor and smashed. The aspidistra pot, she thought.

Dangerous as it was, she had to go down and see what was happening, but as she reached the bottom stair there was a deafening report as the gun went off. Then there was silence.

337

'Owen!'

Stella stood as though turned to stone. Then she edged towards the parlour door, but was afraid to go into the room.

The pungent stench of cordite assailed her nostrils as she stood, numbed to the bone, unable to move. Then a man's hand gripped the edge of the door and, beyond her line of vision, he hauled himself up.

Griff! He'd killed Owen. Now he'd kill her!

Far away, she could hear men shouting and fists pounding on the front door. Too late!

She must save herself – hide!

But she couldn't move a muscle.

Stella closed her eyes, uttering a prayer. A hoarse voice called her name. 'Stella?'

Her eyes opened, and then she was filled with relief. Owen was hanging on to the door, his face pale and bloody.

'Owen!' she shrilled. 'I thought you were dead.'

He held out the front-door key. 'Let them in,' he said faintly. 'I think I've had it.' Then he collapsed on to the linoleum.

'Owen!'

Stella had the presence of mind to dash to the front door and open it. Men in dark uniforms poured in, their faces grim. She sank on to the staircase, her head in her hands, weeping with relief that she and Owen were safe.

It was a few minutes before it dawned on her that Griff, her brother, must be dead.

Owen had killed him.

Chapter Thirty

February was the worst month for a funeral, yet the miserable weather seemed a fitting background for the conclusion of Griff's wretched life. Stella attended the ceremony, with Babs for moral support. There was no one else, and it broke her heart to realise how empty her brother's life had been. Standing at the graveside with Babs, Stella hung her head.

How shaming. The siege at Victor Street, the inquest and the police enquiry had people talking, gossiping, blaming. Would she ever be able to put it all behind her?

A week or two after the funeral, Stella opened her front door one morning to find Owen Walters on the step.

She'd thought never to set eyes on him again, and at the sight of him the hurt of the last few months came rushing back. Thankfully, he wasn't in uniform. That would've been too much to bear. The last time she'd seen him, he had been facing the coroner's questions.

'What do you want?' She couldn't keep the raw hostility out of her voice.

'Can I come in?' he asked.

Reluctantly Stella allowed him to pass over the threshold, and followed him into the living room. 'Why are you here?' she asked abruptly. 'The police have finished their enquiries, haven't they? Haven't I suffered enough?'

'Here as a friend, I am, Stella.'

Stella laughed bitterly. 'I haven't any friends, not any more. I'm lucky to have a job after what happened.'

He glanced around. 'Where are the children?'

'Up the park with Babs.'

'Pity,' he said. 'I was hoping to see them. They're a couple of good kids.'

'Say what you've come to say,' Stella snapped.

'How are you?'

'How do you think? My name's been bandied about in the local paper, with hints of the smutty reputation Ted invented for me. People point the finger everywhere I go.'

'You could sue the paper, you know.'

'What with?' Stella tossed her head with scorn. 'The sixpence in my purse?'

'I'm sorry all this has happened.'

'Huh! *You*'re sorry! My brother's branded a murderer. My home's tainted with his death. I'll never be able to forget that, neither will my children.'

'Listen, Stella,' Owen said hastily, 'I didn't kill him, you must know that. The coroner—'

'I don't want to hear another word about it,' she broke in. 'I can't stand any more.'

'You *must* hear this,' he went on, his tone determined. 'Griff could've shot me easily during that last fight. At one point he had me at his mercy. Instead he turned the gun on himself.'

'Oh, God!' Stella put a hand to her head as though in pain. 'Suicide, to add to everything else. Is there no end to the shame he's brought on me and my family? People will be talking about us for years.'

'I'm sorry.'

'You keep saying that,' Stella snapped. 'It doesn't help.'

'I just didn't want you to believe I was responsible for your brother's death.'

'You're a policeman, aren't you?' she replied dully. 'Why would it concern you what I believe?'

'It does. You concern me, Stella, very deeply. I mean . . . if ever you need me . . . anything I can do for you—'

'You've done enough, haven't you?' Stella rapped out. 'You came into my home under false pretences. You lied, deceived me, caused my brother's death – yes, you *did*, Owen! I don't need help from *you*.'

'Stella, listen to me, please.'

'No! You'd better go. There's nothing more to say.'

'Well, *I* think there is, see,' Owen retorted frankly. 'I can't walk away, with us feeling the way we do about each other.'

'*What?*'

'Oh, come on now, Stella, you're not going to stand by there and blatantly deny what you feel for me, are you?'

Speechless at the turn in their conversation, Stella flopped on to a chair and stared up at him.

'When we were facing Griff and that gun, Stella, you said you didn't know what you'd do if anything happened to me.' He lifted a hand. 'Now, don't deny it.'

Stella was angry that she'd given herself away in a moment of despair. 'If I said that,' she parried, 'it was because I was frightened. I thought we were both going to die that day.'

'Oh, no!' Owen smiled faintly. 'It was more than fright, much more. I know because I fell in love with you, too, Stella.'

Stella set her mouth in a firm line. 'When we first met and talked in this room, I won't deny I was drawn to you. I thought you were a man I could trust.' She couldn't contain a bitter laugh. 'How wrong I was.'

'I had a job to do,' Owen said angrily. 'I didn't know then that I'd fall in love with you. And for you to deny now that you feel something for me is like lying, too, Stella.'

Stella was silent. She'd been so attracted to him, enough to dream of a future together. She was still drawn to him, she couldn't deny it.

'A man who can cover up the truth as easily as you can isn't to be trusted,' she said.

'You *can* trust me, Stella, I swear by all that's holy.'

'It's easy for you to say that,' Stella said. 'Rolls off your tongue like honey. No, you're no different from any of the others, Owen. Men's lies have pushed me to the brink of despair, ruined my life. But no more!'

'My job—'

'Oh, yes! Your job!' Stella repeated. 'That comes before everything, doesn't it? And always will.'

Owen's lips thinned. 'My profession *does* mean a lot to me,' he agreed. 'And I'm damned good at it. I intend to go far.'

'I don't doubt it. You'll not let anything stand in your way. What are a few lies, anyway? Never mind about other people's feelings.'

Owen's face paled, Stella didn't know whether from anger or shame.

'I *do* love you, Stella,' he said softly. 'How could I help it? I've watched your tenderness with your children; your devotion to your friend, Babs. There's so much love in you, Stella, you deserve happiness.'

'I *was* badly hurt by Eddie,' she said. 'I never want that to happen to me again.'

'I know that.' She was touched suddenly by the emotion that quivered in his voice. 'And all I'm asking is a chance to prove myself worthy of you. I'll never deceive you again, I promise.'

His emotion sparked her own, yet she wasn't ready to surrender to her feelings. Her suffering over these last months had strengthened her, and she was thankful for it.

'I need time to straighten out my life,' she said. 'Time to find a way to live a normal life again, me and my children.'

'Can you do that without love?'

'My children love me.' Stella lifted her chin in defiance. 'Danny and Rosie are all that matter now. They have a lot of happiness to catch up on, too.'

'And what about you?' Owen took a step closer, and Stella tensed. 'You matter, too, Stella. You're so young and beautiful. You need to be taken care of and loved.'

Stella said nothing, thinking of the way she'd loved Eddie,

believing in him steadfastly, never realising he'd stopped loving her. 'What I deserve and what I get,' she replied despondently, 'may be two different things.'

She did want to be loved, though – but wholeheartedly. Was she being foolish to let false love of the past curdle happiness in the future?

Something of her thoughts must have been expressed in her face, for Owen spoke again, his voice soft and husky. 'Can I see you again, Stella?'

Stella gazed up at him. Perhaps it was foolish to reject him. She was hurting now, her heart stung almost to hopelessness by the perfidy of selfish men, but in a month or two, when spring came and the sap was rising, would she regret turning him away? Yet caution kept her silent.

Owen gave a deep sigh. 'I'm not giving up, Stella,' he said. There was a ring of certitude in his voice that impressed her. 'I love you, and I'll always be around, watching, waiting.'

Stella sighed too, and stood up.

'Right, then,' she said lightly. 'I suppose you'd better have a cup of tea while you're waiting.'